D1384042

At Random

Lee Zacharias

FUGITIVE POETS PRESS
Greensboro, North Carolina

This is a work of fiction. All characters and incidents are products of the author's imagination, and any resemblance to actual persons or events is coincidental.

Published by

Fugitive Poets Press
Greensboro, NC

ISBN 978-1-938045-07-3

First Edition

A portion of this novel appeared in *The Southern Review* in slightly different form under the title "At Random."

Acknowledgments:

For their assistance in researching this novel, I am grateful to Raymond Bell of the Greensboro Police Department, Geoffrey Mangum, Sidney J. Stern, the late James Tucker, Betty Watson, Douglas Dreishspoon, Michael Bohen, Michael Gaspeny, and the Montagnard-Dega Association in Greensboro. Gerald Cannon Hickey's books on Montagnard culture in Vietnam and the *Greensboro News and Record's* coverage of the Montagnards in North Carolina were most helpful, as were the films *Remembering the King of Fire* and *Living in Exile.* I have adapted a few lines of dialogue about life in the Central Highlands from interviews in these films.

My thanks also to Peggy Parris for her advice on an early portion of the manuscript, to Michael Parker, Dave Shaw, and Craig Nova for their generous reading and suggestions, to Les Butchart for rescuing the book from a box on my shelf, and always to my mother, my husband, and my sons, Max and Al Gaspeny, for their love and support.

for Michael

At Random

November 16, 1991

In daylight the road between the nameless bar and East Side Pawn was surely bleak, but on a rainy November night the pavement shimmered beneath a sea of neon colors. To the couple in the car, the little strip of civilization appeared like an oasis from a landscape of deserted warehouses and dead-end turns, but instead of stopping the man drove on.

"Where are you going?" the woman said at last.

She turned to gauge his expression, for it flustered him to be lost, and the fluster often took the form of irritation. At the least he would be annoyed that she had asked. Three weeks ago he had lost his job, and in everything since he had been quick to perceive injustice or slight. It was that seeming look of irritation which impressed itself upon her even as she anticipated the jolt and swiveled her head. At the same instant the boy dove out of darkness. She knew it was a boy, though it happened so fast she saw no more than his denim jacket and dark hair. The wheel thunked, and the body flew across the hood.

"Jesus Christ," her husband said.

Later it seemed to her that for a full minute they sat listening to the motor tick while they waited for the shock to release them into action, but she was wrong. Before the car stopped, she had flung her door open. She was on her knees, blind in the headlamps that lit only rain, feeling with her hands along the slick street and cinder shoulder. Behind the car her husband knelt over a dark form. "I can't tell if he's alive or not," he said in a voice so weak it guttered. He stood. “We’ll need to find a phone.” Her hair stuck to her face in wet strands; she had lost her shoes. In the rain she couldn’t tell if she was crying, but she knew it was a boy because they had a boy at home.

Chapter 1

It was her son's name that Eva whispered, crouched beside the boy while Guy searched out a phone. She was reluctant to touch him, for fear that she might injure him in some further way. The flashlight was dead. She had nothing to cover him with, but she held her umbrella over his head, murmuring, "It's okay, you're going to be okay." She couldn't tell if he was breathing. He seemed smaller than she'd thought, smaller than her son Nick, who was eight but big for his age. It was her son she thought about.

She remembered the night in the hospital just after he was born, how she seemed to swim out of sleep and there he was, wrapped like a gift inside the nurse's arms, and she said, "Hello, it's my little barracuda," her voice already rich with love. "You hold them like a football," the nurse instructed. (Like a *football?* Eva had never held a football in her life.) "Bonding well with baby," the nurse wrote on Eva's chart, all the joy and wonder Eva had thought possible for anyone to feel scaled down to an ordinary biological process.

He had seemed so fragile. For a week every time she passed the hammer in the basement stairwell she was seized by a vision of Nickie's skull. She didn't know whether she was more horrified by the vision or herself, and she wanted Guy to move it, but she couldn't ask for fear he would confirm that she was crazy. It was just that Nickie was so tiny—she was overwhelmed by the tangle of love and responsibility such a small and precious creature made. She grew into the job, of course, and Nickie grew so obviously sturdy that the weight of her guardianship seemed scarcely more than a set of routine maxims (take your raincoat, wear your helmet, call me when you get there). But now, as she crouched in the rain, her child suddenly seemed as vulnerable as he had eight years ago, when she was so nuts with postpartum hormones she was afraid she would pick up a hammer and smash his skull. She must be a monster after all. The child beside her was surely dead or dying, and what she thought about was her son.

Her legs ached. Water puddled on the pavement, her dress was soaked, and she was cold. She wondered if the boy was cold, wishing again she had a blanket. Never move the victim; always keep him warm. What else? She knew to put baking soda on a bee sting and ice on a burn; she kept syrup of ipecac in the medicine chest and the number of Poison Control taped to the phone. If her son choked, she could do the Heimlich; in ninth grade health she'd even practiced mouth to mouth (like every other girl in the class Eva had prayed to draw Bucky Stiles as her partner, but that was more than thirty years ago, and the class had resuscitated a giggly boy-boy, girl-girl). She and Guy carried no flares; she probably hadn't checked the batteries in the flashlight for a year. Who knew how long it would take the ambulance to arrive, how far Guy would have to walk before he could call?

Her eyes filled, and she bent over the boy. "It's okay," she promised, touching his wet hair, longer than Nick's and thick. His arm was flung out at an ominous angle. She couldn't feel any blood, but perhaps the rain washed it away. "We're getting you help, they're coming, they're almost here." The umbrella tipped, and to help him she had to sit up and take her hand away.

Pity tore her chest. She couldn't bear to think about his parents—watching television maybe or asleep. It seemed hideous that they should not yet know. If Nickie—Nick, he was growing up, he wanted them to call him Nick now—she would want to be with him if anything happened to her son.

Hurry up she willed. She closed her eyes, repeating *Don't die, don't die, don't die* until she felt as if she must be screaming, but the hysteria passed like the initial shock; she had been sitting here beside him for so long that in another way she felt quite calm. It felt hours since Guy had left, so many that it seemed as if everything else in her life had been a dream and all she had ever really done was to wait beside this boy.

"Hurry up," she whispered again, disoriented now, wandering her mind like an unmapped building, where in one room she found her husband, in another her son, in yet another her husband and her son. Down this hall were the boy's parents and their unsuspected grief, around the corner the labyrinth of guilt and consequence she and Guy would soon inhabit. Yet in another room it was only Saturday night and raining, and she sat on the floor like an abandoned date with aching legs and ruined clothing. And at the same time she seemed to occupy one room at a time, she was in all of them at once, including that last room, where all the minutes she had waited turned to hours and she had waited so long she was bored.

She felt so sorry for Guy. No one could have stopped. Lost, impatient with the stubbornness with which he nurtured error, she had wished that she were driving. Again she saw the boy fly across the hood. What made him pitch forward like that? If he'd gone over the handlebars of a bicycle they would have found the bike. And whose parents would let their child go bicycling at midnight in the rain?

It seemed so unbelievably unfair that she should not know his name. If only she knew his name she thought he would not die, and it wasn't fair, it was so unfair, so horribly unfair that he should have to depend upon her ignorance to save him.

No fair, that's not fair, the childhood refrain, to which she always answered, "Of course it's not fair. Fair is where you go to see horses and cows." But she hadn't taken Nick to see the horses and cows for at least two years, and he didn't think that was fair either.

She forced herself to concentrate. If she knew what the boy was doing, she might know why he was there. Skateboarding? Nick maintained a wistful reverence toward skateboards, something he'd given up on wanting even before the desire set in. Safety was the price you paid for parents who protected you. This boy might be cold and wet or even dead, but her son was warm and dry, asleep in the room she'd repainted last year, when he outgrew the dinosaurs on his wallpaper border, while downstairs the babysitter ate microwave popcorn and watched MTV. They had promised to be home by midnight. She didn't suppose Guy would remember to call Courtney.

He was only a child. She glanced at the crumpled form beside her and swallowed tears. She was afraid she would vomit, and so she lowered her head and wept until she heard the siren.

Guy walked as briskly as he could to the lighted strip they had passed. That he found it so efficiently despite having no sense of direction registered without awareness; he was only slightly more conscious that he had been right not to stop before: it was a rough neighborhood. Eva never gave him the least benefit of doubt. But he didn't think about her or himself or even the boy. He had found his way back by concentrating on a single image. It was a trick of empowerment he'd learned from sales: you could do anything you could visualize yourself doing. Over and over he watched himself place his finger in the dial.

"Mister?" the bartender asked as he stepped inside the tavern.

"Do you have a telephone?" Guy replied, but already he'd seen it, on the wall outside the toilet. It was a touch-tone phone, of course, and for a moment as he stood with the receiver in his hand it seemed as if his failure to anticipate this detail was a defect of character so great that he would not be able to carry through, all the incompetence, the mistakes of judgment, false assumptions, and petty misdeeds of his life having joined into an endless train of fate that pinned him to this moment. Smoke stung his eyes. In his ears the throb of his pulse confused itself with jukebox rap and the muted crack of pool balls from a back room.

"Who you calling, white boy?" A young man with eyes concealed behind dark glasses took a step toward him, but immediately the bartender said, "The phone be working. Leave the gentlemens make his call."

Guy pressed 911. Without thinking he had memorized the street signs so he wouldn't have to inquire where he was. It was hard to tell in the dark, but he didn't think the boy he'd killed was black, and he was grateful for that. He was the only white man in the room.

The dispatcher asked how long he'd walked. More than ten minutes, less than fifteen, Guy estimated. Another reason not to have sent Eva, who had no sense of time, though she couldn't forgive his misturns and muddled circles.

"Whitey must think this Southern Bell," someone muttered as Guy hung up. It was unthinkable that he bring the police inside, and although it was still raining, he stepped outside to wait.

The squad car arrived almost immediately. A lone officer got out, a black man so light skinned it took Guy a moment to realize he was black. In his uniform he gave the impression of being taller than he was, thick through the shoulders, barrel-chested, with tapered legs and narrow feet. The name on the bar pinned to his pocket was McThune.

"You the party who called to report an accident?"

Guy stated his name and address.

"Occupation?"

It was the question he'd been dreading for three weeks. "I was a district manager for the *Random Herald.*"

Through the rain sluicing off the brim of his hat McThune appeared displeased. The *Random Herald* no longer existed. It had merged with the *Gazette* in a corporate buyout, and Guy's job had been eliminated, though he persisted in thinking of it as fired.

"I'm unemployed," he admitted.

"Were you the driver of the vehicle?"

"Yes sir." The *sir* rankled in Guy's mouth. He was forty-seven, but he had a teenaged boy's instinctive animosity for cops.

"Step into the light please." Guy moved closer to the street. "I'm going to ask you to perform a few simple tests." Guy walked a straight line, tracked McThune's pen with his eyes, touched his index fingers to his nose.

"Have you had anything to drink tonight?"

"Not for several hours."

"Have you had anything to drink tonight?"

Guy made an effort to keep his voice even. "I had a drink before dinner and a glass of wine with, that would have been around seven, at least four and a half hours before the accident." He felt as if a shot of Novocain had begun to wear off. He was impatient to know what happened to the boy, and his impatience might easily border on anger. It was obvious he wasn't drunk. He'd been to the opera for Christ's sake, and he and Eva had Cokes at the intermission.

"What time did the accident occur?"

"Twenty minutes ago. I had to walk to a phone."

"Did you check your watch?"

"No." With his tongue Guy dislodged his dry upper lip from a tooth. "But I have a very good sense of time."

McThune's eyes traveled to Guy's feet and back, as if measuring the extent of his mistake. "You hit a pedestrian?"

"A kid. He ran in front of the car, and I couldn't stop." There was a taste like chalk at the back of Guy's throat. "I feel terrible. I have a boy myself."

"All right, I'm going to have you direct me back to the site so I can get a look at the scene and check out the victim's condition. After that, if you wouldn't mind, I'd like you to come downtown and take a little test."

"Is that necessary?"

"Your compliance is voluntary, but a refusal is admissible as evidence in court."

The clot of fear inside Guy's chest sent his voice careening. "He just ran right out. Believe me, I would have stopped if I could."

"I'll take your statement. Let's check out the scene, and then I'd like you to come to the station."

There were no witnesses except Eva. What if he couldn't prove that it wasn't his fault? "I don't have any reason to refuse. The kid tripped or something. It could have happened to anybody."

"Just try to stay calm and remember exactly what happened."

He was perfectly calm, Guy thought angrily. "The kid ran right in front of the car," he repeated, his voice fading. He could hardly expect a cop to sympathize with a guy who'd just killed a kid. It wasn't his fault, but that didn't make him any less guilty. His stomach plunged, and bile filled his mouth.

"Let's go," McThune said as Guy doubled over the gutter.

The ambulance arrived before the police. As it approached, Eva made the mistake of looking into the headlights, and then, when she turned back to the boy, her vision whirled with residual blindness. She rose to move out of the way, but the driver called her back to hold the umbrella. She had only a glimpse of the boy's face before the paramedic eclipsed his upper body. He looked foreign in a way she couldn't place. The radio crackled, and she strained to hear the driver. "No respiratory function; BP extremely weak. Blood in the mouth, evident multiple trauma, assume massive internal injuries, possible hypovolemic." The umbrella trembled.

A police car wailed to the side of the road. Somehow Eva had assumed that Guy would return before the police and EMS arrived, but now an officer was walking toward the ambulance as Guy hung back, standing beside the squad car, surveying the scene as if from a great distance, not seeming to locate either her or the boy. When she returned her attention to the boy, he was strapped to a board, his shirt and jacket cut away, face distorted by a clear green bag.

"What've we got?" McThune asked.

"Multiple trauma, probable hypovolemic shock. We're attempting to stabilize for transport."

McThune glanced at the boy as a second car pulled in, shook his head and wiped rain from his face. "Hell of a night."

Then Eva was running beside the gurney to the ambulance, still holding the umbrella.

Guy hadn't moved. "Is he dead?" he asked when she came to stand beside him. His hair stuck to his skull.

"I think he might be, but they're trying to revive him." She stared at the three officers in conference with the medic, the rain covers for their hats neon disks in the garish dark. The landscape churned with red and blue lights and the steady rain that splattered through the intermittent bark and rasp of radio static. A sob escaped her. "I don't know how this happened."

"It was an accident," Guy said coldly.

She sucked her breath until she could speak. "What did the police say?" She glanced at him as two more cars arrived. "Guy? Did you tell them what happened?"

"He wanted to know if I'd been drinking."

"Well, they always ask that…don't they?"

"I've got to go downtown."

As the ambulance pulled out, the siren cut mournfully through the rain, and a gust of emptiness blew through Eva. Suddenly it seemed as if the time she'd spent waiting with the boy had been no time at all, not nearly enough. Already he was gone, passed from her hands into the vast, impersonal institutions of the hospital and the state.

Guy was cracking his knuckles. Eighteen years they had fallen asleep to the rhythm of each other's breath, yet as she returned her attention to him he seemed only vaguely familiar. "I'm sure it's just routine," she said.

McThune had slipped into his car. Finally he came around to her.

"The dispatcher's sending another car to complete the site investigation. I'd like for you to come with your husband so that I can take your statement."

"The boy," Eva said, eyes riveted on his face. "Is he going to die?"

"We're sending a unit to the hospital." She nodded. "You ought to get out of the rain," McThune advised and invited them to wait in the back of his vehicle.

Guy slumped on the seat beside her, his face turned toward the window. The car had the smell of wet wool and rubber boots, an odor that never failed to bring elementary school back to Eva. She had been a dutiful student, easily intimidated, overly respectful, more frightened by a misplaced homework assignment than she was of the officer outside. They had done nothing wrong.

"Did you call Courtney?" she asked.

Guy continued to stare at the steamy window. "Why would I call Courtney?"

"We were supposed to be home by midnight." He had been the rebel. Yet in the last year or so, as one thing after another faltered or fell short, he seemed not merely depressed (*she* was depressed; her career wasn't going so well either) but cowed.

She groped for his hand. "It's okay. I'll call from the station." He was so touchy—it was understandable; he'd lost his job. But she was afraid he would lose his temper too.

"It wasn't your fault," she said.

At the station Guy's blood alcohol registered .02, and McThune asked Eva to wait while he took her husband's statement.

The interview took place in a closet furnished with a narrow table and three plastic seats. If he had imagined the setting, Guy would have pictured a common room, an enormous space of desked off territories, ringing typewriters and phones, less an image he'd absorbed from TV (actually he didn't watch much except sports), than a grafting of old cop shows with his memory of the city room before carpeting, partitions, and the muted click and hum of electronics had given newspapers the bland face of an insurance office. The chair was too small for him. He was tall and lanky, a fact that contributed to the boyish impression he still made in his late 40s, and the standard issue seats of public places made him feel gawky and adolescent. On the other side of the table, McThune had removed his hat. He was bald, a fact that discovered late seemed disconcerting. "How fast were you driving?"

"Not fast."

"Give me a number."

"Twenty, maybe twenty-five."

"What was the posted speed?"

"Thirty-five," Guy guessed. He didn't remember seeing a sign. "We were lost; it was raining. I wasn't speeding."

"Would you say you were driving too fast for conditions?"

"I don't think so, no."

"But you couldn't stop."

"The kid ran in front of the car—he must have tripped or something, he seemed to just vault up over the hood."

"Before the impact?"

Guy hesitated.

"Did he hit you or did you hit him?"

The scene was so vivid: how could he not be sure? "I think we hit him."

"Did you see him before you hit him?"

"Yes." He would never forget it, the boy trapped in the headlights, eyes feral with fear. Or maybe it was shock—there hadn't been enough time for fear.

"But you couldn't stop."

"No."

"Why's that?"

Guy resisted an impulse to grind his teeth. "I told you—he ran right in front of the car."

"I thought he was airborne."

There was a cigarette butt floating in a half-empty Styrofoam cup. It was disgusting, but for the first time in the eight years since he'd quit, Guy wished he had a cigarette. "He was running, and he tripped."

"Were his feet on the ground when you hit him?"

"I'm not sure."

"So you saw him only a moment before the impact."

"That's right." He was beginning to sweat, though his clothes were still damp and he felt chilled.

"Why was that?"

"I'm not sure I understand the question."

"Was it because of the rain? Was he behind something? Did something obstruct your vision?"

Guy shifted in his seat, and the chair's metal cleat caught a loop of the stained nylon carpet. "He must have been behind something."

"What?"

"I don't know."

"Vegetation? A building maybe. A car?"

"No." His head had begun to hurt, but the pain felt old, as if it had been there a long time and he'd just worn through to it. "I couldn't see what it was, but I know it wasn't a car."

"A pile of rubbish?"

"Brush," Guy decided, but when he replayed the scene, the brush was only an impenetrable darkness.

"You're sure." There was something distracting about McThune's mouth. A narrow scar split his upper lip, a seam so fine Guy had to strain to see it.

"No." Years ago McThune might have guarded him in a pick-up game of basketball. He thought he remembered the mouth twisted by a taunt, and then the moment when he pivoted with the rebound as the guard moved in too close and the mouth connected with his elbow.

He tried again. "I don't know. It was dark, and I was unfamiliar with the street. Maybe he was just wearing dark clothes." How often in his own neighborhood had a dark-clad jogger suddenly loomed in his headlights? He couldn't picture what the boy had been wearing, though he was certain that fifteen minutes ago he had known every detail of the boy's appearance, known it as vividly as one knows a dream that is irretrievably lost the instant the dreamer attempts to fit its images to words.

Though he was telling the truth, he felt tangled in lies. It had happened too fast to process. He couldn't separate the details, but he was certain of the shape: the boy ran out; he couldn't stop, and the reason he couldn't was that no one could have.

McThune was tapping his pen. Guy saw the narrow, almost feminine fingers on the ball. "Okay, you saw him a moment before you hit him. Did you brake?"

"Of course." *Yes* was the right answer; *of course* sounded snide. Look, he wanted to say, I understand you're just doing your job, but don't you think the only decent thing for us to do right now is get over to the hospital and find out what's happened to that boy? It pissed him off to have his grief polluted by paranoia; and it pissed him off to be pissed off. His animosity toward cops was part of a larger aversion for authority, and though there wasn't a thing he could have done to save his job when the paper was sold, he knew that Eva would never be sure it wasn't his attitude that canned him.

"Did you skid?"

"Yes."

"Before or after you hit the boy?"

He wasn't sure.

"The pavement was wet?"

"Yes."

"Was it raining?"

"Yes."

"You're sure you saw the victim."

"Yes."

"But you couldn't stop."

"That's right."

"Maybe the rain kept you from seeing him sooner."

That was it. There was no obstruction; it was raining, and the kid was wearing dark clothes.

McThune made a note. "How fast were you going at the moment of impact?"

"I don't know."

"But before you braked you were going twenty-five."

"Or twenty. I don't think I was going more than twenty."

"The pavement was wet, you were going twenty miles an hour, and when you braked you skidded."

"That's right." The questions were no longer worded as questions, but as traps he had set for himself.

"You didn't brake sooner because the rain kept you from seeing the victim."

"Yes."

McThune slapped his notebook shut and stood. "You were unfamiliar with the street. It was raining, it was dark, visibility was impaired. Now I've been following what you said very carefully, and it sounds to me like you're telling me you were driving too fast for conditions."

Guy felt more resigned than angry. He was tired, and a vein throbbed behind his right eye. "In my opinion I was not driving too fast for conditions."

McThune walked to the door and stared into the hall for a moment before he turned. "Mister Ferrin, you hit a child. Believe me, you were driving too fast for conditions." He resumed his seat, softening his tone to accommodate a note of empathetic suasion. "By your own admission you'd been drinking. We're talking about an accident with serious bodily injury. Now you tell me why it's not your fault."

"I wasn't drinking."

McThune consulted his notes. "A drink before dinner, a glass of wine with."

Guy took a deep breath. "I think I want a lawyer." He should have asked for a lawyer as soon as they reached the station. Eva was the one who thought of things. Why hadn't she suggested it?

There was a knock on the door, and another officer stuck his head in. McThune stepped outside. It was a report from the hospital, Guy felt sure, though he wasn't at all sure that the police would tell him if the boy had died. Probably they would wait to catch him off guard.

"The kid?" he asked anyway when McThune opened the door and indicated he was to come out.

"Still in ER."

Guy's breath thickened. He thought of Nick and realized that if anything like this had happened to his son he wouldn't have cared whose fault it was, he would have killed the guy who did it.

Though the public phone was in plain view of the sergeant's desk, the book had been stolen; when Eva tipped the apparatus up, only a scrap of paper clung to the rod inside the plastic binder. She would have to call home first. Luckily the officer had reminded her to remove her purse from their car, or she would have no change. The phone rang a dozen times before Courtney mumbled "Hullo?" Waiting, Eva forced herself to trace the girl's steps as she stumbled through the darkened living room toward the sound, picking up just at the moment when Eva could no longer contain her alarm. "Oh, Mrs. Ferrin."

"I'm sorry we're late. There's been an accident." Eva

asked after Nick and obtained Mrs. Lloyd's number, which she wrote on the back of her hand. Her hair was beginning to dry and frizz. Her knees and hands were scraped. Somehow she had lost her shoes.

Courtney's mother answered on the first ring.

"Hello, this is Eva Summer, Nick Ferrin's mother? Courtney is babysitting for us tonight?" Hysteria bubbled up in Eva's throat. "I know you must be worried, it's so late. There's been an accident."

"An accident?" Mrs. Lloyd's voice lurched.

"Courtney's fine," Eva promised. "She wasn't in the car."

"I've been so worried."

I'm sure you have," Eva said, "and I'm very sorry, but I'm afraid we're going to be a while longer."

"She didn't leave us your number, and it's unlisted. Courtney's supposed to leave a number."

"I'm sorry." Eva closed her eyes. "I promise we'll be home as soon as we can."

"It's pretty late."

"I know, and I'm sorry, but we're at the police station right now."

"Courtney's not allowed to sit past midnight, you know."

"I'm sorry. We hit a little boy...." Eva's voice quavered.

"I doubt I'll be able to get her up for church tomorrow."

Well, scratch Courtney from the sitter list, Eva thought bitterly as she hung up. *Bitch.* She remembered asking her best friend Claudia to recommend a babysitter after Nick was born. Claudia had been the first to know when Eva got pregnant; six months pregnant with her second, she'd been so excited she'd accompanied Eva to the doctor for the test. "They'll be so close," she rejoiced as she sketched out their mutual motherhood on the spot, the picnics in the park and summer mornings at the pool. They'd shared secrets for years; they knew each other's kitchens as intimately as their own. Yet when Eva asked for the name of a sitter, Claudia changed the subject. That was Eva's introduction to the List, an asset more precious than heirloom silver, never to be let outside the family, no matter how much like sisters best friends were.

When she turned around, McThune was standing behind her. "What happened to your shoes?" he asked.

"I don't know. How is the boy?"

"Still in ER."

He had made it to the hospital. She had been afraid he would die on the way. Now he couldn't die. No matter how bad it was, they would save him. "How will they find out who he is?"

"He's a foreign kid, Montagnard looked like to me. We'll send an officer to ask around the community, probably one of the churches or social service agencies."

Montagnard. They were from somewhere in Vietnam. The *Herald* had run a series of articles on them when they first came over. "I was just thinking about his parents. It seemed so horrible out there on the road—all that time, and they still don't know anything has happened to him."

"It probably wasn't as much time as you think." McThune held a door.

Eva paused just inside. "I kept thinking about my own son." Her eyes dropped to his patent leather holster as he indicated the chair Guy had occupied. "The thing is I can't figure out why he was there. It was so late, and there was nothing but warehouses and vacant lots."

He took out a notebook and a pen. "Would you like a cup of coffee?" Eva shook her head. "What were you doing there?"

It was easier not to look at the gun when he sat. "We took the wrong exit from the interstate and got lost."

"What was your destination?"

"Home." If you're ever anyplace where anyone has a gun, leave immediately and tell your parents, they had instructed Nick long ago, so long she thought maybe they should wake him up to remind him as soon as they got home. Once when he was small the couple across the street invited them for a cookout, which the couple spoiled by arguing, one of those tedious evenings when the visitor feels summoned less as a guest than witness to a long dispute. At some point during the evening, while their children played together upstairs, the woman had complained to Eva that despite her concern for the safety of their three-year-old son her husband kept a revolver in their nightstand drawer. Later, when Eva said to Nick, "Jason's daddy has a gun," by way of explaining why he would never play at Jason's house again, Nick replied, "I know. Jason showed me." Eva never forgave the woman. She was glad when the couple split up and moved away.

"Where were you traveling from?"

"Dill Creek. We went to the opera."

"Who was driving?"

"My husband." She smoothed the damp silk bunched at her knee.

"Did your husband have anything to drink?"

"We went out to dinner. We had a drink while we were waiting for our table and a glass of wine with the meal." The room smelled stale, foul with cigarette smoke and the unrepentant breath of hardened felons.

McThune studied his notes. "To the best of your knowledge then your husband had one glass of wine with dinner and one drink before, is that correct?"

"Yes."

"What time did you eat?"

"About seven. The opera started at eight."

"Did either you or your husband have anything to drink after dinner?"

"No."

"Did your husband leave your presence at any time between dinner and the accident, did he go to the men's room, say?"

"Once, but...."

"Let's come back to the accident. How fast were you traveling?"

Eva's face felt stiff. "My husband did not have a drink when he went to the bathroom." As McThune looked up, his features swam inside a corona. She no longer wore her contact lenses full time, and they burned her eyes. "If he had, your machine would have registered it."

"The BAC has been noted." He returned his attention to his notebook. "How fast was your vehicle traveling?"

"Not very." Her voice was cool, though she supposed she should forgive him. He would have gone to school to learn how to interview; if he seemed more sympathetic, it would only be technique.

"Give me a number."

She shook her head. "I'm not good with estimates."

"Try."

"Fifteen maybe?"

"Your husband says twenty."

"It could have been twenty. It was below the speed limit, I'm sure." Eva wished she could ask how Guy was holding up, but McThune was still writing.

"Did you see the child?"

"I think so, just before we hit him, yes."

"What happened?"

"I don't know. I turned my head, and when I looked back he was already there. It was like he flew off a bicycle or something."

"Did you see a bicycle?"

"No."

"Skateboard?"

"I thought of that. But no."

"Was he running? Did he look frightened, like he might have been running away from something?"

"I didn't see his face until we hit him." It was Guy's face Eva saw now, and the expression wasn't irritation but shock. A shiver slipped down her spine. "He looked surprised. Like he couldn't believe...." She wiped at her eyes. "When will we know? "

"We've got an officer at the hospital who'll keep us advised if there's any change in the victim's condition." McThune looked at her, not unkindly. "You'd be surprised, even twenty miles an hour. Especially kids, they take the trauma lower, there's usually more vital organs involved. Was the victim airborne when you hit him?"

"What do you mean?"

"Were his feet on the ground?" He was writing.

"I'm sorry. It just happened so fast. We were lost, and I thought my husband might be mad. It's not a good side of town...." It was the black side of town. Not until that moment had it registered that he was black.

"Did you hit him, or did he hit you?"

"He hit us," she answered, surprised. She hadn't been able to frame it that way for herself, but as soon as he said it she knew.

"Your husband says that you hit him."

"No." She shook her head. "I mean, it happened so fast I can see how he would think that, but that's not what happened."

"Did your husband see the boy?"

"I'm sure he did."

"Did he say anything that would indicate he saw him?"

"No, but...."

"Did he brake?"

"Yes. He had this look."

"What look was that?"

She shook her head.

"Did the car skid?"

"Maybe." Tears sprang to her eyes. How could anything that happened so fast happen so irrevocably?

"Take your time," he offered. She tightened her lips and gave him a pinched nod. He softened his voice. "Can you tell me what happened after you hit the boy?"

"There was a big thump, and the car jerked. I saw him fly up over the hood."

"And then?"

"We stopped and looked for him. My husband found him. He was behind the car. I don't know why I was looking in front."

"Once you stopped did either you or your husband move the car?"

"No. The only thing, I had an umbrella, I went back to get it, and I turned off the lights so the battery wouldn't run down."

"The ignition was off?"

"I don't remember. I might have turned that off too. My door was open, and I shut it."

"What happened when you found the boy?"

"My husband couldn't tell if he was alive. He went to look for a phone. I was afraid to move him, so I got the umbrella."

"Is there anything you've left out?"

"I don't think so. Just...." When she hesitated, he looked up. "It wasn't my husband's fault."

"Okay, Mrs. Ferrin." He returned his attention to his notebook. After a few minutes he passed her a sheet of paper. "Read that over, and if you feel it's accurate I'd like you to sign it."

She found her reading glasses in her bag, then picked up the pen. "It's fine. Only my name's not Ferrin, it's Summer."

He looked at her the way the receptionist at the orthopedist's office had when Nickie broke his wrist. "I'm just trying to determine who will be responsible for the bill," the receptionist had said. Nineteen ninety and she'd acted as if she'd never heard of a husband and wife with different names before. "Summer is your maiden name?"

"My first husband's name." She flushed, irked to find herself explaining, as if she'd revealed that she and Guy were not the irreproachable middle-class couple they pretended to be. "I was using it professionally before I met Guy."

"What do you do?"

"I'm the curator of the Gardell College Gallery."

McThune stood and handed her his card. "Okay, Mrs.—

Ms.?—Summer. If you think of anything else, give me a call."

"We're free to go then?"

"You are."

"What do you mean?" She followed him down the hall to an office where Guy slumped in a chair. McThune removed a pair of handcuffs from the drawer.

"You're under arrest for driving while impaired." For a moment the room went still. Eva's vision reeled. The top of her scalp seemed to lift as all the oxygen drained from the air. "You have the right to remain silent."

She swallowed a breath so big it tore her chest, and the words fell out. "You don't understand. We feel terrible about what happened, but...."

"Eva." Guy's voice was weary; pouches of exhaustion sagged beneath his eyes. He lurched to his feet. In his disheveled clothes he looked drunk.

"I'll call a lawyer," she promised. When Guy had been fingerprinted and photographed, she met them at the magistrate's office. "Bond is set for $500," the magistrate announced, but as they were on their way out, another officer came in and whispered to McThune. McThune turned to the magistrate.

"We have a confirmed death."

Eva put her hands to her face and began to cry.

"Charge is upgraded to felony death by motor vehicle," McThune announced, and immediately the magistrate said, "Bond for $500 is revoked. Mr. Ferrin, I order that you be held on a new bond of $20,000. Your first appearance will be in district court at 9 a.m., Monday, November 18. Hearing for probable cause is scheduled for 9 a.m., Thursday, January 2,

1992."

"I'll get a bondsman and a lawyer," Eva promised as McThune led Guy from the room. "It wasn't your fault," she called.

McThune turned around.

"Lady, when you hit a kid, it's always your fault."

Chapter 2

It was almost five when Guy and Eva left the station. The bondsman had taken a check for $3000, but they had to put up collateral for the remainder of the bond, and the only thing they had worth $17,000 was the equity in their house. Not Guy's Camry, which would be impounded and was probably damaged anyway, certainly not Eva's car, not their rugs, paintings, or art deco, not the silver or the china, her camera or their computer, all those things that had until then fostered a feeling of privilege and wellbeing.

There were Nick's savings bonds, of course, and Guy had invested a modest inheritance from his mother, which he would need now that he'd lost his pension, though if he didn't find another job, it might have to help them through the next year. Their savings account would barely cover the check.

"We'll call Jerry Beck," she promised in the cab on the way home. "He'll know how to handle it."

Guy slumped on the seat beside her. He hadn't spoken since the arrest.

"If Jerry's who you want." One of the advantages of their fictitious affluence: a number of their neighbors and friends were lawyers. They wouldn't have to wait until business hours on Monday. More than once Jerry had done them a legal favor, mostly by way of allowing them to throw his name around. "I'm so sorry." She was about to add it wasn't fair, but that's what she said when he lost his job, and Guy had responded, "Life isn't fair," rendering her resentment foolish, though he'd seethed with resentment himself. There were only so many times she could tell him the accident wasn't his fault, and it seemed inappropriate to bring up the boy, though she wondered again who he was and if his parents knew yet or whether they were asleep and hadn't even missed him, at the same time she knew that Guy must be wondering the same thing. Preoccupied, he could seem abrupt and cold, but he was neither, and she knew that, blameless as he was, he would never forgive himself. It was Guy who couldn't read features about children with terminal diseases, who sent money to the fund for every local family disaster. If anything, he was more protective of Nick than she was.

The rain had stopped, and birds were beginning to stir in the trees. Their street looked peaceful, washed with silver beneath a canopy of glittering black branches. An unfamiliar car was in their driveway, and it took Eva a minute to realize that Courtney's mother must have driven over, but almost instantly her relief was annulled by the bad taste her conversation with the woman had left. She had completely forgotten that she still had to deal with the sitter, and having to speak to anyone else before she and Guy could close the door, look in on their son, and fall into bed seemed an ordeal beyond human endurance.

She turned toward Guy. "I forgot we have to pay Courtney. What time did we leave?" How many hours since they had possessed the kind of innocence they would never have again? "My god, we owe her almost fifty dollars." At least they wouldn't need to take her home. She tipped the driver and opened the door. "I'd give a lot if we could just go in and see Nickie."

Guy didn't look at her. "I'd give a lot more if this whole goddamn night had never happened."

She touched his wrist, her throat too tight to speak.

Behind the porchlight the house was dark. Eva used her key and gave the door a tentative push, calling out "We're home" as she always did, not to scare the sitter.

A woman with curly brown hair sat up on the sofa as Eva snapped on the lamp. "What time is it?"

"Five," Eva said guiltily. Guy had gone straight upstairs. "I'm terribly sorry."

"You're back," Courtney mumbled in a voice furred with sleep when she came blinking through the French doors beside the fireplace, the warp of the den upholstery imprinted on her cheek.

"I'm sorry," Eva repeated. She opened her purse and bent over the desk. "I'm going to have to give you a check." She wrote a check for seventy-five dollars, which Courtney folded into her pocket without inspecting.

"What happened?" Mrs. Lloyd asked, her voice muffled as she bent to tie her shoes.

"We had an accident. I was hoping we'd be home sooner, but...." The words wobbled in Eva's mouth. Her eyes strayed to the needlepoint footstool by the fireplace. "The boy died." She refused to look up to see their expressions.

There was a long pause. Mrs. Lloyd turned to her daughter. "Have you got everything? You aren't forgetting your math book, are you?"

"I didn't bring my math."

"Are you sure? Why don't you go back and look?"

"We didn't have any math."

"I just don't want you to forget. You know how you are."

"Could we go home?" Courtney sighed. "I'm tired."

"I know." Mrs. Lloyd gave Eva a pointed look. "We really don't permit her to sit past midnight."

Eva saw them to the door and watched the overhead light come on in their car, then turned out the porch light. For a moment she stood at the foot of the steps, listening to the house, already quiet, but not yet so quiet she could hear it creak. Then she switched off the living room lamp and went upstairs. Their room was dark. She went into Nickie's room, stepping carefully in case he was in his sleeping bag on the floor. He often slept on the floor since a counselor at his summer day camp had remarked it was good for the back. It amused her, the habits he appropriated from the briefest exposure to others. After Gregory Whitt's birthday sleepover, he'd taken to requesting a cup of milky coffee in the morning to help him wake up, and when she had protested, "Honey, you're too young to need caffeine to wake up," he said, "But Mom, I'm tired."

Would he do drugs if his friends did? Those perilous years, the teen years, still seemed unimaginably distant.

He was in the bed, draped half over the side, sleeping with his mouth open. She touched his cheek. She wanted to turn on the light to look at him, but didn't. He was a deep sleeper; should he awake, she need only say, "Go back to sleep," but she was afraid that Guy would accuse her of being mawkish, and so she made herself cross the hall. Dropping her damp underwear at her feet, she felt for the nightshirt on the hook in her closet. When she got into bed Guy was already asleep.

When she woke, the light through the shades was golden and the clock read 10 a.m. Guy was gone. She checked Nick's room even before she used the bathroom. Empty, save the stuffed animals, Legos, books, and dirty clothes on the carpet. It smelled of peanut butter and funky socks. Downstairs she found an open cereal box and a puddle of milk on the counter. On the breakfast room table the Sunday paper still lay in its plastic bag. She switched off the light over the table off and found Nick in the den, watching the Lone Ranger.

"Hi, sweetie. Where's daddy?"

"I don't know," he said without taking his eyes off the TV.

She fought an urge to panic. "Is he in the house?"

"I don't know."

"Have you seen him?"

"Oh, yeah," Nickie said. "He's raking May's leaves. He's going to take me fishing this afternoon."

"That's nice." She frowned. Her eyes felt squinchy, and the back of her throat burned. On top of everything else she was going to catch cold. "When did he promise to take you fishing?"

"I don't know."

"I mean," she prodded gently, "was it this morning?"

"How come you slept so late? I had to fix breakfast for myself."

"I know you did, baby, I'm sorry. Mom and Dad had kind of a late night, we were tired." She resisted the temptation to praise him for being so self-sufficient (he was eight, not four) as well as the urge to remind him to rinse his bowl and put the cereal and milk away. For a moment she watched the screen. She had never noticed that neither the masked man nor Tonto cast shadows; the great west seemed to be a stage-set indoors. "What did you and Courtney do?"

"Huh?"

"Did you have a good time?"

"We watched 'Cops' and played Monopoly." Without

glancing up he added, "I won. I had Boardwalk and all the railroads. How was the opera?"

How could Courtney let him watch a show like "Cops"? She wanted to snatch him up and hug him and never let him go. "It was fine, but the last scene went on forever, and your daddy had to pee." He seemed so much bigger than she remembered. He had slept on his hair wrong; at the crown it stood up in brown spikes. She couldn't see his eyes; they were still fixed on the masked man, and without intending to she said, "You know, there are a lot of dirty clothes on your floor, and I want you to put them in the laundry."

"Mom!"

"What?"

"I'm watching this show."

"I didn't mean this minute." She started toward the door. "I just think from now on you should keep your room picked up."

He didn't answer.

"Okay," she said and came back to kiss his hair, but he jerked away, and she had to go over the conversation in her mind to discover whether she'd called him Nickie out of habit, but no, he was just absorbed and she'd interrupted.

In the kitchen she made tea and opened the paper, turning at once to the local section, then pushing it away. The accident had happened too late for today's paper, and anyway the thought of reading about it made her sick. The death of a child—it wouldn't be in City-State; it would be splashed across the front page.

She looked at the clock. Both she and Guy had hectic schedules—even since Guy left the paper he complained of not having enough time—but now she wasn't sure what to do with herself until he came in. Surely it was too wet to rake. But even if he was just keeping busy, he deserved the distraction, and tidying May Pleasants' yard was a generous thing for him to do. May had been disabled by a series of minor strokes the year after they moved in, and when her husband died Guy had taken over the yard work. If the police wanted to know what kind of character Guy possessed they should ask May Pleasants.

Nick was still in the den when Guy came in, and she let him stay, though in general she and Guy discouraged TV. Nick was a great reader, and tended to discipline himself with television by losing interest and doing something else. Still, he was a somewhat lonely child, she thought. None of the children on their block were his age. When she and Guy moved in, most of the neighbors had been elderly; now a generation of twenty- and thirty-somethings were buying up the old houses, enclosing the screened porches, redoing kitchens, adding bathrooms and big decks. With its bungalows, big front porches, and sidewalk clutter of strollers and bikes, her best friend Claudia's neighborhood felt more homey. She and Claudia had assumed their sons would grow up best friends, but they couldn't walk to each other's houses, and Gregory hung out with the kids on his street, whose parents didn't have to make playdates.

At the sink Guy drew a glass of water. He hadn't shaved, and his face looked dirty. His sweatshirt exposed an inch of white tee shirt where it met his sweatpants at the back. He owned a sweatshirt that fit, but he had a perverse habit of ignoring clothes that hadn't shrunk or lost their buttons.

"I see we've had a change in the weather," she said.

"New and improved." He sounded so normal that for a moment she wondered if she'd dreamed the whole thing.

"What time did you get up?"

"Eight-thirty. Where's Nick?"

"In the den. He thinks you're taking him fishing today."

"Today. Tomorrow, tomorrow, and tomorrow." The joke fell flat.

She looked away. He was waiting for her to bring up last night so he could blame her for ruining his day. He hadn't been that keen on the opera in the first place. She had ordered the tickets. They had gone out to eat even though they couldn't afford to in order to assure themselves that his luck was going to turn. "How's May?"

"I didn't see her."

She sneezed. "I'm catching cold," she said and left it at that.

"I'm not surprised."

She met his eyes. "I presume you haven't told Nick."

"No." He seemed unperturbed. It struck her as odd that she should misread his mood. After eighteen years she would have thought they'd anticipate each other's every notion.

She folded the paper. "I suppose we ought to talk about what we're going to tell him."

"What do you think?" He sat.

"We have to tell him something. It was too late for today's paper, but won't it be on TV? You don't want him to hear it from another kid."

"Why don't we just tell him the truth?"

"All of it?"

"I've always believed that honesty is the best policy." His voice went slightly faint on the pious note that generally annoyed her, his habit of turning a simple answer into a platitude.

"You don't think it will upset him to know we killed a child?"

"Hell yes, it's going to upset him."

"Well I know that." Eva scratched a crusty spot on her placemat. "What I mean is, do you think it would change the way he sees us?"

"Don't be ridiculous."

"I mean," she said, feeling helpless to explain exactly what she did mean, "he wouldn't stop loving us, but he's always trusted us. We're supposed to protect him."

Guy slammed his chair back. "Jesus Christ, Eva."

"I'm sorry," she said, though it seemed to her the conversation had taken a turn she couldn't follow, and the refrain was beginning to wear. "I didn't mean to make you feel bad. Anyway, I feel as implicated as you do. I was in the car. It could as easily have been me as you."

"You wouldn't have got us lost."

Lurking behind his tone of self-reproach was an accusation whose anger surprised her. She changed the subject. "Do you think we should call the police to see if they've identified the boy?"

"Would they tell you?"

"I don't know. If the family's been notified...." Stricken, they met each other's eyes. "If anything ever happened to Nick,..." Guy said in a ragged voice.

Eva's eyes brimmed as she covered his hand with hers. "I know."

Guy made himself a cup of coffee. What he was going to hate most was the fuss. Like picking a scab. All that scratching at the surface while the real wound festered inside. Last night he'd been shocked to be charged, but this morning he'd discovered it didn't matter. He'd killed a kid. He would learn to live with it because he had to, but he'd be damned if he'd worry the details or mawk it up with words. It wasn't his fault, but it was his. Still, because of Nick he cared what would happen. For his son's sake he didn't want to go to jail. Or maybe he wouldn't go to jail but it would cost everything they had and then how would Nick go to college? He shook the thought from his mind—Eva's pattern, worst-case scenarios stretched to fill the next forty years. He was guilty of a lot of things, but he would not compound them with self-pity.

When he thought of the boy he had killed, it was with a mixture of remorse and grief and a surprising amount of righteousness and anger. It was the kid's own fault. His stomach soured. But what child should have to forfeit his life for a moment's negligence that every kid committed?

Eva had changed into a sweater and a pair of black leggings when she came back down, though on a normal Sunday morning she would have been in sweatshirt and jeans. He knew how her mind worked better than she did. She hadn't even reached for her jeans; her life had, without deliberation, come to seem too exposed. In a way becoming a criminal or a criminal's wife made you a public person. He looked down at his dirty red sweatshirt and gray sweatpants. He could live with the guilt, he would learn to, but he wasn't prepared to become a public person. One thing he'd enjoyed since losing his job was not having to wear a tie every day, something he'd realized last night as he dressed for the opera.

Eva seemed to be waiting for him to request the information she was dying to give him. "Okay," he said, "tell me," and was unreasonably pleased to see that she looked sheepish. It alarmed him. He was taking pleasure in being a bastard. He supposed it was to punish her because he'd been the one driving, which was lower than low—it was what she sometimes accused him of being when they argued, it was petty.

"I called the police station," she said. "He was nine. A Montagnard boy named Y Bhan Buon To—it's spelled *Y* but you say it *E*. The family's been notified, but the parents don't speak much English. He has a twelve-year-old brother who broke the news."

"That's terrific, that makes my day." Guy's eyes flashed, and she seemed to brace herself at the same time she shrank against the stove. "If you're going to run over a kid, why not pick one whose parents have to have a translator tell them their son is dead, how about if they're people who've just been through twenty years of war and a pile of paperwork ass-deep to get to a country where they can't understand the fucking cop who rings the doorbell to tell them some maniac's mowed down their kid! Thanks a lot, Eva."

"Goddamn you." For a moment they stared balefully at each other. Her voice tempered. "You're not a maniac."

There was a whimper from the doorway, and they turned to see Nick, eyes glassy with fear, sucking on the neckband of his T-shirt. They couldn't exchange a sharp word over a leaky faucet or lapsed promise without Nick chewing on his shirt or hyperventilating, pushing between them, sobbing, begging them to stop. It never failed to make Guy feel guilty, though usually it pissed Eva off.

"Oh, honey," Eva said. "Go on back to the den. We aren't fighting. Daddy's just upset." Guy shot her a malevolent look. "Guy." She turned to Nick, then back to him. "I think we should tell him. Do you want to be the one, or should I?"

"At least he understands English," Guy muttered and exhaled loudly. "I'm sorry." His voice broke, and he dropped to a chair. For a moment the room filled with the awful shudder of his sobs.

Eva rubbed his shoulders and turned to Nick. "It's okay, honey. Take your shirt out of your mouth. Your dad and I had an accident last night. A boy ran out in front of our car. It was a terrible thing, and we both feel very sad."

"What happened to him?"

"He died."

Nick paused to consider. "How old was he?"

"Nine."

Again Nick seemed to mull the information over. "He should have looked both ways."

"That's true," Eva said. A sound that could have been a laugh or a sob caught in her throat. "I guess that's it. He didn't look both ways."

Nick crossed the room to stand beside his father. The neckband of his shirt was wet. "It wasn't your fault."

Guy raised his head and patted Nick's shoulder. "Thank you, son."

"What time do you want to go fishing?"

"Nick," Eva chided.

"How about two o'clock?"

"Can we take Tyler?"

"Sure."

"Yes!" Nick raced back to the den.

Eva shook her head. "Honey, you don't have to take Nick fishing."

“I promised.”

“That was before the accident.”

“A promise is a promise.”

She tightened her lips. “You’re going to be stubborn, aren’t you?”

“I’m not being stubborn. I just think a person ought to keep his promises.” The pious note again, with its subtext of self-congratulation and accusal.

“And you’re going to take Tyler? All they do is bicker. What you ought to be doing is talking to Jerry Beck.”

“I don’t want to get my friends involved in this.”

“He’s a lawyer, for god’s sake. It’s his profession to be involved in things like this.” She pushed a stray hair back. “Or would you rather get someone else? Maybe you’d prefer someone we don’t know.”

He shrugged. “Maybe I shouldn’t even get a lawyer. Maybe I should just plead guilty.”

“Are you out of your mind? This is a felony.” Her breath had the sound of a sigh. “Of course you feel guilty. I understand that. I feel guilty. But the accident wasn’t your fault.”

“Tell that to his parents.”

“Tell your son you killed a nine-year-old boy because you were drunk.”

His shoulders sagged. “Okay,” he said after a minute. “You win.” He rubbed his eyes. “How long do you suppose it’ll be before the trial?”

“Call Jerry.” He nodded. “I’ll take the kids fishing.”

“You don’t mind?”

“Of course I mind.” He gave her a weak smile, and she was relieved to see that he knew she was kidding. She cut through the living room to the den, where the contents of Nick's tackle box were spread across the carpet.

"Nick!"

"What?"

"Pick up your stuff. You know you're not supposed to have your tackle box in the house."

"Okay." He didn't move.

"I'm tired of stepping on fishhooks and tangling my feet up in line. From now on I want that box to stay in the garage." He didn't answer. "Do you understand me?"

"Yes." He sighed.

"I don't want to have to tell you again."

"Okay," he said.

"I mean it. The next time I step on a fishhook I'm throwing everything out."

"Okay!"

"Okay," she said, knowing that within a week they would have the conversation again. "Put it in the garage and call Tyler. I'm going to take you fishing."

"What about Dad?"

"Daddy has some business to take care of."

"He said he was going to take me."

"Nick."

Nick brightened. "What kind of business? Did he find a new job?"

She reached out to ruff up his light brown hair. He had Guy's hair and her mouth, which meant that he would probably need orthodontia. Her mouth was full of crowns because her parents couldn't afford braces. "No, honey."

Jerry Beck was more cynical about the law than anyone Guy knew, though the trait seemed to serve him well in its practice. A casual observer might have dismissed him as a hypocrite: a passionate family man and chronic philanderer whose vulgarity and impeccable manners spoke of the prep school boy he'd been. Depravity filled him with delight. But it was not the duality in his character that struck Guy as strange (for who, should he look deep enough, wouldn't find some schism), rather the rhapsodic embrace of its extremes. He lacked the subtlety of an ordinary, mixed-up human nature.

"Drunk driving death," Jerry translated when Guy named the charge.

"I wasn't drunk. My blood alcohol was .02. I didn't think they could arrest you for less than .10." Suddenly Guy remembered a story Jerry had told at a party last summer, the inside tale, full of winks and chuckles, of a minor scandal Guy remembered only vaguely from the *Herald*, something about a local Jaycee whose Mercedes jumped a curb, tore up the country club's seventh green, and sideswiped a fleet of golf carts before coming to rest in the pond, after which an unidentified woman wearing nothing but his necktie waded to shore and disappeared. The police had found improbable cause to test him for drunk driving. Recalling Jerry's glee, Guy began to regret that he'd called. He would have preferred a lawyer whose view of innocence was more exalted.

"Ten's per se, but you can be arrested for less. Don't worry. You're not going to be convicted on .02, and the cop knows it. He's just covering his ass. Some reporter finds out you had a Scotch before dinner and writes in the papers you were drinking, people get upset, the MADD folks rile everybody up, and the public wants to know why the cop let the guy go. This way everybody's happy. You know how it works, I mean that's your game, right?"

No, Guy thought, he did not know how it works. In his fifteen years at the paper, not one of their acquaintances had ever seemed to comprehend that he was a salesman, not a reporter. "Happy?"

"Hey, it's a rough break, you feel bad, anybody would. All I'm saying is on the legal score I don't think you've got big worries. What time's your first appearance? Have you called your insurance agent?"

"Not till the office opens tomorrow morning."

"Good. Talk to your agent, and when it's over—chances are it'll never even go to court—we'll get together, watch the Bowl games and drink a few brews."

"Thanks, Jere."

Jerry chuckled. "Don't thank me yet. This isn't a parking ticket. It's going to cost you out your ass."

Eva changed her clothes and returned to the kitchen to put away Nick's lunch things before they left. "Where's the wagon?" he asked when he came in from rigging up and opened the refrigerator.

"We have to take my car. The Camry's at the police station."

"At the police station!" Nick's eyes went wide.

"We had an accident, remember? The police need to keep the car for evidence."

"But it wasn't Dad's fault."

"I know," she said as Nick set the milk jug on the counter. "Honey, what are you doing?"

"I'm hungry."

"You just ate lunch." She emptied the sack of cookies he'd left open into the jar. "Did you get the rods? Where do you want to go?"

"Lake Stuart."

She was tempted to remind him that if he'd gone with his father he would have had to fish in Willow Creek. Guy hated Lake Stuart, ever since he'd let Nick keep a bass an inch too short and wound up in a shouting match with the warden.

She had just put the tackle box and bucket in her trunk when Nick appeared in the driveway. Brow creased with disapproval, he watched her angle the rods into the back seat.

"If the accident wasn't Dad's fault, how come they get to keep our car?"

"We'll get it back." They would sell it or trade it, Eva was sure. She couldn't imagine that either one of them would ever drive it again. "Ready?"

As soon as they pulled up to Tyler's, Nick disappeared upstairs, and Eva had to hunt out Tyler's room, where Nick was already absorbed in a game of Nintendo. "I thought you wanted to go fishing."

"In a minute," Nick said.

"I didn't see your mother when I came in," Eva said to Tyler, who lay on his stomach next to Nick on the sleeping bag spread across his bed. His room was neater than Nick's, she noted. "Shouldn't we tell her you're leaving?" After a minute she said, "Tyler, it's time to go. I want you to help me find your mother."

"Mom!"

A minute later his mother appeared in the doorway,

wrapped in a terrycloth robe. "I hate weekends," she said to Eva in a voice slack with fatigue. "Why can't they have school seven days a week?"

"Boy, this sure is an old car," Tyler observed as soon as they were seated.

"It's very reliable," Nick said from the back seat, where he'd squeezed in with the rods, and Eva was touched, though for the first time it occurred to her to wonder if he wasn't secretly embarrassed. It was fourteen years old, the upholstery was torn, and a hole in of one of the rocker panels had nearly rusted through. She had planned to trade it when she finished the book on the nude in Western art she'd spent a decade researching and writing, but that was more than two years ago, and the book hadn't sold. The public just wasn't buying big, expensive art books, editors told her. It wouldn't matter so much, but Gardell had reclassified her job from an administrative to faculty position, and all of a sudden she needed a book to satisfy the college requirements for promotion and tenure.

Tyler was flipping his door lock up and down. "You got any Guns and Roses?"

"They're awesome," Nick said. "It makes such cool noises when they smash their guitars."

Eva thought Guns and Roses should have more respect for property—and she'd loved Jimi Hendrix! She felt middle-aged.

"I don't have a tape deck," she said to Tyler. "Did you fasten your seatbelts?"

"Tom Petty's my favorite," Nick confided.

"Tom Petty sucks," Tyler said.

As soon as Eva parked in the gravel lot above Lake Stuart, Nick announced, "You forgot to stop and get bait."

"Didn't you dig worms?"

"In November?"

"I guess not," she sighed. Only last week she'd picked a late tomato. The boys weren't even wearing jackets. "You should have told me before we got here." Her throat burned; tomorrow her nose would be stopped up. It made her feel small to notice—as if she lacked the dignity to experience tragedy uncorrupted by trifling complaint. She shifted into reverse. "Isn't there a place on Clark's Chapel Road?"

"They sell bass minnows at the Parker Lake Marina."

"Parker Lake! Come on, Nick, there's got to be someplace closer."

"It's not my fault. You should have stopped on the way."

"Parker Lake's not on the way."

"So? We could have got livers at the Winn Dixie and fished for hybrids."

"I don't want to fish for hybrids," Tyler said. "Last summer on my uncle's boat I caught a five-hundred pound swordfish."

"Did not," Nick said. "My uncle said he's going to take me bonefishing in the Keys."

"What's the matter with the place on Clark's Chapel Road? The 76," Eva said. "Don't they sell minnows?"

"I caught a bonefish that weighed a hundred pounds."

Nick rolled his eyes. "Dumbo, the world record's nineteen."

The tanks in front of the 76 were dry. "I told you," Nick said.

Eva went inside. "Do you have minnows?" The clerk looked up from his magazine. He was wearing his baseball cap backwards, and sprouts of hair were caught in the plastic tab. Nick put an orange soda and a bag of Cheetos on the counter.

"Minnows," she repeated.

He shook his head. "We got nightcrawlers in the refrigerator and crickets in the back room."

"Crickets!" Tyler upset a display of leaders on the pegboard hung with plastic packages of hooks.

"Tyler, pick that up. Nick, put the Cheetos back." Eva turned to the clerk. "Give us a dozen nightcrawlers."

Nick pulled a long face.

"What?" she said.

"This is the best time of year. It's my last chance to catch a big bass."

"Nickie!" She was perilously close to tears, something he seemed to recognize, for he softened his tone.

"It's okay, Mom. We'll fish for bream. It'll be fun."

At the lake Eva helped them lug the equipment down the hill. The grass wet her shoes, and they had to watch out for patches of slick red clay. She wished she'd remembered to bring chairs. "An hour, boys," she said when they were settled.

She dropped a line in the water, felt a tug, and pulled up a bare hook. She threaded another worm and wiped her hands on her jeans, having forgotten to remind Nick to bring a rag. She hadn't brought a book because she didn't think she could concentrate, but maybe fishing would keep her busy. Once she and Nick had caught fifty fish here in an afternoon, or maybe it was twenty-five fish twice, not one of them as big as his hand. What she really wanted, she realized, was to stop by Claudia's. It wouldn't help, but she needed to play the accident over. She wanted to talk. Or maybe she just wanted sympathy, which she could hardly ask from Guy, who needed sympathy himself.

What she wanted was to be told not that it would be okay—

nothing could make it okay—but that they didn't deserve to have it happen. Only somehow she always had to take Nick here or pick him up, had to cook dinner or check his homework, or else she'd brought work home from the office, and as a result she hadn't seen Claudia in more than a month or maybe even longer and not really to talk to since last summer, when their sons played on the same baseball team, and once a week they lingered together in the stands. It seemed impossible that should be months ago already. One of their friends had left her husband, and they'd been breathless with shock. It was all they could talk about, though they possessed few details. Neither of them had talked to Kay, though Kay's husband had spoken bitterly to Claudia's husband Bill, and those details Bill passed on they had picked over and over, trying to puzzle out what could have happened. Eva had been divorced, Claudia pointed out, but that was different. Not after twenty years of marriage and two children not yet ten years old. The five years she'd spent married to Brooks Summer seemed as long past, nearly as insignificant as the boy she had dated in high school. She'd known Claudia fifteen years. And though couples split all the time, Kay had always made such a show of her marriage; other couples measured their affection against the Courtlands' and went home wanting. But according to Bill Whitt, who heard it from John Courtland, Kay had been sleeping with another man for a year.

It wasn't reasonable for life to be so busy that you couldn't see your friends. Of course, Eva had never been as close to Kay or Kay's friend Sally DeMik as she was to Claudia, but at one time, the four of them had made something of a crowd. They were Claudia's friends, Claudia having introduced her to them the first year Eva spent in Random, and in retrospect Eva had to admit that Kay and Sally had never made her feel entirely included. Random girls both, they'd been friends since high school, and there was something adolescent in their friendship, an exhibitionistic exclusiveness that Eva found annoying. But she'd assumed that Claudia still saw them on occasion, until last summer, when, sitting in the bleachers, Claudia observed that probably she and Eva were as surprised to realize Kay had grown away from them as they were to learn that she'd left John.

What she needed was to be told that none of it was her fault—not the accident, not her book or Guy's job or the friends who'd drifted away. She would rent a movie for Nick on the way home and go by Claudia's after she found out what Jerry Beck had said to Guy.

The only thing was she had to go to the grocery store. There was nothing in the house for dinner.

"Mom," Nick screamed, "your bobber's going under!"

"Oh."

"Set the hook!" She jerked the rod. There was another wriggle and then the line went dead. Nick's face dimmed. "You have to jerk when you feel the pull."

"I didn't feel a pull." A minute later she lost another fish and reeled in. Guy was right, she thought, the thing to do was carry on, but in the meantime she had a class to prepare as well as another show coming up (it wasn't enough to run the gallery, Gardell had given her first one and now two classes to teach), when all she wanted to do was think.

"Aren't you going to fish?" Nick asked.

"You catch one for me," she said and found a rock to sit on.

Before her the lake spread out, the color of army canvas

beneath a lustrous blue sky. On the far shore the trees had thinned, though a few flags of brilliant color remained against the dark pines. New and improved, like Guy said. Though the damp stone sent a chill up through her jeans, it was hard to imagine yesterday's rain. She tried to picture a scene of some comparable everyday beauty in Vietnam. If she could understand Y Bhan Buon To's life, maybe she could comprehend his death, but for all the familiarity summoned by the word Vietnam, she had no real image of the landscape. She had watched the war in black and white.

But possibly, she realized with a start, Y Bhan Buon To had never seen Vietnam. The war had ended years before he was born. She tried but couldn't remember the capsule history the *Herald* had printed when the Montagnards arrived. It didn't seem as if they'd been here very long, though the war was over so long ago that the POW debate that had recently resurfaced in the papers read more like déjà vu than news. Imagine waiting all these years, not knowing whether your husband was alive.

Imagine sleeping soundly, not knowing that your son had died.

Neither her first husband nor Guy had served in Vietnam. The only boy that she had known at all well who did was Warren Hossick. The name came back, though she couldn't assemble his face from its parts. Dark hair, narrow forehead, black-framed glasses that magnified his eyes. In her senior year in college, she had gone out with him a few times. They had lost touch by the time they graduated, but when he arrived in Vietnam he began to write. He was not especially gifted with language, and as she recalled his letters were really rather dull. His descriptions of the jungle and the war were more like lists, perfunctory, reportorial, matter-of-fact. The best parts of the letters were about her. He began to recall their courtship (no more than a few casual dates—they had been in the same German class, and they used to study together; she had not realized he considered those sessions dates until they went to the movies and he kissed her goodnight), things she not only didn't remember but was relatively certain had never happened. It was in his recounting of their time together that he summoned the sensory detail that might have made Vietnam real: the way she had inclined her head in a certain lamplight, the smell of her hair in the rain, a little humming sound she had made while memorizing the impossibly long and gutteral German nouns. In the beginning she had written him back for the romance of writing to someone in combat. Also she liked him well enough, but when he told her that he loved her, she knew she shouldn't have answered his letters. He didn't love her, of course—even then she had realized he was only homesick and scared—but she didn't want to trivialize his feelings or take away whatever fantasy he might need to survive.

That was part of why she did what she did. The other part was that she fell in love with herself, or rather with the self described in Warren Hossick's letters, so much lovelier than the everyday self she thought she knew all too well, though in fact she'd scarcely known herself at all, certainly not well enough to recognize either motive. She never pretended that she loved him, but she continued to write and her letters grew longer. She began to notice things she had never noticed in order to write about them; if she did not begin to feel what she had never felt in order to write about that, she became more accurate in naming those things which evoked her feelings. No doubt they were all very trite—storms, sad jazz, the sound of wheels on wet pavement—

but she was too young to know that, and the letters she began to send seemed those the girl he pined for might have written, a young woman with sensibilities so exquisite they could inspire love from a battlefield halfway around the globe. She kept writing even after she met Brooks, because it seemed to her that it would be cruel to break it off when Warren had no chance to find a girlfriend to replace her. To her the letters had become a journal, and she told him things that, because she told him, she had no need to tell Brooks Summer, or perhaps they were things she already sensed she could not tell Brooks. When Warren returned, she had thought they would see each other again—maybe she even hoped they would fall in love, and then, when she knew they wouldn't because she was in love with Brooks Summer, she thought that when Warren got back they would simply acknowledge with something like wry affection their bond of mutual folly and go on with their lives. Instead Brooks found one of the letters and stormed about her apartment (technically it was still hers though by then he was spending every night there) until she agreed to burn Warren's letters and never write to him again. Although she pled for a last epistle announcing her engagement, Brooks was adamant: hadn't she already shown she couldn't be trusted? Because grad school had proved boring and lonely—in an attempt to be practical she had enrolled in education—and because she was in love, she gave in, but by the time they married that September, on some level she knew that she did not and would never love Brooks Summer. When she left him five years later she went back to school in museum studies.

Now when she recalled the episode, it was always with distaste for the silly girl who had enchanted her and Warren.

She assumed that he had gone on with his life, for to entertain the thought of anything else seemed a deplorable act of self-dramatization. Deliberately she had not looked for his name when she went to the Wall. If it was there, she had no right to know it.

Yet surely she should be forgiven. She had been so young, and if Warren's picture of her had falsified and flattered, it had also been essential to her, much more than any sense of self she'd gained from her failed first marriage.

"Mom, Mom!" Nick was yelling. "I got one. Get the camera."

Startled, Eva looked up. Nick was holding up a tiny sunfish with a bright orange belly. "I didn't bring it, honey." When he released the fish, she glanced at her watch. "It's about time to pack it in, boys." She'd wasted half an afternoon. What meaning could a ridiculous episode from her past possibly have for her now?

"We can't go," Nick protested. "They just started biting."

"Fifteen minutes then," Eva said, but at the end of fifteen minutes Nick had caught four and Tyler two and Tyler didn't want to leave until he'd caught up with Nick. "Come on," she said. "Help me load up," but the boys had started squabbling again, and she had to speak sharply to Nick, who scuffed his way up the hill, complaining, "Dad would have let me stay."

"You're not with Dad, you're with me," Eva said, and he answered belligerently, "I know it."

"We have to go by the grocery store," she said when they'd dropped Tyler off. "We need something for dinner."

"Do I have to come?"

"Yes."

"Why?"

"Because it'll take too long if I have to take you home and then come back."

Nick sighed. "Can I wait in the car?"

"I'd rather you didn't."

"Why?"

"Because—oh, Nickie, just quit asking, it'll only take a minute. I'm tired. I've caught cold, and I feel sick." Once or twice she had let him wait in the car, then sped through her errand with a growing dread that she would come out to find him missing. He was eight, but would she feel any different when he was twelve?

"Okay," he said brightly, and in the store he steered the cart through the aisles, then carried the bag out to the car.

When they got home Guy was out running. Eva dialed Claudia but got no answer. Tomorrow Guy would probably meet with Jerry Beck, they would call the insurance company, the boy's obituary would appear in the paper, along with a story about the accident, but in the meantime the evening stretched interminably before her—a daunting prospect for someone whose major complaint about her life was that she had no time. Everything had changed, but at least for the rest of the day there was nothing that could be done about it, just as last night while she waited in the rain there was nothing to be done for the boy. She wished she knew who his parents were, though to no purpose. They wouldn't want her condolences. She read a draft of a student paper and realized that she didn't have the concentration to comment, though she had a heavy week in store and needed to catch up. When Guy returned, he went straight to the shower. They ate without saying much; he did the dishes, then turned on a football game in the den, which he watched with Nick until Nick's bedtime. "I'll read," he said. Though Nick could read to himself, they maintained the bedtime story hour.

When he came down, Eva asked, "Did you call Jerry? What did he say?"

"I don't have to go to court tomorrow morning."

"You mean the charges have been dropped?"

"No. If you have a lawyer, you waive your first appearance."

She tried not to show her disappointment. "Did he say anything else?"

"I won't be convicted."

"Of course you won't. Did you tell him we want to pay him?"

Guy studied her a moment before he picked up the remote. "This isn't exactly the kind of favor you do for a friend."

Eva realized what her problem was. The shock had worn off, and with nothing to do—nothing she was capable of doing—she was depressed.

Chapter 3

Y Bhan Buon To

Y Bhan Buon To, 9, of 2617-D Jamaica Avenue died November 17, 1991, at Alwyn Chandler Memorial Hospital.

Surviving are parents Y Rung Kbuor and H'deo Buon To, brother Y Nuh Buon To and sister H'nghai Buon To of the home, and paternal grandmother of Vietnam.

Funeral arrangements are incomplete.

Eva turned back to the front page. There it was:

Montagnard Boy Struck and Killed By Automobile
Police Say Alcohol Involved

A 9-year-old boy died early Sunday morning after being struck by an automobile on Lanyan Road.

Y Bhan Buon To, whose parents were among the 200 Montagnard refugees who arrived in Random almost four years ago, was pronounced dead at Alwyn Chandler Memorial Hospital after attempts to resuscitate him failed.

The accident occurred sometime before midnight Saturday. The driver, Guy L. Ferrin of 2216 Jefferson Road, Random, was charged with felony death by motor vehicle and released on a $20,000 bond. According to police Ferrin admitted he had been drinking that evening. Neither Ferrin nor his wife, who was with him in the car, was injured.

Random police officer Aaron McThune was the first to arrive on the scene. Ferrin maintains

that the boy ran into the path of the car and in the rain he could not stop.

According to the boy's brother, Y Nuh Buon To, the victim was angry after having been punished for eating some ice cream. Police speculate that the boy may have been running away when Ferrin's car struck him.

"These people have suffered so much," said Betty Paxton, a volunteer tutoring the Montagnards in English. "It's amazing, all they went through to get here, the stress of being separated from their families and learning a new language and culture. This is a tragedy for the entire Montagnard community."

Eva studied the picture of Y Bhan Buon To. A smile as big as Southeast Asia split his face, lit by enormous black eyes that beckoned her from beneath his chopped off bangs. A school portrait from the look of it, but without the cowering squint that tended to make the comeliest of schoolchildren resemble blind fish brought up from caves. The paper trembled in her hands. She got up and went to the sink, but couldn't remember what she'd gotten up for. Restlessly she crossed the kitchen, picked up a sponge, and wiped the stove. When Guy came in from escorting Nick to the bus stop she was sitting at the breakfast table again, staring at the empty bird feeder outside.

"Did you see it?" Her throat scratched.

He nodded.

She turned away and pressed her lips to keep back tears as the face from the paper shed its smile and reproached her through the windshield on the boy's flight over the hood of their car. She had never seen a more beautiful child. When she turned back her voice heated. "It's disgusting. 'Ferrin admitted to drinking earlier that evening.' And the quote—they make it sound as if you've committed a crime against the entire Third World."

He poured himself a cup of coffee. "I have to call the insurance company and go down to Jerry's office."

"Are you sure we shouldn't go to court? Maybe the judge will dismiss the charges." When he didn't respond, she wrinkled her brow. "Well, if we're not going, I'm going to stop by Sears on my way to work and buy a new answering machine." The old one had broken six months ago, and now that the world had stopped calling her, Eva hadn't bothered to replace it. "We should have one anyway while you're looking for a job."

"Are you kidding? Who do you think is going to hire me now?"

"Damnit." She slapped the flat of her hand against the table. "I'd like to wring that reporter's neck."

"She's just doing her job."

Eva glanced at the by-line. Janet Sarver. The new management had increased the number of women reporters. As a woman was she supposed to applaud? Four years ago she had been as excited as all the other women at Gardell to hire their first female Dean, but now that same Dean had reclassified Eva's job. What had once been a full-time position was now just a course release, so that when Eva failed to make tenure the Dean could appoint a new curator to run the gallery from her office. It had nothing to do with Eva, though she'd heard the Dean had asked why she would want to write a book on an art form that traditionally exploited women. Two editors had rejected it because it lacked a strong feminist perspective, and only last summer an editor who had liked it confided, "We're just not buying books on Western art. Now if it was a non-western book...."

From her office Eva tried to call Claudia again but got no answer. After a minute she picked up the phone and called home.

"Hello, this is Eva Summer. If you would like to leave a message for me, Guy Ferrin, or Nick, please wait for the tone."

"It works," she said into the receiver and hung up.

"At least something around here does." Amy Trent, the adjunct photography instructor, flung herself into a chair. Though the gallery had moved from its cramped quarters to the posh new library addition last summer, Eva still conducted its affairs from a basement office in the old brick art building across the quad. It was the closest thing to a department office the art faculty and students could find.

"I'm working, Amy." Eva picked up the copy for the Clarence Hines show, which had to be at the printer by five. She had a meeting of the gallery Friends at noon, not that it would accomplish anything. Old Charlie Hairston would clear his throat to say, "Well, I don't know about this modern art," then the rest of the Friends would agree that while they certainly felt the gallery should keep abreast of current trends it had gotten too far out, at the same time the students complained it was stodgy, the faculty had their own ideas, and those were deeply divided.

"I'd like to have your job—sucking up to the rich at cocktail parties."

"Believe me," Eva said, "that's work."

"All so they can give you their little Rembrandt etchings that everybody's sick of seeing." Amy pushed her wiry red-gold hair back. "The bulb in the fucking projector is burned out."

"Did you check the supply closet?" Eva wished her cold would either worsen or get better; it was a shadow cold that bred a shallow headache and left her feeling dull.

Amy hurled herself to her feet. "I'm not in charge of the equipment."

"Check the closet," Eva said before Amy could sit back down. She wasn't in charge of the equipment either. That was the problem. No one was.

When she got to the YMCA at five to pick up Nick, he pulled a crumpled note from his backpack and thrust it toward her. "You're supposed to read this."

> **Dear Parents,**
> **This is to remind you that your child has a report on _______ due tomorrow. Children should consult at least two sources. Their reports may be typed, but they should use their own words to describe what they've learned.**

The teacher had written "Venus" in the blank.

"Nick," she said. "This says you have a report due tomorrow."

He bent over the drinking fountain.

"How long have you known about this?"

"I don't know." The running water drowned his words.

"Why didn't you tell me about it before?"

"I forgot."

Eva sighed. Less than two days ago she and Guy had hit and killed a child, and not only did the world not end, their own lives went right on, and it didn't matter whether she felt up to hers or not. "We'll have to stop at the library. You need to remember these things. I've got work to do, I can't spend the whole night helping you with homework."

Nick came up wiping his chin. The knees were out of his jeans again, his hands were inky, and a sullage of red Kool-Aid had washed down the front of the twenty-five dollar sweatshirt she'd bought at the National Aquarium when they visited her mother in Baltimore last summer. *"I forgot,"* he said.

She retrieved her car keys from her purse as they started down the walk. "Where's your lunchbox?"

"I left it at school."

She sighed. "Oh, Nickie, what am I going to do with you?"

At the library all the children's books on the planets were checked out.

"We'd better Xerox what we find in the encyclopedia," Eva said. "Do you have any books on the solar system at home?"

"I don't know. Can I look for fishing books?"

"After we look up Venus."

"I wanted to do Pluto, but Shenika got that." Nick spun on the swivel chair in front of the computer that served the children's room. There were dents in the carpet where the card catalogue had stood, and the plush animals who used to preside over the top—Curious George, Babar, the Velveteen Rabbit—had been flung in a grimy heap in the preschool corner beside the beanbag chairs.

Instinctively Eva reached out to stop him. "Too bad. At least we know Pluto's the farthest planet from the sun."

"No it's not."

"Yes it is, honey." She visualized the planets as they'd appeared in her grade school textbook, the lines of bold serif type that brought back the sour smell of the ink and slick paper.

Pluto was a speck at the edge of the page, Mars was the red planet, Saturn had rings, and Jupiter was veiled in clouds. She couldn't remember anything about Venus except the Temple, Botticelli, and Frankie Avalon.

"No it's not. Neptune is the farthest planet from the sun."

"Let me show you," Eva insisted, but when she looked up Pluto in *The World Book Encyclopedia* she discovered that on January 23, 1979, it had entered Neptune's orbit. "You're right, I'm wrong."

"That's okay," Nick assured her, but she felt unsettled. For more than a decade she had not lived in the same universe she thought.

She replaced the volume and selected another. "Here's Venus."

"Cool. Now can I look up the fishing books?"

"Okay, but you don't have much time." As Nick disappeared into the stacks, Eva picked up volume M. Nothing under Montagnards. She checked the computer. Nothing. She hit search again and typed in "Vietnam." Eight titles. That couldn't be right. Surely the public library had more than eight books on Vietnam. If she got a chance between meetings, she would try the college library tomorrow.

When she turned around, Gregory Whitt was standing at the circulation desk with his mother.

"Claudia!" Eva was ecstatic.

Claudia turned her head. She looked different. The ash blonde hair she had worn in a chin-length bob for as long as Eva had known her touched her shoulders, and it struck Eva that they must not have seen each other for longer than she'd thought.

"Oh hi, Eva. How are you?" Her voice sounded wan.

"Not good," Eva admitted. "I'm so glad to see you! I've been trying to call."

"I haven't been home." Claudia's gaze roamed from the bulletin board to the shelves of Hardy Boys and Nancy Drews, then seemed to settle on the hamster cage behind the circulation desk. She was wearing a long cranberry-colored coat that Eva hadn't seen before.

"I know." Eva took a deep breath. "Did you see this morning's paper?"

Behind a row of books Nick and Gregory had found each other, and Claudia turned toward the muted chord of the boys' conversation.

"The most terrible thing," Eva began as the librarian picked up a microphone to announce that the children's room would close in five minutes. "I've really missed you."

"Gregory," Claudia called. "They're going to close. You have to check your book out now." She turned back to Eva. "What did you say?"

"There's just never any time." Eva scarcely paused. "We had an accident—it was in the paper, did you see it? Guy can't talk about it, he's too upset. He's been arrested."

"Gregory," Claudia called again.

"Maybe we could have lunch tomorrow? I have to help Nick with a report for school, but I'll call you later." Mentally she calculated: dinner, Nick's report, the insurance list for the Hines show. She'd gotten the catalogue copy to the print shop, but she still had papers to grade and a class to prepare. "I've got a meeting at one, but I could go early. Or else we could have coffee later. I really need to talk."

Claudia shifted feet. "Ready, Greg?" With a covert glance at the librarian she returned her attention to Eva. "Did you know Bill and I have separated?"

"No." Involuntarily Eva reached for the counter as her breath caught. "When?"

"A week ago." Claudia's blue-gray eyes were still focused somewhere past Eva's shoulder.

"I had no idea."

"I wondered whether I should tell you."

Not tell her? How long might it have been before she found out? Claudia was her best friend. It was unthinkable that she would hear from someone else. "I know I've been busy. I'm teaching two classes now, and since the gallery moved last year—there's a lot more space, we do more shows—I'm sorry I haven't called."

Claudia's eyes strayed toward the window, where the last of the day's light was losing color. "The last four years haven't been good."

Four years? On the spot Eva tried to recollect each instance she'd seen Claudia and Bill in the last four years. Four years ago the boys had been four—Nick was still in daycare. Saturday mornings she and Claudia drank tea while Nick and Gregory drove their Tonkas through the sandbox; they shopped the kids' sales at T.J. Maxx and the boys ran amok with the shopping carts and hid beneath the counters; for lunch they made Spaghettios and hot dogs and laughed when they saw they'd cut their own meat into bite-sized pieces; Saturday nights they put the kids to bed at each other's houses so the adults could sit down to beer and a late supper. Or else they went to the movies and shared a sitter. It wasn't possible that Claudia's marriage had soured four years ago. Only last summer she and Claudia had been sitting in the bleachers speculating on what had happened to the Courtlands as if such a thing were inconceivable to them. Claudia had said as much. In August she and Bill had left the children with her parents and spent a week in Spain. They were always taking little honeymoons that Eva could only envy.

"Mom." Nick yanked her sleeve. "They're closing."

"How do you feel?" Eva finally recovered enough to ask.

"Euphoric!" Claudia burst out, then lowered her voice again. "Except for Bill. He's been such a pain."

Eva couldn't fit her mind around it. "I just don't know what to say. I'm stunned."

Claudia pushed the door to the children's room open, and together they walked down the stairs. The streetlights had come on, tinting the dusk a sulfurous and gloomy yellow. In another month it would be dark by the time she picked Nick up at the Y.

"Are you in the house?"

"I'm at a friend's."

"What about the kids?" Eva glanced at Gregory, walking ahead of them with Nick. For the first three months of his life Nick had worn Gregory's outgrown sleepers, though by his second birthday he was the one passing hand-me-downs to Greg.

"They're in the house."

"With Bill?" Eva was shocked all over again. Before Gregory's older sister, Caroline, was born, Claudia had suffered a series of miscarriages. For years while Eva seemed to be on the fast track in her career Claudia had obsessed on becoming a mother. It wasn't plausible that she would leave her children.

"Bill's moved in with John Courtland." Just last summer John had been the one pouring his heart out to Bill. "I guess I feel more sympathy for John, since he's the one who got dumped," Claudia had confided as she and Eva gossiped in the bleachers. She opened the door to her van. "We're taking turns staying at the house with the kids."

"Do you want to talk?"

Claudia slid into the driver's seat. "Sure. Give me a call."

"How do I reach you?"

"Just call the house. If Bill's there he'll give me the message."

As Eva drove up Kirby Boulevard she glanced at Nick, already lost in one of the fishing books he'd checked out, and asked if he had understood the conversation. She didn't want him to internalize a half-impression and worry, the way he freaked at the slightest friction between her and Guy.

"What conversation?" Briefly he looked up. The freckles on his face had faded since last summer. His brown eyes were darker than hers or Guy's, which were not really brown but hazel. "Gregory and Caroline's mom and dad aren't living together anymore." At a friend's. Eva wondered if she meant Kay. Claudia hadn't given her a phone number or address, and Eva didn't know where Kay lived since she'd left John. She and Claudia had always coveted the Courtlands' house, a turreted Queen Anne sparkling with leaded glass and painted in subtle shades of putty, with a wraparound front porch that overlooked Wilson Park. "Would you leave a house like that?" they had asked each other last summer.

"I know. Gregory told me."

"Just now?"

"Uh-uh."

"When?" she persisted.

"I don't know."

"Well, when did you see Gregory?"

"Oh yeah," Nick said. "He was at Zack's birthday party." He studied the illustration. "His mom and dad are mad at each other."

Zack's birthday party had been a week ago. "Well, honey, it's more than that," Eva said, sneaking one more glance. "A lot of moms and dads get mad at each other, but that doesn't mean they're not going to live together anymore." He turned a page. "You don't have to worry. Your mom and dad love each other."

"I know." He looked up."Did you know you can catch a catfish with a vitamin pill?"

Eva shook her head. Every time she thought that she had anticipated exactly what would worry her son, he left her spinning with the realization that she had no idea how his mind worked. "I promise," she said. "We'll always want to live together with you."

"Where have you been?" Guy rose from where he'd been sitting on the stairs as Nick dropped his backpack and disappeared into the kitchen. His voice was sharp. "I was beginning to worry."

"At the library—Nick has a report due tomorrow that he forgot. I think we need to have another talk with him about keeping track of his assignments." Guy had been the one to pick Nick up from Zack's party. She wanted to ask if he knew about Claudia and Bill (if he had she would never forgive him), but instead she asked, "Did you see Jerry Beck? What happened in court?"

A ripple of annoyance crossed Guy's face. "Of course I saw Jerry Beck."

"Well you don't have to take my head off." She retrieved Nick's backpack and set it on the antique trunk in the hallway, then followed him to the kitchen. "What did he say?"

"He said...."

"Nick!" Briefly Eva returned her attention to Guy as Nick looked up from the breakfast room table, where he'd made himself a bowl of cereal he was dribbling on the open library book. "I'm sorry. I want to hear this, but...."

"What?" Nick said.

"You have a report due tomorrow. You may not read your fishing books until you've gone upstairs and found that book on the planets and read what we Xeroxed from the encyclopedia and taken notes."

"Can't I finish my snack?"

"No!" Eva said at the same instant that Guy said, "Yes."

"Honey," Eva said.

"I just think he should be allowed to finish his snack," Guy said, and Eva burst into tears.

"What did I say?"

"I'll go right up," Nick promised. He scraped his chair back. "Don't cry, Mom." He touched her arm.

Eva sniffed. "It's okay. Finish your cereal."

"What's the matter?" Guy asked.

"What's the matter!"

"Really," he said, placing an awkward arm across her shoulder. "Is it the accident?"

"Our son has a report due that he should have started working on two weeks ago, his room is a pigsty, he forgot his lunchbox, I can't seem to make him understand the simplest responsibilities—he manipulates us, he has too many privileges, he has too many things, he won't put the least effort into anything...."

"I know."

She was crying harder, because everything she said was true, but that wasn't why she was crying. Nick had frozen at the foot of the stairs.

"He's alive." Eva looked up. "He's alive because we've kept him alive, he's going to stay alive, and he doesn't appreciate it!"

Guy tightened his arm. "I know, baby."

"I can't stop thinking about that boy. I keep seeing his face, the way it looked when he flew over the hood. Like he couldn't believe we did this to him."

"You didn't see him." Gently Guy released her.

"I know I didn't, but I did. It was like a dream, maybe, but I saw it. I recognized him in the paper. He was such a beautiful boy."

"Nick," Guy said quietly, "go upstairs and do what your mother said. I'll help you with your report later."

"I can't stop thinking about his family." She toed the rag rug spread over the pine floor. Crying had stopped her nose up. "I don't know anything about the Montagnards, do you?"

"Not really."

"They're from Vietnam—there were some articles in the paper when they first came over."

"I remember. They fought with the Green Berets in the war."

"They don't look like the rest of the Vietnamese—they have broader features." She looked up. "I saw his face."

"You never got a good look at him. It happened too fast."

She pushed Nick's cereal bowl aside and sat. "I want to

do something for his family—I know that's tacky, like we could make it up, and I don't mean it like that, but if we could do something anonymous...."

Guy shook his head. "We can't."

"Why not?"

"I talked to the insurance adjustor. We can't do anything that would admit or imply fault. We're not supposed to have any contact with the family."

Eva bristled. "I think that's sick. We kill their son, and we can't even tell them that we're sorry?"

"That's right."

Her mouth flattened.

"Okay, it's sick." Guy leaned against the refrigerator, knocking a magnet to the floor. "But that's the way it is. It's better for them if we don't foul up the company's procedure."

"But we have to do something. We could make a contribution to the community—didn't the cop say there was one? I could do volunteer work."

"When? You don't have enough time to get your own work done. Look, Eva, I'm going to court. The criminal case is only the beginning. After that we'll probably be sued." It was such a reversal of roles she felt as if he'd turned into a stranger. Only two months ago it was she telling him that she was putting a moratorium on their charitable contributions, because the paper had been sold, his pink slip was surely on the way, and he was handing twenty-five dollar checks to every supplicant who knocked on the door.

"I guess I thought maybe the charges would have been dropped." The wistfulness in her voice struck her ear as childish. "I'm sorry. I know you'd be the first to do something if we could." There had to be something they could do. "What did Jerry say?"

"I won't be convicted of drunk driving death."

"Well, that's a relief," she said. Of course he wouldn't. How could he be?

"True, but it's not quite that simple. I should have sounded the horn."

"He couldn't have gotten out of the way. It happened so fast...."

"There's a statute. Essentially it says that drivers have to exercise due caution to avoid hitting pedestrians, especially kids. Jerry looked it up. You're supposed to anticipate that kids act irrationally. I should have sounded the horn."

"It wouldn't have done any good."

"That doesn't matter. If the judge is pissed off, and he probably will be, he can send me back to district court for failing to exercise due caution."

"Is it a felony?"

"Misdemeanor." He sat.

"Well, that's something at least. What's the penalty for a misdemeanor? Can they put you in jail?" They couldn't put him in jail. He hadn't done anything.

"Not for too long. There was something weird though... something I couldn't quite put my finger on, and afterwards Jerry didn't ask me to come over and watch football again."

"Men. They think the world depends on sports." Eva used her placemat to sop up Nick's mess.

"Yesterday he was insistent on it, and today it was like he forgot all about it."

"There's a TV here. So what if you don't get to watch the

Redskins on Jerry Beck's forty-six inch screen?"

"I don't know. There was something weird."

"Anyway, we're in this together."

He squeezed her hand as Nick bounded down the stairs.

"Finished my report, Mom." He spread a wrinkled sheet of notebook paper on the table.

On it he had written, "Venus is the second closest planet to the sun."

"That's it?" she said.

"It's all I could find."

"Well, you'd better find some more."

He sulked.

"Son," Guy said.

"You stay out of this," Eva said.

"I told him I'd help him."

Eva stood. "I'm going to put this in as positive a framework as I can. Nickie, I love you. That encyclopedia article had plenty of information, you just didn't read it. Now get your butt upstairs, read that article, find that other book, and don't you dare come down here again until you've written at least a page and a half."

"I said I'd help him," Guy protested as Nick marched up the stairs.

"He doesn't need any help." Eva picked up Nick's bowl.

"You're too hard on him."

"You're twice as hard on him when you're mad." At the sink she rinsed the dish. A soggy brown sludge had collected in the strainer, and she emptied it onto a paper towel. Someone, Guy, had made a peanut butter sandwich earlier. The counter was sticky. She knew it was peanut butter because he'd left the jar open on the counter.

"But I'm not mad," Guy said.

She didn't want to be mad, at either of them. She turned her back on the counter, and the edge left her voice. "There's nothing for dinner—I ended up going to the library instead of the store. What do you want on your pizza?"

"I'll order it. Relax."

She sat at the table again. The day's mail was still unopened. Pre-approved credit, an acre of rainforest that was hers to save for less than it cost to make her morning coffee. "I can't believe we're talking about pizza."

He massaged her shoulders, loosening the knot between the blades, relaxing the muscles of her neck. But she wanted the knot; she wanted every pinch of tension.

"I just can't stand the way everything is so bloody normal at the same time...."

Guy dropped his hands. "I shouldn't have hit the kid."

"It wasn't your fault!" How many times would she have to say it? She stood and put the cereal in the pantry. "There's something else. I was going to tell you earlier, but.... Did you know that Claudia and Bill have separated?"

"Are you joking?" So he hadn't known.

"I ran into her at the library, and she told me, even though I think she was trying to avoid it—there was something funny about the way she acted." It was the same thing he had said about Jerry Beck, and she'd dismissed it. "Can you imagine? What if I hadn't run into her?"

"I'm floored." He looked floored.

"And you know what else? Nick already knew. Gregory told him at Zack's birthday party."

Slowly he shook his head. "I guess it just goes to show you never know what goes on in someone else's marriage."

"You must have seen them when you picked Nick up at the party."

"I talked to Bill for a minute or so. He didn't say a word."

"He's living with John Courtland." Eva sketched the arrangement Claudia had described. "It sounds so weird—like the kids live by themselves and the parents come by to babysit. She didn't even tell me where she's staying." *With a friend.* Eva was her friend.

"Did she say why it happened?"

"Not really. Can you imagine how I would have felt if I'd heard from someone else?"

"I have to say I'm shocked," he repeated, though the color had come back to his face. "I'm just sorry to hear it."

"It's like an epidemic." Three years before Nick was born first Claudia, then Sally DeMik and Kay Courtland had gotten pregnant. "Must be something in the water," they joked, and Eva laughed, "I hope not," though soon, secretly, she was trying to get pregnant herself. She hadn't confided in Claudia for fear that she wouldn't; she was a few years older than the others, and time was running out. Or else she was afraid she would and after all the miscarriages Claudia had endured, Claudia would think Eva got things too easily.

"Ten to one there's another man involved," Guy said.

Eva shook her head. "No way." Years ago one of the librarians at Gardell had a crush on Claudia. The attention had been good for the ego, Claudia admitted, "but I could never do anything to hurt Bill." The confession had surprised Eva. They were not in the habit of talking about sex. Claudia rarely spoke of quarrels. That had been in the first years after Eva and Guy had moved to Random, when he'd taken his adjustment out on her. But that was years ago, and the bond between them had not merely survived, it had deepened. Despite the infidelities that had attended the demise of their first marriages—which had come apart in what she now thought of as an era of infidelity, one she tended to associate with the North, simply because the heady politics of the '60s and its sexual revolution seemed to have passed the bland New South city of Random by—neither she nor Guy had ever been unfaithful. The idea was inconceivable to her. True, they spoke impatiently and wounded each other all the time—he was overly sensitive, and so was she—but she would never do anything deliberate to hurt him. They had learned to trust each other. Along with Nick that trust was the most precious thing she had. "I'm sure she'd wait until after she left to start dating. Anyway, why assume it's another man? It could be another woman."

Guy shook his head. "Another man," he insisted. Eva had to admit it was impossible to imagine Bill with another woman. She wouldn't exactly call him a prude—he had too quick a wit—but it was true that his idea of a good time was a bike ride with the kids or a night spent volunteering at the homeless shelter; just the sight of him could make her twinge with guilt over a tub of moldy leftovers she'd tossed into the garbage instead of scrubbing out for the recycling bin. She had never heard a four-letter word cross his lips or seen him drink more than two beers, though he was hardly more wholesome than Claudia, whom as far as Eva could see he had always bent over backwards to please.

"Why does everyone think the only reason people leave each other is to change partners?" she asked, though she couldn't think of any other reason Claudia might have for leaving Bill herself.

In the middle of that night she woke whimpering and reached for Guy, who held her as she pressed herself wordlessly against him. He smelled of sleep, and the rumples of his pajamas felt warm against her skin. She lay in his arms and wept, grateful for the reassurances he crooned, the damp hum of his breath in her hair, even though he could not really reassure her, because if Claudia and Bill could come apart then they could too, and everything she told Nick was a lie: neither he nor she could guarantee anyone, least of all themselves, anything at all.

Chapter 4

Although Guy had always found her features too coolly patrician to be sexy, most men considered Claudia Whitt a sleeping fox. He supposed she was pretty enough, a tall but somewhat shapeless dishwater blonde who neither dressed nor wore her hair to her advantage. He didn't trust her. Years ago he had caught her in a lie, a small one to be sure, an excuse to her husband that put the blame for some minor tardiness on Eva, but the offense, committed in his presence and Eva's absence, shocked him, for the fact of the lie seemed far more significant than the size of it. He had considered his confidence, his warning that Eva should not expect too much of the friendship, an act of loyalty. It still stung him that Eva had found it necessary to forgive not Claudia but him, for although he had come to recognize that in some way Claudia was essential to her, he had known for years that she was not essential to Claudia in the same way. Now Claudia had left her husband without telling Eva, and Eva was hurt.

The truth was Claudia hadn't called Eva in six months, but Eva's job kept her so busy she blamed herself. He couldn't have guessed this when he met her, but Eva had no self-confidence. She had never seen how superior she was to her friends. (If he thought Claudia superficial, he harbored a genuine dislike for Kay Courtland and Sally DeMik. Rich girls spoiled rotten, both of them.) Once, when he'd remarked casually that Claudia had no sense of style, Eva had narrowed her eyes at him and said, "What have you got against women?" Nothing, he could say now, though it was true that for years he had blamed his mother, a chronic invalid, for emasculating his father with her needs and had wound up hating his first wife. Eva protested when he dismissed his ex as a space cadet, but she didn't know Pauline. It was impossible for anyone like Eva to believe that a Pauline could sleep eighteen hours each day and spend the remaining six eating Cool Whip from the carton while she watched TV. Eva was a worker.

For a time he supposed he'd held that against her. At least he'd resented her success. Her achievements had cast a long shadow and for too long a time, though he believed it to be a much shorter time than she recalled, he supposed he had gotten in her way just to make sure that she remembered he was there. When they'd met she was working at the Carnegie Museum while she finished her M.A. He'd been a Ph.D. student in English at Pitt (Eva liked to think he'd been the star pupil, but in fact he had done nothing to distinguish himself beyond one minor publication). The job at Gardell had been a gamble, a small college with an empty room, a recent bequest, and a closet full of gifts it wanted turned into a museum. Supposedly he came along to write his dissertation, though he'd already known he never would, for what he learned in grad school was that he hated academia more than he loved literature. He should have finished anyway, if only to forestall his later sense of failure, but it was 1975, and at thirty-one he was still arrogant with youth and the heady *now* of recent times. He couldn't see the point; those were days of burning bridges. And while he hadn't minded teaching, had enjoyed it on a level that felt more physical than intellectual—like exercise it both energized and exhausted—he couldn't front a life spent reading freshman themes and haggling through committee meetings. The self-importance of his professors turned him off. He was a coach's son; he wanted something more robust. When he failed to find a job in Random, he had gone to work as a temporary, sweeping out warehouses and unloading trucks, supplementing the minimum wage and irregular assignments with a paper route. To his surprise the route had suited him, the solitude, getting up at 3 a.m., driving a hundred miles down country roads before the sun came up, then watching it rise with the sense that he'd already done what the day required and everything else that came to him was free; he had even taken pride in his ability to throw a route clean, something Eva didn't understand, though any male would, a satisfaction in the act of throwing so purely physical it transformed itself to spirit. But the term paperboy had rankled beneath the skin, even though Eva knew instinctively not to make jokes and the time had passed when the daily news was delivered to the door by pubescent boys on Schwinns. Seven years of college, and he was making his living the same way he had bankrolled his Moon Pies and Lotta Colas in sixth grade. All the while she was racking up, or so it seemed during the years when she was the darling of the campus, taking a collection with no coherence and turning it into something any college would be proud of, expanding, courting donors, getting grants, discovering this unrecognized and that forgotten artist, always trying for the tour that would put Gardell on the map, giving party after party—and none of the artists, administrators, or collectors who came to his house and drank his liquor ever bothered to learn his name. It had worn at his temper.

Still, he had gotten over it. Within two years he'd turned the route into a respectable occupation, moving up to district manager—so it wasn't a big-buck career, it was a decent job by any standards but her friends'. He'd even missed the route, enough not to mind the days when one of his carriers was out and he had to cover, and he'd enjoyed sales more than he could have guessed, the quotas, the Super Saturdays, canvassing neighborhoods so unlike his own. In its way it was missionary work, and he discovered an affinity for it, a gift for connecting with the undereducated and the poor, for whom he felt a rapport bred on the sandlots of his childhood, a partiality that he had not been able to summon for Pitt's roster of eighteen-year-old white middle-class students. And then, when Nick was born, it was as if his life had started over, his smudgy slate of debits and demerits miraculously wiped clean. He wouldn't have wanted a career that bound him to a clientele of privileged students, the sick or wrongly accused, any of those paying needy the professional classes served; he would have been miserable in a job that indentured to others the time he treasured with his son. Only now the job was gone, and Eva wasn't faring so well either. He felt for her. Unlike him she'd done what she was supposed to. It wasn't her fault that the college changed the rules.

Claudia Whitt had no idea what it was like to fail because she'd never had to try. Her father had been a bigwig; she'd grown up in Westchester County and married Bill the day after she graduated from her fancy Eastern college. How could she possibly understand Eva's life? She hadn't held a job since she was a teenaged camp counselor, though she'd never forgiven Bill for moving her to North Carolina to take over the family's textile mill when his father died. She was forever making little digs about the South, something Guy, who had grown up in Savannah, resented less for himself than on Bill's behalf, though Bill himself only laughed and pretended he'd grown up without a pair of shoes, drinking moonshine out of Mason jars and beating Bibles.

Still she had seemed quite fond of Bill, and Guy was genuinely shocked to hear that they had split. He was sorry. No matter what reservations he had about her, she had to harbor at least as many about him. Years ago, in the worst throes of his adjustment to Random, before he and Eva married, he suspected she had thought Eva ought to send him packing. Why Eva hadn't he didn't know.

Instead of feeling defeated by her luck, Eva should think about her accomplishments. So she hadn't made it as a painter; she had a great eye and a knack for the business of art. They had bought their house off the sale of an Edgar Barefoot painting he'd thought she was nuts to pay a hundred dollars for at auction back when they were poor—at least the painting had covered the down payment. Gardell had no idea how astutely she had invested its money; he alone knew how hard she'd worked, for one of her many gifts was a modesty that made everything she did look easy. Sometimes it convinced even him. A dozen years ago, when she'd scandalized the college by accepting the gallery's first nude, a little drawing by Pierre Ribéra that nearly got her fired, she'd come back to write the first comprehensive study of the nude in Western Art since Kenneth Clark. Now half the board the new Dean had appointed to the gallery thought her too conservative; they'd have every show feature images of women's body parts disfigured by disease or sexist beauty standards. Aesthetics, she complained, had become a dirty word. Even so, if she'd gotten her book published, the college would have canonized her instead of threatening to replace her. It made him mad on her behalf.

Still, she should be proud. She had bought this house. So what if they couldn't afford to remodel a bathroom even he knew was substandard, she ought to think about what she had done—stripping woodwork, refinishing the floors, painting, hanging paper—and while he sometimes complained they lived too well (he had grown up with two brothers in a brick ranch not half its size), the truth was he'd gotten used to it, he liked the space, and he could see that she'd transformed it into something a thousand times more beautiful than it had been. Her renovations had inspired him to reclaim the yard, pulling out the tangled vines and yanking stumps, knocking down a crumbling stone barbecue, so Nick could have a play space.

They were both proud of Nick, though the truth was they wouldn't have him if she hadn't insisted. He already had a daughter, Molly—Good Golly Miss Molly, he used to call her—and he hadn't felt the call to reproduce again, for it had hurt too much to leave her when he and Pauline split, not to mention that he had been convinced he didn't make enough money to raise another child. He'd done his best not to let the divorce affect his relationship with Molly, but it was never the same after Pauline moved back to North Dakota, and his ex had tried to thwart his influence from the start. Or maybe that wasn't fair, maybe it just happened when one parent was there every day and the other only when the court permitted (no father now would agree to the terms he'd accepted, though back then they'd been standard); somehow as her teens wore on he felt her slip away. Or maybe that was just the way it was with fathers and daughters. He was afraid that Pauline had instilled in Molly her own lack of ambition, for his daughter had dropped out of college after her sophomore year and married a musician who couldn't seem to hold a steady job. She lived in Minneapolis, and though she was often in his thoughts he sometimes let a month slip by between calls. Eva should be proud that because of her he was a better person—he'd been wrong about his mother, who'd become invisible even to herself in a house full of men, a gracious but fragile woman whose misfortune was to marry a high school basketball coach and give birth to three sports-crazed sons.

There were so many things she ought to take pride in. Only, better person or not, he could no longer count himself as one.

He hadn't told her, but he had yet to type his résumé, because every time he looked at his credentials he felt so sick with failure that he couldn't face sending it out. The unwritten dissertation that laid the years of graduate school to waste, the two years of his thirties when any euphemism he could use was only a transparent term for paperboy. This company might be a good bet, Eva would come home saying, or why don't you go back to teaching, there must be lots of community colleges that don't require doctorates. Worst of all was the hint that he should go back to finish the degree. Even if he wanted to, even if they could afford it, it was too late. He would have to submit to the humiliation of course work all over again, and then did she really think anyone would hire a fifty-something assistant professor whose only teaching experience had come as a T.A.? How about an SI Department at one of the colleges, she would say, you could get back into sports writing, which he had done briefly while married to Pauline, and he would say yes, this was a good idea, that was a real lead, he'd look into it, knowing that he wouldn't. He hadn't minded selling papers, but he'd be damned if he'd sell pots and pans. Textbooks, she suggested, picking up on the pathetic squeamishness that passed for his ideals, but he was too attached to Nick to want to make his living on the road. He was forty-seven. For God's sake, hadn't she read Arthur Miller?

The truth was he didn't know what would become of him, and when she woke whimpering and clung to him in the night he held her without speaking, because he needed her and he was afraid that she would talk to Claudia Whitt and discover that she didn't need him.

From her office Eva called the newspaper to get the dates of the features it had run on the Montagnards. When she left the Dean's office after their meeting, instead of returning to her office she went to the library, where she copied the articles from microfilm. There were no books on Montagnards, but at the university library across town she found three, and she stayed there reading until it was time to pick up Nick.

Although the books were ethno-linguistic studies too dense and technical for her purpose, she did learn that they had been the original people of Vietnam, there before the third century B.C., when a renegade Chinese general conquered the northern mountains, established a capital, and proclaimed himself emperor of Nam Viet. The Vietnamese were descended from the Chinese who had migrated when the Han Dynasty incorporated Vietnam; from their arrival they had scorned the native population, whose twenty-nine tribes ultimately numbered anywhere from two hundred thousand to three million. For twenty centuries the Montagnards had battled the Vietnamese while living a semi-nomadic life as hunters and swidden farmers in the country's central highlands.

Hurriedly she skimmed the account of World War II in

Indochina. Later, after the French colonialists withdrew, the Montagnards were caught between the Vietnamese and the Viet Cong, who promised autonomy, then forced them into labor gangs. No wonder they'd been so eager to support the Special Forces when the Americans arrived.

Eva shifted, and her chair made a loud squeak. The reading room was overheated. Though the collection was limited, she preferred the library at Gardell, with its tall colonial windows and fat leather chairs, a card catalog still in wooden drawers, the art that she had chosen hanging in the alcoves that supplemented the main gallery off the entrance hall. The university library reminded her of the police station, shadowless and fluorescent. Like the police station it smelled of air filters instead of air.

In battle the Montagnards had proved both fearless and fiercely loyal. By the time the Americans pulled out of Southeast Asia, more than half the forty-five thousand Montagnard recruits had been killed.

It was getting late. She flipped ahead to see how many pages were left, though what she wanted most to know was what happened after the Vietnam War, when the communist regime began its resettlement and systematic suppression of Montagnard culture. They wound up in America, or some of them did; an entire group of two hundred survivors arrived in Random at the end of 1986, sponsored by an interdenominational group called the Christian Relocation Service, and that was the last she knew until Y Bhan Buon To stepped in front of their car.

"They don't use the term Montagnard," she explained to Guy later that evening, sitting at the breakfast table with the books and Xeroxed articles as he unloaded the dishwasher before she started dinner. Her eyes lingered on a picture of a group of children playing with a toy helicopter and shell casings. In the late '70s, when the remainder of the Montagnard army attempted to flee through Cambodia, most had been killed by the Khmer Rouge. "That was given to them by the French. Their name for themselves is Dega, it means 'the first people', because they were there before the Chinese colonialists. Did you know the first place they asked to be taken when they got here was the library? I mean these were people who spent their whole lives fighting a guerilla war!" Her face was hot.

He put her colander in a cupboard, and she got up to remove it, hanging it on its hook by the sink. It irked him to be asked where something was, but he never put anything in the same place twice. She was always halfway through a sauce when she couldn't find her whisk, in the middle of a stir-fry without the lid that fit her wok. It drove her crazy.

"Claudia called," he said.

Her voice leapt. "When?"

"About 4."

She could have been home if she hadn't gone to the university. And to what purpose?

Firmly she closed the book on the children of Ban Me Thuot. Guy didn't want to know about the Montagnards. What good did it do her to know the sketchy history she'd been able to piece together?

"Is she going to call back? What did she say?"

Claudia had asked for Eva, but when Guy told her that Eva was out she talked to him instead. He was sorry she missed the call, because now that Claudia had done her unloading on him she wouldn't need to unload on Eva. She had talked because she wanted to talk, not because she cared who listened.

"She said she met a man she wanted to kiss."

"You were right then," Eva said wistfully.

He was sorry to be right. It gave him no pleasure at all. "She said she knew if she didn't go ahead and kiss him she would just hold it against Bill."

So she'd kissed him and blamed Bill anyway, because she felt guilty. "I hated having sex with him," she'd said. "I mean we got along, the marriage was okay, but I couldn't stand to have him touch me. I was actually glad that we were getting older because I thought when I was fifty I could say I didn't want to have sex anymore."

Telling him how old and dead she'd felt, she cried. "She sounded sad. I felt sorry for her."

"I don't know," Eva said doubtfully, casting her eyes downward. "It sounds as if maybe we ought to feel sorry for Bill."

He did feel sorry for Bill. It was bad enough to lose your wife without having her tell your friends you flunked in bed. "I feel sorry for both of them."

"Me too," Eva said, though she still seemed uncertain. He understood: she didn't know what to feel. She hadn't talked to Claudia or Bill. She didn't know what happened. "Did she say anything else?"

Claudia had talked for half an hour, but that was the gist of it. "Not really."

Eva looked disappointed. "Did you tell her about the accident?"

"It didn't seem like a good time." He closed the dishwasher.

"No, I suppose not," Eva said and rose to begin dinner.

Though she had a brochure to design, after dinner she invited Nick to play Monopoly. When he was younger they always spent the after-dinner hour in play, graduating from rattles to blocks to firetrucks, then pirate ships made of Legos. Now she felt as if she scarcely ever saw him.

"Better watch out," Guy advised, pausing on his way through the living room. "Your mother's a shark."

"You're more likely to be trampled by an elephant or get struck by lightning six times than you are to get killed by a shark." Guy and Eva exchanged smiles as Nick moved his race car to Pacific Avenue.

"Are you going to buy it?" Eva asked, though she already knew. He spent his allowance before he got it, but was invariably reluctant to part with his play money. She on the other hand had already mortgaged St. Charles Place to make the last six dollars of her Short Line rent. He preferred railroads and utilities; she favored houses and hotels. The gamble of long-term growth against the certainty of steady income. Who won the game was always a matter of who landed on Free Parking.

The third time he landed on Free Parking she was in jail, hoping to roll a ten. "I earned my money," she teased as he scooped up the pot.

"So have I." His voice was full of unexpected dander. "I've been going around and around this board."

"I thought you wanted to play." When he didn't answer, she changed the subject. "What did you do with your tooth?" At dinner when she noticed the new gap, he'd sent her to his lunchbox, where she found his tooth in with the banana peel and cookie crumbs and crumpled plastic wrap.

"It's under my pillow." He was still counting his take, but

straightened to confront her. "How come the tooth fairy brings Mandy five dollars and me only one?"

Good question. Why would the tooth fairy bring Mandy Morris five dollars and Nick Ferrin only one? "When I was a girl, the tooth fairy brought me a dime." Two years ago she had had to ask Claudia the fairy's going rate: a dollar per tooth, plus a bonus for the first. Nick had shrieked with joy when he reached beneath his pillow and touched the two crisp bills. "Quick! Turn on the light," he'd ordered. "These might not be ones."

Now that the pot was empty she rolled double fives. When she threw again he thrust his palm out even before she moved.

"Mom?" he asked as she mortgaged Indiana. "What happens when you die?"

Her breath caught beneath her ribs. "Oh." In the other room she heard water running, Guy still doing dishes. "Well...."

He regarded her intently.

Though neither of them was much of a believer, Guy tending toward the agnostic, she more toward a latent atheism, they had agreed several years ago that Nick ought to have some religious training. As a child she'd been jealous of the children who had churches—it seemed like having lots of cousins. Her parents had both been only children who did not belong to church, but Guy had served as an Episcopal acolyte, and so the year that Nick turned three they'd enrolled him in Sunday School at St. Thomas. She had enjoyed kneeling in the shafts of ruby light that fell from the stained glass lancets and was moved by the formal beauty of the communion. The first solemn chords of Bach issuing from the organ could stir her to tears, but her appreciation was aesthetic, and in the adult Sunday School she sat rigid with hypocrisy and guilt. Guy had chafed at the clubby atmosphere of the coffee hour. After the service, while Nick received his religious instruction, they took to slipping away and walking together in the park. The magnolias were in bloom before she remembered to ask her son what he'd learned. Not much, as it turned out, for he had responded with such ignorance to her questions about the Garden of Eden, her queries regarding Moses and Noah (surely they had covered the baby in the bulrushes and merry couples on the ark) that at last she knelt before him and asked, "Nickie, do you know who Jesus was?"

"No, but I've heard the name."

Their attendance had grown spotty, and finally they hadn't gone back.

What happens when you die? Ashes to ashes. Dust to dust. A few particles of the earth's energy replenished. She thought of the funerals she had been to, the way the mourners stood outside the church when the services were over, chatting, putting on their sunglasses, delaying the moment when they would have to go back to work.

"Well, a lot of people believe...."

"I know." He rocked back on his haunches. "If you live a good life you go to Heaven."

"That's right." She didn't know much about Montagnard religion except that it was animistic. But according to her reading, many of the Dega no longer practiced the traditional faith, having been converted to Christianity by missionaries before the war. Whatever faith they followed, she hoped Y Rung Kbuor and H'deo Buon To believed in Heaven.

"What if you're bad?"

Gravely he regarded her, and just as gravely she watched

his expression. "And if you're bad a lot of people believe you go to Hell, but...." What was it that the priest had said to them in St. Thomas's adult ed? God's grace reaches far. It is more difficult than you think to avoid Heaven. *My god.* "Sweetheart, just because I get mad when you forget your homework...."

"I wonder where that boy went."

"Oh, Nickie." She wanted to scatter the deeds and money spread between them, to press his face into her chest and feel his warm pulse beat against her skin. "I don't think children ever go to Hell."

"Even if they're bad?"

He wanted a simple answer, not a meditation on the relativity of good and bad and absolute of evil. "Even if they're bad."

"Good," he said and rolled the dice.

"Would you like to go back to church?"

"Nope." He plunked his car down on St. Charles. "How much?" She glanced at property spread out beside her last few dollars. "You're in luck. It's mortgaged."

"I'll pay you anyway," he offered.

"You can't do that. It's against the rules. Don't you want to win?"

"I'm gonna win," he said.

He wanted to win but not so soon, because if he won the game would be over and she would disappear into her work. "I'll tell you what. We'll open an account and put it into escrow."

Happily he handed her ten dollars. "Here's my theory. I think when you die you get to live again, only you might not be a person, but no matter what you are you don't remember, so that's why it can't be proven scientifically."

Eva smiled. "That's called reincarnation." To his generation it would probably seem just another way to recycle.

"I just hope I don't ever come back as a worm, because worms don't have a brain."

She watched his tongue probe the space left by his tooth. What good would it do if Y Bhan Buon To came back but didn't remember and neither Guy nor she nor his parents knew? "Have you been thinking about dying?"

"Sometimes."

"Because you're going to live a very long time," she promised. She closed her hand around the dice and watched him as he bent to tend to his play fortune. *Grief,* she thought. That was what happened when you died. The grief we leave behind is the immortality we're given.

If he were to die, her grief would be so deep and so wide she would never get across it. But he hadn't died, and for that she bowed her head in thanks and tried not to let him see that she was weeping.

Perhaps the most annoying consequence of Guy's unemployment was his relentless presence in the house. Eva couldn't listen to music while she cleaned; she had to shut the study door whenever she used her computer; a hundred times a day he breached her concentration to ask where she kept the envelopes or the aspirin. He couldn't even leave without disturbing her, because he had to ask to use her car. "Take it," she insisted, but irritation at having to be asked infused her voice, and he understood instead that she didn't want him to drive it. Everything they said distorted itself and hid inside some other meaning. She had used her cold as an excuse to stay home to catch up with the paperwork she could never get done at the office, and she was relieved when he decided to go to the bookstore.

He had been gone only a few minutes when the doorbell rang. As soon as she opened the door she knew who it was. He was short and wiry with thick black hair chopped off in bangs like his brother's, dressed in a black nylon jacket with his shirt tail hanging out, red sweatpants, and purple high-top sneakers. For a minute they looked each other over. Eva's nose was chapped and red; she felt self-conscious.

"Guy L. Ferrin," he said.

A thick accent cloaked his words, but she recognized a semblance of Guy's name and pressed her lips together as she nodded. He was as beautiful as his brother's picture. More, because his eyes were alive and sunlight caught the sheen of his skin. "He's not here right now."

"Okay. I wait." She didn't know what to do but ask him in. He peered into the dining and living rooms that opened off each side of the front hall. Old as the house was, with doors that wouldn't close all the way and windows that wouldn't open, its skimpy closets and short circuits, it lacked the feel of luxury, but gave off the appearance. The silver serving pieces they had inherited from Guy's mother gleamed from behind the doors of the dining room hutch. He couldn't see that in the upstairs bathroom the toilet tank was cracked, the sink pitted and stained where hot water leaked rusty tears from one faucet and cold out of the other, but there was no point in replacing the fixtures because the tile was broken and the plumbing shot; they couldn't fix anything without fixing everything, and that they couldn't afford. Never mind that her friends had houses just as big and bigger. If the students she invited over once a year could assume that she was rich, Y Bhan Buon To's brother would have to think she and Guy obscenely privileged.

Reluctantly she guided him into the living room, where he examined the family pictures on a table. The wooden half shutters cast striped shadows across the gleaming hardwood floor.

"Could I get you something to drink?" she asked, wondering what and landing on, "Tea, maybe?" She had no idea what to do with him. He seemed not to know what to say, and she was uncertain whether he could understand her. "I think we have some Cokes, well, they're diet Cokes. Coca Cola?"

"Coke," he agreed, and she busied herself in the kitchen, prying ice from the tray.

When she returned with the glass he was gone. She found him in the den, playing with the remote control for the TV. "Nintendo," he said.

"We don't have Nintendo." He smiled. "No Nintendo," she repeated and sat across from him. "I have a boy though." She wanted to tell him she was sorry about his brother but decided to wait until he told her who he was. "He's eight." When he didn't answer she asked, "How long have you been in America?" His eyes jumped with fright. "You came from Vietnam?" Vigorously he shook his head. "No?"

"I am American."

Eva smiled encouragingly. "Of course. Now you're an American."

"My family Êdê. My sister marry to Go."

She was having difficulty understanding. "I see."

"Not like she husband."

"Oh." Eva fingered the cuff of her sweater. The lithograph

hung behind the boy's head was crooked, as was the lampshade. Rough-housing. She complained about it; she forbade it, but Guy was worse than Nick; he egged him on. She restrained herself from reaching out to straighten either. Again she thought about telling him she was sorry about his brother, but couldn't form the words.

"My parent make H'nghai marry Go."

Was the father a tyrant? According to the paper his brother was running away.

"Tell me your name," she said.

"Y Nuh Buon To. 2617-D Jamaica Avenue. Random, North Carolina, U.S.A."

"Y Nuh Buon To," she repeated slowly.

"Nuh."

"Nuh. Is your sister here? In America I mean."

"Get American divorce."

She and Claudia, Eva thought. But Claudia's father had never forced her to marry Bill.

Well, she and Guy made bad first marriages themselves. Did she think no one else had the right to start over? She thought again of Claudia saying, "I could never do anything to hurt Bill." At the time she and Guy had not yet married. They had lived together years before they married and had Nick. What a long time ago that had been. She had changed, he had changed. Why should Claudia seem bound by what she had been?

"Do you go to school? School," she repeated.

"Grade five."

"Excuse me a minute," she said as she heard the car in the driveway. She waited on the porch. "There's someone to see you," she announced. "His brother."

"Whose brother?"

"*His* brother." Her voice was thin. "The boy's. Y Bhan Buon To."

Guy's face clotted. "Are you kidding?"

"Of course I'm not kidding."

"Goddamnit, Eva...."

"It's not my fault. He came to the door. I couldn't just turn him away."

"I don't see why not. What does he want?"

"I don't know. He was looking for you."

In disgust he turned away, gazing at the azalea garden along the side yard.

"What else was I supposed to do?"

"Does he have a gun?"

"He's just a boy." It hadn't occurred to her that he might be armed. Why not? Students were suspended every day for bringing guns to school, and not just high school either. Earlier that fall the paper had reported that a Random teacher found a knife in a second grader's book bag. Eva couldn't stand to think about it—you weren't supposed to have to send your children into a combat zone to learn their ABCs and long division. Guy was right; she shouldn't have let him in. It was only logical that the boy might mean them harm, though she was certain that he didn't.

"He's in fifth grade, he drinks Coke, he wants to be an American and play Nintendo. He has a sister. We didn't mention the accident."

As if he had been summoned, Y Nuh Buon To opened the door behind them. Eva turned. "Nuh, this is my husband." The boy looked blank. "My husband," she said again. "Guy Ferrin.

You were looking for him."

"Guy L. Ferrin?"

"Look." Guy stepped in front of Eva. "I understand how you feel, but you have to understand it was an accident." A shiver ran down Eva's back. "Your brother ran out in front of our car."

"We're so very sorry about what happened," Eva chimed. The words felt artificial. She should have told him she was sorry as soon as he came to the door. "We're very sad."

Nuh looked Guy over. "My sister."

"Yes, you were telling me about your sister." Eva stepped from behind Guy. "It's cold. We should go back inside."

In the living room Nuh pitched himself back in one of the wingback chairs as if he expected it to recline and eyed the Coke that she had left on the coffee table. She sat on the sofa, but Guy remained standing in the doorway. "Why did you come here?" he asked.

Nuh's face lit as if he'd been waiting to be asked. He smiled, baring big, square white teeth. "Insurance."

"Insurance?"

"American insurance."

"I think he wants money," Eva said without turning toward Guy.

"I don't have the money," Guy explained. "There's paperwork. It's the insurance company that pays."

"H'nghai not like she husband."

"Your sister," Eva pursued. "She wants money?"

"Get divorce."

"Oh," Eva said slowly. "I see. But, Nuh, we don't have the insurance money. It's like Guy said. The company pays."

He nodded. "American insurance."

Eva rose to stand beside Guy, who had come a few steps into the room. "Did your parents send you here?"

The boy's eyes glazed with evident fright.

"Your parents," Eva persisted. "Do they know that you're here?"

He hung his head. "Please...no parent."

After a minute Eva said, "No, we won't tell your parents."

He raised his face, but Eva couldn't tell if he was relieved. "You must miss your brother." Nuh looked puzzled. "Your brother. What happened to him—it wasn't my husband's fault, but we feel very bad." Guy tucked his arm around her shoulder. "It's a school day," Eva observed. "Why aren't you in school?"

He frowned. "Grade five."

"Yes, but aren't you supposed to be there?"

He beamed a beatific smile of utter incomprehension.

"If you don't want us to tell your parents, you have to let me drive you to school," Eva said as Guy's hold tightened. Nuh's eyes recoiled. "Then let me drive you to school."

His shoulders sagged. "Okay," he said. It was the clearest word he'd spoken.

At Whitney Elementary School she delivered him to the office and asked to speak to the principal, a plump gray-haired woman with puckered features.

"I've brought Y Nuh Buon To to school," Eva explained, "and I wanted to speak to his teacher if I could, or well, I guess she'd be in class. Maybe I could talk to you?"

The principal ushered Eva into her office and indicated a chair beneath the usual bland portraits of departed officials. The dry heat stung her nostrils. "What can I do for you?"

"Well, it's just—I wanted to put in a word for him, I don't want him to get in trouble." The principal's expression disappeared into the pudding of her face. "You may know his brother's been killed." Eva looked down. Of course the woman knew. "He came to our house. My husband was driving the car that hit his brother." Eva clapped her hand to her mouth as, unexpectedly, tears spilled over. After a minute she found a Kleenex in the pocket of her jacket and blew her nose. "I'm sorry. It was an accident. He ran in front of our car, and we couldn't stop." The principal's blue eyes were unreadable.

"Maybe you could give me some information about the family?" Eva asked after a few moments.

The woman's face closed. "That would be impossible."

"Our insurance company says we can't have any contact with the family, but he came to the door. I couldn't just send him away. It was hard to understand his accent, but I gathered that his sister is unhappily married. I think she needs money...." How, Eva wondered, did he communicate with his teacher and his classmates?

"Our records are strictly confidential."

"Of course," Eva said. "Yes, of course, I understand, they would be." She rose, feeling foolish. "I'm sorry to have taken your time, but anyway I hope you won't punish him for skipping."

"We do not punish our children."

On the sidewalk Eva hesitated, then turned around, and went back to the school office. "May I use a phone book?" she asked the secretary and committed the address of Christian Relocation Services to memory. In her car she found a map beneath the seat.

The office was between a small appliance repair and a

for-lease sign in an aging strip mall. Inside the light was dusty, and Eva thought the faint essence in the air smelled like a shoe repair, though her nose was so stopped up she didn't know how she could smell anything. She had to lean over a narrow counter to discover the receptionist seated at a gray steel desk below.

"May I see the director?" she asked.

"Do you have an appointment?"

"No."

"She's in a meeting. Maybe I can help you."

"I'm here about the Buon To family—the family of the Montagnard boy who got killed. I believe you've worked with the Montagnards since their resettlement?"

"Isn't it sad? They've been through so much."

"Maybe I could make an appointment."

"At least they got the guy who did it." The receptionist turned her head as the inner door opened. A man who seemed to shamble after his own shaggy white eyebrows emerged followed by a woman in faded jeans, Birkenstocks, and woolly socks who shook his hand and then glanced at Eva.

"Excuse me," Eva said, "are you the director?"

"Carole Eisen. Can I help you?" The director took a step forward and extended her hand. Though she gave an impression of youth, her skin had the papery texture of middle age. Her hair was cut so short Eva could see her scalp.

"I hope so. I'm here about the Buon To family."

"Do you want to make a donation? The family doesn't have insurance. There's a fund to help cover the medical bills."

"Oh," Eva said faintly. She hadn't thought about medical bills. The boy was dead. But surely their liability would cover those. Friday the adjustor had met with them to tape their statements. Even if it didn't cover everything, they would find some way to pay—they had a moral debt. She firmed her voice. "No, I can't make a donation, but I'd like to speak to you if I may." She followed Carole Eisen into her office. "The paper said the Buon Tos came over in 1986, is that right?" Eva shifted to avoid a sharp spring on the sofa where Carole Eisen invited her to sit. The office looked like a thrift shop with all the bags and boxes spilling clothing.

"Rung came over with the first group. The family arrived just a few months ago. He was one of the first to get them out. So many of the Montagnard men are still waiting." Carole Eisen inched forward in her chair, turning her narrow, deep-socketed face pretty. She was thinner than Eva would have expected if she assumed, and she realized she must, that the Christian generosity of spirit would manifest itself in a generosity of flesh. "Are you familiar with U.S. immigration policy?"

"I suppose there must be a lot of red tape." Eva's cold was worse.

"On both sides. We tend to blame the U.S. for bureaucracy, but the Montagnards are a poor people, and Vietnamese officials are used to being bribed. They're unbelievably slow to grant exit visas."

She felt feverish, and the walls had begun to shimmy. The sharp smell of leather or whatever memory the air held burned her eyes.

"As you undoubtedly know, the Montagnards fought with the Americans. The Communist officials are not exactly disposed to favorable treatment."

"The Vietnamese have always hated the Montagnards."

A ray of interest crossed the director's face and she leaned into her knees. "You know about the Montagnards then?"

"Not a lot. I looked up a couple of things in the library."

"Are you conducting research?"

Eva shifted under her gaze. "Not exactly."

"You seem interested. We could use volunteers."

Guy would be furious. She'd gone too far already. "I'm sorry, but...."

"Mostly we need tutors and drivers."

"I can't."

"You drove here," Carole Eisen pointed out. "You speak English. Those are all the skills it takes."

Eva shook her head.

Carole Eisen gave her a pleasant smile that seemed to disguise a frown. "I'm sorry—why did you say you were here? I'm not sure I understand what you want."

"I don't think I know," Eva confessed. "Information about the family maybe? I just took Y Nuh Buon To to school. He came to visit."

"Oh, Nuh. He's a charmer, isn't he? A very bright boy. How do you know him?"

And his brother, Eva wanted to ask, his brother Y Bhan, was he a charmer? A bright boy? "I wondered about the names. He told me to call him Nuh. He and his brother seemed to have had the same name."

"All Rhadé males are given the name Y. It's like an honorific—dropping it is a sign of familiarity, like using *tu* in French. The women's names all begin with a silent h."

H'deo. H'nghai. Nuh had pronounced it "Nigh."

"He told me about his sister."

The phone rang. Carole Eisen listened for a few minutes,

then said, "Ray Hanner is the liaison with the landlords."

When she hung up Eva asked, "How old is the sister?"

"Sixteen or seventeen, I think. It's hard to know the exact ages. How did you come to meet Nuh?"

"Is she here?"

"Oh yes. She and her husband live with the family."

"Nuh says she's unhappy."

"They've lost their whole world. A great many of the Montagnards are depressed."

"With her husband, I mean."

"I'm sorry to hear that. Are you a counselor?"

"No." When it became apparent that Carole Eisen was waiting for her to go on, she added, "I'm the curator of the Gardell College Gallery."

"Oh. You're working on an exhibit then."

"No—well, I'm always working on an exhibit, but it's not on Montagnards."

"You should consider one. The Montagnard-Dega Cultural Association does some wonderful things. They've put on a number of performances at the schools. Have you seen their textiles? In Vietnam each woman would have her own back loom. They grew the cotton themselves." The director rested her elbows on her thighs. "They'd be thrilled to have an exhibit. They're very anxious for people to know their story."

"I'd like to see the textiles." Eva couldn't do a craft show at Gardell, but maybe the historical museum downtown could do something. She leaned forward. "If I understood Nuh right, her parents made her get married." At sixteen or seventeen, and now she wanted a divorce.

"Many of the Montagnard tribes—the Buon Tos are Rhadé;

I'm not sure what tribe H'nghai's husband belongs to, but many of the tribes practice arranged marriages."

"Oh, I see." She had thought the father was a tyrant.

Carole Eisen inched toward Eva. "You still haven't told me how you know Nuh."

Her tone was more insistent, and Eva could see she was torn between her desire to disseminate information and her puzzlement. But if Eva told, Carole Eisen might order her from the office or turn stony like the principal; she wouldn't learn any more than she already knew. Though for all she knew what she took as the principal's hostility might have merely been discomfort. Her confession had put the woman in an awkward situation. "My son knows him from school," she said, surprised to find the lie so readily at her tongue.

"He seems like a nice boy, but I was wondering—he didn't seem very sad about his brother. I don't mean he seemed callous. He was charming really." The image of his smile flashed before her: puckish was the word. "I just can't tell how he feels."

"Montagnards are a friendly but very private people. They hide a lot with smiles, and they're likely to tell you what they think you'll be pleased to hear. So many of them have had to struggle with adjustment—the stress they're subjected to is horrendous, and just like you and me, some handle it better than others. We've tried to employ counselors, but the cultural taboo against revealing problems to strangers is so ingrained. It's a very close knit society."

Some handle it better than others, Eva thought. Was she handling it better? Or worse? How was Guy handling it? He was her husband, and she didn't know.

Self-consciously she glanced around the room, at the used

appliances and household goods trailing cords from the open metal shelves. “The father—what does he do?”

“He works. They all work, none of them are on welfare, I hope people realize that. They’re very resilient, very enterprising, and most of them are resentful not to have found better jobs. They’re extremely intelligent, but the communication problem is overwhelming. The language—languages—are just so different, and it makes it difficult for them to learn more than manual skills. I believe Rung works as a custodian for one of the textile mills. They’re a fine family. You don’t need to be concerned about Nuh’s relationship with your son.”

Eva’s face flushed. “Oh no, I didn’t mean, I wasn’t—I didn’t come here to check out the family!”

Carole Eisen cocked her head. “I don’t think I understand why you are here.”

“I’m glad my son knows Nuh. I’m interested is all.”

The director’s face seemed to remain deliberately neutral. At last she said, “We’d be glad to have you volunteer.”

“Maybe I could think about it,” Eva said to put her off. “It must be hard for the kids at school—I don’t see how they could even understand their teachers. What will happen with a boy like Nuh? Will he be able to find a better job when he grows up?”

“It is hard. Not just the language problem. Some of these kids have spent their whole lives carrying machine guns in the jungle.They’ve never been to school, and now all of a sudden they’re supposed to sit at a desk all day long. But they’ll catch up.”

Eva tried to imagine what it would be like to have to sit in a classroom if you’d never done it before. Even Nick had trouble. What if he were suddenly snatched from his comfortable life and plunked down in another culture? He couldn't remember to do his homework; he pouted when he didn't get his way; he fell apart if she and Guy exchanged the least cross word. He'd never make it.

"In many ways resettlement is even harder on children than the adults."

For that matter, what made Eva think she would fare any better than Nick?

"The adults have a strong sense of their own culture—they worked to preserve it, it's one of the things that sustained them while they were living in the forest—but the children want to be like their peers and fit in at school while at home there's so much pressure to maintain Montagnard ways. It's an excruciating conflict."

"Oh yes," Eva said. "I picked up on that. He was very proud of being American."

"They had a lot of faith in the Americans."

"Well, they were our allies," Eva said. "We brought them here."

Carole Eisen directed a level gaze her way. "I assure you that if conditions in Vietnam were different, they would much rather have stayed home. Under the circumstances, I'd say it was the least we could do."

Under the circumstances? "I know they thought we'd come back. It seems amazing. I mean the war's been over for so long."

Carole scooted forward, as if she'd been waiting for this moment.

"They thought we'd come back because the special assistant to the American ambassador promised them we would. Her tone heated though her voice didn't rise. "It would never have occurred to them not to believe him because to a Montagnard a promise is binding. They don't have our cynicism about American politics. Did you know that when American soldiers were ambushed, they literally shielded our men's bodies with their own? That's the kind of loyalty they gave us, and we turned around and left them waiting for reinforcements we never intended to deliver."

"Oh." Eva swallowed.

"The Montagnards who are here are still trying to contact the other half of the army in the jungle, to tell them their president was killed sixteen years ago, their cabinet's over here, and the Americans are never coming. Until they do the rest of the army will keep fighting."

"My God."

"Perhaps you can understand why our agency feels so protective toward them." Carole Eisen scooted back and added, "I don't believe I caught your name."

"Eva Summer."

"And you're with Gardell College? There's a real need for tutors."

"Well, I'd have to think it over," Eva said again, ashamed of her evasion. She stood. "Thank you for your time."

"A couple hours a week." The director rose and extended her dry hand again. "I'm sure we could accomodate your schedule."

"I'll let you know," Eva said weakly. She'd done it now.

Chapter 5

While Eva was out Guy set to work revising his résumé. That way he could say yes when Eva asked, yes he'd worked on the job search when she wanted to know what he'd done with his day. Y Nuh Buon To's visit had shaken him badly, and he wanted to have something else for her to talk about when she got home.

The résumé was so old he had never entered it on disk, and he spent an annoying amount of time figuring out line breaks and tabs. Then there was the problem of what to include. Wasn't his M.A. in English just an admission that he had failed to get the Ph.D.? He'd worked as a sportswriter when he first graduated from college. Poor pay and lousy hours, but he'd enjoyed it, though Pauline had hectored him so relentlessly about his schedule that in the end he could barely separate the pleasure of the work from the pleasure of pissing her off. Still something of her complaint must have stuck: she had accused him of immaturity, of wasting his life hanging out on playgrounds with boys. A man who watched junior high football for a living was incapable of adult dialogue, she implied, an idea to which in general he subscribed, although her idea of adult dialogue had consisted of an endless paean in praise of her. "Isn't my hair beautiful?" she used to ask. "What do you really think of my legs?" She'd been especially vain about her lustrous curtain of dark hair and sensitive about the spider veins that splotched her thighs after she bore Molly. All the same, when they divorced, he quit his job, grew a beard, and enrolled in graduate school, where he must have thought he would learn a grown-up trade. The beard had suited him no better than academia. Years ago he'd resumed playing basketball and softball. (Now he'd slowed down so much he was injured all the time—it was painful to think he might not have another season of basketball left in him.) But even when he'd applied to the *Random Herald*, he had left his experience as a sportswriter out.

Well, it was ancient history and too late now, but to take up space he decided to include it. Somewhere he had a file of old clippings that would give him dates. He tried the attic, and after knocking over a dusty fan and poking through a box of family photographs that had come to him when his mother died, he found what he wanted.

Maybe it wasn't mature or important work, but he'd been good at it and he'd loved it, he remembered as he read: game stories, sidebars; for a year he'd penned a column for an alternative paper in Athens long since defunct. Nineteen sixty-eight. The championship game between Valdosta and East Paul. He could still see Harley Trumbo's turnaround jump shot. The kid should have made it to the pros, but his first college season he busted up his knee, and after a series of surgeries and two more seasons on the bench, he'd dropped out of school. Guy had no idea what had happened to him since. So perhaps it was important that he had been there to take note. Surely it had been important to Harley Trumbo.

When he went downstairs to warm a cup of coffee, the light on the new answering machine was flashing. He hadn't heard the phone ring in the attic. When he punched play, Jerry Beck's voice asked him to call back, but before he could pick up the receiver the doorbell rang and Bill Whitt exploded into the front hall.

"That bitch!" Bill yanked the refrigerator open with a vicious clinking of bottles and jars, slammed a can of Budweiser on the breakfast room table, and sat. "She can't even wait till she leaves the house! She's got to call lover-boy from the kitchen with the kids in the next room!"

"Man, I'm sorry." Guy took his coffee from the microwave and joined Bill at the table. "Eva told me—she ran into Claudia. We were both stunned."

Bill's eyes blazed. Overnight the lids seemed to have grown an extra fold. "What did she tell Eva?"

"Just that you were separated." Guy decided not to mention Claudia's call. He wondered if he should get a beer to seem more sympathetic, but it was a little early for alcohol and he'd already brought his coffee mug to the table. He needed to finish his résumé. Now that he'd started, he wanted to get it over with.

"Yeah, I bet." Bill's mouth flattened into an expression of nihilistic accusation.

"She said you were living with John Courtland."

"Oh yeah—I'm living with John Courtland." Bill's voice was as flatly nihilistic as his face. He wiped his sweaty forehead on his shirt. He was a bunchy, round-faced man with thin blond hair and watery blue eyes who had trouble keeping his shirts tucked in, and anger fit him as poorly as his clothes. "How do you like these apples? We spend a month finding her an apartment so she can walk out on me and the kids, then at the last minute she decides it would be too disruptive for them to have to visit her, so all of a sudden I'm evicted and she's pissed off because I ask John if I can bunk at his place for a few days or weeks or however long she means for this insanity to go on."

Guy shook his head. "Why doesn't she want you to stay with John?"

"How the hell do I know what she wants or why? Are you sure you didn't know about this? She didn't talk to Eva?" Bill slit his eyes.

"Eva didn't have a clue. She was really hurt."

"She was hurt!" Bill slapped his can onto the table so hard the salt and pepper shakers jumped. "You know how I found out? I run into Sally DeMik at the grocery store, because, hey, I'm a good boy, I do my share around the house, I cook, I shop. The fucking bitch doesn't talk to me, she talks to Sally DeMik."

Guy's felt his eyebrows lift. "You mean...?"

"So I don't get it, I go home and say, 'You wouldn't believe this weird conversation I just had with Sally DeMik at Harris Teeter,' and just like that she looks up and says, 'I want a divorce.'"

Guy wagged his head in disbelief. "Jesus."

"These women, they get together and one of them starts boohooing about she's so unhappy, she's unfulfilled, the next thing you know they're all unhappy, they've got to shack up with someone new to keep from feeling stifled, except that's not what they call it, hell no, they call it growing, they're not fucking around, they're finding their inner space."

"I don't know what to say," Guy said, in part because he understood that was what he should say. He wasn't supposed to participate in the conversation; he was just supposed to make sympathetic noises.

Bill drained his can. "So tell me this: how come the only way they can find this inner space is to have some other guy's prick shoved up inside it?"

Guy shifted uncomfortably. He had forgotten to drink his

coffee, and he went to the refrigerator and brought back two beers. He could always do his résumé tomorrow. It wasn't as if anyone had requested it. Eva could hardly claim there was any rush.

"First it's Kay Courtland, she's having such a good time leaving John she's got to talk Sally DeMik into ditching Frank. You better watch out. Next thing you know the three of them will be going to work on Eva." Bill wiped his mouth and popped the tab on his second can.

"You mean Sally and Frank DeMik split up?"

"Hell, she threw him out in August, where have you been?"

Sally and Frank were nothing to him, but Eva would be shocked.

"I'm warning you, pal. You're next."

Guy tucked the corners of his mouth into what he intended as a modest expression of demurral, but Bill waved it away.

"Look how they operate. They've got to do everything in a group—first one of them has a kid, they all have to have kids together. Now one of them ditches her husband, they've all got to ditch their husbands, because, hey, they've got their kids, what do they need husbands for? Fourteen years ago it was art classes. Then that women's group." Bill's mouth twisted. "They're like a goddamn pack of cheerleaders hanging out in the high school bathroom."

Sally DeMik looked like a cheerleader with her pert nose and tits. She had the bouncy brunette bob and saucy look-at-me smile. When Guy tried to imagine her undressed he couldn't get past a pair of pink day-of-the-week panties.

"How are the kids taking it?" Guy sipped his beer. He hadn't had a drink since the accident. He wondered what Eva would say if she came home in the middle of the afternoon and found them drunk.

"What do you think? Greg's puking and crying his eyes out, he can't eat, he can't sleep, and you know what the kid's mother has to say? 'Oh good, he's able to express his feelings.'"

Guy shook his head again. "What about Caroline?"

"In a shell, but she feels it as much as Greg does, maybe more. You know what really gets me? Half the nights of the week my kids need me, and I'm not there."

"I'm really sorry, man." He was.

"The woman's forty years old—she's got a ten-year-old daughter for Christ's sake—and she's shacked up with a twenty-nine-year-old housepainter who wears a frigging earring."

The front door opened with a whoosh of weatherstripping, and Guy looked up. "I'm home. Did the mail come?" Eva strolled into the kitchen still taking off her jacket. "Bill!" Awkwardly he rose to receive her hug. Condolence melted through her features. "I'm so sorry."

Guy turned his head, and they exchanged a self-conscious glance, as if to kiss each other might seem cruel, a show of what they had managed to hold on to that Bill Whitt had not. "Want a beer?" he asked as her glance fell across the table. He had intended to greet her with the news that he'd worked on his résumé. She made him feel like a kid whose mother knows without asking that he hasn't done his chores.

She shook her head and hung her jacket on the clothes tree in the hall. "Nick's got a birthday party at Skateworld. I've got to pick him up at school." For a moment she hesitated, then sat.

"Did you talk to Claudia?" Bill demanded.

"No." Her nose was chapped around the nostrils. She cut

a trim figure in her knit pants and sweater, but her face was beginning to age, her skin looked dry, and her once glossy brown hair was streaked with gray. In Guy's opinion the way she'd taken to wearing it pulled back made her look severe. She had always been so much sexier than she gave herself credit for—though at the time he met her, conditioned by the generous portions of Pauline's flesh, he'd preferred women with ample breasts and wide, soft asses. Thin women made him nervous with their brusque energy and hard stomachs. The tight navels and compact breasts with their crisp brown nipples seemed to him more stingy than appealing. He liked the subtle loosening in Eva's thighs and belly since Nick, the stretching of her breasts that tipped their weight and spread the areolas, the clotted color of her dusky auburn nipples. "We just ran into each other at the library."

"Did she tell you about her boyfriend?"

Eva shook her head again. "I didn't know she had one until she told Guy." Bill's eyes shifted from her to Guy, and guiltily she looked down.

"She called the other day, and Eva wasn't home," Guy admitted.

"No sweat." Bill shrugged, a bit too elaborately. "She's your friend."

Eva reached across the table. "You're both our friends, Bill."

"So what did she say?" he asked after a moment's pause meant to feign indifference.

"Nothing much." Guy shifted.

Eva fiddled with her wedding ring. "She said the last four years hadn't been good."

"Four years?" Bill's voice sparked. "Four years? Where the hell does she get these numbers? You want to know when it went bad? September 7, that's when."

"Oh." The syllable made a soft popping sound, like a bubble bursting in Eva's mouth. "That's her birthday." For years she and Guy had celebrated with the Whitts, though in the last few years there had been so many childhood illnesses and cancelled sitters that last year neither couple had remembered to engage one, but at the least Eva always delivered a card and a bottle of wine. This year she had a lecture at the gallery, but on her way to pick up the visiting artist for dinner she'd stopped by. They'd joked about the big 4-0 as they stood chatting on the porch. She herself had turned forty nearly six years before, but Claudia took age hard, and Eva had made sure to buy an especially expensive chardonnay. "I guess it really hit her."

Bill cut his eyes to indicate that only he could appreciate how hard. "That week she gets her hair dyed, buys a bunch of makeup and new clothes, and by the next week she's got a boyfriend."

Claudia spoke more longingly about her high school and college years than anyone Eva knew. Once as the four of them sat around the Whitts' fireplace on a Saturday evening, she'd actually asked, "Don't you wish you were sixteen again?" and without an instant's hesitation they had collectively gasped, "No!" Thirty, yes, but Eva didn't even wish she were twenty-five. That was the night she had realized the real difference between Claudia and herself was not her job, not her friend's free time or money, but Claudia's untouchable naiveté.

"For two months she's yelling and weeping—one day she hates me, the next day she says she can't do this to me and the kids, she's a bad person, and I'm thinking damn right, you're a bad person, but instead I have to say no I understand, it's okay, or else she starts screaming all over again about how I've ruined her life. Did I ask her to have kids? Did I ask her not to have a career?" Bill thunked his empty can.

Though Guy's can was still half full, he got up to get Bill another. He glanced at the clock, and reluctantly Eva rose. She wished he would volunteer to get Nick, but that was selfish—Bill wanted to talk to him, not her. All the same it didn't seem fair that he should be the one to talk to both Claudia and Bill. Especially when she knew what he would say when she asked what else Bill had said: "Nothing much."

"I have to pick up Nick. Bill...." She gave him another lingering look of consolation as he stood for her goodbye hug. "I just want you to know how sorry we both are."

By the time she got back Bill was gone, and as she expected when she asked Guy what else Bill had said, he replied, "Not much." She had no way of knowing that in fact it was true, that as soon as she left Bill seemed to lose his desire to talk and changed the subject to baseball. "We've got a team to field," he said, in reference to the kids' team Guy had agreed to help him coach next summer. Shortly after that he had carried his empty beer cans to the trash and taken his car keys from his pocket.

Guy hadn't opened another, but all the same she would have to be the one to get Nick at six. He couldn't have taken Nick to the party even if Bill had wanted to talk to her instead of him: he'd been drinking.

By the time Guy remembered he was supposed to call Jerry Beck it was after five, and the office didn't answer.

"Call him at home," Eva suggested, but Guy didn't want

to bother him after hours again. "Well, what did he want?"

"I don't know."

"Then why don't you call him and find out?"

"I'll find out tomorrow."

"You are so stubborn," she said, opening the refrigerator to begin dinner. It was the sort of remark that ordinarily she might have made in grudging recognition of his character and her exasperated endearment to it, but if there was a lilt of endearment in her voice he missed it.

He wanted to talk but didn't know what to say that wouldn't sound like a speech. Then he remembered. "I worked on my résumé today."

"I thought you'd finished that."

He heard the inaudible sigh but was undaunted. "I added some stuff that I'd forgotten."

"Good," she said without interest.

"Yeah, I dug out my old sports clips."

"Oh." She was zesting a lemon, and a spray of fragrant yellow oil rose around her face. He leaned against the refrigerator. "You know, I wasn't bad. It made me feel good to look at them, to be able to tell myself, 'By God, you may be down right now, but....'"

He had gone too far. Still holding the lemon, she turned to look at him with a mixture of horror and pity.

"I was good at what I did," he finished, but his voice went lame, it came out imploring and whiny.

"Guy, that was high school," she said.

She thought he was talking about—he had played basketball in high school. He had been so obsessed that in one of his ritual self-purges he had deliberately chosen a college with a team he wouldn't be good enough to make. Even so it had taken him six years to graduate, because Pauline had gotten pregnant and when they got married he'd dropped out to take a job. "No," he cried, almost joyful with relief. "I meant my clips, you know, from when I was a sportswriter."

But she only said, "Of course you were good. Why would you think you weren't? You should have stuck with it."

She put a lid on the pot of water heating on the stove, oblivious to the outrage that cramped his chest and stung his eyes. She knew perfectly well why he hadn't stuck with it. He had told her. His first wife convinced him it was puerile.

"I have to get Nick," she said. "I'll put the pasta on when I get home."

In the morning he called Jerry Beck.

"Can I tell him who's calling?" the receptionist asked, then connected him with a secretary who asked the same question. Though he knew it was routine, the screening made him feel singled out and small.

"Guy! How are you?" Jerry said heartily when he came on the line. It was the same question the doctor had asked Guy's mother each day when she lay in the hospital with her last illness, and every day she had responded "Fine" in the cracked whisper that was all the voice she had left. Guy had willed that just once she should answer "I'm dying, you ass," though he supposed the doctor only would have chided, "That's not what I meant."

"Sorry I didn't return your call yesterday. I had an unexpected visitor."

"No problem. Listen, I wasn't thinking the other day. I've

got more work than I can handle. I'm going to have to back off this case."

"Come again?" Guy said.

"I'm going to have to drop your case."

"That's what I thought you said." Guy studied the creased spines of the paperbacks on their office shelves.

"I'm sorry as hell," Jerry was saying, "but I'm up to my eyeballs in work. I'm just not going to have the time to devote to your case."

"The thing I don't understand," Guy said slowly, "is how you decide which case you're going to drop."

"It's nothing personal," Jerry assured him. "You just happen to be one of the last cases I took on."

"Bullshit." For a long minute there was silence.

"Look, I can refer you. Like I said, due caution is the worst that's going to come down— they slap you on the wrist, you get off with a traffic fine. Chances are the Grand Jury won't even indict."

"I thought you said it wouldn't go to the Grand Jury. You said the charges would be thrown out at the hearing for probable cause."

"Well...." Jerry drew the syllable out.

"What does that mean?"

"The D.A. plays hardball. I don't think he's going to schedule."

"What do you mean?"

"Nothing, really. Like I said I've got too many cases."

"What is it? You don't want to represent a guy who's killed a kid?"

"Hell, you know me, the guiltier the better." Once Jerry had explained the philosophy of his practice to Eva. He didn't take domestic cases because the lawyer was always the middle guy, caught between two parties who couldn't get enough revenge. Criminal law was more to his taste, and he preferred that his clients be guilty because the innocent were a pain in the ass, so outraged to be accused that a lawyer could never do enough for them, whereas the guilty, Jerry had reported with a gleeful little smirk, "the guilty know they're guilty—they're grateful as hell for any little favor."

"I'd defend an ax murderer," he was saying now. "It's just Marissa..."

Marissa was his wife.

"...you know how crazy she is about kids."

They had four, or was it five? Jerry drove a mid-life crisis, a sportscar Eva called the penismobile, while Marissa tooled around town in a mini-van plastered with pro-life bumper stickers.

"So Marissa told you to drop the case."

"Not exactly. I'm thinking about running for city council."

"I thought you'd bagged that idea."

"Well...."

"You used to tell Eva you couldn't run for office because you'd catch hell from Marissa if you came out pro-choice."

"Well, abortion's not really a local issue."

"The hell it isn't." For over a year the Ob-Gyn who delivered Nick had been trying to get a court order to keep Operation Rescue from picketing his house, though Guy hadn't paid the case much attention and was surprised at the sudden anger he felt now. "Anyway, city council's just a warm up. You've got your eye on the state house."

"I'm considering it."

"What's Marissa going to say when you come out pro-choice?"

"We're working out a compromise."

"Who's doing the compromising?"

"I'm considering my position."

"You mean you're changing your stance."

"I thought you were married," Jerry said.

Guy was staring at the copy of *V* he had read in grad school. Because he had read it Eva did. "I don't get it," she'd said flatly when she finished, and now it seemed to him that the grave and skeptical look she gave him had been what he deserved. "What about your little honeys? What happens when one of them gets pregnant, how do you hide that from Marissa once you've outlawed abortion?"

"You're upset," Jerry said. "I'll be glad to talk this over after you've calmed down."

"Fuck you," Guy said and slammed the receiver into its cradle. He was still fuming when Eva got home with Nick and a bag of groceries at noon.

"What's the matter?" he demanded.

"Nick has a stomach ache. I picked him up at school." She set the bag on the counter and returned to the hall to pick up the jacket Nick had dropped inside the door.

"Did you take him to the doctor?"

"No."

"Why not?"

"It's just a stomach ache." She didn't want to tell him how her throat had closed with fear when the school nurse identified herself on the phone, how a chill had prickled down her back as the receiver went clammy in her hand.

"How do you know?"

"Because I asked him." She unpacked her groceries. "Nick, I'm going to give you some 7- Up. Do you want me to make a bed on the couch so you can watch your movie?"

"Uh huh."

"Where did you get the movie?" Guy felt Nick's ears and forehead with his hand. "Shouldn't we take his temperature?"

"Blockbuster." Her forehead wrinkled as Guy crossed his arms. "He doesn't have a fever. I checked."

"You took a sick kid to Blockbuster?"

"Come on, Nick. Let's get you set up in the den." When she came back to the kitchen she put the sodas in the pantry and some water on to boil. "I assume you called Jerry Beck. Is that what's eating you?"

"There's nothing eating me."

"Fine. Just tell me what Jerry said."

"He's dropping the case."

She turned from the stove. "What?"

"Mom!"

Her mouth still hung open as she tuned an ear toward the den. "What, honey?"

"The movie's all messed up."

"Just a minute," she promised Guy and went to adjust the tracking. "Why?" she asked when she came back.

"Politically incorrect."

The teakettle whistled, and she stirred the water into a packet of Jell-O. "That's what he said? He used those words?"

Guy shrugged and moved out of the way so she could open the freezer. "He's thinking about running for city council."

Eva emptied the ice tray into the bowl, and Guy put it back. "Fill it please." He took the tray to the sink, then slammed it into the freezer so hard the water spilled. "Thank you," she said tartly.

"Listen, goddamnit. I happen to have some very serious problems."

She closed her eyes and counted. "I'm sorry I asked you to fill the ice tray," she said in a milder voice when she was done. "Truly," she added. "I know you're upset." She paused. "Jerry Beck can think about city council all he wants, but he won't run. He's scared of Marissa."

"Not any more. He's going to come out against abortion."

"Well, that prick." She scooped the last slivers of ice from the Jell-O bowl and set it in the refrigerator.

"He's a sleaze," Guy agreed.

Briefly she touched his shoulder. "We'll call someone else. It's not like there's any shortage of lawyers."

"I'm going to lose," he said.

"You think that's why Jerry pulled out?" She sucked her lip.

"Yes," he lied, because if he didn't she would dismiss his apprehension, which had come to him just now and not as a worry but a sudden feeling in the gut, just the way he'd had the gut feeling he'd be canned the minute he heard the Anchor Media Group might be interested in buying the *Herald.* It was the same feeling Eva had experienced when the first press returned her book—"It'll never be published," she'd despaired, and he had said, "Don't be silly." Now he was obligated to repeat at each rejection, "Someone will take it yet, you'll see," though he no longer believed it himself. And because he knew his own falseness, he couldn't bear the same reassurance from her.

"But you didn't do anything wrong! You can't just give up hope."

He sat at the table and shook his head slowly. "I can't believe it. I'm going to lose."

"Don't be ridiculous," she said, but then she added, "So what if Jerry Beck won't take the case? The nicest thing you could say about him is that he's a hypocrite. It's not like he's anybody's idea of a moral standard."

"I thought you liked him."

"I did. You could always count on him to say something outrageous at a party. But that's kind of sick." She sat beside him. She had laughed when Jerry told her what a pain the innocent were. Now it made her ill. How could she claim to have any more integrity than he did?

Guy looked up. "You're a good woman, Eva."

She lowered her eyes, emitting a sad laugh. "Well, I'd never let Sally DeMik be the one to tell you I was leaving you, if that's what you mean."

"Can you believe that?" he said.

"It's unbelievable," she agreed. For a while neither spoke. She flexed her fingers. "He actually found out from Sally DeMik."

"From what he said, until Sally told him he didn't have a clue."

"Incredible—his wife decides to leave him and he has to run into Sally DeMik at the grocery store to find out."

"I just can't believe it," he said.

"It's amazing." They shared a companionable silence. Sitting together at the breakfast table, she saw herself in Claudia's kitchen, pouring tea from her blue pot, pulling a spoon from a drawer, opening a cupboard to unload the dishwasher on any one of a hundred Saturday nights. Bill and Claudia had renovated the house before moving in, bumping out the kitchen wall to accommodate a breakfast table, stripping layers of linoleum from the pine floor, installing cabinets with recessed fluorescent lighting that gave the room a cozy glow. The memory of the light hit her with unexpected vividness. It was the same color as the light given off by the fixture over the kitchen table in Guy's parents' house in Savannah. It was a hideous lamp, a swag of heavy glass suspended in an enameled metal cage that everyone in the household struck his head on, but each Thanksgiving the cheery white light had shone through the windows above the sink, welcoming them like weary sailors as they crossed the ocean of dark lawn between their car and the back door. A pang of loss seared her chest and throat. There would be no more evenings at the Whitts', just as there were no more holidays in Savannah, for after Guy's mother died his dad had sold the house and moved to an apartment above the marina on Tybee Island. "Do you think it's true?"

"No."

"You don't?" His answer surprised her. "I was completely convinced by his sincerity."

"I know he's sincere. But I just don't think something like that can happen without you suspect something."

"That seems contradictory."

"Not really."

"You say you believe he didn't suspect a thing; then you say it couldn't have happened unless he suspected."

"What's contradictory about that?"

"Maybe I'm just confused," she offered. She did feel

confused. "Maybe I don't understand what you're saying."

She wasn't looking at him just then, so it would have been unfair to accuse him of having led her—just when she thought they were having a good time, or at least a moment's balm in the face of a bad one—but she heard the little smirk of victory on his face as he said, "It wouldn't be the first time."

She stood so abruptly her chair hit the floor. "That's the last time," he said.

He came out to her car while she sat in the driveway, sobbing. She rolled down her window to hear.

He bent to stick his face in. "Nick wants to go find a friend." She couldn't tell whether the neutrality in his voice was the result of effort.

"He has a stomach ache," she said, feeling her face turn stony.

"He says he feels better."

"That's too bad."

"Is that what you want me to say to him?"

"How am I supposed to know what to say to him?" she cried, nearly bumping his head as she whipped hers around to face him. "I don't know what's happening. What am I supposed to do, go in and tell him goodbye?"

"There's no reason for you to leave."

"Then give me a reason to stay."

"I don't think I should have to."

"Why don't you just do it anyway?"

"You threw a chair."

"I didn't throw it. It fell."

He spread his hands on the door of the car. "I just can't win with you, can I?"

She lowered her face to the steering wheel. "Why do you think someone always has to win?"

"I'm opposed to violence," he said stiffly as he straightened, shoving his hands in his pockets. "I don't think it's called for, and it makes me really angry when you throw things."

"I didn't throw it. And it makes me really angry when you make such uncalled for and cutting remarks."

"There are more acceptable ways to express your anger."

"I'm sure there are. I wasn't looking for one."

He sighed and stared off to the distance. "Come back in the house."

"Why?" she said, though part of her wanted not to hold out. He was right; she couldn't let him win.

"Because I want you to," he admitted. When he opened the door she stepped out of the car, and he put his arm around her. "Because I love you."

"I love you," she said, but with a note of futility and sadness. "Why do we have to fight? Ever since...." She stopped herself. She'd been about to say "you lost your job," which would be sure to set him off. Instead she squeezed his hand. "We'll get through this."

"Why don't you call Claudia?" he suggested as they walked up the front steps arm in arm. "She could probably use someone to talk to, and it would make you feel better."

"I don't know how to reach her unless I catch her at the house." Twice she had called, and Bill had answered. Though Claudia had told her to leave a message, his voice had scared her off, and she'd hung up without a word. She'd called a second time because the first left her feeling abashed, somehow caught out, as if he would know who had called—there were phones that did that now, let people know who chickened out—but when he answered she lost her nerve and hung up again. After that she was too ashamed to call back. And yesterday's visit hardly served to convince her that he was the affable middleman Claudia had implied.

"Why don't you try?"

Nick met them at the door. "Can I go?"

"I don't think so," Eva said. He pulled a long face. "You're supposed to be sick."

"But, Mom, I feel better." He had put on his shoes. The untied laces trailed across the floor.

"He does seem better," Guy noticed.

"No."

"Why not?" Nick whined.

"Because," Eva said.

"Because why?" Nick persisted, and Guy said, "I don't think it would hurt."

"I won't go any farther than Britton's," Nick promised, eyes limpid with honor.

"No," she said.

He huffed up the stairs. A second later they heard his door slam.

"Are you afraid he's got some kind of bug?" Guy wondered, and her eyes darkened as she said heatedly, "I don't think there's anything wrong with him. There wasn't any reason for him to come home from school, he's just bored with the Y, and who can blame him?"

"So you don't want to reward him for faking," Guy observed.

"I don't want him crossing the street!"

They stared at each other.

"I don't want him crossing the street," she repeated, quietly this time, watching for his reaction.

"I understand."

"Aren't you going to point out that I used to let him cross?" He shook his head.

"You don't think I'm being paranoid?"

"I do. But I understand."

She moved into the dining room and sank to a chair. "I'm sorry about Jerry."

He crossed his arms. "These things happen."

"I recommended him."

"You couldn't know."

"What I don't understand," she said, turning in her seat, "is why you're afraid you're going to lose. Three days ago you were talking about pleading guilty."

"I was upset."

"The point is you're not guilty. Any court is going to see that. I know how you feel, but the case hasn't got anything to do with you. It doesn't change what kind of person you are. You didn't become a monster because the street was slick and some kid was out where he shouldn't have been. What about his parents? What's the matter with them, their kid's out in the rain in the middle of the night?"

"They didn't know he was out."

"You think that's an excuse? You think Nick would ever be out in the rain at midnight and we wouldn't know?"

"The paper said he was running away."

"So tell me why he was running away. Our son doesn't run away." Her voice wheeled. "They were his *parents.* They had an obligation to protect him."

"Sometimes you can't protect your kids."

"No." She was creasing and recreasing an advertising circular left on the table, reading and rereading as if she could make sense of the words. *No money down. No payments until after Christmas.* Did anyone think there was such a thing as a note that didn't come due? "I don't believe that. Don't tell me that. I won't accept it."

He kneaded the back of her neck and when she didn't respond walked to the windows, staring out at a dead spot in one of the bushes.

"You're right," he said after a minute, turning back. "If I lose, I lose. I wasn't thinking in moral terms anyway. I was thinking about the money."

"Money," she echoed with a faint note of surprise. She was the one who always thought about money, and she hadn't given it a thought. "I suppose that is an issue."

"It could be very expensive."

"I suppose," she said tentatively, "it could cost everything we've got."

"I don't think that's an unreasonable guess."

She gazed down the length of the table to the silver tea service on the buffet. Everything they owned seemed to reflect in the polished cherry surface, to weave itself into the pattern of the Indian rug. For the last two, incontinent years of their dog's life she had vowed to replace the soiled twenty-year-old carpet remnant beneath the dining room table the minute Lucky died, and that was exactly what she did, driving directly to the rug store from the vet's, where it took her less than twenty minutes to select a bold Heriz and divest herself of eighteen hundred dollars. Without preface she had marched into the house and begun stacking the Chippendale chairs they inherited from Guy's mother, announcing, "I said I was going to do it, and I did."

"I didn't say a word," he'd responded, and she spat, "Well, hell, it'll help me get over the dog."

Of course, she hadn't known as she handed her credit card to the dealer that Guy would lose his job and hers would be reclassified. The scene came back to her now with a twist: if they lost everything would it mean she had to go back and mourn the dog?

She took her hands from the table and raised her chin. "It's only a house," she said.

It was only a house. Still, it had never struck her, really struck her, that they could lose it, despite the fact that she'd been threatening to lose it for years—"We could lose the house," she wailed each time something else broke and they discovered that all it would take to fix the problem was another few thousand. She had stopped saying it only a month ago, when he lost his job.

But now, as she looked for some preliminary task to get ready for her mother's visit—on top of everything else her mother was coming for Thanksgiving—she tried to peruse the rooms as if they belonged to a vacation cottage she would soon have to abandon to others after having come to feel that it was hers. In the paper she read the follow up to the hard luck feature of the week, about a man with Crohn's disease. Within days of the initial story the FHA had suspended payments on his mobile home, Social Security agreed to reopen his disability case, and readers donated a portable heater, money, clothing, and so many canned goods to his family that the surplus would be given to the Urban Ministry.

Well, no canned goods for them, Eva thought. The public might be willing to open its hearts to a sick man in a trailer, but hardly to a healthy, college-educated couple in a four-bedroom house on Jefferson Road. She had no more than a vague idea of what the property might be worth. Last summer the house on the corner had sold for two-seventy, but it was larger than theirs, with more and better bathrooms. One-seventy maybe. It seemed like an incredible amount of money, but nine years ago they had paid eighty-five, and over the years it had swallowed at least another sixty. New roof; new gutters; in the dining room a leak had required a ten-foot section of plaster crown molding to be recast. The garage had needed siding and new doors. When the floor of the old screened porch collapsed, they'd enclosed it for a den and built a smaller porch out back; when the ancient window-unit in the stairwell conked out, they put in central air. Nothing extravagant, nothing ostentatious, but the rooms had been built to gracious proportions, and she had a flair for decor. She loved the house, impractical as it had proven—when the particular foibles of her generation were tallied, she suspected its penchant for old houses would rank right near the top. But in 1981, flush with money from the Edgar Barefoot painting, she had no idea what kind of dream she was buying into. She had stripped woodwork, hung paper, and learned how to rag paint; wielding only a putty knife and wet towel, she had taken up the hideous old vinyl kitchen floor. She knew the house's bones like her own. She and Guy had married in front of the living room fireplace; Nick had been conceived in the master bedroom upstairs. She had worked so hard and Guy had worked so hard just to make a place for himself in Random, she had thought when they moved in that surely they had earned what all of her friends had: a house, a child, a comfortable middle-class life. She'd never been happier than the year she was pregnant. In that giddy year it had not seemed possible that she'd overreached.

But the last three years they'd been overextended, not so much in debt as unable to save, for long before the paper was bought out it had reduced hours and cancelled benefits. She had to add Guy to her medical plan, which upped the monthly bill by more than a hundred dollars, just when the college reclassified her position and cut her salary by twenty-five percent because supposedly she was on a nine-month contract now. They had Nick's bonds and the seven thousand dollars Guy had invested when his father sold the house, the rest of his share having financed the new den, but the unpaid balance on her credit card was rising, and the balance in their savings account had dwindled to less than two hundred dollars. Already they had fallen below the minimum required to maintain free checking, and she was doing something she hadn't really had to do since they moved to Random: pinching pennies at the grocery. Not much of a hardship tale, but still, working as they had, living where they did, surrounded by such plenty, she felt betrayed by something, some promise, though exactly what it was or who had made it she could not say.

Yet when she thought of Y Bhan Buon To, it seemed unreasonable that they should ever have enjoyed such a prosperous and carefree life.

She decided to polish the silver and filled the sink with water, carrying the tea service, the assorted bowls and trays to the kitchen counter. It occurred to her as she worked that she could sell the silver and china—wasn't that what people who possessed such things did first when they fell on hard times? But the price of silver had fallen. These items were worth far more to her than whatever price they'd bring. They had inherited the flatware from Guy's mother, a woman who, though never even moderately wealthy, had been what people used to call a real lady, who never went to the store without a hat and gloves back when women did that, who had acquired the utensils for gracious living one place setting at a time. They had come to Guy by default. At the time of her death one brother had recently divorced and the youngest was a ne'er-do-well who'd dropped out of college and never married; he was forever talking about moving to the Florida Keys to become a fishing guide, but never got farther than the Tybee Island Marina, where he worked the counter, slinging hot dogs and selling bait. And so at the age of forty-two Eva, who'd grown up eating dinner off stained Melmac in a cramped row house in Baltimore, had come into the finery her friends had been showered with when they married twenty years before. She wondered what would become of Claudia's china and silver. A couple she'd known as free spirits in the '60s fought bitterly over their household possessions when they divorced. "Did he ever cook—what does he want with my Revereware?" the woman fumed to Eva. Cash value. Maybe it mattered even more when the investment of emotions went bad.

When she finished the silver, she decided to risk another call to the Whitt house. To her surprise Claudia answered.

"Oh, hi Eva," she said in the anemic voice Eva recalled from the library.

"I was just wondering how you were doing."

"Fine."

"Good." In a rush to cover the ensuing silence Eva added,

"Guy said you called."

"Oh...yes." Eva looped the cord over her arm and pressed the receiver to her ear. She could barely hear. "I did."

"I'm sorry I missed you. I was wondering if you'd want to get together."

"I guess so."

"Tomorrow?"

"Tomorrow?" Claudia sounded exhausted.

"Or would you rather have lunch next week? How about Monday?"

"Actually Monday wouldn't be good."

"Tuesday?"

But Tuesday wasn't good either, and Wednesday Eva's mother was coming, and when Eva suggested coffee instead of lunch, Claudia couldn't figure out a time.

"Maybe we could get together after the holiday then," Eva said, disappointed.

There was another pause. "I might have time for coffee Monday." But just as Eva was agreeing, Claudia said, "Actually, maybe we should make it Tuesday after all."

"Four?"

"Three would be better for me." Eva had a meeting. "Oh." Claudia's voice went flat. "Well." She prolonged the syllable into a sigh. "I guess I could make it at four."

Eva replaced the receiver, a little unsettled. When she turned around she nearly tripped over Nick. She barely caught the unreasonable fury that had formed inside her mouth. "Sweetie, you startled me." Her eyes strayed to the breakfast table. I thought I asked you to pick up your baseball cards."

"I will." He poured himself a glass of juice.

"Nick!" she called as he started up the stairs.

"What?" He returned to the room.

"Put the orange juice away and pick up your cards."

"I'm going to."

"Now." Angrily he opened the refrigerator, then moved the cards from the table to the counter. "Away," she said.

With a loud sigh he picked them up again. "Can I go to Britton's?"

She was sorry, even though she couldn't see where she was wrong. She softened her voice. "Why don't you call Britton and ask him to come here?"

"He never wants to come here. I don't have Nintendo."

"Why can't you trade baseball cards or play Monopoly? Why do you have to play electronic games?" She had anticipated when she and Guy ruled against Nintendo that Nick might sulk or whine, not that he would lay his social exclusion at her feet. It was true. He nearly always played at other kids' houses. When he was five she had wondered if it might be their art—did his friends go home and tell their parents that they had pictures of naked women on their walls? But it wasn't that. As many toys as Nick had, the other kids had more.

"Britton doesn't want to do anything else."

But it wasn't entirely that either. He liked to go to other kids' houses because he had more freedom there.

She sighed.

"So can I go?"

"Honey, I don't know. It gets dark so early...."

"You know you're going to have to let me out of the house sometime," he said flatly, and as she reached for the support of the counter her mouth opened into a gasp that made no sound.

Chapter 6

That night Eva dreamed that she had returned to Brooks Summer. Immediately she knew she'd made a mistake, knew too that she was dreaming, though she was powerless to stop the dream's progress. She missed Guy. In her dream he had disappeared, moved without a forwarding address, she didn't know how to get him back, and the rushing panic of her grief would neither let her sleep nor waken. Somehow she learned that he was teaching at a university in San Francisco. At the campus information desk a young woman with the doleful eyes and long straight hair of a '60s flower child informed her that Guy kept office hours from one to two; she would find his office in an old house at the corner of Pimino and Newton. Eva searched for the intersection in a San Francisco she could not map—there were no hills, from nowhere could she glimpse either ocean or bay. Though she looked and looked she could not locate the building, and in desperation she began to weep, for by the logic of a dream that had redesigned the landscape and renamed the streets, she had only that one chance, and if she did not find him by 2 p.m. she would lose him forever.

She woke sweating and reached to his side of the bed, where her hand struck bone, and he grunted and rolled over. She listened for the reassuring whistle of his breath, then rose and went downstairs. Although it was November, the air felt spongy, and the sweat trapped beneath her hair made her skin feel unclean. With a loud tock the minute hand on the kitchen clock lurched forward. Four-thirty. She poured herself a glass of juice. Often the natural sugar soothed her back to sleep, but instead she dozed just in time to wake to the insistent beep of the alarm with a clubbed and Lethean feeling. It took her several minutes to retrieve the dream, but when she recounted it for Guy, he only frowned and said, "Was there a Newton Street in San Francisco?"

At the gallery she had to hang the Clarence Hines show. The opening was Sunday, and she could hardly hang it while her mother was here. A shadow of guilt played at her conscience. Her mother's plane was scheduled to take off only two hours before the reception began, and while there was no reason her mother should attend—Ruby would demand all of Eva's attention and refuse to meet anyone—all the same, a better daughter would have invited her mother to stay.

But Eva's cold was improved, and if, as she often claimed, her job was two percent art and ninety-seven percent placation, today she was grateful for the remaining one percent, the physical labor. She spent much of the morning on the elevator, transporting the paintings to the gallery from the storage room downstairs, then ferrying the crates back to storage. Three times she paced the gallery off. After lunch she could hang the smaller works herself, but she would have to flag someone down to help with the larger pieces.

When she got back to her office, the phone was ringing. "I don't think tomorrow is going to be possible for me," Claudia said.

"Another time?" Eva suggested.

"Well." Claudia seemed to hesitate. With evident reluctance she admitted, "I'll be at the house tonight. I guess you could come over."

"What time?"

"I don't know. The kids need supper."

"I'll bring a pizza," Eva promised.

Half an hour later Claudia called again. "I got to thinking—Monday night, kids and homework. Maybe we should make it tomorrow after all."

"Claudia!"

"What?"

"Tomorrow are you going to call me back and cancel again?"

"Eva, my life is difficult right now."

"I know that." It took Eva a moment to realize that the muffled sounds coming through the wire were sobs. "I'm sorry. Tomorrow at four?"

"Actually it probably would be better for me if we just postponed it."

"Sure," Eva said, trying to keep disappointment from staining her voice.

"I'll give you a call."

Guy was gone when Eva got home, but he'd left the mail on the dining room table.

Something from their insurance company about the Camry. Eva wondered if the Buon Tos had received their check yet. One hundred five thousand dollars: one hundred thousand for bodily harm, five for medical expenses. It was nothing. The Buon Tos had lost their son. Not their only son, but if she had another child would she be willing to part with Nick? Her heart went cold inside her chest, and gooseflesh rose along her arms. She tasted metal.

Then what would she give up to give their son back?

She would be willing to lose her house, but what house could be enough, a house was sticks and stones, a house was nothing. She would sacrifice her career, she would starve, she would wear a hairshirt and walk barefoot over coals, but that was nothing, there was nothing she could forfeit that might begin to repay what they had stolen. Except Nick.

An electric current passed through her body. *Never.* No matter how many children she had.

She had no idea how long she stood in the front hall. When she recovered enough to go to the kitchen to start dinner, the counter was sticky again and dishes spilled up over the top of the sink; she had to stack them to wash the skillet. Her back ached from handling the heavy art work all day. After dinner she had recommendations to write. It seemed unreasonable that Guy should be home all day and not clean up his mess, but if she said anything he would only accuse her of trying to make him feel bad. In the weeks since he'd lost his job he'd taken to doing less around the house instead of more, almost as if to challenge her into the confrontation that would reveal her insensitivity. It wasn't deliberate, of course—he was crippled by depression. Still. She was depressed too. How come she didn't get to be disabled?

She drank a glass of wine before she went to bed and didn't dream at all.

In the late morning Claudia called her at the office. "I've got a few minutes free right now if you want to have lunch."

Eva eyed the yogurt and apple on her desk. "Where?"

"I'm at the mall. I'll meet you at the food court."

"I can be there in twenty minutes."

"That long." Claudia sighed.

It would take her five to walk to her car. "Fifteen," she said. "I'll hurry."

She made it in seventeen. Rushing past the cosmetic counters in Belk's, she felt the burnished elegance of the lighting sweep her into the dizzying, parti-colored world. She was too old to have been a mall rat in her teens—in those days shopping centers had yet to steal the hearts out of cities—nor had she and Claudia been mall moms. Crowds made her claustrophobic, but on a Monday not quite noon, she had no trouble negotiating aisles or the entrance to the escalator. The place always reminded her of church, for in the silky light the imitation sparkle of the goods recalled the luster her imitation birthstone ring had taken on as she sat twisting it as a girl in the heavenly air of the Basilica of the Assumption of the Blessed Virgin Mary. She had not been raised Catholic, but her mother thought the church pretty; no doubt her mother had been seeing one of the parishioners, for they hadn't gone to church before or after that one brief stint.

On the top floor she cruised the food court several times to be sure she hadn't missed anyone and took a table. The line of kids at the pizza franchise wound around a corner. Apparently no one ate peanut butter sandwiches and Hostess cupcakes in the high school cafeteria anymore. As the line advanced, she glanced at her watch. She didn't want to feel slighted, but there was something slippery about the way Claudia kept rescheduling.

"There you are," she said with a relieved smile when Claudia appeared at last. "I was beginning to think you were avoiding me."

"Oh, have you been waiting?" Claudia's hair was subtly lighter, frosted maybe. Eva hadn't noticed last week in the library.

"What's your pleasure?" Eva waved toward the row of international vendors decked out like sidewalk cafes. Taco Bell, Pita Palace, Signore Pizza, Frank 'n Stein, Wok and Roll. It was so American it was funny.

"You go ahead." As Claudia opened her hand into a weak wave, Eva saw that her nails were painted scarlet. "I'm not hungry."

"You've lost weight," Eva observed.

"Isn't it great? Next summer I'm going to get a bikini."

Actually Eva thought Claudia looked drawn, the skin beneath the blusher on her cheeks a jaundiced gray, like tallow. She had lost fifteen pounds at least; her clavicle arched beneath her clingy sweater. "I think I'll get some hot and sour soup. Can I bring you an eggroll?" Claudia shook her head.

"I hear Bill and Guy got together," Claudia said when she returned.

Eva nodded, wondering what Bill had said as she took the Styrofoam cup of coffee off her tray and set it in front of Claudia.

"That's good. I guess." Claudia stroked her crimson nails with the flat of her other hand. "How have you been? Did you sell your book?"

"No." Eva couldn't recall Claudia's having asked before, but she didn't want to talk about her book today. There was too much text for a coffee table volume and too many plates for anything but. Or else the editor loved it but couldn't get house support. For too long it had dimmed her landscape and dulled her days, but now that the accident had come between her and that failure, the landscape was so dark it seemed to her that she would gladly go back to gray. "How are you doing?"

Claudia seemed to taste the question. "Better."

"How are the kids?"

Claudia fanned her hair in a gesture that reminded Eva of Kay Courtland, whose thick, curly auburn mane had been the curse of her high school years, or so she said, and now her glory. "Fine. I mean of course they're both sad right now, but Gregory's able to express his feelings, he'll be okay. Caroline's got a lot of bottled-up anger, but she'll adjust. They're getting older—this was a good time for me to do it."

She made it sound as if she had been waiting.

"It's good to see you." Claudia's eyes looked different. Beneath her shaped brows her glance kept darting, and it took Eva a minute to realize that she was wearing shadow and mascara. "I feel better when I see my friends. I know a lot of people think I'm a rat, but you've been through it, you know how much courage it takes."

"Well," Eva said uncomfortably, not wanting to diminish Claudia's pain or claim credit she didn't deserve. "I was younger though, I didn't have kids." She had never thought of it in terms of courage. She and Brooks had separated at a time when everything in the world seemed to be coming apart. She'd been married, and then it seemed as if the marriage, along with a lot of other things, just came to an end. The era had been marked by impermanence. She couldn't remember feeling as disrupted then as she did now. "I guess I'm just sorry to know you've been unhappy so long."

"I haven't been unhappy."

Eva was confused. "Oh. I thought...."

Claudia fanned her hair again. Eva had to admit the longer length and lighter color became her. She looked pretty despite her sharp bones and waxy pallor. "I think most women envy me. They just don't have the nerve to admit it."

Eva picked up her fork. The line at Wok and Roll had been too long, and she'd come back with a Greek salad, though Claudia's untouched coffee made her feel she was wolfing chocolate cake instead of lettuce. "Do you think it was Bill or just marriage?"

"Marriage," Claudia said quickly. "I mean our marriage was like most marriages, it was okay." She gave the word an extra beat that made it seem not okay at all. "That's why the kids are having a hard time. They never heard us argue."

"Oh, well, if that's the test of a good marriage...." Eva's lips crooked into a rueful smile.

"Caroline's mad at me, and Bill's been such a pain. I don't know why he can't be more supportive."

Eva was flabbergasted, but she said, "In what way? Do you need money?"

Claudia slid a finger forward on the table. "Well I'm having to watch my money, of course. Bill's given me ten thousand for right now. He hopes we'll get back together. He's unhappy, and Caroline picks up on that. It's just making it really hard. Did you know he's staying with John Courtland?"

"I heard." Only four and a half months ago they had been sitting in the bleachers speculating on what went wrong between John and Kay.

"I wish Bill hadn't moved in with him. I'm afraid he'll make Bill mad at me."

In astonishment Eva dropped her fork. "What makes you think he needs John to get mad at you?"

"What do you mean?" Claudia's wide-set eyes narrowed.

"You left him."

"He could be more understanding."

"I don't think that's the way it works," Eva said.

"I felt stifled." Eva stared as Claudia brushed a strand of hair back. "Marriage is boring. I'm sorry if that offends people, but it's true." Two mothers with strollers took the table next to them, and she lowered her voice. "We always did it on Saturday night, like it was a date or something. After a while I was glad if I got my period or we went out and I could say it was too late when we got home." She glanced at the mothers as they bent to arrange the blankets around their babies and sat back. "What about you and Guy? Do you have a good sex life?"

No one asked such questions. Eva had never even considered it herself in quite that way, yes or no, good or bad. "We've always been close," she said. It was true, but as she spoke she wondered how true. They did have a good sexual relationship, or had until Guy lost his job. But how good was good? Very good? Outstanding? There had been times when she would have liked more of this or less of that but didn't say so. Was that a problem, or was sex what had held them together? After so many years she didn't expect skyrockets every single time, but she had treasured the intimacy, a sweet shyness that seemed to take root after their initial boldness withered; what had once passed for liberation, for a lack of inhibition, seemed to her now solipsistic and superficial. Sex had always been natural between them, but the act of it had come to mean something more. As a lover Guy never betrayed the impatience he was quick to show in nearly every other commerce. They really did make love. "I think it's helped us through a lot."

Claudia's eyes wandered again as one of the women at the

next table removed a jar of baby food from her diaper bag. "Did I tell you I'm seeing someone else?"

"Yes. Well, I mean Guy...."

"It has nothing to do with leaving Bill."

"Oh, no," Eva agreed, adding timidly, "Do you think it could have anything to do with age?"

Claudia tossed her hair in another gesture reminiscent of Kay Courtland. "No. It makes me mad that people think that."

Eva picked up her fork. "I was surprised to hear about Sally and Frank."

A smile that was part grimace ridged the corners of Claudia's mouth. "I know, it's embarrassing, everybody's doing it—it's like an epidemic." She leaned into the table. "Did you know she's been having affairs for years, and none of us knew? I wish I had. Don't you think Bill is really kind of repulsive?"

"Well, I never thought about him that way," Eva hedged. She wouldn't have been attracted to Bill Whitt—he was their friend—but he was far from repulsive. Physically he and Claudia had seemed a match, both good-looking people careless of their appearance. In a way, it had been a quality she admired.

"He's such a slob. He's starting to go bald, but he's got this hairy little gut. Derek—that's the guy I'm seeing now, he's an artist, he does faux finishes—Derek works out all the time, he's gorgeous." Claudia's eyes went soft as she lingered on the word.

Bill had said her boyfriend was a housepainter, but a lot of artists wound up painting houses. Eva shouldn't be so snobbish just because she ran a gallery. If she didn't get tenure she might end up painting houses herself. Faux finishing was about her speed—she hadn't painted in so many years that when she thought about picking up a brush again her stomach cramped and her breath came in ragged quivers. It was easier to accept what she knew to be the truth at a remove: as an artist she was competent, even skilled, but nothing more. She lacked the originality of vision.

She swallowed a chunk of vinegary feta. She wanted to sympathize, but Claudia didn't want sympathy; she wanted agreement, and not just agreement but like and enthusiastic feeling. "You don't sound like yourself," she said weakly.

"I'm in love!" Claudia burst out. "Being around Derek I've learned so much these past weeks. Being around Derek—he's such an open person."

"Well, I'm glad you feel good."

"I feel great. Everytime I hear a knock on the door I keep thinking that it's going to be a policeman saying the party's over, you have to go back to your husband and kids now. But you know what? No one's coming, I can do what I want!"

Eva had started at the word policeman. She pushed the rest of her salad aside. Everything Claudia said seemed to open more distance between them. At the same time she understood how Claudia felt. How many times since her career had gone bad had she wished for something, anything, to lift her from the doldrums of routine, to blast through her despondency and restore her. Falling in love: you couldn't beat it for entertainment value. But Eva loved Guy; she didn't want to lose him.

"I love fucking now, I love getting fucked." Claudia's lips made savory little movements as she sampled the word, and all of a sudden Eva felt like reaching across the table and slapping her. How could you take such indiscretions seriously? What was she supposed to say? And it wasn't marriage that was boring, for marriage was full of unexpected twists and small daily dramas; it wasn't so much their partners people got bored with as themselves. They got to know each other and thought everything was over, all their stories told, every opinion charted. But circumstances changed, people changed, and then the bonds either deepened or they broke. Looking at Claudia now, Eva remembered helping her paper Gregory's room with stripes and circus wagons. When they finished Claudia had said, "I think I would be so happy if I could redo my whole house in bright primary colors." Once, just moments after blurting, "These kids don't let me have a minute for myself," Claudia had pressed a neighbor's baby to her cheek and said, "Sometimes I think I would be so happy if I just had three children"—had said these things not ironically but wistfully, and repeating them to Guy, Eva could only laugh and shake her head. Maybe Claudia's problem was that she had never known what she wanted. "I hope you'll be careful," Eva said. "That's a word with more than one meaning, you know."

"What about you? Have you always been happy?"

Once Claudia wouldn't have needed to ask such a question; she would have assumed that she knew. Eva thought for a long time before she answered. "I suppose I do envy you the distraction. Things haven't been so good these last years starting with my book and now...."

"Oh your book," Claudia said. "You'll sell it." She craned her neck toward the mall's central chasm and gathered her jacket. "Sorry I have to run, but it's Derek's birthday, and I want to make him a special dessert."

"Did you know Guy lost his job?"

Claudia hesitated, halfway out of her chair. "No."

"Over a month ago."

"Well, Eva, there's a lot going on in my life right now."

"I know that."

"I'm so happy! I just wish Bill would quit being such a pain. I used to wish he'd die, but then I'd have the kids all the time." Claudia stood.

How could she say such a thing? Eva wanted to shake her and scream What makes you think that leaving your husband is such a big deal? Has it ever occurred to you that other people have problems too? But how could she condemn Claudia for aggrandizing her separation? Didn't she herself feel threatened by it? Didn't she herself think it was a very big deal? She thought again of Claudia's kitchen, the two of them sitting at the table over tea. It wasn't so much that Claudia had dismissed her time with Bill; it was that Eva felt Claudia had dismissed all the time she's spent with Eva too. "I guess you haven't been reading the paper," she said. "We had an accident." She thought she'd mentioned it at the library, but maybe she hadn't.

"I'm sorry." Claudia paused, still looking out past the food court. "Was anyone hurt?"

"We hit and killed a nine-year-old boy."

For a moment Eva thought Claudia hadn't heard, but then their eyes met, and Claudia dropped back to her seat.

"He ran right in front of our car. Guy's been charged...." Eva started to cry. "He's been charged with drunk driving death."

"That's terrible!" The mothers at the next table paused with their forks in the air and stared. "Couldn't you make him let you drive?"

Mid-sniffle, Eva stiffened. "He wasn't drunk!"

"Oh, it's a mistake then," Claudia said, visibly relieved. She stood again. "You'll get it straightened out." She hesitated, as if she couldn't think of anything else to say. "Anyway I'm glad we got together. I feel better when I see my friends."

That evening Guy rose from the breakfast table as the sound of squabbling carried from the den. Cleaning house always turned Eva bitchy. Her mother was arriving for the holiday tomorrow, and as usual she was knocking herself out. He wouldn't mind half as much if she would just admit she was in a foul mood.

"Daddy doesn't pick up his shoes," Nick was saying.

"That's not the point," Eva said.

"What's the problem?" he asked from the doorway.

Eva was standing in front of the TV, blocking Nick's view. "There's no problem."

"That's not what it sounds like to me."

"There's no problem." Eva's voice sharpened. "Nick just needs to pick up his things so I can vacuum."

Nick pressed himself into a corner of the sofa, trying to make himself invisible.

"He heard you, he'll do it."

"He hasn't done it."

"Get off his back. You're not going to vacuum tonight. Let him pick his room up in the morning."

"In the morning he has school."

The stagy coldness of her tone pissed him off. "You want it picked up so bad, you pick it up."

"Thanks for your support," Eva snapped and brushed past him.

He followed her upstairs and closed the door to their bedroom. "Look. I agree he needs to be more responsible. All I want is for you to quit sniping at him."

"I am not sniping. I'm just not going to spend all day picking up after you both."

"Oh, now it's both of us."

She crossed from her bureau to the bed and sat, folding her arms across her chest. "Do we have to do this?"

"You're like a broken record."

"Oh yeah?" She dropped her arms and stood to face him. "Well let me tell you something. There is something very simple he could do, something you could do, and neither one of you would ever have to hear me snipe again."

"And what's that?"

"He could pick up his room. You could put your Kleenex in the trash and your jacket in the closet. When you open a bag of cookies you could put the cookies in the jar and wipe the counter, you could...."

"There you go again." He closed his hand over the bedpost. "I'm sorry your mother's coming, but you don't have to take it out on us."

"Okay. Have it your way: my mother drives me nuts. What about you?"

"I've told you before. I don't mind your mother."

"That's not what I meant. If you're going to blame my mood on my mother, why can't we talk about—" she faltered—"how things have affected yours?"

He dug his foot into the rug. "Go ahead and say it. I killed a kid. It's made me impossible to live with."

"You were in a bad mood before the accident."

"So were you."

"I haven't sold my book. I've been doing my job for sixteen

years, and all of a sudden I'm an untenured assistant professor who doesn't have a Ph.D. I built their fucking gallery!"

He tried to put his arm around her, but she stepped aside and began picking loose change up off the bureau. He softened his voice. "I'm not saying you don't have reason to feel the way you do."

"You think I'm saying you don't? I understand. But it's not fair to say that when you're mad it's because Nick did something wrong and when I'm mad it's my mood."

She couldn't hear herself, or she would know the difference. "You go back and forth. Ever since the accident. One minute you're hugging him, the next you're screaming in his face."

"Okay, I nag," she admitted and dropped the coins into a saucer. "That doesn't change the fact that I asked Nick to pick up his things two hours ago and he still hasn't done it." Why did they do this? It was the pattern of every fight, which wore itself out before either of them would give in. The fight had acquired a life of its own, the ability to revive itself spontaneously, because it was always the same fight, and it never resolved but only ran down.

"Just tell me what you want."

"I want you to stay out of it when I'm talking to Nick. I want you to pick up after yourself and set a better example "

"Jesus!"

"You asked what I wanted."

"You want too much." He turned on his heel and slammed the door behind him.

At least he was playing basketball tomorrow. He had begun to live for the games, though he came home from more and more of them beat up. His legs were dead, but he could still shoot; he hadn't had to quit yet. He needed the games. Eva had been depressed for two years, but she wanted to blame him for being depressed for a month. She'd just love it if she had a rich, accomodating husband like all her friends.

Except that her friends had all dumped their rich, accommodating husbands. Claudia's separation hit Eva especially hard because she wanted to believe her friends had everything. Especially now that her own hopes had been thwarted. She had her own problems. It was unreasonable to ask her to be available to nurse him through his. Still, she might think. He'd lost his job; he'd killed a child; he was looking at a possible ten years in prison. What if he really did go to jail? Nick would be eighteen years old when he got out.

And what would happen to Eva? But that wasn't even a question. She would take care of herself—in a way he was sorry to know that. Despite what he said, she'd do a fine job with Nick. He couldn't convince her that her slump was temporary, though he had to admit it had gone on longer than he could have imagined. But she was more competent, more resilient than she believed herself to be; she'd be fine. He ought to be glad, but it made him mad, to think of his wife and son managing so well without him. That was why he had to act like such a jerk: he had to make her pay for his vulnerability and her vigor.

Eva's mother was the last to deplane, and for a moment Eva almost hoped she wasn't on the flight. Maybe her mother was sick, nothing serious, just a cold that made her head too clogged for flying; she would go to the desk, and they would tell her Ruby wasn't coming. She was ashamed of the thought. Besides, Ruby's tickets were nonrefundable. Eva should have cancelled the visit herself. She should have called and offered to reimburse her mother, told her it wasn't a good time, would have if her mother didn't threaten never to speak to her again at the least affront, real or imagined. She wasn't up to this visit. While in theory she loved her mother, in her presence Eva grew cranky and sullen; by the end of each reunion she disliked herself even more than she disliked her mother's relentless chatter. It was easier to love her mother by proxy.

Still, she never failed to be amused at the first sight of Ruby, who was lurching toward her, balancing a coat, purse, flight bag, and overstuffed tote. She'd been coloring and perming her hair too long; the black frizz was dry and dull, so thin Eva could see her scalp and the scaly patches burned along her forehead. At the age of seventy-four she dressed like a go-go girl. Her psychedelic tent dress was short enough to show the loose skin at her knees, and she was wearing the kind of bead earrings that made Eva think of opium den curtains. Eva often wondered if her mother's taste in clothes had driven her to her own, so impeccable it was dull, natural fabrics, beautifully tailored buttonholes, conservative colors and lines. At times she longed to look more bohemian, but every time she reached for a broomstick skirt or tie-dyed shirt a vision of the item on Ruby froze her hand on the rack.

"Hi, Ma." Dutifully Eva pecked her cheek and reached for the canvas shopping bag and coat. In the last few years her mother had shrunk. Once they had been the same height, but now Eva seemed to tower.

"Wait, I've got it. Here." Her mother rummaged in the tote while Eva tried to hold it. She thrust a plastic bag at Eva.

"I got these socks on sale at Kmart. Fifty percent off, already marked down to a dollar, plus I got the senior discount. If they don't fit Nickie, you can wear them."

Ruby was already fishing for something else as Eva bent to rescue the socks and tried to propel the two of them from the path of other travelers. "Just put them back in the bag until we get to the house, okay?"

"Where is Nickie?" Ruby straightened, squinting around as if he might be hiding behind the rows of seats.

"He's at school, Ma. They don't get out till 3."

"Ohhh." Her mother's habit of drawing out the syllable always seemed to imply an ineffable disappointment. "Well he has to get an education, doesn't he? I've always been proud to have been a part of your education, after all, I'd say it's enriched your life." She paused for the thanks that Eva could never make herself deliver. Sometimes Eva fantasized saying "You know, if you would only stop congratulating yourself, I'd give you the gratitude you want," but Ruby would bristle at the implication, and the truth was that Eva was an ingrate.

"How's he doing in school anyway? Here." Ruby fumbled at her purse, producing a fistful of coupons which she pressed into Eva's hand. "If you don't use this stuff, just give them to someone who does." There was something birdlike, a glittery suspicion, in the way she was peering around. "Where's the washroom?"

"Back here." Eva extricated herself from the crowd moving up the concourse and waited for her mother.

"Hold this." Ruby pushed her squishy purse and flight bag toward Eva.

Still talking, she disappeared into a stall, and Eva stared at herself in the mirror. She couldn't get used to her hair, which didn't seem to be turning gray so much as streaky. Dun streaks made the brown look darker than her hair had ever been, and no matter how often she shampooed it looked dirty. Also she'd quit wearing her contact lenses just this fall, and she still looked strange to herself in her schoolboy glasses. She wouldn't have minded looking older, but instead of an older version of herself she looked like someone else, whereas Guy looked the same as ever, the only change an appealing silver sparkle in his sandy brown hair.

"Are those new glasses?" her mother asked as she emerged.

"Bifocals," Eva admitted.

"Imagine my baby wearing bifocals." Ruby washed her hands. "It seems like just yesterday you were born. How come you picked red frames?"

"I don't know." Eva couldn't remember why herself.

"Well, they're different, I'll say that. You know, if you haven't got anything planned for dinner tonight that meat pie you make is good. I mean if you're wondering what to feed me, tomorrow being Thanksgiving and all, I imagine you're planning a big meal. Did you make a pumpkin pie?"

"I bought some salmon. I thought I'd just broil it with some lemon butter and dill."

"Anything's fine, you don't need to go to any trouble for me. You know, I told Mary about that meat pie—that pie was so good, it's something I never get at home, you just don't bother cooking like that for one."

"Maybe we could have the meat pie on Saturday," Eva suggested, though on Saturday she had intended to go out. They had reached the baggage claim. Already she felt tired.

"I hope they didn't lose my luggage. What luggage are you

using nowdays?"

"The same."

"Ohhh." With a jerk the conveyor belt rattled into motion, and around them the crowd pressed in. Ruby placed her coat on top of the oversized tote. "I thought you'd have some new stuff by now. Did you sell your book?"

"No."

"Those tapestry suitcases are pretty. You used to do all that traveling on business. When somebody picks you up at the airport you want to look like somebody special." Ruby gripped her arm.

"I see it," Eva said and reached for her mother's suitcase.

"I see you still have the same car," Ruby said when they reached the lot.

Same car, same luggage, Eva thought as she hoisted the suitcases into the trunk. She hated the feeling her mother bred in her that every purchase was only a momentary stay against beggary and destitution.

"I thought you'd be driving the Camry."

Eva winced as Ruby fitted herself into the front seat. She hadn't told her mother about the accident. "It's in the shop," she mumbled.

"You know it used to be the woman that drove the good car. The man had an old clunker he drove to work. Speaking of the man—do you ever hear anything from that Brooks?" Ruby tugged at the dizzying fabric of her dress, hot pink and electric yellow.

"No." Eva checked the rearview mirror.

"After all, you put him through school. What's he doing

now, is he using his education? You know, I read in the paper about this other gal that put her husband through school, he was a doctor. She sued him for half his future income, and you know those doctors make a lot."

"Brooks isn't a doctor." The last Eva knew, he was another unemployed Ph.D., but she found the innocence with which her mother revered higher education touching. Ruby seemed to think it came with a warranty, itself a magic ticket. For her mother education was a product, one that never varied in quality no matter where you bought it or how poorly it was used.

"Aren't people with doctorates called doctor? What did you say he's doing now?"

"I don't know." She had no reason or desire to know, but still it seemed odd that a connection once so binding could be completely broken. Maybe Claudia could walk out on Bill, Kay on John and Sally on Frank because it felt safe: because of the children their ties could never be completely severed.

"Well, I hate to say it, after all it was your life, but I never thought too much of him. Now Guy I can talk to, he doesn't act so high and mighty, like everybody has to be as educated as him. And he pays a lot of attention to Nickie, that counts for a lot. He's a lucky little boy. Your father never paid a bit of attention to you."

Sometimes Eva wondered if she and Guy had been drawn to each other because both had experienced such lopsided childhoods; in each of their families one parent had eclipsed the other, worn the other away.

Her mother had not aged well. Hard to believe now, but Ruby had once had lover after lover. As a child Eva remembered meeting them whenever she was out with her mother, this one here for ice cream, that one for the zoo, always fading into the background while her mother and her "friend" whispered and giggled and cast furtive glances. She was astonished to recall how brazen Ruby had been—she had never bribed, never threatened, never warned her daughter not to tell, though Eva never told anyway. She wouldn't have dreamed of telling, of hurting her father in such a way, though perhaps Ruby was right; perhaps she never told because he paid her no attention; perhaps she hadn't felt close enough to share the ugly secret. Still he must have known. They had been a bad match, her mother and father, her mother's restless energy and her father's lethargic, sickly constitution. As Eva grew older Ruby grew fretful; she began to say that she needed her freedom, she was going to leave her husband, she was going to marry Rich or Earl or Don, whoever her lover of the moment happened to be, she wasn't going to put up with Walter, Eva's father, anymore, but either she didn't have the nerve or perhaps, Eva thought, she really didn't want to, because she never did, and then in what Eva had always considered a supreme irony, when her father finally died, Ruby was over the hill, looking used up, her hair already thin and frazzled, her neck and breasts crepey beneath her teeny-bopper clothes. As far as Eva knew her mother had not had another lover since.

"Did you say Guy was at work?" Ruby asked.

"No."

Her father had called her "Princess Pie." That's what she remembered: her father lying on the slip-covered sofa, with the acrid smell of the fertilizer plant clinging to his work twills, saying, "Turn on the TV, Princess Pie." He had been an Orioles fan, though she couldn't remember his ever going to a game, couldn't remember him anywhere but lying on the sofa in the darkened living room before the television's ashy flicker.

"I thought he must be at work since he didn't come with you. Got to make a living, you know."

"Guy lost his job." Eva had postponed the announcement because she didn't want to talk about it. When she'd tried to tell Claudia, Claudia had barely listened, and even so Eva wouldn't confide in her own mother.

"Lost his job." Her mother frowned, the pleats above her mouth a reminder of where Eva's faint pinch of lines was headed. "What do you mean?"

"The paper got bought out."

"Well, you tell him not to feel bad. These days a lot of people are in the same boat. What's he going to do?"

"I don't know. Just do me a favor and don't mention it, all right?" Guy might give her a little credit when he got on her for nagging Nick: he might notice what a concentrated effort she had made not to hound him about the job search, and it was harder than he knew to keep from asking, from suggesting, from hoping or worrying out loud, from bringing it up at all. That was the trouble with her mother: there was nothing she wouldn't bring up. Eva might have found her lack of discretion refreshing if Ruby didn't feel that being related gave her the right.

"I mean, is he looking for a job? What about other newspapers in the area? He's a good worker, they'd be glad to have him."

"Ma, over a hundred people lost their jobs. That's a lot of slack for a couple of small town weeklies to absorb."

"And they say the economy's getting better." Ruby's face twitched. "That Bush, I'll tell you, I don't know how he got elected—people are losing their homes, they can't pay for a doctor when they're sick, you should see my gas bill, over a hundred dollars and it's not even winter yet. And he says we're turning the corner."

"You voted for him," Eva said.

"What do you mean?"

"You voted for him. That's how he got elected."

"Well, but I'm just one vote, and I'll tell you one thing, I won't vote for him again."

Eva smiled into the rearview mirror. "You always say that."

"What?"

"You always say you aren't going to vote for the Republican, and then you do."

"Well, you can't just vote for any jackass the Democrats put up."

"Sure you can. I do."

Her mother looked at her. "Did you get new glasses?"

"Bifocals," Eva said again.

"Imagine that," her mother said as Eva pulled into the driveway. "It seems like just yesterday you were born."

Guy came out to unload the luggage.

"I hear you lost your job," Ruby said as he stooped to hug her.

"Hi, Ruby." Guy picked up her suitcases. "It's good to see you."

"Have you thought about social work?" Ruby trailed him toward the house. They hadn't had a killing frost yet, and the impatiens were still in bloom in Eva's urns. "You know, it was different in the Depression, people helped each other then. These days nobody wants to know anybody else's troubles. I sure hope you kids don't lose your house."

As Guy held the door, he and Eva traded smiles.

"That's a beautiful dress," he told Ruby before he headed upstairs with her bags.

"I like Guy," Ruby said to Eva, twirling to display the full effect. For her age Ruby had a good figure, but even at Eva's age the flesh began to loosen from the bones. "He always says things like 'it's nice to see you' and 'that's a nice dress.'"

Meaning you never do. "It's a very colorful dress," Eva said.

"Half price." Ruby followed Eva into the kitchen. "Guy's got a nice personality. That Brooks Summer, I never said anything, but I never cared for him, I mean as far as I know he never abused you or nothing, but he was a snob if you ask me."

"Guy's great," Eva said faintly, grateful to him for knowing just how to court her mother, and at the same time, for the same reason, ticked off. He could afford to be gracious: as soon as he set the suitcases in the guestroom he'd be off to the basketball court. She couldn't even go to the bathroom without her mother talking at her through the door. She hated herself, but her mother's presence squeezed her small.

Guy reappeared in his shorts as she turned the coffeemaker on. "I'm off."

"Have fun," Eva said gracelessly.

"I'll get Nick at school and drop him off."

"I don't mind doing it," Eva said, but he said, "That's okay, you stay here and visit." He was better tempered than she was and didn't smirk.

After cake and coffee she helped her mother unpack. The smaller suitcase was full of shirts for Nick. "I thought Guy went to pick him up," Ruby said when they came back downstairs and she had parked herself on the stool at the end of the kitchen counter.

"He did."

"Where is he?"

"Probably in the den." Eva would have to speak to Nick. He had passed the age where a visit from his grandmother could excite him, and as for the many gifts she bore, what eight-year-old gave a hoot about socks? All the same, he could be reasoned with; he would understand if she told him to make his grandma feel good. She had noticed that she liked thinking of Ruby as his grandmother. She was still Eva's mother but one step removed.

Eva went to the French doors that opened off the living room. Nick had turned on a cartoon. There were ink stains on his sweatshirt, and his face was smeared with dirt. "Your grandma's here. Don't you want to come say hello?"

"Not especially."

"Nick!" She sat beside him.

"What?"

"You'll hurt her feelings," Eva said, thinking what about his feelings, why doesn't she come in here to say hello to him? In his whole life Ruby had never read him a story or played a game with him. So what if it didn't bother him? It bothered Eva. She sat beside her son. She shouldn't have asked of course; she should have told him. Anyone who knew anything about parenting knew that. *Parenting.* People used words like that these days, attractive and intelligent people, people that otherwise you thought you might like. Or else they left their husbands and if their husbands didn't like it they said their husbands should be more supportive. It was no wonder her book couldn't be published. She didn't speak the same language that everyone else knew.

"What?" Nick repeated when she didn't move. She could see the stupid smile that had crept onto her face reflected in his eyes. More curious than impatient now, he was waiting for her to speak. In a minute she was going to. In a minute she was going to get up and tell him to change his shirt and wash his face. In a minute she would do what she was supposed to, she would parent, she would tell him to turn off the TV, get his butt into the breakfast room, and give his grandmother a kiss. She put her arm around him. His shoulder stiffened, but then he relaxed beneath her touch. *In a minute.* In the meantime she just sat beside him on the sofa. Together they watched Elmer Fudd blow the fucking fur off his tormentor as the darkening sky drained the room of color and they watched the flickering red and blue light of the cartoon and sat.

Chapter 7

Thanksgiving Day. The holiday with something for everyone: football for the men and cooking for the women, or so Eva used to joke back in the days when they spent their Thanksgivings in Savannah, where Guy, his brothers, nephews, and father had commandeered the den while the wives basted the turkey and juggled casseroles in the oven. It was a tradition lost on Eva's mother, who had been an adequate cook while Eva was growing up but in the years since seemed to have forgotten how. Still in her bathrobe and a pair of soiled pink terrycloth slippers, she sat on her stool at the counter watching Eva cook.

"I don't know about this permanent. I don't think it took too good." She pulled at the frizz along her forehead and peered into Eva's mixing bowl. "What's that?"

"Corn pudding."

"So what did you say Guy is going to do now?" her mother asked. "He has a nice personality. I always thought he would be good at social work."

"He'd have to go back to school." Why did her mother always have to remind her she'd put Brooks through graduate school? But even if Guy wanted to go, they couldn't afford it. Eva poured the pudding into a Pyrex dish. Pudding mixed, sweet potatoes cooked and waiting to be candied, beets in the refrigerator in their sweet and sour syrup; the greens would wait until the afternoon. What she needed to do now was make the pie.

"A lot of people are having to be retrained. I feel sorry for young people, I really do."

"We're not young." As Eva measured out the flour, a fine white dust sifted to the floor and settled on the sleeve of her sweatshirt. Her nose itched.

"Wait till you're seventy-four. Although for an old gal I think I'm pretty spunky." Ruby paused. "Would you say I'm spunky?"

Eva rubbed the bridge of her nose with a floury knuckle. "Sure."

"I think I'm darn spunky. You look at where I was when your father died and where I am now. I bet Guy thinks I'm spunky." She paused. "What are you making now?"

"Pie crust."

"Ohhh." Ruby stretched to see into the Cuisinart. The yoke of her nightgown had bunched beneath her robe and was ballooning out the top. "What kind of pie?"

"Pecan."

"I always liked pumpkin myself. I used to make good pumpkin pie, remember?"

"It was delicious," Eva said. She was partial to pumpkin herself.

"How come you're making pecan?"

"Guy doesn't like pumpkin."

"I bet he'd like my pumpkin pie."

No, Eva thought, he wouldn't, but he would take a sliver and praise it, and her mother would be allowed to think he loved it; so Eva wouldn't be able to make pecan; she would have to make pumpkin, and Guy wouldn't eat it, and Nick wouldn't eat it because Guy wouldn't, and Guy would wonder why she'd made his least favorite pie, and her mother would never know the difference. "Pecan is Guy's favorite. His mother used to make it."

"Ohhh, his mother." Invariably Ruby's voice cooled at references to Guy's mother. You would think that he'd betrayed her just by having one. "I bet your school has a program. Guy could work part time and go to school at night."

"What program?"

"Social work. He could get a job with the state or the city. Those government jobs have good benefits. Guy's got a nice personality, he'd be good at it."

"Well, I'm not sure he'd like it." Eva added a tablespoon of water to the dough. Guy hated to have anyone tell him his or her problems. "Besides, I'm not sure that's the best field to go into right now with the way social services are being cut back."

"You don't know whether he'd like it or not." Ruby wrinkled her lips. "Well, I'm not going to vote for that Bush."

"You told me."

"I used to make good crust," Ruby said as Eva floured her pastry cloth and rolled out the dough. "Remember all the pies I used to make?"

Already there were routines that Nick did not remember. It would serve Eva right if she too felt crushed one day, all the time she'd spent pushing him on swings, the songs she'd sung, the stories she'd read, the pictures they had drawn, the fun they'd had forgotten.

When the doorbell rang Eva's hands were full of flour. "Guy," she called, but he would hardly hear her over the TV if he hadn't heard the bell. "Mom, could you get that?" she asked as it rang again.

"Honey, I don't know who it is."

"I don't either."

"What would I say?"

"Just find out who it is. I'll be there in a minute. Oh, for God's sake." Eva wiped her hands on a dishtowel.

It was Y Nuh Buon To. Eva saw him through the glass as Ruby tiptoed up behind her.

"It's some foreigner," Ruby whispered. "Don't open the door."

"Don't be ridiculous," Eva said as she yanked the door open. It was a nice day, warmer again, perhaps as high as seventy. Nuh wore a plaid cowboy shirt that was too tight across his narrow shoulders.

"Hello. No school today," he announced as he entered the house. Ruby had backed against the wall.

"That's right. It's Thanksgiving. That's a holiday for Americans." Eva sounded like an idiot. Worse: as if she thought she were talking to one. And Carole Eisen thought she had the skills it took to tutor.

"I am American. Also for me is Thanksgiving."

In spite of herself Eva smiled. They were still standing in the hallway. Ruby was clutching the front of her robe as if she thought he might mean to tear it off. "Mom, this is Y Nuh Buon To. This is my mother, Ruby Johns."

"Very pleased, John," he said and held out his hand.

"Hi, Mom." Nick emerged from the den, one sock sliding down his ankle.

He and Nuh were eyeing each other curiously like dogs sniffing each other on a corner. Nick was as tall as Nuh. "Nintendo?" Nuh asked.

"Nah. I don't like it that much." Nick turned to Eva.

"Nick, this is Y Nuh Buon To. Nuh, this is my son Nick." Gratefully she looked up as Guy appeared behind Nick. The sound of the football game drifted from the den.

Guy stiffened as he caught sight of Nuh. "Son," he said, and Nuh flinched, eyes widening with fright.

Eva made sure to keep her voice gentle as she addressed him, leaning forward. "Do your parents know you're here?"

"No parents."

Her brow creased. He seemed to understand them much better than she did him, and it unnerved her, made her feel inadequate and embarrassed.

"My sister," he said.

"Son." Guy's tone softened. "We're very sorry for your loss, but we just can't let you come here like this."

Nuh shifted his eyes to Nick and let his gaze travel down to the sagging sock. "Reebok," he said.

"Oh God." Eva put her hand to her face, masking a sound that was half laugh, half sob as tears sprang to her eyes. "Nuh. I'm sorry, I don't want to get you in trouble, but I am going to have to call your parents. Do they have a phone? A telephone?"

"No phone."

"I want to talk to you," Guy said pointedly and motioned Eva into the den. He closed the French doors behind them and muted the football game. "What the hell do you mean letting him come here like this?"

"I didn't let him come here."

"What's he doing here then?"

"Eva?" It was Ruby's voice outside. Eva could see her robe through the lace curtains.

"Eva, where are you?"

Impatiently Eva flipped her head toward the door. "You're all right, Ma."

"Get rid of him," Guy said.

"Why me? Why not you?"

"Eva?" Ruby called again.

"You don't know what I'm going through."

"Yes I do."

"No," he said, "you don't."

"Eva?"

"Okay then. I don't." She sat. "Nobody knows what anyone else goes through. We're all alone."

"Don't give me that crap. I'm the one who killed him. I'm alone. You're not."

As his eyes blazed down at her Eva thought that at the moment she could easily kill him.

She looked away. "Have it your way. In the meantime he's waiting, and my mother's going nuts. Do you have any suggestions?"

"Get rid of him."

"Well, I really don't know how to do that unless I drive him home, and I don't know where he lives, and I don't know if he'll be able to tell me. I seem to have a hard time understanding what he says." She looked at him. His face seemed lumpy. There was a faint streak of pink at the corner of one eye. Neither of them had been sleeping well. "Look, I agree, he needs to go home. I don't think his parents know where he is." The hairs on the back of her neck prickled. His parents didn't seem to know where any of their kids were, she thought, first in anger, then with shame. "The only thing is I'm cooking Thanksgiving dinner. Why don't you take him?"

"Because," Guy said evenly, "under the circumstances I really don't think I should be driving one of their kids."

There was nothing she could say.

When she opened the door to the den, Nick and Nuh were gone. She found her mother reparked on her stool in the kitchen with the dough where she left it, half rolled, already beginning to crack where a thin waxy yellow crust had dried across the surface. "Where are the boys?" Eva asked, touching her tongue to the strange form of the plural.

"I don't know," Ruby said. "That foreign boy—does he go to Nickie's school?"

"They must be upstairs. I'm going to have to drive Nuh home."

Ruby rose, plucking at the worn fleece of her robe. "I'll come with you. Just let me take a bath and set my hair."

"No." Eva eyed the eggs and Karo syrup sitting on the counter. "I'll tell you what—there's the recipe. It would be a really big help to me if you could finish making the pie."

"Me?" Ruby shrank.

"All you have to do is beat the eggs, add the syrup and pecans and a little bit of butter. It says everything you do right on the card."

"But I might not do it the way Guy likes it."

"There's nothing to it."

"You said it was his mother's recipe."

Eva's mouth jerked in exasperation. "It's not his mother's ashes for God's sake."

"Well, honey, I never made pecan pie before. Now if you had a can of pumpkin...."

"Okay." Eva sighed. "Look, I don't have any idea where Nuh lives, I don't know how long this will take. I'll just have to do the pie and the turkey when I get back."

Ruby tugged at her hair. "What time did you plan to eat? You don't want to undercook the turkey."

Eva closed her eyes. It was no good wishing what she'd spent the last two weeks wishing for, that none of it had happened. All she wanted was to act, whatever it took to stop feeling helpless. "I don't serve raw poultry," she said through clenched teeth. "I have many faults, but serving bloody turkey has never been one of them. We'll eat the goddamn thing at midnight if that's when it's ready unless you want to make the pie."

"I wish you wouldn't talk that way."

"I'm sorry," Eva snapped.

"It just sounds so common. That foreign boy—is he one of Nickie's playmates? You'd think parents would know enough not to send their kids to someone else's house on Thanksgiving."

"No, he's not one of Nick's playmates," Eva said, but when she went upstairs to find Nuh, he and Nick were seated on the floor of Nick's room building something out of Legos and engaged in an unfathomable conversation. Nick seemed to have no difficulty understanding Nuh at all.

"Mom!" A rim of light shone along his cheekbone. "Nuh likes to fish! Can he go with us this weekend, please please please?"

"Your grandma's here this weekend," Eva said. "I need to take him home now. Come on, Nuh, I don't want your parents to worry."

"No worry," Nuh assured her with a dazzling smile. Bitterly Eva thought *I bet*, then checked herself. She had no right to judge. She didn't know the parents, she didn't know the culture.

When they were seated in her Corolla, she turned toward him, heart pounding. "Our family uses seatbelts," she said in a choked voice. He didn't seem to understand, so she went around to pull the strap out. As she bent over him she caught a whiff of something musky, not unpleasant, just the spoor of a different diet, though he seemed so much younger to her than twelve, too young for anything but the familiar kid smell of sour dirt, peanut butter, and grape jelly.

When she was behind the wheel again instead of putting the car into reverse she turned toward him. "Tell me about your brother."

He smiled.

"Your brother, Bhan." He examined the air vents.

"Do you miss him?" She could never be sure when he really didn't understand and when he chose not to. "What kind of games did you play? Did he have pets? What was his favorite food?" Her heart was racing.

Y Nuh laughed, a high-pitched hee-hee-hee. "Guns and Roses," he said finally. "Nintendo. Reebok."

Eva wanted to cry. After a minute she backed down the drive. "You'll have to tell me where you live."

He smiled.

"Where you live. Do you know the address?"

"Twenty-six seventeen-D Jamaica Avenue," he said. "Random, North Carolina, USA. Y Nuh Buon To. Whitney Elementary School. Miss Harvell grade five."

Sadly she smiled back. "Do you know how to get there?"

"Bus," he said.

Her throat was full of phlegm. "That's okay. I have a map."

She turned the corner and pulled into the parking lot at the church. She had to lean across him to get the map from the glovebox, but instead of unfolding it she turned toward him again. "What was the name of your village? In Vietnam. Did you live in a village?"

He fingered some of the papers she had spilled. "Site Two."

Eva recognized the name from one of the newspaper features she had copied. "You were in the refugee camp?"

"Êdê-Kpâ." She shook her head, and he unleashed his smile again. "Thailand."

"That's right, the camp is in Thailand." A note of excitement crept into her voice. "But I thought—I mean from what I read the women and children were left behind. Did you live there with your family? Where were you born?"

"Aduôn aê Ban Me Thuot."

Was he speaking Rhadé, or were the indecipherable words a name? "That's the name of your village?"

"Gone." He smiled again.

She was clutching the map. "But before it was gone—that was your home?"

His smile evolved into a shrug. "Many home."

"Was your father part of the resistance? Where was your village?"

"Highland." His smile widened, and he raised his hands to his chopped off hair. "In the jungle I am different. No—" he made a snipping motion and rubbed his face. "Hair very long. Dirty. I dig food." He slapped himself across one arm. "Many ant."

Eva was breathless. "Your brother—did he dig food?"

"Yes. No." Nuh cocked an eyebrow in a gesture she would have understood in any language, and they both smiled.

"He was younger than you," Eva agreed.

"In jungle beautiful flower." Nuh inhaled deeply. "Many beautiful flower."

"What kind of food did you dig for?"

"Root. Like that."

"Were you hungry?"

Vigorously he nodded. "Many bad water. I throw in the leafs, green okay drink, brown no good. In Highland everything is different."

Eva nodded. What she wanted was to know was every detail of the difference.

He slapped himself again. "Ant. Many ant."

"How long were you?..." She didn't know how to say what she meant. It was a stupid question anyway. Time meant nothing to children; even for adults in such a situation the only answer would probably be "long." Guy, perhaps, would have been able to count the minutes with his internal clock; she herself could never say how long she had spent at the grocery, let alone fleeing through a jungle. "I know you had to travel through Cambodia to get to Site Two. I read about that. The Khmer Rouge...."

"Hunt elephant." He raised an imaginary rifle and sited through the windshield.

She pictured Barnum and Bailey, elephants standing trunks to shoulders, embroidered satin saddles, Turkish dancing girls on top.

"Many animal. Rabbit, pig, elephant, tiger. So many killing. Sad."

"You had to eat." He was a *boy.*

"Daytimes okay, but nighttimes is bad dream."

Eva was wringing her hands.

"See eyes, the animal I kill. Many animal." He shook his head.

"Oh, Nuh."

After a minute he said, "Look," and bent down to show her where the sole had come loose on his shoe. "I wait insurance."

Eva winced. "It will come," she promised. Why hadn't it come already? Consulting the map, she set out, noting the way Nuh sat up straight in his seat, watching through the window as if he were a fairytale boy marking his route through the forest. She wanted to stop the car to hug him and promise him all the Reeboks and Nintendos it would take for him to feel safe, but she was afraid even to reach across the gearshift.

"How is your sister?" Her voice was full of gravel, her words couldn't find their footing.

"H'nghai not like she husband."

She cleared her throat. "You know, Nuh, you really can't keep coming to see us." On Monday she would call the insurance company to find out what was taking so long. Guy was supposed to be handling it, but he had yet to look for a new lawyer, and when she reminded him he said his court date wasn't till January. She was afraid he would wait until January to find one.

Nuh gave her his beatific, uncomprehending smile, though she was sure he understood.

"Your parents have already lost one son. You can't do things that are going to make them worry about you." His dark brown eyes studied her with great attention. "Do you understand?"

"She drove past a bleak apartment complex at the corner

of Jamaica Avenue and Sibley Boulevard. She circled the block twice before she saw the driveway that ran along the back. The front yard was deserted, but in the grassless courtyards behind the green asbestos-shingled buildings, children, all of whom appeared to be Montagnard, were playing. Several men sat smoking on the back stoops. A bent screen leaned against an old wringer washer in the yard, and blankets hung at the windows. She pulled into an empty parking space, and before she could speak he hopped from the car and sped across the yard while she sat undecided. She had intended to escort him, to introduce herself and explain how she happened to be there—it seemed the only responsible action, but was it the right one? How come Guy, who had been so adamant about protecting her the night of the accident, not allowing her to go off in search of a phone, how come he hadn't thought about what might happen to her when she brought the boy home? How did they know what state of mind his parents were in? When Nuh opened a door and disappeared inside she assured herself that she'd got him home safe, that the most appropriate course of action would be to drive on and leave his parents in peace, but once she had she felt like a coward.

On the way home she stopped by the twenty-four-hour grocery and picked a pumpkin pie out of the freezer.

Her mother hadn't moved from the kitchen stool. "That sure took long enough," she said, looking up from the circular she was reading. But she had moved; she had changed from her robe into a green pantsuit strewn with mylar appliqués. "Did you say that foreign boy was one of Nickie's friends?"

"No."

"Well, you know how it is when you get old," Ruby said.

"First the memory goes..."

"He's a Montagnard boy," Eva said.

"...then the hearing goes, then your eyesight. I just hope when my time comes I don't get cancer. "

Eva scraped the half rolled pie dough into a plastic bag and threw the bag in the garbage.

"They're from Vietnam. His name is Y Nuh Buon To." She turned to her mother. "Two weeks ago Guy hit and killed his little brother."

"Did I tell you about Gladys Ricowski?" Ruby reached out to tap her on the wrist, but Eva stood just out of reach. "God, I hope I don't get like her."

"Did you hear me?" Eva said. "Two weeks ago Guy hit and killed a nine-year-old Montagnard boy. He's been charged with felony death by motor vehicle. That's why we don't have the Camry."

Her mother touched her collarbone. The lipstick that had bled into the lines around her mouth trembled; her eyes looked trapped inside their sockets. "Oh my," she said finally. "Guy's always been so good with Nickie."

"The boy ran out in the rain, and we couldn't stop."

"Kids," Ruby said, and the color came back to her cheeks, "they don't look. Remember when Billy Zweigert got hit by that car? Did you know he's a lawyer now?"

"You're not listening to me."

Ruby uttered a loud sigh. "Do you think you'll lose your house?"

"I don't know."

"Well, at least you have insurance. A lot of folks...."

"Can you imagine how we feel?"

"Well now, honey, you can't blame yourself. There's a lot of people—I'll tell you these days there's some people wouldn't even stop."

"Do you realize that Guy could be sentenced to ten years in prison?" It was true, but neither she nor Guy had voiced the possibility before, and doing so now she felt dishonest. Jerry Beck had promised Guy wouldn't be convicted. "That's the rest of Nick's childhood."

"He's a lucky little boy. I was telling Mary how much attention he gets. Your father never paid attention like that to you."

"The way I feel, I don't want to let him out of my sight. Other times I can't bear the sight of him! Because he's alive, and I think about that, I think about that boy, and then I think what right does he have...?"

Ruby picked at one of her appliqués. "Oh honey, you're just upset."

"Of course I'm upset!"

"I know—you carry these things the rest of your life. But life goes on, Eva. Believe me, I know. When your father died..."

"What's my father got to do with it?"

"Well, it's no picnic being alone, you know. Your father...."

"You didn't even love my father," Eva cried. "You go on about what a poor lonely widow you are when you never even loved him."

Ruby shifted position on the stool. "What difference does that make? We lived together nearly thirty years."

"Did you ever consider how unfair that was to Dad?"

"He didn't mind."

Eva shook her head.

"Besides, there are different kinds of love. How's your friend, that one I met—Claudia?" her mother said, scraping at a spot of dough hardening on the counter.

Eva dropped to a chair at the breakfast table. "She left her husband."

Ruby rose from her stool to sit beside Eva. "Did I tell you Wanda Sterling got divorced again?"

"She left him and her kids to take up with some guy who's eleven years younger and doesn't have a steady job." Eva's acrimony caught her by surprise. Bill had a right to be angry, but why was she mad? It wasn't as if Claudia had done anything to her. Even Guy had expressed some sympathy for her. Why couldn't Eva? "That's not what she says, of course, but the kids are with Bill most of the time."

Well, so what? People were supposed to act like jerks when their marriages broke up. They were supposed to say things they didn't mean. You were supposed to listen and forget it.

"So you think that's what I should have done?" Her mother's tone turned cold. "I've got news for you, little girl. Your father wouldn't have taken care of you, and what do you think I would have done, a little kid, no skills, no money—I didn't get to go to college like you did, Miss Smarty, I didn't get to graduate from high school before I had to quit and go to work, and I'll tell you one thing—you could have kissed that fancy education good-bye if I'd of done like you'd of had me to and left."

"I didn't say you should have left him."

"They warned me, you know—you're so worried about your father, well, he was a good enough man I guess, but he was sick, and you think he wanted you to go to college? 'What do you want to let her do that for?' he said. 'As soon as they get a little education they think they're too good for you.'"

"Would you please listen to me? I'm not criticizing you." But did she ever have a thought about Ruby that wasn't critical? She didn't want to feel too good for her mother, but for God's sake why couldn't her mother ever just listen? "All I'm trying to say is that Guy and I are in a lot of trouble right now. He's lost his job, he's accidentally killed a child. He's in a terrible state, and we can't even talk. I don't know what's going to happen to us. It's up to me to support this family, and if I don't get tenure what am I going to do for the next twenty years? We're in a mess, and there doesn't seem to be anything I can do to fix it, and there isn't anybody I can even talk to because you know what? you're right, everybody's got their own problems, they don't want to hear mine—they're afraid it could happen to them."

Awkwardly Ruby rose to touch her shoulder. "I know, honey. I'm sorry."

Eva looked up. "Are you?"

"Of course I am. I'm your mother."

Eva wiped her glasses. "Tell me what to do."

"Well, I think Guy ought to look into social work."

Eva's laugh loosed the sound of a sob as she sniffed back tears. Whatever made her think the world had changed? When she rose and opened her arms into a hug the scent that she inhaled—a mixture of coffee, plaque, new perm, Avon perfume, and Arrid—was as familiar as her own. It was the smell of her mother's flesh, and it outlasted every peccadillo she remembered and every pie crust she forgot.

"I love you, Mom," she said.

Chapter 8

Sunday the weather turned cold. Guy woke to the hiss of the radiator and a thin gray light that meant he had overslept. He liked to begin his run before the sun rose. It was a matter of necessity in summer, when Random's heavy cloak of humidity sapped his strength and dulled his stride, but even when it was unnecessary to avoid the day's heat, the dawn run defined for him what he knew to be the essential truth of his life: he had inherited his mother's tendency to depression, and morning was the only time of day he consistently felt optimistic. Especially in winter, as he ran along the trail beside Willow Creek, the sky's gathering band of amber and rush of blood beneath his skin let him take from the coloration of the coming day a deeper sense that he was running from darkness into light. If he started early enough, Eva and Nick would still be asleep after he'd showered and settled at the table with coffee and paper, and those moments alone with the sense of them upstairs and the lilt his humming heart gave to the hour were his favorite time of day.

The hardwood floor was cold, and the sulphur light on the street behind theirs glared through the stairwell window as he slipped into the sweats he'd left outside the bedroom door, then sat on the top step to tie his shoes. In spite of the cold he was moving slowly. Much earlier he had awakened with a dream and gone back to sleep. Rather, he'd awakened with the sense of having had a dream, for he could not remember the dream itself or even fragments, though he knew it had been an erotic dream from the pleasurable tingling in his scrotum. Beside him Eva made a little mewing sound as she slept. He didn't know whether she had been the woman in the dream, only that whatever desire it had entailed must have come to satisfaction, because he'd drifted off suffused with a feeling of warmth and well being.

Now he wondered if Eva had figured in the dream. They hadn't made love for a month. More than a month. His fault, he acknowledged as he let himself out of the house and began stretching on the lawn. The frosty grass crackled beneath his feet, and in the crystalline air his breath puffed like cartoon thoughts. He'd been too depressed to feel desire, but miraculously he felt as if his depression had lifted overnight, as if the dream had somehow cured him, and as he began to trot up the first hill he felt the return of potence in the pumping of his legs and pounding of his Nikes. Above the strip of light behind the trees, the sky's brilliant plot of stars was disappearing. The cold bit his face and sent a buzz of warmth from his heart down to his limbs. It was going to be one of those mornings when he could run forever.

He had been looking at things wrong. Not so much the accident—the death of the boy would always weigh and heavily, but that could not be changed, and it was time to move beyond it. The first order of business was to get the court case cleared away. He would not be convicted of drunk driving death. There was no evidence of recklessness, and the Breathalyzer proved he had not been intoxicated. Chances were he would not even be indicted. And if he should be convicted of the lesser charge, the misdemeanor, failing to exercise due caution, well then he would pay his fine, and that would be that, the legal business over. Or if he should be sent to jail, he could handle that, he would serve his thirty days, or sixty—how stiff could the sentence for a misdemeanor be? Any attorney would know, and that was the first thing he had to do—tomorrow he would engage another lawyer. And if it cost everything they had, the truth was, except the house, they really didn't have much, nothing he would miss anyway; they didn't have so much they couldn't start over. Which brought him to the second order of business: as soon as his case was settled he would get another job, what he didn't know, but surely there were lots of things he could do, and if none of them presented themselves right away, he could always work as a temp until he found something better. For that matter, he could temp now. He had resisted doing it again because it seemed a measure of defeat, a return to that grim period of his life when he and Eva first moved to Random, but now it seemed like a vital first step on his journey forward.

Though the copper stain of sunlight on the creek had paled to lemon by the time he turned from street to trail, the crispness of the air and percussion of his feet cleared the last webs of gloom from his mind. Christmas was less than a month away. His family was gathering at his brother Curt's new house in Jacksonville. Originally he and Eva had planned to take Nick on from there to Disney World, but they hadn't mentioned the trip of late, probably because neither wanted to be the one to say they shouldn't spend the money. He would tell her today that they should go. It would be a mistake to change their plans; they needed this vacation. In fact, when he got back, he was going to call the airlines. He missed his daughter. She hadn't been East more than once since his mother's funeral five years before, though he managed to get to Minneapolis for a weekend each summer. Surely Molly and Brian would welcome a break from the Minnesota winter. He would call her when he got home and offer to pay their airfare.

By the time he left the trail to loop back through the neighborhood, he had begun to anticipate his arrival. Eva would be stirring, her hair spilled across the pillow in the bedroom's golden light. His mother-in-law was there, but so what? They could be quiet. And if not this morning, then later. He thought about her body, so unfailingly generous in sex. She was just shy of average height but slightly built so that she gave the impression of being smaller. When they met he'd thought her too thin. The first time she'd taken off her clothes, the shapeliness of her torso surprised him. She had beautiful breasts, much larger than they looked inside her clothes, round and densely muscled, with a tracing of blue veins and long, dusky auburn nipples that he loved to tease and stroke until they jutted through her shirt before he raised it up to suck them. She liked lingerie, and before Nick had stretched her flesh instead of bras she wore silky little camisoles and matching panties. He missed that easy touch of her through clothes, though the relaxing of her breasts since Nick aroused him. It took her a long time to come, but when she did, the little whimper of vulnerability that escaped her lips tore his heart, and then she opened like a flower. In sex there was no duplicity, no selfishness in her. It was as if when they made love he was reminded who she was. He'd been a bastard to her ever since he lost his job.

When he opened the front door, his mother-in-law seemed to be speaking to him from the kitchen in mid-sentence. It was one of her least endearing habits, beginning a conversation before the other person had a chance to enter the room. He liked Ruby, liked the idea of her at least, but in the mornings her chatter rang against his teeth and droned inside his skull; he couldn't think or read the paper; her voice was a rasp that rubbed him raw. Once or twice he had snapped at her, then later flushed with shame. He pretended not to hear her and hurried up the stairs.

In the bedroom Eva was standing with her back to him before an open dresser drawer; he was just in time to glimpse the soft woggle of one breast as she leaned forward to step into a pair of panties. The lust that had been building through his run gave a sharp twitch at the base of his penis. He crossed the room, stooping to place a kiss at the nape of her neck.

"Is she up? I thought I heard her talking." Eva stiffened slightly as his hands slid down her shoulders.

"Shhh." He dipped his face to her ear in a merry whisper, but when he touched the tip of his tongue inside the lobe, her back went rigid, and she turned around, giving him a full frontal view. Her panties were the high-waisted kind that showed her legs up to her pelvis.

"Oh brother," she said flatly.

"What?" It was hard to feign innocence with his cock raised like a fist inside his sweatpants.

Turning her back, she took a bra from the open drawer and shut it. Quickly she thrust her arms inside the straps, but as she tipped herself into the cups, he slid his palm beneath one breast inside the silky fabric. "Your hand's cold," she said. When he curled his thumb and forefinger around the teat, she pulled away. "Cut it out."

"You have the prettiest body."

She stepped around him to pluck her jeans from the hook

on the back of the door. "She's up."

"Please," he said. He had never said please, never begged, before—he had never had to. She should understand that he needed this. It wasn't just physical, he needed her.

She took a sweater from the closet. He was almost dizzy with desire. If she would just let him touch, if she would just unhook the bra and let him suck, if she would allow him to put first one and then the other of those russet nipples in his mouth, he wouldn't care if they couldn't make love.

"Guy," she said, exasperation drawing two long syllables from the word.

Her mother's feet sounded on the stairs. "Eva, are you up? Did Guy go for his run? I thought I heard him come in."

Eva's face stiffened. "Yes, I'm up, Ma, I'll be there in a minute."

"It's okay," he promised, though his cock felt so hard he thought it might explode.

"What time is it?" Ruby called. "Guy sure gets up early, don't he?"

"No, it is not okay," Eva said tightly almost at the same time she called back, "I'm getting dressed, Ma. I'll be there in a minute." Her eyes were bright with tears. "You see?" she hissed. "You see?" She jerked the sweater over her head. As he closed the distance between them—all he was going to do was put his arm around her shoulder, he wasn't going to touch her precious tits, he was going to express sympathy, goddamnit—she gave him a murderous look and yanked the door open.

He whacked off in the toilet and deliberately didn't pick up his sweats or socks.

As soon as her mother boarded the plane Eva drove to the store to pick up the trays for the Hines reception. Usually she made the dip and cut the cheese and crudités herself, but she hadn't wanted to risk hurting her mother's feelings, since the only excuse she could give for not inviting Ruby to stay was the real reason: her mother would be in the way. The plane had been delayed, and all the way home she listened for planes overhead with a crackling dread that her mother's flight would crash on takeoff, or else there would be a bomb scare, the plane would be evacuated, and Ruby would discover them gone—Eva didn't know which was worse—all because she and Nick hadn't stayed to watch it taxi. The temperature hadn't climbed above twenty-five all day, though earlier that week it had been seventy. The steering wheel was so cold it hurt her fingers; she'd left her gloves in the pocket of her other coat, and her hands looked rough and blotchy. She hoped the wings of her mother's plane hadn't been de-iced too early.

Nick disappeared upstairs the instant they got home, still sulking because Bill Whitt had called to invite him to a movie with the kids and Eva had insisted that he see his grandmother off instead. She wondered if Bill knew that Gregory had spent Friday night and Saturday with them. Claudia had surprised her by calling on Friday afternoon to ask if she would mind. She never minded taking Greg, though Claudia hadn't said where she was going, and Eva had been under the impression that Claudia would pick him up at noon when Claudia hadn't actually shown till after five—not that it mattered; Guy had stayed with the boys so that she could take her mother shopping. But she'd been in the middle of making her meat pie when Guy answered the door, and by the time she could move the skillet off the burner and dust the flour from her hands, Claudia and Greg were at the curb, and all she did was wave goodbye. And if she really didn't mind, why did she feel put upon?

Guy stayed in the den while she carried the wine and soft drinks to the car. The house had the dour-smelling air of an everlasting chill, though with her mother prattling away at her all weekend she and Guy had had no need to avoid each other. She should be glad to escape. It still made her mad: he didn't touch her for a month, didn't speak except to snap, then expected her to fall into bed with him while her mother lay in wait for her just outside the door. No doubt he considered her insensitive to his needs, but she had needs too, and one of them was not to have somebody demanding something of her every minute. If he were reasonable he could hardly be mad. There was no need for either of them to be mad unless the other was. Why did it have to be so complicated?

She sighed and shut the car door and went back into the house.

"I'm going now." She stood in the doorway to the den. "When you're hungry, there's still some turkey in the fridge—you can make sandwiches for you and Nick, there's salad stuff, or if you want you can heat that little bit of sweet potatoes and corn pudding."

"Did your mother get off okay?"

"Her plane was late."

"I'm sorry."

"Well...." She fingered the keys inside her pocket.

"Rough visit, huh?" A note of sympathy crept into his voice.

"It was okay."

"Still, a bad time for company." He raised his eyes to meet

hers. "I want you to have a good time tonight. You deserve it."

"I don't go to these things for pleasure."

"But you enjoy them. I mean it, I want you to have a good time."

She was forgiven. Her relief was nettled, since she had done nothing to be forgiven for. "Well, I guess I'll see you later."

"Sure." He picked up the remote. "I'll be here."

What was that supposed to mean? she wondered as she drove up the street. Or was it a joke, since she had the car?

By the time she finished laying out the refreshments the first people were in the gallery, a student couple, the boy in baggy gabardine pants and punk-dyed yellow hair, the girl with nose and eyebrow rings and a maroon buzz cut. Her name was Gwyneth; she had been in Eva's Renaissance Through Modern class last year. The boy, Jemmy Miller, was in the same survey now; he had a paper due tomorrow. Holding hands like high school sweethearts, they stepped back to view the large green canvas on the back wall. Like all Hines's paintings, there was something cold about it, diaphanous colors laid over thin black lines whose overlapping arches spoke too mechanically of the drawing compass despite the radiance they framed, a light that summoned the image of a woman's figure, though the figure was not there. The light reminded Eva of the Sulamith Wülfing cards sold in headshops in the '70s. Both Wülfing and Hines had found a formula and stuck with it. Vaguely she remembered the pale, bespectacled young man who had graduated from Gardell a few years after she arrived. He'd gone on to take an M.F.A. and teach at a college in Ohio until his death eighteen months before. His parents were endowing a scholarship in his honor.

The gallery was filling. Charlie Hairston, chairman of the

Friends, had buttonholed her to point out Gwyneth when she caught sight of Sally DeMik chatting in the corner with another of the Friends, Bernice Yow.

"Excuse me," she said. "There's someone I have to talk to."

She was halfway to Sally before she realized that the trendy woman in the long knit skirt and boots talking to Bernice's husband was Kay Courtland. Kay had cut her thick red hair; it was nearly shingled at the nape though the natural curl had been left to frame her face.

"Hi, Kay," she said.

"Oh hi, Eva."

"I love your haircut," Eva offered. She never would have expected Kay to cut her hair off, but the bob became her.

"Thanks." Absently Kay feathered the back up with her fingers.

"How are you?" Eva asked. Sally and Bernice were still chatting, apparently without having seen her.

"Good. How are you?" Kay's smile seemed unfocused, and unexpectedly Eva remembered something Claudia had once said about her—"I wish Kay would stop playing the professional Southern belle."

"Oh. Good." In the shallow silence that ensued Eva realized they didn't know what to say to each other. She hadn't seen Kay since Kay left John, and she felt acutely the unacknowledged fact that lay between them. It seemed inappropriate to mention the separation unless Kay did. She wondered if Kay was thinking the same thing about the accident. Though probably, like Claudia, she had passed right over it in the paper, if she read the paper. "I haven't seen you in a long time," Eva finally blurted, then, to cover her embarrassment, "You haven't been coming to the openings."

Sally, Eva noted, had drifted toward the table. Like Claudia she'd lost weight. She was wearing wool shorts with tights and an expensive-looking vest that called attention to her narrow waist.

"I've been busy." Kay's green eyes darkened, and Eva was afraid she'd sounded critical. She felt dowdy and dull and wished she'd worn another outfit. Her dress was printed with blue roses, her Tennessee Williams dress Guy called it—maybe that was why she'd liked it, because he did, but looking now from Sally back to Kay, she felt blindsided. Neither one of them would ever wear a floral print or flats. Sally's shoes were clogs with wooden soles and handsome-looking brown suede uppers.

"Oh, there's Judy Nichols. Good to see you," Kay called as she followed Sally to the table, and for a moment Eva's vision tunneled; she felt conspicuously alone. When it widened Kay was tilting her head to hear something Judy Nichols had just said; when she looked again both Sally and Kay were chatting with the Hineses. It figured. Kay and Sally had roomed together at Gardell; Sally had majored in art education. For a moment she wondered if Clarence had been in their class, but no, they'd graduated a few years before Eva arrived. Why hadn't Kay just said they knew the family? Kay made her feel that she'd been rude, when she'd only observed a benign truth: neither Kay nor Sally had been to an opening in years.

But she was being over sensitive again. Kay had done no such thing, and Sally simply hadn't seen her. She was picking up Guy's habit of imagining slights.

"If I could have your attention," she began, and after a while the whir of conversation subsided enough for her to give an account of Clarence's career and announce the scholarship. The family lined up behind her, looking reverent. Clarence had died of a congenital heart defect; he'd actually outlived his predicted years, though Eva didn't suppose that made his loss any easier to bear. They had been specific in requesting that she mention the heart defect; and though they didn't say so, Eva suspected they wanted everyone to know that although he was gay he had not died of AIDS. She wondered if setting the record straight made his death less painful. She thought of the Buon Tos and was ashamed of herself, stewing over who talked to whom and clothes. When the speeches were done, she would seek out Sally just to prove how paranoid she was being in her uneasy sense that she'd been snubbed.

When she looked up she was astonished to see Claudia framed inside the gallery's double doors. Impatiently she waited out the titter of applause as Claudia scanned the room. Then she had to turn around to shake hands with each Hines and Clarence's partner from Ohio. When at last she was able to excuse herself, Jemmy Miller blocked her way.

"I finished my paper." He had a sloughing patch of eczema at his temple and a habit of not meeting people's eyes that made his narrow face look feral. She looked around for Claudia, who was laughing about something with Kay and Sally. "Are you going to be home later? You said you'd read a draft."

"Tonight?"

"It's due tomorrow."

"I know when it's due," she said.

His voice sparked. "I work better under pressure."

Sally and Claudia had linked arms. Sally whispered something to Kay, who stood in front of them, blocking Eva's view. She was afraid they would leave before she could make her way to them. The gallery was beginning to clear out.

"It's on Modigliani's sculpture. He was a pretty cool dude, you know?"

"Jemmy, it's Sunday night."

"Gwyn'll drop me off as soon as I type it. I can do the revisions when the computer lab opens in the morning."

"No," she said. She caught up to Claudia at the display case in the hallway just outside the gallery.

Sally had disappeared. Claudia's scuffed leather bomber hung loosely from her shoulders. She was wearing faded jeans ripped across one knee and like Sally had on clogs.

"Hi. I saw you come in during the presentation." Eva sounded winded. "Sorry I missed you when you came by for Gregory yesterday. My mom was here."

"No problem." Claudia hadn't said where she was going when she'd called to ask if Gregory could spend the night. Eva would have said no to anyone else. Her mother was there; she had company. She was surprised that Claudia would ask. She had told Claudia that Ruby was coming.

"I didn't expect to see you," Eva said. "What do you think of the show?"

"Oh." Claudia's voice had a new trill. "I'll have to come back. I was going to meet Sally and Kay, but Caroline couldn't find her ballet shoes, and Bill has to take her to her lesson tomorrow. I just got here."

"Ready, Claudia?" Kay called from the coatrack. "Where's Sally?"

"In the bathroom." Claudia glanced at Eva. "Have you tried the Renaissance Grille yet? We're having dinner there."

"How nice." Her voice was faint.

"It's *very* nice."

The mincing twist in her voice pierced Eva's heart. Out of the corner of one eye Eva saw Sally emerge from the ladies' room. She turned back to Claudia. "I hope you had a good time this weekend."

"I had a wonderful time. By the way, Valerie Rider says hello. I would have come by earlier for Greg, but Sally had us all over for wine and cheese."

Eva had been Valerie's friend too—before Val moved to California, the five of them had made a sort of crowd. "How is Val?" she said woodenly.

"Great. Just great." Claudia's eyes sparkled. "Remember Wyn, the guy she was engaged to? Did you know he's divorced? They got back together."

Of course she didn't know. How would she?

"Coming, Claud?" Sally called.

"I've got to run," Claudia said. "That's a cute dress." Kay had gone ahead, but as they reached the outer door Claudia turned to Sally. "Doesn't Eva look pretty tonight?"

"Hello, Eva," Sally said coldly as she and Claudia linked arms.

"Bye," Claudia called, and the two of them stepped outside.

Tears burned behind Eva's eyes, nearly blinding her as she turned back toward the gallery.

Her throat ached, but she managed not to cry while she cleared the table and policed the hallway for stray cups, glad there were only a few stragglers left. She managed not to cry as she drove home and when she went upstairs to say goodnight to Nick and even when Guy asked if she'd had a good time and she answered in a dead voice, "Not really." But she was crying openly by the time Jemmy Miller arrived at the door with his Modigliani paper.

Guy brought it to her in the den, where she was huddled on the sofa with a pile of Kleenex in her lap. "Did you promise to read a student paper tonight?"

"No," she sobbed. Her spattered glasses slid off the cushion where she'd set them. Her eyes and nose were raw and swollen.

"I didn't think so. He seemed to think he was supposed to wait while you read it."

"He...." She broke down again.

"It's okay. I sent him away." Guy laid the paper on the end table by the sofa and sat in the chair in front of the TV, turning to face her. "So you had a confrontation with a student, is that it?"

"No."

"You had a confrontation with Claudia." His voice was elaborate with patience, though for at least ten minutes after she'd begun to sob he had ignored her, eyes firmly fixed on the TV, no doubt hoping that if he didn't invite her to explain she would stop. When at last he'd turned to ask "Did something happen?" his tone was stained with resignation, but by then she was crying so hard her words had bumped together, broken off, and made no sense, and all she could blubber was "Claudia." Then the doorbell rang.

"No." She blew her nose and added another Kleenex to the heap. "She snubbed me."

"Claudia snubbed you?" His tone was incredulous.

She shook her head again. "I mean Sally snubbed me, and Claudia was with her."

His mouth gave an impatient jerk. "Sweetheart, you have to expect stuff like that from Sally. I know you think she's a friend of yours, but she's a snob."

"You never liked my friends."

He released a loud, impatient sigh. "That's because I'm on your side."

"I know," she whimpered. "You're very supportive."

"Sally DeMik is a bitch. You can't let what she does get to you."

"But Claudia...."

"Honey, Claudia is going through a rough time right now."

"I know that!" But if Claudia was going through a rough time, she should need Eva more than ever. "But she doesn't have time for me, she never has time to talk, tonight she was going to dinner with Sally and Kay, and yesterday...." She wept.

"What happened yesterday?"

Yesterday Sally had given a party for Valerie Rider and hadn't invited Eva, and Claudia had asked Eva to babysit while she went.

"I'm not excusing her."

"We used to go to dinner together!" So what if she hadn't known Val as long as the others had, how could Claudia tell Eva about Sally's party without knowing Eva would be hurt? It wasn't just that Sally had snubbed her. Sally had wanted her to know that she'd been snubbed. What Guy said was true—Sally could be a bitch. She was different from Kay that way; Kay had such gracious manners that Claudia herself once complained Kay was insincere. Eva had thought that Claudia was confiding a basic reservation, when now she realized it was more likely that Claudia had just been venting because she and Kay had had a spat. Somehow Eva had never thought of Claudia's having a relationship with Kay or Sally that was separate from the group's before.

"I know you did," he said. "But you have to remember Claudia has a lot more in common with Sally and Kay right now."

"You mean they've dumped their husbands." Eva's voice was bitter. If it had been the accident—if he had told her that they'd read in the paper that Guy was arrested for drunk driving, if he had told her that because of him, because of what he had done, she was being shunned—she could have accepted that. Somehow she would even have preferred that. But it wasn't that, it wasn't the accident—if her friends had even read about it, they'd forgotten and never thought about her or Guy at all. It wasn't anything she'd done. She was married, and they were not. Her tears had dried, and she burst into a fresh set. "So what are you trying to say? If I want to have friends, I have to dump you too?"

"Don't be silly."

"Claudia's my best friend! I need her right now."

"I know you do. I'm very sorry this happened." He rubbed her shoulders. "I love you." After a minute he let his hand drop. "I'm kind of tired tonight. I'm going to bed."

She couldn't look at him. "I think I'll stay up a while."

There was nothing on TV, and after fifteen minutes she turned it off and read Jemmy's paper. It was terrible, of course, and she let him know so in the margins, though in the morning when she reread it, she discovered it wasn't that bad. She used half a bottle of White Out trying to erase her vitriolic comments before she decided just to tell him she'd lost it and request another copy. It was his fault anyway. She'd told him not to bring it over.

Chapter 9

Guy studied the phone book. There were twenty-two pages of attorneys listed in the Yellow Pages, counting ads.

Don't take chances with your legal rights. Are you considering bankruptcy? See our ad page 27. Antitrust/Unfair Competition. Free initial consultation. Over 25 years Experience. Dog Bites. Defective Products. Sexual Harassment. When your reputation is at stake. Accidents. Assaults and Homicides. Sex Offenses. Slip and Fall. We want to help. Family and Divorce. Qualified representation at reasonable cost. Speeding, DWI and Drug Crimes. Don't settle for less.

Guy closed the book. He could call Jerry Beck for a referral; he could call another friend; he could choose a name at random. He flipped to the page of criminal attorneys, closed his eyes, and put his finger down. Menard, Hoth and Turner. Before he could give himself a chance to change his mind he reached for the phone.

When he had an appointment, he tried Molly again. Twice he had reached her answering machine, but she hadn't called him back. She worked odd hours, waiting tables at a restaurant called the Neon Giraffe—at least she told him it was a restaurant, though with a name like that he thought it more likely a bar, and he wondered if she told him it was a restaurant to protect him. In either case he worried about her driving home, though when he asked if Brian couldn't pick her up, she laughed him off, and he didn't want to alienate her by fussing. His son-in-law was getting more gigs now, she'd reminded, and when Trash—that was the name of the latest band—wasn't playing Brian worked construction and had to hit the sack early. Guy couldn't tell if she meant to send a subtle message: her husband was not the bum her father thought. If she thought that was what he thought. In fact he had no opinion. He didn't know his son-in-law that well, though it seemed to him that any man worthy of his daughter would have the sense not to let her drive home alone so late at night, an opinion he was careful not to share with Molly, even though he knew his fear was rational enough: an attractive young woman with a purse full of tips leaving an empty parking lot by herself at 1 or 2 a.m. That was if the bar or maybe restaurant didn't get robbed after hours while she was cleaning up. Sometimes he thought she was lucky to live so far away. She was often absent from his thoughts, but when he did think about her he worried more than he had when she was little.

She picked up the phone on the second ring. "Oh hi, Dad." Her buoyant voice filled his heart with light. She had a natural optimism she could not have inherited from him or Pauline. More than likely she got it from his father, though in his father he found the same cheer relentless and annoying. "Sorry I didn't call. I didn't get your messages till late."

"Did you have a good Thanksgiving?"

"It was great. We had Brian's parents. I cooked my first turkey."

"How's the weather?"

"Not too bad. How is it there?"

"Cold." When he was younger he had disdained his parents' obsession with the weather, had considered it a measure of the banality at the core of their lives. He supposed his daughter thought the core of his life banal too.

"I thought it would be warm!" Molly protested. Somewhere along the way she'd shed her Georgia drawl. Pauline, who'd traveled all the way to the University of Georgia to get away from home, had run right back to North Dakota the minute they divorced. She'd made a Yankee of his daughter, who assumed that whatever went for Miami Beach went for the whole South.

"Do you have snow?"

"Not that much."

"Where's the mailbox?" The mailbox had become a joke, the detail about the Minnesota weather that had stuck with him, snow so deep and packed people had to stoop to mail a letter.

"Still above sea level."

In his memory of Pittsburgh winters, the snow was stained with piss and rimed with soot, still piled in grungy mountains in the parking lot at Three Rivers Stadium long after the first pitch had been thrown out. The recollection was enough to make him shiver. "Maybe you'd like to come South."

"What do you mean?" Her voice turned guarded.

"For a visit," he explained. "You and Brian. Sometime after the New Year, or—" he was inspired—"what about Christmas? If you don't have plans. Your uncle Curt's invited the whole family to Jacksonville. I could send you tickets."

"You mean you want us to fly to Florida?"

"Why not?"

"Gee, I don't know," Molly said. "The Neon's closed Christmas Day, I wouldn't have any problem getting off, but...."

"Have you and Brian been to Disney World?" He knew

they hadn't. "We were planning to take Nick on to Orlando."

"Brian might have a gig. But Florida...." Molly gave the word a longing twist.

"You don't have to decide right away."

"I'll check with Bri," she promised.

He needed to check with Eva. He hadn't had a chance to talk with her about the trip yet.

But how could she object? She'd thought Florida was a great idea when they first decided. Curt would be glad to see Molly, and it wasn't as if they would be imposing. With Barry and his father there, they'd already planned to stay in a motel. Plus Eva had invited her mother for Thanksgiving. What could she say if he wanted his daughter for Christmas? Still, he knew that she assumed the Florida trip was off.

He planned to tell her when she got home from work, but Nick had some homework project that kept her distracted until she began dinner, and he watched the news in the den. "What are we having?" he asked when she set the steaming wok on a trivet. "It smells great."

"Chicken with snow peas and red peppers."

"Yum," Nick said as Guy echoed, "Aren't we lucky!" and poured his son a glass of milk.

Eva sat. "Nick, you forgot the plates."

"I'll get them." Guy opened the cabinet.

At the table Nick took a swig of milk. Guy distributed the plates and dished up one for Eva.

"Did you call the insurance adjustor?" she asked.

He had called Molly and a lawyer, but he had forgotten the adjustor.

"I'll do it tomorrow," he promised as he motioned Nick to

pass his plate. "It's hot, buddy. Better let me serve you." When Guy had filled his own plate he turned to Eva. "By the way, I made an appointment with a lawyer." The receptionist at Menard, Hoth, and Turner had put him down for Wednesday with Gordon Weems.

"Good." She raised her fork but set it down without eating. "I just don't know why it's taking so long to for them to settle. When that big branch fell on the Camry they sent a check right away."

"Don't forget there's been a holiday." He never should have mentioned calling the adjustor, but he didn't want any more visits from Y Nuh Buon To, and so after the boy's appearance on Thanksgiving he had made a big fuss about calling first thing Friday morning, only to discover that the office was closed for the holiday weekend.

"If you want me to call, just say so."

"I'll take care of it," he said.

Nick drizzled soy sauce over his rice. "This is good, Mom."

Eva sighed. Guy had forgotten about her troubles of last night, but he could see now that they were planted squarely in front of her. A prickle of adrenalin ran up his neck. He should have known that she'd spend today mooning about what happened with Claudia at the gallery.

"No kidding," he echoed. "It's not just good, it's great."

Eva's head was tilted to one side, her mouth drawn into a disagreeable line. The film of cooking oil on her glasses reflected dully in the light.

It was a mistake, he knew it was a mistake even before he spoke, but he was anxious to get things settled. "Speaking of calls, I talked to Molly. We should talk about our Christmas plans. I need to call Curt."

"Tonight?" Eva's eyes fell somewhere to the right of her plate. "Nick, you didn't wipe the table."

"Yes I did."

"No, you did not." Eva skimmed her fingers along the surface.

"I did so."

"I don't know how many times I have to tell you. When you set the table, you're supposed to wipe it. It's part of the job."

"Could we just eat?" Guy asked. "You've fixed this beautiful dinner. Let's not spoil it."

Eva pursed her lips, letting a minute of taut silence pass before she spoke. "Nick, I'm going to tell you one more time: before you set the table you are to wipe it. Not with your hand and not with a dry napkin. I want you to wet a paper towel, and I want you to remember, tomorrow and the next day and the day after that."

Tears slid down Nick's cheeks. "I did wipe it."

Eva ran her napkin along the table and held it up for him to see.

"Goddamnit, if he says he wiped it, he wiped it." The knot of fury tied around Guy's stomach rose to cramp his chest. As soon as Nick bolted from the table, Guy picked up his plate and carried it to the counter. He didn't wait for her to make the usual show of scraping her own plate into the garbage before he stomped up the stairs and knocked on Nick's closed door.

"What?" Nick's voice was muffled.

He pushed the door open. Eva was right: the room was a disaster. Disorder seemed to be growing from the baseboards and creeping toward the door. The sheets had been pulled off the mattress, where Nick lay huddled on a grayish pad beneath a wad of twisted blankets. Guy sat on the edge of the bed. A grubby shoal of stuffed animals and dirty laundry choked the space between mattress and wall.

"How you doing, Niggs?"

The pillow swallowed his answer.

"I think there's a show on whales tonight if you want to watch."

He sniffled.

"I'll tell you what, why don't you get your jacket, and I'll take you out for a cheeseburger."

"Okay." Nick wiped his nose on his sleeve.

As soon as Guy had retrieved his wallet and keys, Eva accosted them in the hall. At least her face no longer wore its little smirk.

"Where are you going?" She avoided Guy's eyes and addressed the question somewhere between him and Nick.

"C'mon, Nick," Guy said as he opened the door. She'd been lying in wait for this fight, and now she had it.

At Wendy's Nick fetched napkins and straws while Guy carried their tray to the table. He handed Nick his burger, but when Nick unwrapped it he set it on the table and cast his eyes down. The boy looked so small and vulnerable Guy felt a fresh wave of anger wash into his throat. Eva had always made him pay for her disappointments and her moods, but it was too much when she tried to do the same to her son. So Nick hadn't wiped the table. He was a kid, for Christ's sake.

"Don't worry," he said. "You didn't do anything."

Nick kept his eyes on the littered carpet. "She's always yelling at me."

"Your mother loves you." A father pulled a high chair up to the next table while the mother distributed fries to the older kids, all of them blond and curly, an ad for family life. "She's just going through a hard time." Despite his anger he felt a pinch of guilt. He hated it when she tried to explain him to Nick; he liked to think that he spoke for himself. "She's pretty upset about Greg's mom and dad. She and his mom were such good friends."

Nick didn't answer. Slowly, almost imperceptibly, the expression on his face seemed to evolve from sorrow into stubbornness. Guy picked up his burger, but Nick made no move to eat. Hey, buddy, help me out here, Guy felt like saying. He set his sandwich down.

"You know how sometimes when one of your friends hurts your feelings and you can't hurt him back you end up hurting someone else instead?"

"Uh-uh."

Guy tried not to show impatience. It was possible Nick really didn't know what he meant. He might not realize that adults got their feelings hurt. When Guy was a kid, he'd thought adults had the world knocked. "Anyway, your mom's not mad at you."

"I know," Nick said, though he still made no move to eat.

"What then?"

Nick looked up, his mouth hung in a pout. "I really like chicken and snow peas!" His face appeared so earnest, so stricken, that Guy almost laughed.

"Me too, buddy. Your mother's one heck of a cook." Guy took a bite of his cold burger.

What had Molly done when he and Pauline fought? She had been nearly six when they divorced, old enough to remember that she'd seen some ugly scenes. Just the other day Eva had told him that Claudia and Bill never fought, told him with a short, ironic laugh that didn't quite cover her wistfulness despite what she knew now. That couldn't be healthy either, kids who didn't know what discord was suddenly told that the happy world they knew was false. It would be his preference not to argue so bitterly in front of Nick, but when did that leave—when did he and Eva ever see each other without Nick around? Nick didn't cause their arguments, but his presence often served to provoke them. He had to know as much, and that was unfair. He shouldn't have to think it was his fault that they argued.

Guy couldn't remember his own parents fighting, though surely there had been occasional harsh words. Or maybe not. Maybe that had been his mother's problem: instead of confronting her husband she withdrew. It hadn't been a happy household despite the harmony at its surface. Funny that when he was younger he had seen that as his mother's fault—her depression hollowed the house, and all their rowdy noise had only intensified the echo of her loneliness and despair. Lately though, he wondered if his father hadn't taken advantage of her morose and self-effacing nature. He had inherited his mother's squeamishness about fights, though not her ability to avoid them. His first marriage had been one long and bloody battle; he and Eva fought more often than she thought, especially now.

"You want a Frosty?" Guy asked.

Nick shook his head and balled up his empty wrapper, having at some point wolfed the burger.

"I'm going to get one."

"Okay," Nick said without enthusiasm.

Guy brought the treats."By the way, I talked to your sister this afternoon. I think we're going to be able get her down here for a visit—maybe she'll even come to Florida for Christmas. Wouldn't that be great?"

Nick touched his tongue to the frozen swirl. "Are we going?"

"I don't see why not." Why should it be a question? Two months ago they'd been planning on it. No one had suggested canceling, but if it wasn't a question why would Nick think that they weren't? He should have consulted Eva before inviting Molly, but she'd been so tied up lately he hadn't had a chance.

"Are we going to Disney World?" Nick asked.

"Do you want to?"

"I've never been there." Nick's tone was neutral, as if he trusted deprivation to speak more eloquently than excitement. Or maybe he was just reluctant to commit, doubtful as everything seemed to have become.

"Well then," Guy said, and it was settled. "Do you remember the last time you saw Molly?"

It had been so long he could never be sure whether Nick really remembered his sister. Sometimes they put him on the phone, though with Molly's schedule Guy often called when no one else was home. She always asked after Nick, but she had been seventeen when he was born, and though she'd spent half of every summer with Guy and Eva when she was younger, by the time Nick came along, what with a boyfriend and a job, she didn't want to leave home. At that age she'd had an attraction to lowlife Guy might have identified with had she been a boy; he could already see his tendency to, maybe not encourage but, approve that side of Nick. Probably it was just as well he hadn't spent much time with his daughter then. Pauline had despaired, but she was so susceptible to hysteria that he'd been able to rationalize the danger. Had he actually had to wait up nights or see firsthand the Deadheads, the ass-length ponytails and doper's eyes, the doo rags and tattoos on the biker types who were probably plugging his young daughter, he might have been more sympathetic. Under the circumstances Molly had married pretty well. The only thing he had against his son-in-law, besides the fact that he lived in Minnesota, was that Brian called him sir and seemed to make no distinction between Guy's generation and his father's.

Nick nodded. "She took me to Putt Putt. We played video games, and Brian let me play his bass."

So he did remember.

"Do you know what day you get out of school?" Guy asked as they dumped their trash and returned to Eva's Corolla. He couldn't wait much longer to call Curt, but surely by this weekend he and Eva would be speaking. They had to go. It was the first time his whole family would gather since his mother died. Curt had remarried last year, he and his wife had bought a new house in Jacksonville, and Guy supposed his reason for wanting to get everyone together was to show it off. No doubt Curt was eager to prove that he had put his life back together. Guy understood—he'd felt the same way when Nick was born.

A new crest of anger rose. What would he have to show now? A felony charge and a wife who wasn't speaking to him. The aftertaste at the back of his mouth went sour as his resentment shifted from Eva to his father. Here he and his brother were in middle age still trying to win their father's approval, and why? Because nothing either Guy or Curt did had ever impressed him, not the athletic accomplishments of their youth (the old man's would always eclipse theirs), not their educations (he had paid for them), not their jobs (before he became a health inspector Curt had been a high school teacher, but the old man had been a coach), not their families (he had raised three kids and managed to stay married). It was Barry, the youngest, the tagalong, the tattletale, the whiner, the brat, the one who flunked out of college and was chronically in debt, always calling on the old man to bail him out, the big talker who was going to Florida to become a fishing guide but never got farther than the Tybee Island Marina and a half-ass job selling bait, who not only never got married but couldn't seem to make any relationship last longer than a month—he was the old man's favorite and had been from the start. Guy wouldn't claim that he and Curt were close; it was odd, given all they'd shared as kids, that their relationship should have turned so formal. Until Guy was in his teens they'd slept in the same bed to leave room for Barry's crib and then the youth bed in the corner. They'd grown up pounding the crap out of each other, but they'd gone everywhere together too, their bond of rivalry as strong as, a part of, their childhood bond of love. Naturally the bond had weakened with age, but just as their resentment of Barry had united them as boys, now they had in common the knowledge that no matter what they did their father saw what they did not. Guy thought maybe he deserved it, but not Curt. All through adulthood, it seemed to him, Curt had walked the straight and narrow.

It would be good to see his brother; he'd been looking forward to the holiday all fall. He liked Florida; he liked the idea of it; he hated being cold. And as long as they were going to Orlando—he glanced at Nick, who was staring out the window, and briefly entertained the thought of driving all the way to the Keys. Because of fishing, Nick idolized Barry, who had introduced him to the sport by letting him fish off the marina dock. Nick had Keys fever, had caught it from Barry, who had driven down to Islamorada with a bunch of his no-account buddies back when he was a teen; they'd chartered a boat, and wasted as they were he'd still managed to land a huge tarpon. Their father had kept the picture of Barry with his big fish when he moved to the apartment over the marina—it was the only family picture on display. More than once Barry had promised to take his nephew to Islamorada, but never had (not that Guy was so sure he and Eva would let their son go off with Barry). The Keys weren't that far. Of course, he had to be back for his court date and Nick had school; plus Molly and Brian would be with them—at least he hoped they would. Still it was a thought. He'd like to see Key West and catch a big tarpon himself.

He'd almost forgotten why he and Nick dined at Wendy's, but when he turned the corner to their street, his mood blackened as he remembered the fight. Sometimes, following a particularly nasty one, he would pass the lighted windows of his neighbors with the sense that they were snug inside houses that rang with family laughter, oblivious to the festering black hole of his marriage next door. It was ridiculous, he knew, but that didn't keep him from feeling like the only desolate man on earth.

The house still smelled of garlic and oil. Downstairs was dark, though a light had been left on over the stove. Eva must have gone upstairs, abandoning the kitchen as it was, cold wok still on the table, Nick's glass of milk three-quarters full. Although it was Guy's job to wash the dishes, sometimes after a fight Eva would scour the entire kitchen as if to punish him. It made no sense, but she'd inherited the martyr complex from her mother. He had no idea what this tactic boded.

Nick had gone upstairs. He followed his son and knocked.

"How about a story?"

"Okay." Nick handed him a Hardy Boys, settling into his wad of gray covers as Guy sat on the edge of the bed. Downstairs a pipe clanked.

Guy cleared his throat and began: "'How would you boys like to fly to Iceland?' Mr. Hardy said."

Nick's face popped up from the bedding with a grin so wide it showed his missing tooth. "Not me. I'm going to Disney World."

Chapter 10

At first Eva didn't know how the Director of Christian Relocation Services reached her, but then she remembered that she'd told Carole Eisen she was the curator at Gardell. And so it took her a minute to understand that the director was not reminding her that she had promised to consider an exhibit of Montagnard crafts. Over the years so many artists and special interest groups called, so many gifts the gallery was offered turned out to be self-promotions in disguise, that she caught herself evading, heard herself murmuring into the receiver, "That's right, I remember speaking to you," without any sense of what Carole Eisen had asked.

"You seemed so interested, and I just can't find anybody else."

Realizing that she hadn't listened, Eva closed a file drawer, though she didn't remember opening it. She had been sitting at her desk, brooding over the scene at the Hines opening again, no longer able to recall precisely what had been said, only the certainty that Sally and Claudia had snubbed her. She'd been unable to think about anything else since it happened. "I'm sorry, I didn't quite catch that." It was coming back to her. She'd promised to consider volunteering. But surely the director understood that whenever you promised to think about something you meant no.

"I know you said you weren't ready to commit to tutoring, but we have a great need for volunteers of all kinds. My driver's sick. If you can spare an hour this morning, I need someone to pinch hit."

"You mean you want me to give one of the Montagnards a ride?"

"Can you? Frankly, I'm desperate."

Eva stared at the piles of paper and slide trays on her desk. The truth, "I'm too busy," sounded lame. She'd been caught shirking even if Carole Eisen couldn't know it. Instead of fighting off her mood with work, she'd been feeling sorry for herself.

A noncommital sigh slipped past her lips. She could not get involved—she absolutely could not, but on what ground could she refuse? *Her husband told her not to.* The thought of Guy brought a queasy congestion to her chest. They hadn't made up when he came in last night, and she had slept in the guest room. "I guess."

"Great. She has an appointment at the Healthcare Ministry at 11. If you're coming from Gardell, you'd go out Gordon Road and make a left on Sibley just past Sibley Mills. Jamaica's the next light. She's at 2617D."

"Who?" Eva cleared a phlegmy bubble from her throat. "Who am I supposed to pick up?"

"H'nghai Buon To. Nuh Buon To's sister. You seemed so concerned about the family...."

Eva swallowed a breath that trapped a hard pocket of air behind her breastbone. Her limbs felt leaden.

"Hello?"

"Yes, I'm here."

"I think it's her first visit, so you'll have to help her with the paperwork and interpret for the doctor."

"But...." She couldn't drive Nuh's sister.

"Don't worry. We're none of us fluent, just do the best you can."

When Carole Eisen hung up, Eva sat staring dumbly at the receiver.

How had this happened? Maybe if she hadn't been so busy moping when the phone rang she could have thought how to refuse; if she hadn't had the fight with Guy—how had *that* happened? Red peppers were on sale, she'd cooked a nice dinner, and the next thing she knew Nick was upstairs sobbing and Guy was stomping from the room. She hadn't done a thing except remind Nick to wipe the table. But she should have known better than to do even that, she should have caught the note of warning in Guy's voice the night before. "I'm very sorry it happened," he had said when she told him how Claudia snubbed her. She'd been foolish enough to think he understood; she'd actually felt grateful, though now she saw that he'd just been making his sympathy official, putting it on record at the same time he put her on notice: he would hold her hand tonight, but by morning she'd better be recovered. Overwhelmed, she put her head down on her desk.

In the bathroom she splashed cold water on her face and cleaned her glasses. It was 10:22, too late to call Carole Eisen back even if she could think up an excuse. An emergency at work, the nurse had called from Nickie's school, she'd cut herself, put her back out, fallen off a ladder. Any one of them would have done.

In the car she had to concentrate on obeying traffic signals as her mind rushed. She didn't have to identify herself; her name hadn't appeared in the paper. What *had* appeared was an editorial urging the legislature to vote in favor of lowering the legal limit for blood alcohol from .10 to .08. It cited Guy's case as a reminder of the lethal consequences of drinking and driving, and now the paper was full of letters to the editor, from everyone who'd ever lost a relative to fanatics in favor of smokers' rights. The Life section had run a three-page feature on the Montagnards, though at least it hadn't mentioned the Buon Tos. Now letters about the community were beginning to come in, a few in support, although the ones that sickened her took the other tack, one so full of hate she'd been surprised the paper would print it. *These people are just filth.*

She wondered if Guy would remember to call the insurance adjustor. Maybe that was what had caused their fight. She should have bitten her tongue and just done it herself.

She passed beneath the dye pipe that spanned the street at Sibley Mills. Once, when she was a teen reading fashion magazines, that name had seemed mythic. Poring over all those ads for clothes made from Sibley fabrics, she had never pictured the factory where the cloth was woven; she had been the perfect consumer, imagining instead the assured, affluent world evoked by the models, the world that at that age she'd thought everyone lived in but herself.

She pulled into the drive that ran along the back of the apartments. The paint on the shingles was chalking, and torn screens hung from the windows, where a web of duct tape held one pane together; the doors were splintery with warped veneer. The place had obviously been neglected before the Montagnards arrived. Why else would the landlord agree to rent an entire complex to them? A mixture of curiosity and trepidation fluttered in her stomach. As she sat, a chicken ran across the empty courtyard. She didn't want to go to the door but couldn't bring herself to honk. She couldn't pick out the door Nuh had entered—if the girl didn't appear, she would have to go around front and knock.

She had just stepped out of the car when a girl in faded navy blue sweatpants and a pink parka opened one of the back doors, a girl so small the clothes would have to be a child's. The sweatpants were too short, and as she came down the walk, Eva saw that she was wearing clear plastic jelly shoes with fuzzy yellow socks.

Eva forced a smile. "Hello. You must be H'nghai. I'm here to drive you to the clinic."

She was sixteen or seventeen Carole had said, though she looked even younger, roundfaced and pretty, with the same broad, flat nose and enormous eyes as her brothers, but her lips were fuller and more finely shaped; there was something softer in her face, more elusive. She returned the smile with a shy duck of her head that didn't let her eyes meet Eva's, seeming to hide behind her bangs, which were thick and lustrous, the kind of hair Eva had always wanted. H'nghai's glossy black mane hung to her waist, gathered at the nape of her neck in a strip of cloth that looked handwoven. In her hands she held a boxy red patent leather purse.

Eva opened H'nghai's door. As she drove she felt keenly both the absence of the radio and presence of the girl. She couldn't think of anything to say. It seemed rude to ask why H'nghai was going to the doctor, and "How do you like America?" sounded trite, though she wondered if H'nghai was as crazy to be Americanized as her brother. She had no idea how much if any English the girl spoke. How in the world was she supposed to interpret for the doctor?

H'nghai watched out the window much the way Nuh had, as if she were memorizing landmarks in order to find her way back.

"Do you speak English?"

H'nghai raised her hand, holding her forefinger and thumb just apart. "Little bit."

"Have you been here before?" As Eva parked H'nghai seemed to dwindle. "It's okay. We'll figure it out."

"Thank you," H'nghai said softly and again when she got out of the car.

The smell of disinfectant hit them as soon as they opened the door. The waiting room was paneled in cheap veneer and carpeted with olive shag two decades out of date, though Eva still thought of the style as doctor's office modern.

"H'nghai Buon To," Eva said when the receptionist appeared at the sliding glass window.

"How do you spell that?"

"Oh. Well, H...apostrophe, I think. The last name's Buon To, B-u-o-n capital T-o." If she was married, why was her last name still Buon To? It didn't strike Eva that a culture which practiced arranged marriage would encourage women to maintain their independence through their maiden names. She looked around for H'nghai, who seemed to have burrowed deeper in her parka although the room was overheated. "Can you spell your name?"

"H'nghai."

"Never mind, I've got it." The receptionist drew a line through the name on her legal pad.

"Have you been here before?"

H'nghai raised her eyes to Eva. "Please."

"I don't think so," Eva said.

"Okay, have her fill this out."

Eva took the clipboard to the corner, where H'nghai planted

herself in front of an aquarium. Nick would know the names of the fish, several small electric blues and a larger yellow one with a funny snout. H'nghai pressed her nose against the glass. "Too small eat."

Eva started, glancing from the aquarium back to the form. "They want you to fill this out," she explained. "Would you like me to help you?"

"Thank you." Dutifully H'nghai took the clipboard and sat with it balanced on top of the ridiculous red purse.

"It's hot. Wouldn't you like to take your coat off?" Eva removed her own jacket and laid it on an empty chair.

"Okay." H'nghai stood to unzip her parka, then carefully picked up purse and clipboard again. Eva almost laughed when she saw the lavender My Little Pony sweatshirt.

She pointed. "This is where your name goes." She wouldn't have expected H'nghai to write, but the girl gripped the pen and bent over the page, bangs sweeping against the paper as she slowly printed her name. The sight of the wobbly, oversized letters tightened Eva's throat, as if in witnessing the effort she had violated some code of privacy. H'nghai was still clutching the pen so tightly her knuckles whitened.

"This line's for your address."

H'nghai's back was rigid. She made no move to write.

"Would you like me to?"

Relief spread across H'nghai's face. "Thank you."

Eva didn't have to ask the street number; she would never forget it. "Do you know your zip code?"

H'nghai scrunched her forehead.

"That's okay. They can look it up. Do you have health insurance?" Carole Eisen had said the family was uninsured.

Eva checked the no box, wondering how people who had spent their lives fleeing through a jungle could possibly comprehend the concept of insurance—though Nuh had certainly grasped it, even if he didn't understand quite how it worked. "It doesn't matter, they'll take care of you anyway." If they didn't, she would.

She paused. "Are you allergic to any medications?" *Have you ever had surgery? Heart disease, diabetes, polio, cancer, hepatitis?* The skin between H'nghai's eyes puckered as she twisted her lips, opened her hands, and shrugged in a gesture so complex Eva wanted to hug her. She left all the boxes blank.

"Sorry stupid."

"You're not stupid," Eva said with conviction. For a reason she would have been unable to explain, she was suddenly certain that H'nghai was not only not stupid but quite smart. She returned to the form. *Women: What was the date of your last period?* Fuck it, she thought as she scanned the crowded room. Let the doctor ask in the privacy of his office if he needed to know. The girl didn't need to be embarrassed any more than she already was.

"Last question: 'What is the reason for your visit?' It means why do you want to see the doctor?"

H'nghai sat up very straight. "Check up," she announced with such clipped charm Eva felt like applauding. She delivered the form to the receptionist, who skimmed it, then raised an accusing eye.

"I'm sorry. She doesn't speak much English. Maybe the doctor can explain the questions—he must have treated Montagnards before."

"Are you a relative?"

Did they look like relatives?

"No." Eva glanced around at H'nghai, whose face was pressed to the glass wall of the aquarium again. "I'm her friend," she said.

"Have a seat. We'll call her in a minute."

When the nurse opened the door and called, "Hannabantoon," Eva looked around. "I think that's you. You're supposed to go with her."

H'nghai stood, gripping her pocketbook and looking frantically at Eva. "Please."

"Okay," Eva agreed, and H'nghai's mouth stretched into a grateful smile. Carole Eisen had said she would need to interpret.

Eva followed her to the scale, which she stepped on without relinquishing her purse or the puffy polyester parka. "Seventy-nine," the nurse announced and wrote the figure on the chart. "You can wait here," the nurse told Eva, pointing to a deacon's bench in the hallway. Eva sat, but when the nurse indicated that H'nghai was to come with her, the girl's face collapsed and she plucked at the sleeve of Eva's sweater. "Please. You."

Eva shook her head. "H'nghai, I can't go with you into the examination room, they won't let me."

H'nghai began to speak softly but rapidly in Rhadé.

"Don't worry, your friend will be right out here," the nurse said. "Come on, you can leave your coat with her."

H'nghai's face drew up in panic, and she pulled at Eva's sleeve again. "H'nghai, you'll be okay. You go with her." Eva watched as H'nghai followed the nurse, looking back over her shoulder. She found medical procedures unnerving herself, and the wait was worst of all, lying there undressed, stripped of all identity except your diseased and naked body. If H'nghai knew that everyone felt that way, it might not be so bad, but she would think it was because she didn't know the language—as if language held any power while you lay as alone as you'd ever been, waiting for the footfall of your fate outside the door. There was something heartbreaking about the trust H'nghai seemed to place in Eva, something at once so sweetly shy and open in her manner that it seemed to reach beyond the dependence forced by her lack of words. She was truly innocent. She had no idea who Eva was.

Eva adjusted the coats beside her, fingers whistling against the nylon. She was overreacting. All she had to do was wait. She would help with any paperwork the office needed. She would drive H'nghai home. Her job was almost done. Relieved to see it that way, she picked up a *Car and Driver*—why did doctors always subscribe to *Car and Driver*?—acutely conscious that she had work to do. Not that she'd been doing it when Carole Eisen called. The momentary thought of Claudia's snub smarted, and she made herself move on. This afternoon she had an appointment to view two canvases out near Dill Creek. (Nick had been appalled to learn that the gallery didn't accept every gift it was offered. "Oh, honey," she'd explained, "you don't understand. People would give us anything if they could and take the write-off. We only have so much storage." His mouth had squared in disapproval. To him, it was bad manners to refuse a gift, and why not? She had taught him to say thank you and keep his opinion to himself if he didn't like his presents.)

She hoped the doctor had arrived. She couldn't see the door of H'nghai's exam room.

Not even eighty pounds including purse and parka. Nick weighed nearly seventy. Eva wondered how long H'nghai had been married. Long enough to know she was unhappy. Well, that didn't have to take long, particularly if your marriage was arranged. She was curious whether H'nghai would have been unhappy in the marriage if she were still in Vietnam, whether she would have known that she could be unhappy. Or was the culture so immutable that whatever happened was just the way things were? Eva hadn't read enough about the Montagnards to know whether the idea of happiness had meaning. It was hard to imagine a culture in which it wouldn't, but where did one locate happiness in a world destroyed by war? The girl's entire life would have been dedicated to survival. Eva wondered if the Montagnards studied civics when they went to their English classes, if they read the Declaration of Independence, all those patriotic things she remembered from third grade. Every morning of elementary school, they had placed their hands across their hearts and pledged allegiance, repeating the words by rote, running the syllables together into sounds that had no sense. What did it mean to the refugee just off the plane, the right to pursue happiness?

"I haven't been unhappy," Claudia had said, or did she say, "I was unhappy," or maybe she said both. Eva was having a hard time reconstructing conversations and events. Throughout the Thanksgiving holiday something about their lunch had nagged at Eva, and now she knew what: Claudia had refused to take responsibility for her marriage; she acted as if she'd made no choices, as if she had been somehow tricked or forced to marry Bill.

Still, it was hard to get what you wanted if you didn't know what that was.

But Claudia did know; she was definite. She didn't want

Bill; she wanted Derek. Sally, not Eva.

The nurse brought another patient, and Eva reclaimed her jacket and H'nghai's parka to make room.

According to Bill, Claudia blamed him for not having a career, though if she had wanted one in all the years that they were friends wouldn't she have mentioned it to Eva? If she had really wanted a career, wouldn't she have gone back to school or got a job? Claudia had majored in English, one of those tracks for people who know what they enjoy but not what they want to do. She had wanted children of course, though she could hardly claim that those were mutually exclusive choices, unless she disapproved of Eva.

But Eva had to work, though she was no longer happy in her job—and it wasn't just the unsold book or the trouble at Gardell. She was tired of the art world. Not of art but of artists, with their pettiness and posturing, tired of the self-importance, insularity, and fads. But maybe the book and her job woes had soured her outlook. After all, once she'd wanted exactly what she had.

She shouldn't be so hard on her students, the ones who expected her to take them seriously when they said, "I want to be the greatest artist who ever lived." Not for their time, not just the best painter or sculptor, nor landscapist nor portraitist, not the greatest abstract expressionist, tops at watercolors or unrivaled in pastels, and never just the best that their talent could make them. They were too young to know whose footsteps they were walking in or how many generations would come crowding up behind. She should be more sympathetic. After all, once she had meant to be an artist too.

Well, she had chosen her life, and it wasn't a bad one. People had choices even if those choices weren't completely free. Even in the mess she and Guy were in there had to be choices; she just hadn't figured out what they were yet. She was still trying when the nurse appeared to say that H'nghai was getting dressed and the doctor would see them in his office.

Obediently Eva rose to follow her around the corner. H'nghai was already seated in the far chair, her face turned down and pinched with fright. A freckled, thickset man younger than Eva, the doctor shook her hand. "I'm Doctor Eudy. It's nice to meet you." He addressed his remarks to her. "What we have here looks like a healthy pregnancy around nineteen weeks along. I think we can estimate that conception occurred late July, with a due date of—" he flipped a calendar—"April 29. We'd like her to gain about 20 pounds, limit caffeine, no alcohol, no tobacco products, eat a balanced diet with plenty of protein, I'm giving her a prescription for vitamins, she can get a list of classes at the checkout desk, and I'll see her in a month."

H'nghai turned her worried face to Eva. "Please, what?"

Eva was stunned. "You're going to have a baby, H'nghai. He's telling you what to eat and how to take care of yourself. Baby," she repeated. Nineteen weeks—the girl was well into her second trimester. Surely she knew that she was pregnant; she must have suspected. Why else would she have made the appointment?

Seventy-nine pounds. She couldn't possibly have a baby. Not only that, she was unhappily married. According to Nuh, she wanted a divorce.

"Baby," Eva repeated, cradling her arms.

H'nghai shook her head. "No baby," she said firmly.

The doctor looked at Eva. Now what? their exchanged

glances seemed to say. Did H'nghai mean she didn't believe them or that she wanted an abortion? Eva was ignorant of the procedures used for second-trimester abortions, though she doubted H'nghai could get one if the doctor wasn't sure she understood. Surely an interpreter could explain. Carole Eisen should be able to provide one. *Maybe* she could supply one. "We're none of us fluent," she had said.

"Perhaps you need some time to discuss the options with your friend."

"Which are?"

Dr. Eudy looked pained. "She's in her second trimester. I would say that if she didn't want to continue the pregnancy, it would be much better if she had decided two months ago." What did that mean? He hadn't said whether the Healthcare Ministry offered abortion services, though they could always call Planned Parenthood for a referral. If that was what H'nghai wanted. She turned to H'nghai, whose entire face was drawn into a concentrated squint.

"My advice would be to go ahead and make the appointment for next month," the doctor said. "If she doesn't need it, she can always cancel."

Eva wanted to press him, but when she looked at H'nghai, her stomach kicked as if she were the one who had received the news, and she was afraid that any questions she might ask would be a form of pressure.

"Please, what?"

"You're supposed to come back in a month, for another check up. Check up," Eva repeated. "To see how the baby is growing." She handed H'nghai her parka.

At the desk the receptionist asked for five dollars, and

H'nghai opened the oversized purse and one by one counted out the bills. The furrow between her eyes had deepened. "Please?"

"We'll talk about it," Eva promised.

But when they were in the car she pulled out without looking and received an angry blast of horn that left her rattled for half a mile. When she glanced at H'nghai, the girl's lips were pressed so tight they had all but disappeared.

"It'll be okay. Please, don't worry." She had no idea where she was driving. "Would you like to go somewhere so we can talk? Do you have time? We could get coffee. Or maybe you're hungry—would you like to have lunch?" She couldn't tell whether H'nghai understood. "I'll buy you lunch. Food." She took a hand from the wheel and patted her middle. "Do you feel like eating or have you been sick?"

"Sick," H'nghai agreed and seemed to brighten.

Eva spotted a strip mall with a sandwich shop and turned into the lot. When she turned off the car, her engine overran. "Come on," she said. "If you can't eat, maybe you could have some soup. I'll buy us lunch."

It was nearly one, and she'd hoped the lunch crowd would be thinning out, but the line at the counter was several people deep.

"What would you like?" Eva read the blackboard. No way could she translate the entire menu. "They have soup, sandwiches, and salads."

"Hot dog?"

Eva scanned the blackboard again. "I don't think they have hot dogs. Their special is tomato-basil soup with half a chicken or tuna salad sandwich. Do you eat chicken?" The image of the chicken running across the apartment courtyard came back with unwelcome clarity.

"Hamburger?"

Eva studied the choices. "I don't think they have a grill."

"Coke?"

"May I take your order?" the girl at the counter said.

"A large Coke," Eva said. She looked at H'nghai, who said, "Please. You." She ordered two specials with chicken salad and a glass of water for herself. At the sound of the cash register, H'nghai opened her pocketbook. Eva shook her head. "This is on me."

H'nghai looked confused.

"I pay." Eva reached out to close H'nghai's purse.

"You pay?" H'nghai seemed perplexed.

"That's right." Eva guided H'nghai to the last free booth. At least the backs were high. She had hoped for some privacy.

"Thank you. Very kind." She pronounced it "bery."

"You're welcome." Eva was glad to realize she could hear only pieces of the conversation behind her. "About the doctor...." Instantly H'nghai's eyes went dim. Eva lowered her voice. "Did you understand what he said? You're going to have a baby."

H'nghai looked away.

"You're almost four and a half months pregnant. In four and a half more months you'll have a baby."

"No."

Eva frowned. "H'nghai, I'm really not sure I know what you mean." It ought to be clear enough, she thought, feeling somewhat foolish, but she still had no idea whether H'nghai didn't understand that she was pregnant or wanted to abort the fetus. "Do you want to have a baby?"

"No baby. Sick."

Now what? Eva thought and let out a long breath. "You're not sick, H'nghai. I mean you might feel sick, but you're not sick. You're pregnant."

H'nghai made the little head-ducking motion again as the girl behind the counter called their number.

"I'll be right back," Eva promised as if she expected H'nghai to disappear When she returned, she placed H'nghai's soup and sandwich in front of her and watched her take a tentative taste of each.

"Thank you. Very good."

"You're welcome." When they had finished eating, Eva pushed her bowl aside and leaned into the table. "Tell me about your husband. Does he know you're pregnant?"

"Katu." H'nghai frowned.

"What does he do? Does he have a job?"

"Job."

"Where?"

After a minute H'nghai shrugged. "Work," she said.

"And you live with your parents?" The apartments couldn't have more than two bedrooms. In Vietnam they would have lived with her parents in a longhouse. The Rhadé were matrilineal, she suddenly recalled. Maybe that was why she kept the name Buon To, though how much power could women have if they weren't free to choose their husbands? "How long have you been married?"

To Eva's surprise H'nghai began to speak rapidly and angrily in Rhadé. "No husband," she finished with a flash of her eyes and emphatic sniff.

Well, that was clear enough, Eva thought, though it gave

her no clue what to say next. "Does he know you're pregnant?" she asked again, but H'nghai only repeated, less stridently, "No husband."

It was 1:35. Eva needed to get going. "I promised to tell you what the doctor said."

Suspicion kindled in H'ghai's eyes. "Sick," she insisted.

"Not sick. And if you want to have the baby, you have to take care of yourself. You can't smoke or drink alcohol, no—" Eva pantomimed smoking.

"No pipe," H'nghai said, "no cigarette."

"That's right. No cigarettes, no alcohol...."

"No beer."

"That's right," Eva said, again relieved that H'nghai finally seemed to understand. "The paper he gave you is a prescription for vitamins—pills you need to keep you healthy."

"Tylenol, extra strength."

"Vitamins. They help the baby grow. I have to get back to work, but I'll take you by the drugstore on your way home."

"Sick." H'nghai's chin had a stubborn set; at least it looked stubborn to Eva.

"Damnit," she said.

H'nghai looked startled.

"You know you're pregnant."

H'nghai's face closed in. She trembled.

"What you're doing—it's called denial. Every day...." Well, even if she could, there was no point in regaling H'nghai with the tragic tales of teenaged girls who managed to hide their pregnancies from everyone and convince themselves they were just gaining weight until they went into labor, delivered a healthy full-term baby in a bathroom stall, and panicked. "It's natural, but the point is it won't keep you from having the baby. You have to accept the fact you're pregnant because if you don't want to have a baby...." She had no idea how to phrase it. It was one thing to say H'nghai had a right not to carry the pregnancy to term and quite another to get between a husband, parents, an entire culture and this girl. What if the Montagnards had a strict taboo against abortion? For all she knew it could be an offense punishable by death or else the women might have potions and do it all the time. Maybe H'nghai would tell her mother, and her mother would instruct her. Except she was so far along. Surely the mother knew, or at least suspected.

"There's a procedure," Eva said lamely. "We can talk about it. The point is in America you don't have to have a baby if you don't want to."

Tentatively H'nghai nodded. "In America is freedom."

"Well, yes, but ...."

H'nghai looked down. "In jungle," she said after a minute, "everything is less. We do like a man do. Very hard life, Dega women. In America is microwave oven, washing machine, divorce. Everything like that. Is freedom."

"Sort of."

H'nghai tipped her head to regard Eva. "You husband?"

It took Eva a minute to realize what she meant. "Oh, yes, I'm married."

"You like husband?"

Eva smiled. "Yes, I like my husband." Almost immediately her smile faded as she remembered that she and Guy weren't speaking.

"Baby?"

"One—my stepdaughter doesn't live with us, she's grown."

Older than you, Eva was startled to think. She rummaged her wallet for a picture of Nick. "Big baby. He's eight." Almost the age of Bhan. She shouldn't have pulled out the picture, but H'nghai's hand was already stretched out to take it, a large hand for a girl so small.

She studied the image. "Pretty." She handed the picture back.

"How old were you when you got married, H'nghai?"

A frown of concentration creased H'nghai face, and then she shrugged.

"Did you get married in Vietnam?"

The frown deepened. It took her a long time to answer questions she understood; the ones she didn't understand, Eva was learning, she answered not at all or very quickly. "Very hard life, Vietnam. Viet Congs, they come to Central Highland, destroy property Montagnard, take our food, and kill our peoples."

"It's terrible, what they did," Eva agreed. Reluctantly she looked at her watch. She would have to call her appointment from the drugstore to say she would be late. "H'nghai, I have to go—I have to go back to work, but I'm going to take you to get your vitamins. You need to take one every day, but I wouldn't show the pills to anyone until you've decided what to do." H'nghai's eyes clouded, and a look of fright sprang to her face. "It'll be okay. Look, I'll give you my phone number." She pulled out her card. "This is my telephone number." Nuh had said they didn't have a phone, but maybe H'nghai knew how to use a pay phone. "The one at the top is at work, the other is home. I'll come by to see you in a couple days, but in the meantime if you need to you can call me."

"Call up say hello?"

"Sure." She had no idea what she would tell Guy if he should answer.

H'nghai studied the paper. "Which you name?"

"Oh." Eva released a giddy laugh. She had forgotten to introduce herself. H'nghai was still studying the page. Eva pointed to her name. "Eva Summer."

"Eva Summer," H'nghai repeated. She smiled. "Call up my friend Eva Summer, say hello."

"Yes, I'm your friend." A stone sank through Eva's gut. She blinked hard and leaned toward H'nghai. "You think about what you want to do. About the baby."

"No baby. Sick," H'nghai insisted, her face as clear as water.

Chapter 11

"Thank you for calling North Insurance. If you know the extension of your party and are using a touch-tone phone you may enter the number now." For two days Guy had been trying to call the adjustor, and each time he was more impatient with the automated phones. He had to wait out the entire menu every time because they still had rotary phones.

Instead of an operator, he reached another recording: "We're sorry. All our operators are busy assisting other customers." He waited twenty minutes before he hung up and then had no choice but to dial again. The music was an orchestral Christmas medley with a very short loop. When he finally got through the secretary told him the adjustor wasn't in and connected him to voice mail.

He wore his suit to meet the new lawyer, surprised to discover that the pants felt tight. In the weeks since he'd last worn it he must have gained weight. He was getting plenty of exercise, but snacking too much. He needed to get out of the house just to keep from getting fat. As soon as he finished with the lawyer, he would go by Day Labor and fill out an application.

He was anxious to get the interview over. Though he fully expected the charges to be dropped at the hearing for probable cause, what he needed from the attorney was guidance up until and through the hearing. It was too bad he couldn't get it over with before they went to Florida—he still had to talk to Eva about the trip—but at least it would be settled as soon as they got back. There was no hole so deep you couldn't climb out, and as far as legal holes went, this wasn't nearly so deep as it had seemed. Any real criminal would have known that, for as Jerry Beck once confided to Eva, every deadbeat knew the bottom line: you didn't have to pay. "You don't have to pay?" Eva had echoed in a shocked voice. Jerry's nod was gleeful. The job of the debt collector was to intimidate the upstanding middle class citizen who had fallen on hard times. Collection agents existed for people like Guy and Eva; civilization depended upon their ignorance and guilt. Jerry knew the system, and if he was even a halfway decent lawyer, Gordon Weems would too.

Gordon Weems. When the receptionist had offered his name, Guy almost asked if she couldn't schedule him with someone else. It seemed like an unlucky moniker for a lawyer; you might as well have a doctor named Death as a lawyer with a worm-dicked name like Weems.

Eva needed her car to get to work; he didn't like to use it any more than he had to anyway. He was tempted to walk, but if he wore his dress shoes his feet would blister, and the thought of showing up at the firm with his shoes in a paper sack like the career women who walked the streets at lunch in their power suits and cross-trainers made him cringe. He rode the bus, something he hadn't done for years, though once it had been his regular form of transportation. On the night Molly was born he and Pauline had taken the bus to the hospital. It seemed a lifetime ago, though the smell of exhaust and sight of the other passengers' slack faces instantly conveyed him back to the desperate days of his first marriage.

Menard, Hoth, and Turner occupied a squatty brick building on a narrow court that looked more like an alley, an edifice so undistinguished it might have been mistaken for an annex to the Main Street Methodist Church were it not for the stenciled gilt lettering on the door. Since Weems was not a Menard, Hoth, or Turner, he assumed the lawyer would be young, probably a kid fresh out of law school sporting Italian shoes, wire-rim glasses, and a fifty dollar haircut.

He was right about the glasses. He'd barely had time to sit before Weems appeared, looking more like work scholarship material from the state university than Law Review at Harvard or Duke. He was younger than Guy, but older than the scars from a bad case of teenaged acne made him appear. His shoulders sloped, and his bark-colored hair was thinning.

Guy's parka slipped from his lap as he rose to shake the lawyer's hand. He had a topcoat—at least Eva said he did, but he could never find it in the closet. There was a dusting of tiny white feathers on his suit.

Weems ushered Guy into a windowless office made dark by cheap paneling and soiled rust-colored carpet. "Have a seat." Guy laid the parka on the chair beside him. "Why don't you tell me what your problem is?"

As Guy spoke he jotted notes.

"Was anyone else injured?"

"No."

"And your wife was with you in the car. Anyone else?"

"No."

"Any previous arrests for DWI?"

"No."

"Other arrests?"

"Not since I was a kid."

Weems looked up.

"I got caught walking across a lawn in Fort Lauderdale with

an open beer on spring break." And he'd spent the night in jail because his father refused to put up the cash to bail him out, supposedly to teach him a lesson. Whether he had learned it was hard to say because by the time the next year's bacchinalia rolled around he was bagging groceries to support the pregnant wife waiting in their ratty two-room apartment to berate him because they didn't have enough money to buy a TV and she was bored.

"When was that?"

"More than twenty-five years ago. I was in college." He was right, Guy decided—Weems had been work scholarship. While Guy and his classmates drove all night to sleep twelve to a room and drink themselves stupid on a motel balcony overlooking ten thousand coeds sunning on the beach, Weems was washing dishes back at the state U. The experience seemed to have robbed him of humor.

"Any treatment for alcoholism or alcohol-related disorders?"

"I'm not an alcoholic," Guy said.

"Good." Weems made another note. "What was the date of the accident?"

"November 16."

"So you've had your first appearance. What's your next court date?"

"January 3. Do you think I can get my car back before then? I need it to go back to work."

"It's been impounded?" The overhead light reflected yellow disks on Weems's glasses as he looked up again. "What's your occupation?"

Guy hesitated. "I was planning to temp. I'm sort of

between jobs."

Weems's narrow lips crimped. Not, Guy supposed, what an attorney liked to hear about a client. "Did you leave your last position voluntarily?"

"I wasn't fired. I was laid off."

"Are you collecting unemployment?"

"Yes."

"For how long?"

What did that have to do with it? "Since October."

"Have you requested a hearing on the revocation of your license?"

"What do you mean?"

"Sometimes the judge will grant limited driving privileges if you can prove that you need your car to work."

Guy's forehead knotted. "I wasn't aware that my license had been revoked."

"The magistrate didn't issue an order?"

"Not that I'm aware of."

The attorney flung his pencil down. "There's an automatic ten-day suspension of your license for per se concentration. A charge of felony death nearly always carries additional revocation of one year. Are you telling me that neither the magistrate nor the judge ordered you to surrender your license?"

"No." Could the judge at first appearance have ordered his license revoked and Jerry failed to tell him? He opened his wallet. "What's per se concentration?"

"Blood alcohol." Weems adjusted his glasses. "The amount of blood alcohol that's considered legally drunk. Right now the figure's 0.10, but the Highway Safety Commission wants to see it lowered to 0.0."

Zero as in zero, zip, nought, nothing, zilch? Legally drunk while stone cold sober? It made no sense.

"It's almost certain to be lowered to .08 when the next General Assembly meets. What'll happen is you'll see it come down in increments over the next ten years or so to .05 or .06."

"Well, that explains it. My blood concentration was .02—way below the legal limit. I couldn't believe I got arrested." Neither the magistrate nor the judge had ordered him to surrender his license because he hadn't been intoxicated. In order to be charged with felony death, he had to have committed a felony that resulted in a death, when the fact was he hadn't even committed a misdemeanor.

Weems aimed a vague frown toward his notes. "Your BAC was...."

"Point-0-two."

"Point-0-two." Still frowning, the lawyer nodded.

"I don't know why I was charged."

"Apparently the officer thought you were impaired."

"But...."

"Let me explain something." Weems leaned toward him, into his desk. "Per se is a figure set by the General Assembly that establishes intoxication whether there's any other evidence of impairment or not. If there is other evidence, you can be charged with DWI no matter what your BAC is."

"What other evidence?" He hadn't flunked any of the drills; he'd puked, but surely he wasn't the first man the cop had seen vomit from shock or nerves.

"An accident," Weems said.

Guy uttered an irritated sigh. "About my car...."

"I'll check on it. Let me send over to the D.A.'s office for a copy of the accident report. That should shed some light on the officer's reasoning, and we can take it from there." The lawyer's lips barely moved when he talked, and Guy wondered if that was why his voice lacked intonation. "In the meantime I'd like a list of any medications you were on, prescription, OTC, anything that might affect the BAC or interact with alcohol. Antihistamines, for example. I'll talk to the D.A. and see if we can't work out a plea."

"I wouldn't be interested in a plea."

Weems's frown deepened. "Felony death—you're looking at a ten-year sentence, out in three; even if you get manslaughter you're going to do a year out of five. I'm going to need twenty thousand up front to make sure you don't do jail time."

Twenty thousand dollars? Where did Weems think a man between jobs was going to get that kind of money? He hadn't had that kind of money lying around when he was working. "Are you talking about a bribe?"

The glasses flashed. "D.A.'s don't take bribes, Mr. Ferrin."

Guy shifted. He felt choked inside his tie, and the waistband of his pants cut into his gut. "Sorry—it was just the way you put it."

"Felony death is a serious charge."

"I know that."

"A lot more serious than DWI—and DWI's a hell of a lot more serious than it used to be. The public's fed up, and the Governor's made cracking down on drunk driving a top priority."

"But that's the point," Guy said wearily. "I wasn't drunk." Stiffer penalties for drunk drivers—who could be against them? It would be like saying you were opposed to civil rights. "There are some things you just can't be against," he could hear himself repeat to Eva, though as soon as he did he heard her dry rejoinder, "Some people manage." They'd been together for so long she'd become a voice in his head, though he doubted he was a voice in hers. "They can't convict me of driving while intoxicated if I wasn't drunk."

"Apparently the officer found you to be impaired," Weems said.

"I wasn't impaired."

"No offense," Weems said, "but even the falling-down drunk says that." He hurried on before Guy could protest. "Okay, you weren't falling-down drunk. Point-0-two is good. It means I can keep you out of jail." He paused, giving Guy a moment to think about the value he would get for his twenty thousand. "The D.A. doesn't want to waste the court's time. He knows I'll ask the judge to consider slight impairment as a mitigating factor before he determines your sentence."

It wasn't driving while intoxicated; it was driving while impaired. The distinction hadn't registered when he was arrested. He was sunk. "I don't expect this case to come to court. I was under the impression that it would be thrown out at the hearing for probable cause."

Weems raised an invisible eyebrow. "Who told you that?"

Jerry Beck had said so, hadn't he? "My lawyer," he started to say, but stopped. It seemed like poor salesmanship. Weems would want to know why he was changing attorneys. "A lawyer friend."

"Criminal lawyer?"

This and that lawyer, favor-for-a-friend lawyer. The truth was Guy didn't know.

"You can forget probable cause. You'll never get a hearing."

"What do you mean?" he asked, though it came back. Jerry had called the D.A. a hardass and said the same thing.

"I know these North Carolina D.A.s. In a case like yours they don't like to give probable cause."

"I don't like to pay my taxes."

Weems leaned into his desk again. "Let me explain something to you. The courts are overcrowded. Every week the Grand Jury meets to consider four or five hundred cases. That's four or five *hundred*, every one of them buried in the pack."

Guy could taste the root of his tongue, rancid with dislike. "January 3. It's already scheduled."

Weems slid back. "Mr. Ferrin, have you ever been called for jury duty? If you have, you have some inkling of how the courts move. Do you honestly believe that a hearing scheduled for the morning of January 3 is going to take place on that day?" He ticked his fingers. "You figure delays—say the arresting officer's not available or maybe there are witnesses who can't be found, the records haven't come yet, the D.A.'s mother died, his dog is sick—you name it. Probable cause judges are as strict as they come—they don't want to send anything to the Grand Jury that's not going to go on to Superior Court. These D.A.s know that. They're not stupid. If they don't have what they want, they don't schedule. All your prosecutor has to do is request a delay. Because the Grand Jury's not like the judge—it's going to do whatever he wants them to, and if he says he's got a case, they're going to see he gets his trial." Weems tapped his blotter. "Believe me, Mr. Ferrin, with a BAC of .02 you are not going to get probable cause."

It made no sense. "Isn't it my right to have one?"

"It is. But it's not a good idea to go out of your way to piss off the D.A. Besides, if you win on probable cause, the police can just arrest you again, which means the magistrate sets bond again, which means you're out another...what? Three thousand dollars."

It was unbelievable. The prick wanted twenty thousand dollars to explain to Guy how the system was going to fuck him.

As if he had read Guy's mind, Weems gave him a level look.

"You play the game by the rules in use, not by the ones in the book."

"I hear you." Guy crossed his legs and plucked a small white feather from his knee. "But I still don't want anything to do with a plea bargain. The idea offends me. First of all, I'm innocent. And second of all, I'm broke."

"I understand how you feel." Again Weems leaned toward Guy. "But I'll tell you this: you do not want to go up to Superior Court broke. Because if you do that, innocent or guilty, you're going to find yourself in Central Prison."

Whose side was the guy on? Of course, there was always the possibility that he knew the system. Actually there was a sinking place inside Guy that believed Weems did know the system. The attorney had only confirmed what Guy already knew, what he had always known, from the time he turned twelve or thirteen: the system, any system, was set up to screw every peon in it.

When he uncrossed his legs, his knee cracked. "For twenty thousand dollars, I think you can afford to look at the report before you decide on a strategy." Where did Weems think he was going to get twenty thousand dollars?

"No problem. I'll have the D.A.'s office send it over. Like

I said, my fee's payable in advance, and I couldn't agree to take the case unless you'd be willing to listen to my advice."

Guy picked up his parka. "I understand."

"Think it over. You've got no priors, no aggravating factors; the D.A. will probably agree to let you plead to misdemeanor due caution. That way you never have to go to court—you'll get two years probation and a five hundred dollar fine."

Compared to the lawyer's fee the fine was nothing. "What if I went to court on the misdemeanor?"

"You aren't charged with the misdemeanor."

"Can't you get the charges reduced? I don't want to plead to something I didn't do."

Weems raised his eyebrow again. "You didn't hit the victim?"

"I hit the kid, okay? But I wasn't drinking, I wasn't speeding, I wasn't violating any law. They can't send me to jail just because I'm broke." The bottom line, he told himself. You didn't have to pay. Civilization depended upon the ignorance and guilt of people like Guy and Eva.

"I'll send for the record. In the meantime, I'd like to know about any medications. Aspirin, Ibuprofen, Benadryl, anything. Oh-two sounds about right, but you can have a very low number and still be impaired. We'll have a better idea of the officer's state of mind when I've seen the report. The BAC's good though. The D.A.'s not going to want to go to court with .02. He'll be glad to take a plea."

"If the D.A. doesn't want to go to court, he can drop the charges."

Weems stood. "Why don't I give you a call when I've seen the report?"

When he got home there was a message from the insurance adjustor, asking Guy to call him. At least he'd left a real number instead of the toll-free clearinghouse. Guy was able to reach him on the first try.

"I've checked on your claim," he said. "We've had the vehicle photographed, so just as soon as the police release it and you get an estimate we should be able process your check."

"I wasn't calling about the Camry. It's come to my attention that the check for liability hasn't been received, and I wondered...."

"Can you hold?" the adjustor asked and without waiting for an answer plugged Guy into the same damn Christmas medley. The only holiday song he'd ever liked was Elvis's "Blue Christmas." It was lunchtime, and by stretching the cord he was able to open the refrigerator. There was no sandwich meat or cheese, and he began a tentative inquiry into the various tubs stacked on the shelves. Generally when he did the dishes he tried to date the leftovers, but Nick made a habit of filching the masking tape from the kitchen drawer, and Guy often put them in unlabeled, promising himself in vain to remember tomorrow lunch that the Greek pasta was in the yogurt carton. Every lid he opened exposed fur.

The adjustor's voice came back. "Thanks for waiting. I had to check the file. That claim has been denied."

"Denied?" An elevator dropped inside his stomach. "There must be some mistake."

"Could you hold again?"

The medley picked up. It seemed like an assault beyond anything he had yet weathered to have to stand there in a kitchen where there was nothing to eat that wouldn't kill him listening to a thousand strings pluck out "Rudolph the Red-nosed Reindeer."

"Sorry," the adjustor said when he returned. "I had another call waiting. The claim for liability has been denied. I'm surprised you weren't notified."

"I don't understand how it could possibly be denied. We've paid our premiums...."

"If you'll give me a minute, I'm trying to explain. Based on the witness's statement...."

"It was an accident, that's what we have insurance for."

"Well, Mr. Ferrin, you told us you weren't responsible for the boy's death."

"I couldn't stop. That's what I told you—he ran out. Of course I'm responsible!" He was shouting.

"Mr. Ferrin...."

"That's the way the law works—it doesn't matter who's at fault, the person who does the hitting gets the ticket. I've been charged with felony death for Christ's sake!"

"But that's just it." The adjustor's voice smoothed itself with patience. "According to the witness, you didn't hit him."

What witness? "Accidental death. It's in the policy." Actually Guy hadn't read the policy.

"The issue is liability. Are you liable for the accident?"

"The boy *died.*"

"It's unfortunate, I'm sure you feel badly, but we just don't see liability here."

"I hit the kid."

"Not according to the witness. You didn't hit the boy; he hit you. It's in the accident report."

There wasn't any witness. His head was ringing. "I don't

know anything about any report. All I know is what happened: the boy ran in front of the car."

"According to the witness, he hit the car when he ran out."

Eva was the only other person there. His breath stalled. Eva was the witness. What in the name of God had she said? "I don't know anything about that. It doesn't mean I'm not liable."

"Well, Mr. Ferrin, actually, I'm afraid it does."

"Oh, for Christ's sake," Guy said. "I hit him, all right? I don't care what the witness says, I've been charged!" And a fucking lawyer who hated his guts because nearly thirty years ago when he was in college he'd driven down to Florida with a bunch of drunks for spring break while the lawyer washed dishes at the dorm cafeteria to pay his tuition and then went home to dose his pimples with Clearasil, who'd never shoplifted a Matchbox car or given a pink belly or knocked up *his* girlfriend, who had graduated from the state university magna cum laude and gone on to law school while his wife worked as a file clerk to put him through, who probably had exactly 2.0 children that he'd begotten without ever having a hard-on in his life and now that same wife drove those kids to soccer practice in a minivan that cost more than Guy and Eva's first house, *that* fucking lawyer, wanted twenty thousand dollars to get the D.A. to let him plead guilty to a crime he didn't commit while murderers and rapists walked free.

Goddamn Eva.

"I'm sorry. All I can tell you is we don't find liability."

"Would you just tell me this? What's his family supposed to do? They don't have any money, they don't even speak English—they're refugees."

"I'm afraid that's not our problem."

"You mean to tell me that a jury can put me in jail while you say I'm not liable?"

"If you're convicted, we would expect you to appeal."

"I may not be convicted. My attorney is recommending that I plead guilty to failing to exercise due caution."

"Oh no," the adjustor said quickly, "we don't want you to do that." Guy's blood pressure had risen; he could feel his heart banging in his ears. He still hadn't taken his suit off, and he yanked at the knot in his tie. "If you plead guilty, based on the report that I have here, we would have to cancel your policy."

"Oh yeah?" Guy nearly laughed. A lot of good the policy had done them. He gripped the receiver. "Well, you know what I have to say to that? BFD!"

"What's wrong?" Eva said as soon as she saw him when she and Nick came in that evening. It was the first sentence she'd spoken to him in two days.

He shook his head.

"Nick, why don't you go watch cartoons?" Eva said. "I can help you with your homework later."

"I don't have any homework."

"Yes you do." She kept her ear cocked until the TV was humming in the den. "What happened?"

He pulled out a chair. Timidly she touched his shoulder, letting her hand remain when in gratitude he reached up to close his over hers.

"Wasn't today the day you were going to see the new lawyer?" He nodded. "And?"

When he opened his mouth, the breath that blocked his

words burst. "He wants twenty grand to keep me out of jail. He wants to arrange a plea bargain with the district attorney."

"Twenty thousand dollars?"

"Twenty thousand five hundred counting the fine."

"What fine?"

"He wants me to plead guilty to failing to exercise due caution. I'll be given two years probation and fined five hundred dollars." She came around to sit beside him, chewing on her lip. "That's the misdemeanor Jerry talked about. It means I was negligent."

"But you weren't."

He shrugged and looked away.

"You weren't," she insisted.

"Somehow there doesn't seem to be anyone except me who finds that relevant."

"I find it relevant." He reached across the table to embrace her hand again. She played at his fingers, lifting them one by one, then shook her head. "That's a lot of money."

"More than we have."

"Well...." A frown left her squinting. "There's always the house." She paused. "It just seems like a hell of a lot of money to get you to plead to something you didn't do."

"I'll say. For twenty thousand dollars he ought to be able to get a formal apology from the President of the United States."

"Maybe we could borrow it," she said without conviction.

"I told him I didn't want to plead. He's going to get the police report and call me."

She slipped her hand from beneath his. "Did you like him?"

"Was I supposed to?"

"I don't know. You're supposed to like your doctor."

"Better yet, you hope your doctor likes you."

She forged a flimsy smile.

"Well, Jerry said it was going to cost a lot." Guy exhaled a brief sigh. "I went ahead and gave him the case. He seems to know his stuff, and I didn't know what else to do."

She couldn't quite cover a wince. "I'm sure you did the right thing."

"Felony death's a serious charge." Was he going to parrot the lawyer to her now? At the first let-me-explain-something-to-you she'd stalk from the room. He tried to imagine her in Weems's office but couldn't, couldn't imagine her as the petitioner. If she'd been driving, she wouldn't have been charged. If she'd been handling it...except she had been. She had told the insurance company he wasn't liable.

"What?" she asked at the change in his expression.

"I talked to the adjustor." He avoided her eyes.

"Did he explain the holdup?"

"In a manner of speaking."

"What does that mean?"

But he didn't want to confront her, not now at least. It would only cause friction between them, when they'd finally begun speaking. It was hard to recall the accident's sequence; he'd had difficulty even just after it happened, and she of all people wouldn't have set out to hurt them, she wouldn't lie about a thing like that. Undoubtedly she had told the police and the adjustor what she thought had happened. "Did you hear from Claudia?" he asked to change the subject.

"No," she said bitterly. "Why would I?"

He had hoped Claudia would have called by now—not to

apologize of course, but if she felt the least bit guilty—and if what Eva said was true she should—he thought she might have called to chat. "I'm sorry."

"I know you are." Her voice softened as she sought his eyes. "I'm sorry about dinner the other night. You were right, I was in a bad mood."

"You were upset," he said generously. "Claudia was your friend. She shouldn't have treated you like that."

"No, she shouldn't."

"Anyway you're right. Our son's got to learn some responsibility. His room's deplorable. His bed doesn't even have sheets."

"I don't know what he does with them. It's not like I don't put them on." She gave a delicate snort. "I love the way the teachers say check their homework and just assume they're actually going to let you know what it is."

"I don't know why he can't be more organized."

"Oh, he'll be okay," she said after a minute. "I hope." Her gaze shifted to the dark window. She was thinking about Claudia again, but no—"You didn't tell me what the insurance adjustor said."

"Oh." There was no way not to tell her. It wasn't the kind of secret he could keep. "Just...did you tell him we didn't hit the boy?"

"What do you mean?"

"What I said." He tried not to sound impatient. "Did you tell the insurance company we didn't hit the boy?"

"That's right." She was nodding. "I told the police, the officer, McThune, kept making me go over it, he kept asking questions until I could put it together step by step. The boy,

Bhan, he was running or something, he must have tripped, I don't know, it was like he just flew up in the air." Her eyes glazed again with distant light. "I saw him go over the hood. That's when he hit us. The way McThune questioned me—he kept asking until it was like a movie, like I could rewind it and slow it down."

Guy turned away.

"What?"

He made himself look at her again. "That's not the way it happened."

"Yes it is."

"No it isn't," he said, though for all he knew, it was. He'd been over it so many times he no longer knew what had happened. "I ought to know. I was driving."

"This should make you feel better."

He turned away again. His voice was low. "Maybe I didn't hit him. To tell you the truth, I don't know anything anymore."

"Oh, honey."

He raised his face. "The adjustor says we're not liable."

"What do you mean?"

"They've rejected the claim."

"For the Camry?" She was frowning.

"No, they'll pay for our car. It's the liability they won't pay. He says because we didn't hit him we're not liable and told me not to plead. If I'm convicted they'll reconsider."

"You mean they're not going to pay the Buon Tos?" Her hand rose to her mouth. "Oh my God. Oh, honey. I'm so sorry."

"It's not your fault," he said.

"It never occurred to me that they could deny the claim." Her face had paled. "I am so, so sorry." But there was nothing else to say, and after a while she got up and started dinner.

Chapter 12

Eva stared at the piece of paper, not sure she could trust what she read. For years she had believed herself to suffer a mild dyslexia, if that was the term for her tendency not to transpose individual letters but to mix up entire words. And once she misread she found it almost impossible to reread correctly, for instead of scrambling words into senseless letters, her faulty reading sent her on with the wrong antecedents, left her to solve crosswords armed with false clues, permitted her to digest hallucination as irrefutable fact. In her son she was inclined to blame such mistakes on carelessness or haste, but in herself she suspected a congenitally crossed wire.

In her hand was a sheet of inexpensive white letter-sized bond. She had pulled the envelope from the basket where she filed the bills until she got around to issuing the checks, which she wrote once a month because the practice forced her to balance the checkbook, at least in theory. In fact she seldom found the time, in which case she would simply mail the mortgage, postponing the rest, sometimes until the electric company or gas threatened to cut off their service. Guy found such threats distressing, but because the problem was time rather than money—after all, she always paid—she considered those notices little more than useful reminders. Today she had made the time. In the past if she'd suspected they might not have the money to cover, she would have put the knowledge off, delaying the decision to withdraw from savings or pay a credit card balance in installments, but now their savings were gone, and while she was pretty sure she could cover the bills today, something was going to bounce this month. What was just a matter of who was last in line.

The three words on the page she held in her hand had been written in the same large, rounded script as the envelope. Immediately upon reading them, she had rescued that from the grocery sack full of detritus she had stationed beside her—the looted window envelopes, outdated sweepstakes tickets, ad enclosures, and tear-off flaps she added to the city landfill each time she paid the bills—but there was no return address, nothing to identify the sender save the stamp (generic flag), postmark (local, over a week back), and Guy's name and address in blue ballpoint pen. The rounded handwriting struck her as feminine only because it lacked identifying characteristics. The envelope was the kind you could buy in a box of a hundred for ninety-nine cents. No doubt she'd thrown it in the basket with the bills when Guy left it lying on the dining room table. She had opened it merely to make sure that it should be discarded.

"Go home Motherfuckers" the neatly folded paper read, and only after she read it several times did the letters in Motherfuckers shift and melt into Montagnards.

Guy wanted to drive to the airport. Yesterday Molly had called to accept his invitation, and he was anxious to buy the kids' tickets. Eva would have handled the transaction by calling the airline's toll-free number, but he was sick of phone menus. He hadn't heard from Gordon Weems, but on Monday he intended to remind the lawyer he wanted his car. They would need it for the holiday, and Weems might as well start to earn his twenty thousand.

In the meantime he wished Eva would hurry up and finish with the bills so he could make sure she didn't need her car. Earlier, as he passed through the living room, he'd made the mistake of speaking to her. He had been thinking about an old classmate who had been killed in a freak accident when they were sophomores in high school, and before he thought to stop himself he'd mused out loud, "Don't you think it would be deeply weird to be dead?" She had turned in her chair, face flattening with displeasure as she flicked her hand toward the bills she'd strewn across the desk and responded, "I think you must lead a much deeper inner life than I do." *Here,* the aggravated hand said, *here is my inner life.* Long ago he had learned that it was in his best interest not to call attention to himself while she was cooking dinner, cleaning house, or paying bills, any one of those tasks that might confirm her life was endless drudgery and his least thought the kind of paltry crime that came of excess leisure.

Well, it was a stupid thing to say, and hardly qualified as deep, but she didn't have to be so hateful. He had been thinking about Larry Spreight a lot the last few days. The boy had been in Guy's civics class, and Guy could still see the slash of sunlight across Larry's empty desk the Monday after he died, though he couldn't recall whether they had ever spoken. Larry hadn't been a part of his crowd; until last week Guy hadn't thought about him for years. He had been electrocuted on one of those mild winter days when the ground is sodden with the hint of spring and a low dome of slate-colored clouds intensifies its colors, a day that might not seem so splendid if it occurred in any other season. It was a Friday, but a bomb scare had let school out early for the weekend, no doubt a childish prank owing to the fertile weather. They had spent the hour after lunch lined up on the football field passing rumors before the principal dismissed them. (Did any joy, he wondered, ever equal that again, that delirious, whooping jubilation with which a fifteen-year-old greets a single hour of unexpected freedom?) Larry was on his way home when he stepped in a puddle and grabbed the door handle of a refrigerated truck idling in the alley; his companion tried to pull him loose but couldn't break the current. Guy, who had gone to the park to play basketball with his friends, was on his own way home when the radio aired the news. He wasn't sure whether it was the grotesqueness of the death or the novelty of listening to his new transistor when he should have been in study hall that caused him to take note, for the victim could have been anyone, an unidentified man whose name and age had been withheld pending notification of the family. Walking home with his radio to his ear, he had thought about how intensely lonely the man must have felt as the first surge of electricity passed through him. As Larry's companion told it around school that Monday, told it over and over, Larry had grabbed the handle, then looked at him and said calmly, "Get me off." Guy remembered the line because he and his friends had seized upon it, uneasily, voraciously, in the way the living do in the face of death, needing to but never feeling quite right in making fun. "Get me off," he and his pals mimicked to each other in exaggerated falsetto, holding their crotches and writhing with imaginary voltage, but by the next day the joke had thinned and their laughter grown patchy. Now Guy found himself thinking about Larry Spreight again, though it wasn't just the fact that Larry had been the first boy he knew who'd died that enabled him to recollect so keenly the taste of that springlike day, its muted green light or fresh, damp fragrance.

Without knowing it he had memorized the day even before the victim had a name, for in a life that must have seemed endless until then it was the first time he had thought about dying.

Over thirty years ago that had been, and Larry Spreight's face had come to him with a start just last week—the moon face with its pale blond crewcut and dark eyes, cheeks so ruddy they looked abraded. It was sentimental, it was stupid, but seeing that face again his first response was guilt, because all those years had passed, and Guy hadn't even missed him.

He was in the kitchen, heating a can of soup for lunch, when Eva came in with her bag of trash, finished with the bills at last, though he could tell by the slope of her shoulders that it wasn't a good time to tell her about Molly.

"We're broke," she said without inflection. She set the bag beside the garbage.

"I'm going to work as soon as I get the Camry," he promised. "I can temp until the trial."

"We have to sell the house."

"With unemployment and Day Labor...."

"Unemployment runs out. We have to scale back our standard of living."

He couldn't argue that. He took the pot off the burner and stepped away from the stove. "I'm sorry."

"If we put it on the market now, maybe it'll sell in time to pay your lawyer."

"Why can't we get one of those loans, what do you call them?"

"Home equity." She shook her head. "I mean I suppose we could, but I don't know how we'd make the payments."

"Surely there's some other way."

She toed the rug. "Not that I can see. We can cash Nick's bonds."

"We can't do that."

She raised her eyes. "We have to do that. The problem is they're not worth more than a couple thousand."

"Maybe so, but they're his." Good thing he had a credit card. He had intended to write a check to the airlines. "I'll sell my mutual funds. You don't want to sell the house."

"I'd rather do that than have to worry every month about how to pay the mortgage."

He pushed the hot soup pot away from the edge of the counter. "Let me sell the mutual funds. They're worth around seven thousand."

"Good. That's a down payment for your lawyer. We're selling the house so we can eat."

"Something will work out." Saying it, he almost believed it. "You can't sell your house."

"Our house," she corrected.

She hadn't met his eyes, and in his effort not to look at hers, he swept the room. Past her, out the window, the dark stain where the gutter leaked caught his attention."By the way, the gutter man hasn't come this year."

"What gutter man?"

"The guy who cleans the gutters. He hasn't come."

An invisible string tugged at the corners of her mouth, creating little ripples of amusement. "He hasn't come because he hasn't been called."

"He never had to be called before."

She narrowed her eyes in on him, though her earlier pique seemed to have passed. Her laugh was almost merry.

"What?" Whatever, he had walked right into it.

She pressed her lips together. "He has to be called," she said at last.

"Oh," he answered, wondering if he was supposed to feel foolish, because if she always called and hadn't, it was her lapse, not his. "You love this house," he pointed out. She shrugged. "Yes, you do. You're proud of it. You found it. You bought it with your money."

"Some find." She leaned her weight against the counter. "It's like a stone around our necks."

"It's a great house," he argued, though usually she was the one to sing its praises while he complained about the disruptions that owning an old house entailed—the recalcitrant gas boiler, the windows that wouldn't open and doors that wouldn't shut, workmen forever trooping in and out. He felt as if they were rehearsing a play, but she'd forgotten her lines, and it threw him off kilter. "Surely we don't have to make the decision right away." A skin had formed across his soup. He stirred the pot and opened the cupboard for a bowl.

"Might as well be now as later. Anyway, it doesn't bother me as much as I thought it would."

It didn't seem to bother her at all. That was what confused him. "Want some soup?" She shook her head. He left the empty bowl sitting on the counter as he came to stand before her. "I'm really sorry about all the trouble this has caused."

"Not your fault," she said shortly. Her voice had a singsong lilt that said we've been through this.

A mourning dove chasing the finches from the feeder outside the window caught his eye. His mother had liked birds. They'd had a birdbath in their backyard in Ardsley Park. He thought of the blackbirds twittering in the canopy of live oaks hung with rags of Spanish moss as he walked up Bull Street on his way to school. It was one of the most vivid memories of his childhood. "I've been thinking about a boy I knew who died in high school," he confided. "I guess it's like a delayed reaction."

"That's some delay."

"No, I mean, you know...." He couldn't say it.

"I know what you mean." She looked up under her eyes at him. It was a look he hadn't seen in a long time. Understanding. Recognition. It held what he needed.

Nick was up the street at Britton's. She had made the excuse of needing some exercise and tried to walk him, but given up without a fight when Guy came to his rescue, pointing out, "He's eight years old, Eva," and gone in the other room to pay the bills.

He lifted her hand, weighing it to see if she resisted. When she didn't, when she looked at him again, more directly now, he led her upstairs, where they made love for the first time in six weeks.

She left the bed while he was still suspended in the pleasant drift of his contentment; vaguely he heard water running in the bathroom, the flush of the toilet, a swish of clothes. When he woke, a few minutes or half an hour later, the smell of bouillon seemed to have seeped inside his skin, and he remembered the cold Campbell's soup still sitting in the kitchen. She was standing at the counter, eating an apple, and when he came into the room, she set it on a paper towel and wiped her chin.

"I'm glad you're up. I need to show you something. It was in with the bills. I meant to show it to you earlier." She disappeared into the living room and came back with the anonymous letter.

He frowned as he read it, twice, three times, and still he

couldn't quite make sense of the message. She was watching him when he looked up, more baffled than shocked. "No return address." She held up the envelope for his inspection.

"Let me see that." He set the letter on the counter, taking the envelope from her hand and turning it over to study the postmark. "Who's it from?"

"You must have left it on the dining room table. I thought maybe it was some kind of announcement—you know, a grand opening or political flier—sometimes they come in handwritten envelopes."

"But what does it mean?" He understood the words, but couldn't seem to fit them to a purpose.

"I think," she said slowly, running a finger through her hair, "it's an expression of support."

He read the words again twice, then folded the letter back into the envelope, which he held with fingers that felt stiff with revulsion. "But who sent it?"

She pursed her lips and puffed her cheeks to exhale through her mouth, a habit that betrayed when she was feeling stressed. "I would say you're not supposed to know."

"But why would somebody be sending me an anonymous letter?"

She blew out another breath. "Your name and address were in the paper."

He recalled the anonymous letter their next-door neighbor, May Pleasants, had shown him not long after she was widowed. Signed a "conserned friend," in the guise of friendly advice it had covered two full pages with venom, poorly written, poorly spelled, filled with near obscenity that was somehow more offensive for missing the mark, for its incompetence at crudeness. "But who sent it?" May had demanded when he told her it was nothing but a vicious piece of hate mail; she was afraid the author was watching her house.

"You don't have to worry about that," he'd assured her. "The person who sent this is a coward—if he wasn't a coward he would have signed his name."

"A man?" she'd asked anxiously. "It says a woman."

But he hadn't thought it was a man; he hadn't thought it was a woman. Because the power of the anonymous letter was that it had no face, and so it took all faces; because someone had sent it though no one had, everyone was tainted.

"Don't," Eva said. He had balled the document up for the trash. She took it from his hand and tried to smooth it on the table.

"Why?"

"Because." She was chewing at her lip. "I mean—shouldn't you save it?"

He frowned. "You mean for evidence?"

Her look was both affirmative and sheepish.

"You think I'm going to take it to the police?"

"Maybe your lawyer, I don't know." She looked down. "I just think you shouldn't throw it out. There might be others."

"It's a kind of support I can do without." She folded the letter back inside its envelope. "It's just one person," he said, his voice louder.

"That's right."

He sat at the table. After a while he said, "You're a teacher." What he meant was that she knew as well as he one person could make a crowd, one student filing a complaint could do anyone more damage than a hundred happy pupils did good.

“I shouldn’t have showed you.” She crossed the room to put his soup back on the stove. He thought about it.

“You probably shouldn’t,” he agreed.

That night he insisted on renting a movie.

“We’re broke,” she protested when he mentioned the idea at dinner.

“That’s why we’re renting one,” he said, not that they often went out to the movies. Before they had Nick, they had gone all the time; now it was a fifty dollar occasion what with dinner and a sitter.

“Can I get one?” Nick asked.

“There are movies on TV,” she said before her spine relaxed and she said, “Sure.”

As Guy always did, he brought home two in case they didn’t like the first, along with a six pack of beer and a bag of microwave popcorn.

“The last of the big spenders,” she scoffed when he unpacked his treats, but she seemed to be in a good mood, and they laughed out loud at the old comedy he’d selected—it was Saturday night, the pickings were slim, and she wasn’t in the mood for the Japanese war drama. The popcorn was good; she drank a beer, and he had two. When the credits rolled, instead of leaping to rewind he remained in his chair, gazing around the subtle cream-and-beige striped den, once their screened porch. He remembered how absorbed Eva had been in picking the wallpaper, the carpet, the blinds, fabric for the sofa. It was the first time in her life she’d designed everything from scratch instead of trying to match what she already had, and he could tell by the sparkle in her eyes how much she enjoyed it. It was a handsome room, though the carpet was already showing wear.

"This is a nice house."

She untucked her feet from beneath her on the sofa. "Let's hope it's worth something."

He watched the names of the gaffers and grips roll by in print too small to read. "Do you want to buy a smaller house, is that it?"

She slipped her shoes on. "I don't think we'll be buying a house." Then where would they live? "In an apartment, I imagine." She sounded tired.

It would be a grievous sacrifice for her. Even for him—the loss of space, loss of privacy. They'd had a nice apartment when they'd first arrived in Random, in a complex near Gardell with a small creek wandering through the grounds. Eva had picked it out—in a city like Random, there just weren't any of the great old apartments like the one they'd had in Pittsburgh. But the complex had offered amenities that the apartment in Pittsburgh couldn't match—tennis courts, a pool, a dishwasher, walk-in closet. Still, below them and on either side were neighbors, and after the airy, high-ceilinged space in Pittsburgh, the rooms seemed cramped, although in those days, before Nick, they hadn't owned nearly as much stuff. Somehow their holdings seemed to triple the day they brought him home, crib, stroller, changing table, high chair, swing, car seat—he couldn't begin to remember all the equipment a contemporary middle-class infant required. On the night Molly had come home, she'd slept in a dresser drawer.

"We should talk about Christmas," he said.

"What about it?" She stopped on her way out of the room, glass and popcorn bowl in hand.

"We told Curt we were coming to Florida. We need to

firm up dates." He took a deep breath. "I've invited Molly and Brian."

"You mean here?" She set the bowl down.

"The whole family's going to be there. It's been years since Curt saw Molly."

She sat, a look of dismay jelling on her face.

"I know you probably think we shouldn't go," he admitted.

"We can't afford to go."

Excluding the kids' airfare, excluding Orlando, the trip wouldn't cost that much, but he'd enticed Molly with the promise of Disney World. Well, motels, of course—Curt didn't have room to sleep everyone, and they couldn't all five of them occupy one room at the Ramada. "We can put it on my credit card."

"Guy," she said.

"We *need* to go."

"We need a lot of things. That doesn't mean we'll get them."

He stared at his socks.

"Have you told your father about the accident?"

"I haven't talked to him."

"Molly?"

"No." He hadn't wanted to worry his daughter, but the way Eva was looking at him doubted; her expression argued against altruism and zeroed in on pride. Without even speaking she had won. He hadn't told because he didn't want his daughter to know that he was vulnerable. He had yet to tell Molly or his father that he'd lost his job, knowing that on the underbreath of his father's concern he would smell the scorched wind of disapproval.

Eva's voice softened. "I'm not trying to tell you you can't see your daughter."

"I know that." He did.

"She's family," she assured him. She stared at the snowy screen until he got up to rewind the movie. "Are they driving?" she asked finally.

"Flying." She would know he had offered to buy the tickets. "It's a Christmas present." His tone was defensive.

"You're a generous man." She blew an extended stream of air out through her lips. "I don't know what to say. She's your daughter—you want to see her. It's late. I don't think we should talk about it now."

"I know I should have talked to you before I called her. I just didn't."

She nodded. Her face was wan; when she closed her eyes for a minute she looked old. There was creping in her neck and around her eyes a fan of lines. It scared him.

On Sunday morning Eva and Nick were at the table with the paper when Guy came in from his run. Nick always read the comics and an outdoor column on the sports page. When she finished the news, ideas, and entertainment sections, she had a habit of skimming the open house directory and making a mental calculation of what their house might be worth, though now that she had reason, she discovered that she had no interest in the real estate listings. What did it matter what the owners were asking for some other four-bedroom house? She was done with speculation; she needed an appraisal. Already she felt the house shrivel under the realtor's cold and practiced eye. But first she had to get it cleaned up: Nick would just have to put his room in order, and Guy would have to agree not to jump on her if she nagged. Out front was a dead ligustrum he'd promised to dig out months ago. Someone would have to tackle the basement, the attic, the garage. Even the thought was exhausting, though surely not all of it had to be done before the realtor arrived.

When she looked up, Nick was sitting with his head grotesquely tipped, his eyes glazed, one hand rammed so deep inside the grimace of his mouth that she leapt to her feet. "Honey, what is it? Does your tooth hurt? Do you have an earache?"

His fist garbled the answer.

"Guy!" she called. She could hear the shower running upstairs as she yanked his hand free. His eyes popped, and he sat there blinking, hand glistening with saliva.

"Are you okay? Nick, what's the matter?" Her limbs were limp with relief, though when Guy reached them her heart was still pounding.

"Son." Water trickled from his hair, and a thick white towel hung from his waist. "What happened? What were you doing?"

"Trying to touch my brain."

Guy and Eva looked at each other. The clock above the sink ticked loudly. "Does your head hurt?" Eva asked.

Guy wiped his wet face. "Why did you want to touch your brain?"

Nick didn't answer. Out of the corner of his eye he was studying the bicycles on the back of the Kmart flier. "I was just wondering why I live inside my head. Everything piles up in there. It makes my brain feel heavy."

Eva's impulse was to smile, but when Guy asked, "What's piled up?" and Nick scowled, she sobered.

"Are you worried about something, sweetie?" Eva began straightening the papers strewn across the table. Of course he was. They could try to protect him, but he had to sense that they were troubled. They hadn't mentioned selling the house to him, but even so he could be wondering where he was going to live or where he'd go to school or if he would ever see his friends again. Maybe if they acknowledged their fears, he could cope with his own.

"I just think it's weird that I see out of my head but can't see out my feet." He turned his attention from them to the flier, clearly done with the subject. "These cheap bikes suck." It was a message. The bike he had was too small; the gears skipped; the chain kept falling off. *He said.* Lately he'd been limping to dramatize its defects.

"There's nothing wrong with the bike you have," Eva said. A year and a half ago, when he got it for his birthday, he'd been thrilled; now it wasn't good enough; he wanted a three-hundred-dollar mountain bike like Britton's. He *would* need a bigger bike sometime soon—which was why she couldn't see paying cycle shop prices. Three hundred dollars for a fancy, brand-name bike that he would just outgrow again. She'd ridden the same used bicycle throughout her childhood, third-hand at least, with a hole in the panel where the horn had been, a twenty-eight inch woman's model that she learned to ride standing up because when she sat on the seat her feet wouldn't reach the pedals. Her father had taught her, running along behind her; he'd sanded the rust off the fenders and frame and enameled it bright blue. She'd had nowhere to store it but the cellar, and every time she rode it she had to bump it up and down the narrow, dank stairs, but if she told Nick, he would think it was just another of those hard-luck stories all parents in the world conspire to use against their children, five miles to school, uphill both ways, and cold potatoes for supper.

"It's a crummy bike. It's so cheap my feet fall off the pedals."

"Well, you're not getting another one, so forget it." Eva took her mug to the sink and for emphasis slammed the door to the cabinet he'd left open.

Guy hated it when she stooped to Nick's level, but Guy had gone upstairs to dress, she noted. "Maybe I'll give it to someone who'll appreciate it." An image of Nuh hunched over the high handlebars with a proud and determined look on his face popped into her head.

"Go ahead!" Nick stomped to the den.

She was thinking about H'nghai when Guy came back down and nipped her on the back of the neck with a kiss. She hadn't gone by the Montagnard apartment complex yet, telling herself she wanted to give H'nghai time to think, but she would have to go tomorrow. She couldn't abandon the girl; she wouldn't.

"Where's Knick-Knock?"

She let out a pent and angry breath.

"What's the matter?"

"Nothing." She opened the dishwasher and began putting dishes away.

"I'll do that."

She stepped aside. "Nick wants a new bike for Christmas."

"What's wrong with that?"

"Nothing, except we can't afford it." She moved so he could reach the cabinet where they kept the glasses. "It's just the way he has of asking—the way he has to belittle the one he's got and try to make us feel guilty."

"Maybe he's afraid he won't get one otherwise."

"He's not going to get one anywise." She perched on the kitchen stool. They were back to money again, but it was as good a time as any to continue the conversation they'd interrupted. Finals began this week. They needed to come to some agreement about Christmas.

"What was he doing when you called upstairs? You gave me quite a scare."

"Oh...." Her hand wobbled in the air. "What he said—trying to touch his brain, I guess. I thought he was choking or having a seizure."

Guy opened the silverware drawer. "He did choke once, remember? You saved his life."

She had. On their way home from Savannah years ago Guy had been walking the dog at a rest stop when she heard a little sound like a click inside Nick's throat and turned toward the back seat to see him, strapped in his baby seat, eyes bulging from their sockets, skin so tight his face looked like a balloon, so disfigured by terror that she screamed, screamed and screamed, all through the eternity it took to unbuckle her seatbelt, unlock and open both their doors, maps and soda cans flying, to lift the bar of his seat and undo the network of straps. By the time Guy reached her Nick was howling in her arms and she was sobbing, the little bit of orange pith that had shot from his throat when she yanked her fist up beneath his ribs lying on the pavement in a glister of spit.

He was her baby. Why was she mad at him all the time?

"I'd give him the bike if we could." She paused. "Why can't

Molly and Brian drive?"

He closed the silverware drawer. "Because."

She knew why: the weather, the roads, their car was old, they didn't have much vacation time, all, she had to admit, perfectly sound reasons, though none of them was the real reason, because the real reason was his infuriating stubbornness and pride. Or maybe that was unfair, because it wasn't only pride, but the intemperate way pride mixed with love. He wanted to do as much for Molly as his father had for him. It was not that Eva begrudged her. Even when Molly was young and he had sometimes used her against Eva (his priorities were unassailable, he'd implied, his selfless concern for a daughter versus her petty obligations to a job), she had understood that resentment would be suicidal. Molly came with him; if she made him choose his daughter would win. She couldn't fault him. But somehow, in respecting their relationship, she had failed to construct her own. Maybe it was because they lived so far away, because Molly had spent only a short time with them each summer, or perhaps because they hadn't actually married until his daughter was sixteen, she never felt quite honest in referring to Molly as her stepdaughter; when she used the word it was always with a tentative inflection, as if she were afraid Guy might correct her. She liked Molly and knew that Molly liked her, but somehow a deeper bond had never formed, and in the last few years when she sometimes found herself chafing over the extravagant gifts Guy wrote on their joint account, she never mentioned her displeasure, perhaps because she sensed her feelings were wrong; after all, they spent infinitely more on Nick than he ever had on Molly.

"It's just...."

"I know," he said. "We don't have the money."

"We *don't* have the money."

He seemed to like the answer less from her mouth. "You always knock yourself out for these family visits." She could tell by the way he wouldn't look at her that he knew he was hedging. "It would be a lot less work for you if we all went to Florida."

Not, she noted, that he offered to pitch in. "The work needs to be done. We're going to have to clean up this whole place to put it on the market."

He glanced at her, visibly annoyed. He would think she was changing the subject, using his daughter's visit to ply her own agenda. "Could we not talk about selling the house? I thought we were talking about Christmas."

"I am talking about Christmas. We used up our savings on your bail. Christmas is going to have to be a very modest affair."

He walked to the window. "We told Curt we'd come. We promised Nick we'd go to Disney World."

"We told Nick we'd think about Disney."

"Same thing," he said.

"It is not the same thing." She softened her tone, trying for the limber voice of reason. "He's going to have to adjust. He's had a privileged life, but our circumstances have changed. He's not going to live in the big house or take the big trips or get the big presents."

Guy brought the flat of his hand to rest on the counter. "Will you knock it off about the house? I'm selling my mutual funds; I said I'd temp until I find something better. But that's not good enough—you want to sell the house to make a point, you want—" his voice began to climb—"to make sure I feel the full effect of having brought ruin on my family. Well, guess what! I feel the full effect!" She clapped her hands over her ears. "But you know what? I've got news for you: it wasn't my fault."

She dropped her hands. "Why can't you just tell Molly what happened? She's bound to find out sooner or later."

He looked away. "I'm not going to jail."

"Of course you aren't."

"Weems guaranteed it."

"I should hope so. You ought to get something for twenty thousand." She was sorry as soon as she said it.

"What's the point of telling her about something she can't do anything about?"

"The point is Molly loves you. You just don't want to admit to her that you don't have life knocked, you don't want anyone to know except me." She turned away. "I don't know why, but it doesn't make me feel closer."

"Okay," he said at last. "I'll call her back and say we aren't going."

"But not why."

"What do you want from me?"

Slowly she exhaled. "I don't know," she admitted.

"You win. I'll tell her whatever you want."

She looked up. His face looked dead, though she only told him what was true. "You don't have to call her." She took the Cuisinart blade he had set on the counter and fit it in the rack. "We'll go."

"No," he said. "You're right. It was a stupid idea. I knew it was stupid. That's why I didn't tell you."

"It's not stupid. She's your daughter. You're in trouble; of course you want to see her."

"They can come here. I'll help you clean the house. We'll

still have to pay plane fare, but it'll save some money."

He couldn't make Molly come to North Carolina after inviting her to Florida. She was looking forward to a Florida vacation. Eva thought about the fall she and Guy met. Her father had died the year before, she and Brooks had only recently split up, and Ruby expected her in Baltimore for Thanksgiving. It seemed a measure of defeat somehow, to be going home alone after being married, and the thought of the two of them at the table with her father's empty chair left a hollow place inside her. She had said as much to Guy, though they had barely begun dating. "I've got a friend in D.C.," he'd said. "Maybe we could get together. You could show me the Smithsonian. Do you know any jazz clubs?" She'd spent Thanksgiving day at her mother's with a lilt of anticipation; the next day she had led him through the National Gallery, won by the way he considered, seriously, each painting she admired; for lunch they ate hot dogs on the street, laughing as the wind blew her hair into the mustard. In the afternoon they went to the Freer, and she couldn't remember ever having a better time. Only later did she learn he had slept at the Y. There wasn't any friend. He could have courted her in Pittsburgh if that was all he wanted. He had gone all that way just to keep her from having a bad time.

"What's the difference?" she said. "We're broke. What does it matter how much we owe? Besides, you're right. We need the vacation."

"I could ask my dad. He'd probably pay the plane fare."

Eva shook her head. "I may be mean, but I'm not so mean I'd make you ask your father for money."

"You're not mean."

The corners of her mouth twitched. "Can I quote you on

that?"

"Well, sometimes you're mean," he amended.

She was not.

Chapter 13

"One and a half baths." The real estate agent, whose name was Ravenna Mink, wrinkled her moist red lips and made a note on her clipboard.

"Well, I know the bathrooms are a problem, but the house does have a lot of nice features." Eva swallowed the last syllables, hating the importunate sound of her voice. She stood just behind Ravenna Mink, in the doorway of the upstairs bath, which she'd been foolish enough to appraise in terms of its ribbon tile and porcelain-handled faucets when another realtor first led her through. That realtor hadn't said anything about outdated plumbing or inadequate storage; she'd used words like "quaint" and "charming"; she'd seen possibilities, not problems. Eva had cleaned the room just that morning, but the tub looked gray; she was acutely aware of the mold speckled along the bottom of the shower curtain, the flaking mirror, the patch of bubbled plaster, the basin's twin teardrops of rust. The leaky faucet had never sounded so loud. It was so old even the plumber had given up.

Ravenna Mink opened the door to the linen cupboard, and the crevice between her eyebrows deepened. "You'll want to clean out these closets." She was a large, middle-aged woman with brass-bright hair and too many rings on her fingers. The polyester pantsuit stretched across her thighs was the color of a caution light. "The house has curb appeal, but I can't stress enough the importance of some basic housekeeping." As Eva stepped aside to let her pass, she flicked the vinyl curtain. "You might replace this." Eva flushed. She knew the house's defects: she lived with them. The bathroom didn't have a fan; it had never seemed that much a hardship. She supposed she should be annoyed with herself for allowing the realtor to make her feel defensive, but she was more annoyed with the realtor. How could people live like this? the brusque swish of Ravenna Mink's wide, caution-colored hips implied. The woman made Eva feel slovenly, as if she had to apologize for a kitchen full of roaches, an STD.

On to the master bedroom, distinguished from the others by its two small closets. Neither door latched, and when Ravenna Mink tested Guy's a pair of running shorts slipped off the knob. Eva cringed at the volcano of shoes and clothing on his closet floor. They had made a deal: she would go to Florida; he would clean the basement. He had used most of Monday to haul the stacks of old insulation, dead geraniums, dried up paint cans, and what-have-you to the curb. Though she still had to empty the attic and garage, she'd cleaned the rest of the house when she got home from work, and at least after a fashion Nick had tidied his room. She hadn't wanted to risk a fight by telling Guy that his closet didn't pass muster, though the sight seemed to leave Ravenna Mink speechless. When at last she turned away, she repeated without looking at Eva, "Basic order."

They crossed the hall to the room where she and Guy kept their computer. Ravenna surveyed the chipped baseboards and shook her head. "You need to get rid of those extension cords, dear. They just focus the buyer's attention on the wiring. These old houses weren't built for today's appliances." She turned. "It's the same problem with the storage. The master suite is so important. Even without the bathroom, if you had a walk-in closet it would help. I'll tell you the same thing I tell all my clients: Lease a storage space. It may not increase the value, but it will help you sell."

They would have to sell, though for now they were supposedly just getting an appraisal. Ravenna Mink seemed to think the place already up for grabs. She hadn't asked why they were putting the house on the market. Perhaps she presumed they were fed up. Would her tone be quite so withering if she realized they couldn't afford it, that for them its possibilities had always been out of reach? Did she understand how excruciating it was for Eva to know that whoever bought it would come armed with architects and contractors, that once their remodeling ordeal was over, they would walk their guests through to show off their garden tubs and custom cabinets, exclaiming, "You wouldn't believe what this place looked like when we bought it"?

"Actually," Eva mumbled, "I was thinking of having a yard sale."

"Good idea. Why don't you do that before we list?"

They had reached Nick's room. After straightening it last night he'd gone off to school this morning leaving his socks and dirty underwear on the floor. Creeping from beneath the bed and the room's perimeter, which seemed to close in on the clean puddle of carpet in the center, lay a fringe of lint and bottle caps and Legos where she didn't dare run the vacuum. "Kids," she felt like joking, but her face was hot.

"My son's room," she said instead, stooping for the underpants. "He's eight. Of course, I'll help him clean it before we put it on the market." She'd repainted the room only last year, but already his light switch was sunk in a cluster of grubby fingerprints, and the flapping poster above his bed exposed a jagged nail hole. "I can spackle that," she added.

"Yes, well, this does need attention," the realtor said, hurrying to the stairs. Downstairs, Eva sat in the wing chair beside the fireplace while Ravenna Mink wrote on her clipboard. When the realtor looked up, Eva was glad to see she had lipstick on her teeth. "Now you'll be cleaning out the garage and attic, and you were going to put some things in storage. We've agreed you'll take care of the interior cosmetic work." They had? "What about the exterior? I noticed the trim could use painting. Were you planning to have that done?"

"Not really," Eva said. "Couldn't we sell as is?"

"We're not just talking about price, you know," the realtor said. "Four bedrooms, one and a half baths—I really wish you had one more—approximately twenty-seven hundred square feet, gas, central air.... We could list at one fifty-nine nine, though if you're at all anxious to move it, I'd recommend dropping to one forty-nine nine. At one forty-nine nine, with the size of the house and the quality of the neighborhood people think they're getting a bargain."

One forty-nine nine then, less commission.

"What about financing? Owner financing can be a real incentive, even a two-year note with a balloon."

Eva hadn't the faintest idea what a balloon was. "We can't," she admitted. "We wouldn't consider selling except we need money."

"Oh." Ravenna smiled with practiced pleasantness, though underneath her face seemed steeped in discontent. "Were you thinking of buying a smaller house then? I've got several I could show you. There's a super little Williamsburg cottage over in Briarwood that just came on the market. The owners are going into a retirement home, they've taken excellent care of it."

Eva avoided the realtor's eyes as she shook her head. "About the trim. You say it won't add to the value?"

"But it might help you move the property. Especially in a sluggish market, and I have to tell you winter is traditionally a slow season."

"But this is a great house. I've done so much work on it," Eva cried. "It's a wonderful neighborhood. Don't a lot of people want old houses?"

"Frankly," Ravenna Mink said, "no."

"But the sidewalks, the trees—we have over fifty azaleas...."

"Mature landscaping," the realor cut her off. "But actually with the gardening craze, many of today's buyers would rather plant themselves; I'm afraid most of them are more interested in bathrooms and storage. Living rooms are getting smaller as bathrooms get bigger. In fact, your newer houses don't have living rooms, they have a great room with a media center built in, maybe a small dining room—I see you have some lovely silver—but people don't really entertain anymore. Exercise rooms are very popular, and people still like big kitchens, though as far as I can tell no one uses them for cooking. I know I certainly don't have time."

"What do you eat?" Eva asked.

"I beg your pardon?"

"People say that," Eva said. "Everybody says they used to cook, they don't cook. I can't figure out what they're eating." If she could figure it out, she'd serve it herself.

"Heavens." Ravenna Mink laughed. "No one eats. It's the healthy lifestyle to stay thin."

The realtor didn't look as if she'd missed many meals. Eva

tried to guess her age. Mid-fifties, maybe. Not that much older than Eva. Eva was too old to have to start over.

Ravenna waved her jeweled hand toward the fireplace. "Of course, these French doors are a plus." Her gaze lingered above the mantel, where Eva had hung their favorite nude. She had wondered when the realtor would get around to the art.

"Rather well endowed, isn't she?" Ravenna Mink gave the painting a twinkling last glance and picked up her clipboard. "Now let's see. We've agreed on one forty-nine nine. No owner financing—how about owner pays closing costs? That can be an incentive. You're going to take care of the cleaning chores—did you say you'd get that faucet fixed? I'd advise it."

Eva frowned. "Well, actually—I mean I'm not sure we're ready to list it yet."

Slowly, heavily, Ravenna Mink looked up. "I see," she said just as the phone rang.

"Excuse me." Eva was glad for the escape as she scurried to the kitchen. "Hello?"

A moment's silence, which seemed to coil just before the voice struck. "Murderer." The word reverberated inside the receiver as Eva sagged against the wall. The line went dead. Earlier there had been another call, just after Guy left for work. That voice had said "If you've had anything to drink before you drive, you've had too much." Immediately the phone rang again. Eva picked it up long enough to stop the ringing and hung up. Her legs were rubbery, she felt fuddled, but after a moment she drew a glass of water and made herself sip. Guy had left for work before he could read the paper. He hadn't seen the article at the bottom of the City-State front page. She had read it first with dread and then with disbelief.

Driver in Fatal Accident Was Drunk

The blood alcohol level of the driver charged in the accident that killed a nine-year-old Montagnard boy last month was twice the legal limit.

Guy L. Ferrin was charged with felony death by motor vehicle after his car struck and killed Y Bhan Buon To, who was walking on Lanyan Road. Ferrin's concentration of blood alcohol at the time of the accident measured 0.20, according to Carver County District Attorney Adam Atwater.

A bill to lower the current per se blood alcohol concentration from 0.10 to 0.08 has broad popular support and is expected to pass the General Assembly. The 1983 Safe Roads Act provides that any person charged with impaired driving or a related offense whose blood alcohol content is at or above per se automatically have his driving privileges revoked for ten days. A charge of felony death by motor vehicle normally requires additional revocation of one year.

Ferrin, who was released under $20,000 bond, was not ordered to surrender his license. Atwater said he did not understand why.

"Every year over 700 people in this state are killed by drunk drivers," Atwater said. "The public's sick of it. We need to see that these people do serious time behind bars. They should never be allowed on our highways again."

The victim, Y Bhan Buon To, was part of the second group of Vietnam's Montagnards to settle in Random and had been in the United States for less than a year.

Neither Ferrin nor his attorney could be reached for comment.

It was a mistake, clearly. Someone had transposed the numbers. Otherwise she would have hidden the article. But he would have to see it; he had to get the mistake corrected.

She'd tried to call the district attorney herself but hadn't gotten through. How could the reporter claim Guy couldn't be reached? They had a machine. He would have told her if anyone had left a message.

They would have to get their phone changed.

But they were selling the house.

It wasn't until she thought about the house that she remembered Ravenna Mink was waiting. She took another sip of water, wiped her mouth, and went back to the living room. The realtor acknowledged her return with a curt smile and a pointed glance at her watch. "When did you plan to make a decision then?"

"I'm sorry?" Eva's heart was still pounding.

"When were you planning to put the house on the market?"

"I don't know." Without intending to she made it sound like a question. "After Christmas I guess." Her mind was busy replaying the voice on the phone. Male, so anonymous she couldn't put an age to it, there was no accent, nothing to suggest race or region, but then the person had uttered just the one word. Was it the same voice as earlier? She couldn't remember the voice, only the shock of it. The accusation had an hallucinatory quality, subliminal, freakish; she would have doubted that she heard it if it hadn't been for the article, the first call, or the anonymous letter—but of course the letter had to be from someone else, someone who also thought them murderers and couldn't approve more.

"Well, Christmas week is slow, but on the other hand if you were thinking about decorating...." The realtor's eyes traveled to the built-in bookcases banked around the double windows at the end of the room. "That space was just made for a tree."

Eva's argument precisely every year when Guy objected to the mess.

"Actually we're going to be in Florida," she heard herself say. She wouldn't have the phone changed; they would just be gone. She would let the answering machine screen all their calls until they left, and when they left she would unplug it.

"Perfect," Ravenna Mink said. "I can show the house while you're out of town. So...." She returned her attention to the clipboard. "You'll complete the interior work, I can't remember whether we agreed on the exterior painting—you don't have to pay top dollar, you know, just a little scraping and a cosmetic coat or two. Your husband might be able to do it himself."

Guy had said she shouldn't have shown him the letter. She wouldn't tell him about the calls, but he would have to see the paper. He no longer read the opinion page, not since the editorial calling for the lowered blood alcohol limit. The letters about the Montagnards had been followed by another just as vicious. *It's time for hard-working American taxpayers to wake up.*

"...even a wreath on the door," Ravenna Mink was saying. "Just a few simple decorations."

The neighbors had their decorations up already, though when Eva was a child no one trimmed the tree until the week before Christmas, or left it up past New Year's Day. Eva wondered if it would make Claudia sad not to be with the kids as a family this year. It made her sad, thinking about the kids. It couldn't be a very happy holiday for them. Or for the Buon Tos. She had gone by the apartments on Monday, feeling conspicuous as she circled twice. The children outside playing had stared as she got out of the car and walked around to knock on the Buon Tos' front door, the front seeming more appropriate, and then, when she had knocked a third time and waited and still there was no answer, returned to try the back. She had been as relieved as she was disappointed when that knock too went unanswered, too daunted to try again that day, and the next she'd had so many complications with insurance for an upcoming show she'd barely had time to get to the Y and pick up Nick before it closed. She needed to get to her office as soon as the realtor left, and she didn't dare go by after school for fear Nuh might be there, but she absolutely had to try again tomorrow morning. She wanted to see H'nghai, even though the thought of knocking at the apartment door again sent cold needles down her skin.

Ravenna Mink was still talking. "You're not just selling a house, it's a home, and if the buyer comes in and you've got a tree and there's a fire in the hearth—I see you don't have gas logs—and the house smells of mulled cider—now that's something you can do any season, just get some potpourri."

"Potpourri," Eva repeated senselessly. "Actually...."

"Even a few drops of vanilla on a cotton ball." Ravenna picked up the clipboard. "You have some vanilla, don't you, dear? Now, what about closing costs?"

"Well, I really need to talk it over with my husband."

"Of course." Ravenna jotted a note. "Owner will consider paying closing costs."

"I mean about selling," Eva said. "We just wanted an appraisal."

The realtor's body went rigid. "I see."

Her ad had said free appraisals! "I mean we're definitely thinking about it," Eva amended. "It's probably more like a question of when."

"Well, you don't want to wait too long," Ravenna said

coolly. "After Christmas the market slows down until spring."

When did the woman think Eva was going to get all the cleaning and painting and storing, not to mention decorating, done? She still had finals, and she had to get everything set for the upcoming show of Polish graphics before they could leave for Florida.

"Soon," Eva mumbled. She sat forward. "So if we did want to list it would be at one forty-nine nine—you wouldn't go for the one sixty?"

Ravenna Mink tugged the polyester fabric strained across her thighs. "Well, that would be up to you, of course, but given the market and those bathrooms...." A little scowl pulled at her face. "For the square footage the house really needs two and a half. But like I say it's up to you. You can list too high and let the house sit there and six months or a year later come down to where you should have been in the first place—and I have to tell you when a house is reduced the buyer has a tendency to wonder what's wrong with it, they think of it as damaged goods. The one thing that never occurs to them is that the owner didn't listen to a professional, experienced realtor."

"Right." Eva wanted the woman out of her house—her house for now, or maybe she shouldn't listen, maybe she should list it at one sixty or even one seventy-five, why not two hundred? Then it could be hers forever, until the bank foreclosed. "I'll let you know."

"You have my card?" The realtor heaved herself to her feet. "I'll call if I don't hear from you—shall we say tomorrow? It's a lovely house, really. I get a lot of calls for this neighborhood."

Eva had just closed the door behind her when the phone rang again, sending a quease through her intestines. She let the machine pick it up, but whoever it was hung up when he heard the message, so she didn't know whether it was another anonymous caller and wished she had answered. When it rang again she snatched it.

"Is Eva Summer there?" A woman's voice with a sharp, country twang.

"Speaking."

"She give us your number."

"Who gave you my number?" Impatiently Eva toed a loose string on the rag rug. "Who is this?"

"Tammi Goins." A note of irritation gnarred inside the woman's voice. "I can't hardly understand what she says, but she wrote down your number."

Eva's shoe stalled on the rug. *Can't understand what she says.* "Is she Asian? Is her name H'nghai?"

"She's one of them Indians from Vietnam, you know, the ones they got living in those apartments down the street. She don't want an ambulance. We need you to come get her."

"What happened?" Eva's mind sped. A miscarriage. Complications from an abortion. Would H'nghai have tried to perform one on herself? She should have gone back on Monday. A thick blade of guilt cleaved her chest.

"He drug her," Tammi said. "Maybe you can get her to report it. I don't think she understands what I say."

"I'll be right there," Eva said and took directions.

On the way the lights all seemed against her; traffic was maddeningly slow. Eva ran through possibilities. Miscarriage, abortion. H'nghai hadn't called, but she had kept Eva's number.

Grimly Eva turned the corner. Drugged her. As in something to induce labor? Tammi Courts hadn't said if

H'nghai was bleeding. Eva turned again on Purgason and began reading numbers.

Thirty-three fifteen was in the middle of a block of small, asbestos shingled houses worn to varying states of decay. The windows were sealed with drapes, though the cloth at the picture window in the house next door stirred as Eva hurried up the walk. The door was answered by a woman with thin brown hair pulled back tight against her skull.

"Tammi?"

"I'm Denise. Tammi's in the back." The woman was younger than she appeared, possibly no more than thirty, with grainy skin and a hard line to her mouth. The room darkened when she closed the door, a cartoon flickering on the TV set in the corner. There was a baby bottle lying on the floor, and the room smelled of dirty diapers.

A toilet flushed, and the woman Eva took to be Tammi entered the room twisting a strand from her fountain of bleached-blonde hair.

"Is H'nghai okay? What happened?"

Tammi gestured toward the street. "I come running when I heard her screaming. I thought it was one of the kids."

"We seen it through the window," Denise explained. "Sliding down the street on her belly, next to naked."

"You mean she was dragged?" Not drugged, dragged.

"Who?"

"Her husband I guess," Denise said. "He was laughing and hollering."

"He practically tore her wrists off." Tammi's face worked. "I never seen anything like it in my life."

"You mean he dragged her with a car?" Eva was incredulous.

"How is she?"

Denise sat in the recliner near the door. "We cut her loose when he stopped. He was hollering at her to get up and walk."

"Where is she?" Eva asked numbly.

"Right here." Tammi jerked her hand toward the sofa. In the dimness Eva had made out the two children on the floor in front of the TV, but she hadn't noticed H'nghai, huddled in the corner of the sofa with a blanket, her eyes fixed on the screen.

"Hello, H'nghai."

H'nghai acknowledged the greeting by raising her eyes, then quickly lowered them, determinedly watching the TV. Her face had been scraped raw, and even in the dim room the sight sent a shock of weakness down Eva's spine.

"Have her to show you her hip and her leg," Denise directed.

"She wouldn't let us call the police. I swear I'd of killed him if he hadn't drove off." Tammi turned to Eva. "We couldn't hardly understand her, so she wrote out your name and number. She's got a bad scrape on her hip and leg and a couple cuts, I cleaned 'em out with peroxide. There's rope burns on her wrists, but I don't think any bones is broken."

Over such a big area the antiseptic wouldn't just sting, it would howl. "You have to let me take you to the clinic," she said to H'nghai.

H'nghai didn't answer. At the least she would need a pelvic, but Eva was reluctant to mention the pregnancy in front of Tammi and Denise. What kept playing in her mind was the fact that H'nghai had memorized her name and number.

"He was making her run behind the car and she fell." On screen something blew up and the children laughed. Tammi bent to scoop up a baby crawling out from behind the sofa and held him to her nose. "Buster, your pants stink. Tiffie, go get me a diaper."

"Are you in pain?" Eva asked. "H'nghai, you need to see a doctor." She unbuttoned her jacket. The house was hot. Even if H'nghai was okay, she could lose the baby.

Or maybe, Eva thought suddenly, that was the idea, maybe her husband didn't want the baby any more than she did, and that was why she didn't want a doctor or the police; getting rid of it could have been the purpose. Her pulse quickened. Surely not. Would you laugh and holler while trying to abort your child? "H'nghai."

H'nghai burrowed deeper. "Fine. Sorry trouble," she whispered.

Eva sat on the other end of the sofa. "I'm concerned about you. You need a doctor." She couldn't look at the fiery flesh without feeling her own face burn.

"She might heal up okay. Buddy-boy messed his face up like that falling off his bike, and you can't even tell." Tammi reached out to lift her daughter by the shoulders and thwack her on the butt. "I said go get me a diaper."

"No doctor. Fine," H'nghai said again as Tammi knelt to strip the baby's pants off.

"Was it your husband?" Eva asked.

Determinedly H'nghai watched the cartoon.

"Tiffany!" Tammi yelled, and her daughter reappeared in the doorway with a diaper in one hand.

"Have her to show you her leg," Denise jiggled her foot. "If she don't keep 'em clean them scrapes is going to fester."

"We can go back to Healthcare." H'nghai's face had a

stubborn set. Her eyes seemed to bore holes in the screen. "I'll pay. You don't have to worry about the bill."

H'nghai had no reason to protect her husband—she wanted a divorce. Eva supposed she was afraid, apparently with good reason. Now Eva wondered if last week, when she'd lapsed into Rhadé talking about her husband, she'd been confiding he was violent. Surely her parents must know the man abused her, unless this was the first time. Nuh had said she needed to pay her father for the divorce. The husband must have paid a bride-price, and if she divorced him the father would have to refund his money. They might as well have sold the girl into slavery.

"H'nghai!" Her voice was unexpectedly sharp.

Unwillingly H'nghai turned her face toward Eva. Her eyes flinched, and she shrank from Eva's gaze at the same time her face seem to square off with stubbornness too. The bitter taste of fury pooled in Eva's throat; her knuckles ached; her heart was a spoon that fed her mouth on cold metal. She wanted to reach out and dig her fingers into H'nghai's bones and rattle the words loose. Horrified, she balled her hands in her pockets. The girl was a *victim.*

"I'll get her something to wear. She didn't have on nothing but her underwear and a tee shirt tore to pieces." Tammi disappeared into the bedroom.

"Better get her Tonya's church dress," Denise called. "Jeans is going to rub."

H'nghai hunched further into the sofa. "Fine," she insisted. "Sorry trouble."

Tammi returned with a flowered dress and a zip-front sweatshirt she held out to H'nghai.

"You can dress back there."

H'nghai stood, pulling the blanket even tighter as she snaked one hand out for the clothing. "Very kind," she said, avoiding Tammi's eyes, and Eva realized she was, more than anything, embarrassed. A wave of compassion as sharp as her anger engulfed her.

Tammi pulled a pair of socks from a laundry basket in the corner. "Buddy, go look in your closet for them shoes you outgrown." She eyed Eva as she explained, "He had the stomach ache this morning and stayed home from school," then shot Buddy a look, and he fled to the bedroom. Eva wondered if Tammi thought she was a truant officer. "Are you one of them social workers they got working with her people? They're good folks, I guess—my daddy's a vet, I know he thinks high of 'em—but it ain't right the way we keep bringing all these people over here. We got our own to take care of. Buddy," she called, "don't you be getting into Tonya's Barbies," then turned back to Eva, who flushed as Tammi met her eyes. "If they want to live in America, they got to learn how to act. This here this morning with her husband...." Tammi's mouth tensed as H'nghai opened the door. "That kind of thing gives them all a bad name."

Eva's face warmed. She turned toward H'nghai. She couldn't see the injured leg because the loose dress hung nearly to her ankles, but the angry purple rings at her wrists were plain enough as H'nghai offered a Barbie doll to Tammi, touching the cascade of shining platinum Dynel hair. "Pretty. Thank you," she added when the boy brought in a pair of torn high-top sneakers and Eva promised to return the clothes.

"Maybe you can get her to go to the police," Tammi said. "They ought to put that SOB in jail."

"How is your leg?" Eva asked when H'nghai was settled in

the car.

"Fine," H'nghai repeated. "Thank you to come. Very kind."

Eva started the car, glancing back at the draped living room window, then drove self- consciously up the street, wondering who else might have witnessed. It was a working class neighborhood, not far from the Montagnard apartments, and she caught herself wondering which curtain hid the author of the anonymous letter, which concealed the bigots who sent their hate mail to the paper. She felt chilly since leaving Tammi's overheated house, and she couldn't get the smell of the baby's diaper out of her nostrils. An image of Ravenna Mink in Eva's bathroom flashed through her mind, and again she tasted anger, no longer acid, more like a mouthful of meal she was tired of chewing but couldn't seem to swallow.

"I'm going to take you to the Healthcare Ministry," Eva said.

"Not need. Tylenol extra strength." H'nghai kept her eyes straight ahead.

"H'nghai, you need more than Tylenol—even if you're okay, you need a doctor to make sure this didn't hurt the baby." All the skin on H'nghai's chin and most of one cheek had been torn off; the flesh beneath was the color of raw steak, and Eva hadn't even seen the leg.

"No baby."

"Bullshit," Eva said and pulled into the gravel parking lot behind a church. She set the emergency brake and with the car still running turned on the seat. "Look, I want to help you. I don't mind coming to get you after your husband's dragged you half-naked through the streets and you won't call the police, but you're going to have to quit pretending you're not pregnant. You need to decide what you want to do about the baby because if you want to keep it you need a doctor, and if you don't—well, if you don't you need a doctor too. You can't try this again."

H'nghai gave her an apprehensive look.

"Did your husband drag you to try to get rid of the baby?"

She didn't answer.

"Did he—did you—try to kill the baby?"

"No," she said with such genuine surprise that Eva said, "Okay then. Because you could have been killed."

H'nghai touched her cheek, not quite covering her pain. "Not so bad."

"Jesus." In disbelief Eva touched her forehead to the steering wheel. When she raised her face, she said, "Why? Are you afraid of your husband, is that it?"

H'nghai looked down.

"What he did is against the law. It doesn't matter if he's your husband." Eva turned toward her. "Does he know you're pregnant? Is he angry about the baby? Why did he do this?"

"Lesson." H'nghai's voice was nearly inaudible. "All the time teach lesson."

"He's hurt you before?"

H'nghai looked out the window. The sky was full of blackbirds, swooping from lawn to lawn, chattering in the trees. Despite her chill, Eva cracked her window. The birds were headed south, but the overcast December day seemed scented with spring after the closed, fecal air of the house.

"This is impossible," she said. "You barely speak English, and I don't know the first word of Rhadé. I don't know what you understand, if you even understand anything I say."

A minute passed, and H'nghai reached her hand out to touch Eva's, still resting on the wheel. Like a language, Eva felt the vibration of the engine pass through her to H'nghai. H'nghai's skin was the color of pecan shells below the bracelet of raw purple where her wrist had been tied with rope, purple with a darker stripe of flecked blood. At the sight of it, Eva turned the ignition off and began to weep.

H'nghai turned her hand over. "My friend sad."

"I want to be your friend," Eva said. But she wasn't. The weight of what she and Guy had done to make sure of that pressed against her lungs. She couldn't bear it, and when she turned toward H'nghai again she said, "I have to tell you something. It's not right that you don't know. When your brother died, your brother Bhan...."

H'nghai's face shadowed. "Very sad. My family cry and cry."

"I know." Several moments passed. Eva took in a long, wobbly breath. "I was there. I was there when he died. I was in the car that hit him." *Say something,* she willed.

"My husband was driving." She waited for H'nghai's anger, but H'nghai said nothing, and if she had been able to turn her head she would have found the girl's face unreadable. "Bhan ran out in front of the car. I could tell you that I'm sorry, but I don't think I know if I want you to forgive me or not. They say you're supposed to forgive yourself, that's the first step, but...." At last she looked at H'nghai, who regarded her with eyes so huge and black almost none of the white showed. "I guess I haven't gotten that far."

It was hopeless. The girl couldn't possibly understand her. And even if she spoke perfect English how could she know what

Eva meant when Eva didn't know herself?

"Anyway, I am sorry, so very very sorry." Her hand was still in H'nghai's, and after a while H'nghai reached her other hand out to touch Eva's wet cheek.

"Very sad Bhan. I not blaming you."

Eva pressed her lips together and cried without sound.

When she was done, H'nghai dropped her hand and raised her dress to show the lacerations on her leg to Eva. "I tell you about Katu, about that," she said. Concentrating on patches, Eva was able to piece the story together.

The man who had dragged her was her husband. He had tied her to the bumper of his car and made her run to keep up and when she fell he dragged her. He had come home angry, yelling that he would teach American men how to treat their wives. She didn't like him. He was jealous. He was always trying to teach her a lesson, to teach her how to be a Katu wife. He was older than she was, quite a bit older, Eva gathered. A Dega man, not Rhadé but Katu. H'nghai's mouth pulled into a little grimace as she pronounced the word. In Vietnam she had not known any Katu. The Katu lived up in the mountains, way, way up, so high—she touched the roof of the car to show how high—other Montagnards called the land broken. The Katu were savages, she said, savages; she spat the word, *moi.* They worshiped a spirit who demanded sacrifices of human blood. They buried their victims alive; they cut the heads off children and bragged about their blood raids. Her husband was the only Katu in the group who had come to America. She called him Katu, though his name, she told Eva, was Go. He did not speak Vietnamese or wouldn't—Eva wasn't sure which—the language most of the different groups of Dega used to communicate with one another.

Rhadé, Roglai, Jarai, and Chru, H'nghai explained, were almost the same, but "Katu very different"—although in some form he communicated with her. He had spoken to her father.

He had wanted a wife. He had no family, no cousins, no *shuya,* to marry. Her father wanted a husband for her, though she was young, hardly older than the girls still playing *kdat klei* in America, though in Vietnam she would have been old enough to go strolling with a boy by the river. At the mention of the river her eyes grew soft.

"I remember that river from very small girl, my mother say, the river we take bath, go look for the wild fruit. My mother say is very beautiful the smell of the flower, the butterfly floating on the water, very blue and clean white sand. We hear the bird, the cicada sing. Long time ago, this. I miss that happy time by the beautiful River Krong Kno."

In America with a friend she had met a boy, American but "dark like Montagnard," she said. His name was Ronnie. She was attending a class to learn English, and he helped her with her vocabulary words; when they watched television together, he explained what was going on.

"Dega," she added, "love television, love movie." Eva understood that her father had been afraid she would marry him, though she couldn't tell whether that had been Ronnie's intention, or even H'nghai's. The courtship rituals in the Highlands Eva had read up on were clear-cut; a walk or even a particular glance might carry a commitment, and though it hardly mattered now, Eva wondered if H'nghai's father might have interpreted the relationship in that context. He was afraid that she would leave her family and go to live with Ronnie's people, "go live American family, forget Montagnard, forget

Dega culture, forget ancestor and homeland." He was afraid he would have grandchildren who did not learn to speak Rhadé, who could not talk to him, who would "eat hot dog and never know taste of wild pig," who wouldn't be able to sing their village songs, wouldn't know how "when you sing one way it mean like this, when you sing another way it mean like that, one way animal, other way Viet Congs. Like that."

He was afraid, H'nghai said, looking up at Eva, "they not know Dega struggle or every sadness we try to forget."

And so her parents arranged for her to marry Katu. They didn't know that Katu was a bad man, "not like Rhadé." Katu would not let her see her girlfriend; he was afraid she would go with her friend to meet other men, American men who "treat wife easy." He was, she repeated, very jealous. He wouldn't let her go to the class to learn English, better for her, he said, "stay Dega." He didn't let her go to the movies or to the Montagnard store, where the men met to play video games and pool. He made her stay home to cook, to watch other children, to wash clothes in the bathtub, too much work. "Like home," she said. "Women do lot of hard job, they carry lot of heavy things on they back, my mother always carry everything, my father carry nothing. Very hard life, Dega women." Her eyes flashed. "Everything with Katu like Katu land, broken."

He meant to show her "Katu way better"; he wanted to show American men they gave their wives "too many freedoms, go shopping, go laundromatic, everything like that. Katu man lead his wife, be boss."

"But he's not your boss," Eva said.

H'nghai looked away. Sometimes when she displeased him, even when he was displeased for no reason, he beat her to teach her a lesson. "Many lesson," she said again. "All the time, lesson."

Eva shook her head. "You can't let him hit you. He can't keep you from taking classes in English—that's terrible—he can't keep you from seeing friends. I don't care if it makes your father unhappy." H'nghai didn't answer. "I'm sorry. I know he's only trying to raise his children to know their culture—I respect his position. I hope he doesn't have grandchildren he can't talk to, who don't know anything about their heritage. That would be sad. But you can't preserve your culture by imprisoning your children in it. This is America. He can't make you marry someone you hate."

H'nghai shrugged. "Too late that."

Where was her fire? One minute she was tough as nails, scrappy, determined; the next she was unreachable and fatalistic. It made Eva want to scream. "It's not too late. What about your divorce? You said you wanted a divorce."

"American divorce," H'nghai agreed, but she looked unconvinced.

"Your brother Nuh—" H'nghai's eyes widened—"I know Nuh, he came to see us. After the accident," Eva explained. "He said you need money. Why? To pay your father back the bride-price?"

"Like that. Katu not wanting cheat."

"How much money?" How much money, Eva thought angrily, did you get to sell your daughter, a girl so artless and lovely she could break your heart? H'nghai shrugged. "Does your father know that Katu beats you?"

H'nghai shook her head.

"If you filed a report with the police, they could keep him

from hurting you." Emphatically H'nghai shook her head again.

"Why?"

H'nghai chewed her lip.

"Does Katu know you're going to have a baby?"

H'nghai turned her face toward Eva. "I not telling Katu anything."

Good for you, Eva thought. "H'nghai, do you want to have the baby? It will make things harder for you."

H'nghai looked down. "Hard life, Dega women."

"I guess so," Eva said. She turned toward H'nghai again. "If you want the baby, you have to let me take you to the clinic."

There was a faint tremor in her jaw; in her lap her hand curled like a snail. "Okay," she said

Chapter 14

Though Day Labor was now Dayco, Inc., nothing much had changed. The crew seemed younger to Guy, of course, and there were more minority faces, but essentially it was made up of the same potheads, dropouts, derelicts, criminals, and fuckups he recalled, along with a few men in their fifties and sixties who had been terminated from their regular jobs, one a dignified alcoholic with the face of a consumptive aristocrat who moved even more carefully than Guy. Dopers and not, they shared a certain dullness of eye, a lassitudinous look that was the mark of those for whom being temporarily down on their luck had become a permanent condition. Nothing much had changed, but he felt different. Fifteen years had passed; he felt physically more fragile. It wasn't so much a matter of stamina—that had not appreciably declined—as a knowledge his bones seemed to carry. They shied from risks, meeting the odd step and long reach with reserve. Heights seemed higher, weights more ungainly, he felt himself drawing in, and it was that drawn-in quality, that sense of his body's trying to preserve itself, that caught him unaware his first day back. It was not really the same as having slowed on the bastketball court or discovering that his legs lacked the old spring—those changes were more like the passing of greatness, such as his puny allotment of that had been, the waning of a talent. He could accept that passing of youth; it was the dwindling of his life that gave him pause. Though he considered himself fit—he exercised, he ate well, didn't drink to excess and had long since given up smoking—

this was a reminder that in the long run none of that would matter. His life had peaked; he was on the downhill journey.

The mood too was unchanged, conversation paced by the same old sports talk, pussy jokes, and ribbing. Even the Hispanics who spoke little English were quick to smile. Physical labor was a universal language. But so was breaktime, and he was the only one of the crew who didn't smoke. He felt a little like a recovering alcoholic hanging out with his old pals at the bar— it doesn't bother him, but it bothers them that he isn't drinking— though even that and his new frangibility didn't fully account for his feeling of estrangement. In a way he couldn't name he simply felt different; the years of steady employment and middle class life had changed him. Still he was glad to be busy and grateful for the camaraderie. The solitude of the last weeks had worn thin. And that too set him apart, at least in his perception. His co-workers were looking forward to day's end, but for him time passed almost too quickly.

They'd been hired to unload a warehouse, and when it was empty they'd be free. He remembered those days when a little more steam could buy an extra hour or two, though even when he'd temped before he hadn't craved that bonus time like the others, for after a day of toil he reached home bone-weary, wanting nothing more than a shower, a six pack, and the tube. In those days he and Eva had still been living in the apartment near Gardell; the TV was in the living room, and while she didn't mind watching PBS, the incessant drone of his blue-collar tastes got on her nerves, though she was cautious of complaint lest he take it as an excuse to quit. She had detested her way through a series of menial office jobs while her first husband finished grad school, and he knew the fear of having to support another man was never far from her mind. No doubt that was the reason she hadn't nagged him to work on his dissertation, though he'd felt its unwritten pages pile their weight between them. She wanted him to finish the Ph.D., but didn't want him to take time off to do it, and as long as they didn't discuss it, she didn't have to confront the contradiction. It baffled her, he could tell, to have fallen in love with a scholar, at least her idea of one, only to find herself living with a grunt. Bad enough that he cracked a beer as soon as he walked in the door at 5; he didn't need to begin the evening's dull drunk at 3:30. He was a morning person, and even when he was young drinking in the afternoon always gave him the feeling of having pressed a cloudy glass jar over the splendor of the day. A steady worker—she need never have feared he would let her support him—he couldn't understand the sacred routines of most temps: getting stoned before work, not the way pot prolonged time, or busting his butt to reach a state of nullification.

In all his first day back had an unsettling effect, for the six hours of humping box springs and sleeper sofas rearranged the relationship with idleness he'd developed over the last weeks, and when he arrived home at three, it was with an impending sense of boredom; he parked the dented Camry, which Weems had gotten released, and felt restless already.

He'd forgotten Eva's appointment with the realtor until the vacant, tidied smell, lemon and wax, hit him. She'd been up before 6 a.m., sniffing peevishly through the house for signs that somebody actually lived in it; now the only thing out of place was the mail strewn across the rug in front of the door. She must have driven to Gardell as soon as the realtor left, before the mailman arrived. Ten-thirty weekdays. Though the mail rarely brought much besides bills and ads, in the weeks since he'd been laid off he had come to know the schedule to the minute. He scooped it up, taking a brief inventory, hunting for the envelope with unfamiliar handwriting and no return address that might mean another anonymous letter. There had been only the one. As far as he knew. Having told Eva she shouldn't have shown him, he was now condemned to wonder what she might be holding back. He tossed the ads unopened and set aside something from AICA, the International Association of Art Critics, for Eva. Only the last item caught his eye, a notice that the carrier had been unable to deliver a piece of certified mail to Guy L. Ferrin. He could call for it at the Post Office tomorrow.

Certified mail would be something official. Something to do with his case.

In the kitchen the light on the answering machine was blinking. He listened to two hangups (anonymous calls?) before a woman's voice said, "This is Barbara Lowdermilk, the nurse at Siler School. Nick has had a fall on the playground and is resting in my office. The skin isn't broken, but there's a little swelling along his forearm, and he has a contusion. I'll try your work numbers; in the meantime if you get this, please come by to pick him up or call me at 228-1983."

The second message was shorter. By the third her voice had a frazzled sound, irritable and impatient.

Why hadn't the nurse reached Eva at Gardell? And why couldn't she think to state the time? He had no idea whether she'd called twenty minutes ago or six hours. It was 3:04. School got out at 3:15. Or was it 3? He had to search for the phone book—in her tizzy over the realtor. Eva seemed to have hidden everything away—and by the time he picked up the receiver he was cursing.

"Mr. Ferrin," the nurse said. "I'm glad you called. I was just about to send Nick back to his class for dismissal."

"You didn't reach my wife?"

"There was no answer at her work number. I called yours and was told it had been disconnected."

"Sorry. I've changed jobs. How's Nick?"

"Comfortable. I had ice on the arm earlier, but there didn't seem to be any need to refill the pack. Be sure you let the office know your new work number when you arrive."

"What happened?"

"He fell off a bridge on the playground equipment at lunch. The monitor brought him in." Lunch hour meant noon or even 11 a.m. Where the hell was Eva? Nick had been in the nurse's office over three, maybe four hours.

"But he's not really hurt?"

"That would be hard to say without an Xray. He doesn't seem to be in pain, but he does have some minor swelling and a contusion."

Guy tried to remember if Eva had mentioned any appointments besides the realtor. Surely she hadn't gone Christmas shopping; they had agreed to skip all but the most essential gifts this year. Just last night she'd been complaining about how much work she had to do before they could get away. He glanced at the clock again. Probably he shouldn't take the time to call an orthopedist before he picked Nick up. It didn't sound as if he needed one anyway. All he had was a bruise. The nurse probably should have sent him back to class instead of leaving all those panicked messages.

The halls were empty by the time he reached the school and

went looking for the nurse's office. The old building reminded him of the school that he had gone to, the same echoing high ceiling, same smell of cafeteria food and paste.

Nick sat up on his cot as soon as Guy came in the room. "Where's Mom? Why didn't she come get me?"

"I don't know where she is. How does your arm feel? Which one is it?"

"The right," the nurse said, coming up behind him. "Let's show your dad."

As Nick extended his arm Guy made out the shadow of a bruise. "Does it hurt?"

"I didn't even cry."

The nurse, who had a pretty complexion, smiled at Nick. "He's been a good little patient, but I imagine he'll be glad to go home."

"It was boring," Nick said. "And I missed my spelling test."

Guy bent over the sign out book. "Well, buddy, this doesn't look to me like anything a little ice cream wouldn't fix. Have you got your bookbag?"

The nurse produced his backpack, lunchbox, and sweatshirt.

"Did you have a jacket?" Guy asked.

"It's not cold out." Nick was dancing at the door. "Let's go."

"Put your sweatshirt on then."

Nick raised his arm for the sleeve and screamed.

The nurse shook her head as Guy met her eyes. "I've seen this happen before—the child seems fine until the bone moves or someone touches it the wrong way. It was two days before I knew my daughter's collarbone was broken, and I'm a nurse."

Was it the right or left wrist Nick had broken before? Guy couldn't recall the name of the orthopedist who had set it.

"Do you remember the name of doctor you saw last time? The one who put the cast on your wrist," he said to Nick.

Weakly Nick shook his head. His face had gone white, and his eyes were suddenly glassy. Guy couldn't tell whether his sudden lethargy came from pain or entitlement.

"There are only certain doctors we can go to." Damn Eva's insurance, Guy thought. She was always telling him you couldn't see this doctor, you had to see that one; if you had an emergency you had to apply for it twenty-four hours in advance. Maybe it wasn't her fault, but he resented her bossy tone. Nick had dropped to a chair and was lolling his head. He'd always been astonishingly stoic when he was sick, and so melodramatic you couldn't trust him when injured. The pain, though, was real. No one could fake a scream like that.

The nurse handed him a form. "I've filled out the top. You can have the orthopedist fill out the rest and sign it. Do you have the accident policy? They usually send the applications home at the start of the year."

"I'll have to ask my wife. Can I use your phone book?" Guy looked under orthopedists, but none of the names seemed familiar. It was late anyway; no doctor was going to take them today. He drove Nick to the Emergency Room.

At Healthcare H'nghai was given a pelvic and treated for multiple abrasions. Eva put the bill on her credit card. Twenty-two dollars. She was grateful for the clinic; at the Emergency Room it would have been over two hundred. H'nghai clutched her sheet of instructions, written in English, while Eva signed the credit slip. The doctor, not Dr. Eudy this time, but a younger one, maybe an intern, had gone over the wound care with Eva, no doubt assuming that she would be involved.

H'nghai had told the doctor she fell. "Sorry so clumsy," she said while the doctor looked sternly at Eva. If H'nghai were a child—but she was a child, Eva thought, sixteen or seventeen. At the same age she had been standing in a high school corridor, praying for Bucky Stiles to walk past her locker, her biggest worry that a geek like Eugene Maiseler might ask her to the prom. If H'nghai had been allowed to remain a child instead of married off, the doctor would be obliged by law to report his suspicion of abuse. She was obviously lying. It was up to Eva to speak, but because H'nghai looked so frightened, because she herself wasn't sure what should be done, Eva kept her secret. Maybe, if the doctor had taken Eva aside, if he had made it easy, but there in the crowded waiting room, where he'd seated himself between them to go over the sheet of printed instructions, with H'nghai's worried eyes fastened on her face, she had consented to the lie, at least for the time being, by saying nothing.

At the drugstore she tried to call Carole Eisen for advice, but the director was out of the office.

Back in the car she suggested the women's shelter. "It's a place where women who are afraid of their husbands go. Their husbands can't hit them there." H'nghai had the bright, expectant look that meant she didn't understand. The raw crimson of her face caused Eva to dart her glances and look away; it made her face ache and the top of her head feel as if it might fly away. "I can't take you home, not home, not back to Katu."

"Home, okay."

"No, I can't. No home." She tried again. "There's a shelter for women whose husbands beat them."

H'nghai frowned. Her jaw was beginning to square into her

stubborn look again.

"But look what he did. H'nghai, you could have been killed. You could have lost the baby."

The girl's chin trembled. "Teach lesson."

"Pooh." Eva put the flat of both hands against the wheel. "You told me yourself Katu is a bad man. You don't want to learn his lessons, H'nghai."

H'nghai looked away.

"What if he did it again, or worse? You ought to go to the police."

H'nghai's face had begun to twitch. "Not go home, Katu very angry."

"That's what I mean," Eva argued.

"Everyone angry. With Katu, my mother, my father...."

"I didn't tell the doctor the truth for now, but you can't ask me to help protect Katu—if you protect him you jeopardize yourself. Put yourself in danger. Make risk for yourself," Eva explained. "Your parents can't be angry with you for protecting yourself."

"All the Dega peoples."

"Why? I don't understand."

"You are thinking, everyone thinking Dega peoples all like Katu."

She had completely misunderstood. That wasn't an angle that had ever occurred to her.

"No," she said. "That's not true. No one will think that. I don't think that." *If they want to live in America, they got to learn how to act. These people are just filth. That's the kind of thing that gives them all a bad name.* She was guilty herself: she blamed H'nghai's father for selling her into marriage when he was only following tradition. Instead of thanking Tammi Courts and her friend Denise for helping H'nghai, she heard their country twangs and faulty grammar and saw nothing but redneck clichés. Guy had killed a child by accident, and everyone in Random assumed he was a monster.

"What about a friend then? Didn't you tell me you were with a friend when you met Ronnie?"

Shyly, expectantly, H'nghai looked up from under her lashes.

Eva had asked for it. The lump in her throat was as big as a fist. "I can't," she said softly. She turned to face H'nghai. "I'm sorry. I am your friend, but I can't take you home. My husband...."

"Like Katu?" H'nghai tilted her head. She was sucking on the Life Savers Eva had bought her at the store, and the pursing of her lips gave her a look of pended judgment.

"Oh, no," Eva cried. "He's not like Katu. I love my husband. He's a good man. It's just—well, it's complicated, that's all." She couldn't explain that Guy had killed her brother and it grieved him but now that he was being made a victim his grief had turned to anger. That he couldn't bear the sight of her brother Nuh and would never forgive his wife if he knew she'd involved herself with H'nghai..

"Please," Eva said. "Won't you let me take you to the shelter? Just for one night. They won't make you press charges if you don't want to, but they have counselors—" surely they had counselors—"people who can advise you, you know, help you, tell you what to do."

H'nghai's brow furrowed.

"I could get your things for you—your clothes," Eva offered, though she was unable to picture herself knocking at the apartment door and explaining why she'd come to whoever answered, the parents or Katu. "I'll call Carole Eisen again, the director of Christian Relocation Services. She can tell us what to do."

H'nghai squinched her lips in thought and canted her raw face still farther to the side. At last she asked, "What you do?"

What would she do? She knew what H'nghai should do, but she couldn't imagine what she would do because she couldn't imagine herself in the same situation. Her husband was incapable of cruelty. It was not because she feared his wrath that she would never let him guess she'd befriended H'nghai. She was willing to betray him—she had no choice now—but not to be so mean that she would let him know. He would have done the same thing in her position. He just didn't know it.

"I would go to the shelter."

H'nghai's face closed. She had heard the lie in Eva's voice.

"What about the baby?" Eva begged. "He could hurt your baby. It's a miracle he didn't."

"Save money, get divorce." Her face wore the look that said she didn't understand, but underneath was the stubborn look that also meant that she was lying, and why not? Eva had lied to her. She was out of arguments. In the end, feeling terrible, Eva drove H'nghai home.

"You promise me—*promise*—if he tries to hurt you, you will call me? You know my number."

H'nghai didn't look at her as she got out of the car. The sheet of wound-care instructions and the bag with the Betadyne and the bandages Eva had bought at the drugstore lay on the floor of the passenger seat.

Eva was so upset as she drove home, tempted to turn

around the whole way, that she was in the driveway before she remembered Nick. She backed out, but when she got to the Y he was neither on the playground nor inside. Though swim time was over she checked the pool and the gym; she read over the sign-out book, trying to remember if Guy had said something about picking up Nick, but Guy had gone to work; he'd left for Dayco before seven.

Nick's name wasn't in the book.

She went back to the playground and looked again, finally catching up with one of the counselors. "Nick? I haven't seen him. Ask Debbie."

Debbie was playing Uno with three of the children in the activity room. "Nick wasn't here today."

"Wasn't here?" Eva echoed. Maybe Dayco hadn't had anything for Guy; he could have picked Nick up at school; maybe they went to play basketball or to a movie. Her breath took a panicky flutter. "Did his dad call?" It was a rule that the parents notify the Y by noon if a child would not be coming.

"No."

On the drive home the accident whirled through Eva's mind. She saw the rain and churning lights, the officers' neon rainhats, heard the wail of the ambulance and raspy bark of the radio dispatches. Sternly she scolded herself; there was no reason to panic. She would call the school when she got home. But by the time she got home everyone at the school would be gone. Again she saw Bhan fly across their hood, even as she promised herself there'd been a mix up, nothing more, some logical explanation. She'd forgotten a birthday party (and would he be mad—he didn't have a present!); he'd gone home from school with a friend. But the school never let kids go home together without a written note from a parent.

It was the evil stranger, he had finally come, the one her mother had warned her about when she was a girl, the bad man who stole good little children. She'd grown up terrified that he lurked in every shadow and hid behind each corner, though as a girl she'd had no idea what unspeakable things the bad man did to good little children.

Her stomach surged.

No one was home, but the answering machine was flashing. Eva's heart leapt, but it was only Claudia saying in a petulant, let-down voice that she guessed she'd talk to Eva some other time.

Eva called the school and got no answer. She drove over. It was well after five, and no one was there. Trembling, she got back in her car.

It was because she had taken H'nghai home to Katu, only instead of Katu doing something terrible to H'nghai, something even worse had happened. She was being punished for what she'd done to H'nghai. For what they'd done to Bhan. Her hands shook so violently she had trouble driving.

When she turned their corner, Guy's burgundy Camry sat in the driveway. She flew up the steps and flung open the front door. "Have you got Nick?"

Guy materialized in the hallway by the kitchen door. "Yes, I've got Nick. Where have you been?"

Relief spread warmth through her arms and legs like a rash. "Thank God!" She sat on the steps, suddenly too weak to stand, her heart still thumping. "Where is he?"

"In the bathroom." His face was rigid. "Where were you?"

"*Where was I?* Looking for you!" She blew her nose. She was crying, though she couldn't tell whether it was from gratitude or the delayed impact of her fear.

"Hi, Mom," Nick called. When she turned her head to look, he was standing at the top of the stairs, holding up his arm to show off a bright orange cast that ran from fingertips to elbow.

She gasped. "Honey, what happened?"

"I broke my arm."

She looked to Guy, who had folded his arms across his chest. She turned back to Nick.

"Does it hurt? Let me see. Isn't that the same arm you broke before?" She looked at Guy again. "How did it happen?"

"He fell off a bridge." Guy's tone was stony. "Where *were* you? The school was calling here all day. The kid spent four and a half hours lying on a cot in the nurse's station. They couldn't get you at your office."

"Fell off a *bridge?* Oh my God." She started up the stairs. "Let me see," she said again to Nick, who met her halfway down, saying, "I didn't break my arm before, I broke my wrist. An arm is better."

She inspected the cast. "Well, it looks pretty official, doesn't it? Did you get to pick the color?"

"Uh huh. I have to wear it for three weeks, and I'm not supposed to get it wet. Does that mean I can't go swimming?" His mouth was stained purple. Guy must have bought him a treat after they saw the orthopedist.

"He fell off a bridge on the playground at lunchtime." Guy had walked to the foot of the stairs, but he looked no less hostile. "The nurse left at least four messages when she couldn't reach you. It's a lucky thing I got home early."

It was indeed lucky, Eva agreed, though what she said was,

"I went to the Y. I was so worried."

"How come you weren't in your office?"

She came down the stairs, but he looked so liverish, instead of stopping she passed right by him to stand in the dining room doorway. "Oh." Vagueness made two syllables of the word as the day with H'nghai came back. She looked at Guy but couldn't think of an answer to his question. "How was Dayco?"

"Fine."

"Well, good." She made an effort to sound chipper. Nick had disappeared upstairs. "Did you take him to Dr. Thurston? What did he say?"

"The receipt's on the dining room table." The anger on his face had fermented. "I took him to the Emergency Room."

If she'd taken H'nghai to the Emergency Room they would have run into each other. Her skin went cold.

"Our orthopedist is Peter Thurston."

"How am I supposed to know who it is? You weren't here."

"It's okay," she said meekly, though she was unable to keep from adding, "Did you call for authorization?"

"He was in the nurse's office with a broken arm for half a day waiting for someone to come get him, goddamnit. No, I didn't call for authorization. I don't even know who you're supposed to call."

She swallowed and felt her brow begin to furrow. "It's just that our insurance doesn't pay for Emergency Room visits unless you get pre-authorization."

"Fuck your insurance."

"Our insurance," she corrected.

"You want it done your way, then you do it. Where were you?"

"I was out," she said, hearing her evasive tone as cowering though it was clear from the jerk of his head that he heard it as defiant. Thank God she hadn't gone to the Emergency Room. "The book's in the drawer by the phone. It lists all the doctors on our plan. He can go to any of the orthopedists listed."

"I've never seen it."

"Yes you have." He followed her to the kitchen, where she pulled the provider list from the drawer by the phone and spread it on the table. "Here it is, Peter Thurston. He set Nick's wrist."

"How am I supposed to find anything around here? I couldn't even find the phone book. You've got everything hidden."

"It was right in the drawer where it's always been." His sigh was loud and exasperated. "How much was it?"

"A little over four hundred."

"Did you use your credit card?"

"I wrote a check." She didn't say anything, but even her expression seemed to piss him off. "Your son fell off a bridge and broke his arm."

"For next time," she begged. "That's all. It's fine. Just for next time, please remember about the insurance."

"Fuck your insurance," he said again. "I've been loading sleeper sofas on a truck all day. My back's killing me, and what happens when I come home?"

She sat at the table and began to cry. "What do I have to do to make you understand? We don't have any money. We owe your lawyer twenty thousand dollars. I've never been in debt, not like this. I don't know what people do."

"They call Mr. Cash." It used to be a joke. Nick had made up a whole Mr. Cash routine from the ads on television. "The bottom line, remember? You don't have to pay."

"You do if you don't know how not to."

Guy opened the refrigerator and took out a can of beer. "I said I'd sell my mutual funds. That should cover the check."

She nodded. "I'm sorry I wasn't in my office."

His voice had mellowed. "It's just that a lot of time Dayco sends us out of town. The school may not be able to reach me."

She nodded again. After a while she stood. "How was it?"

"Dayco? Fine. I don't mind that kind of work."

She crossed the kitchen and opened the door to the pantry. "Just be careful. You don't want to hurt yourself." She pulled a can of tuna from a shelf and looked to see if she had olives.

"I've loaded trucks before."

"You were younger before." The box of spaghetti was only a third full. She knelt to see if she had another. "When Nick broke his wrist he only had to wear the cast for two weeks. That's the difference a couple of years makes in your bones." She got to her feet with a box of spaghetti and went to the bottom of the stairs. "Nick! Honey, are you in pain? Do you want a Tylenol?"

"I gave him one," Guy said as she came back to the kitchen. "What are you fixing? I'm starving."

"A tuna pasta." She stood at the counter, thinking about H'nghai again. She had lied, she had said she would go to the shelter when she didn't know what she would do because he had never made her know, and H'nghai had recognized the difference and dismissed her. Even so she shouldn't have taken the girl back to the apartment. According to Tammi Courts, Katu had laughed when they cut H'nghai loose. Laughed and driven off, and if Eva was lucky he wouldn't come home, because anything that happened to H'nghai tonight was on her conscience. She should have brought H'nghai here; it was the only thing to do, and if she hadn't said no at first H'nghai would have come. Only—she looked at Guy.

"What?" he asked.

Even if he had never been arrested and the insurance company had settled, she couldn't have brought H'nghai home. No matter what had happened afterwards, he could not have borne to see her, not because of his anger, but because of his guilt. The problem was not that he would never forgive her for H'nghai, but that she would remind him he could not forgive himself. She could live with his anger. It was his guilt that broke her heart.

"You're a good man," she said. "I'm lucky to have you. Tell Nick to set the table." What was she thinking? Nick couldn't set the table. He had a broken arm.

"I'll do it," Guy said as her glance fell across her placemat. There, folded neatly, because the realtor had been coming, lay the morning paper. Her heart struck against her ribcage like a fist. She had completely forgotten. At least the article wasn't on top. *Driver in Fatal Accident Was Drunk.*

She held her breath as he put it on the seat of the extra chair and set their places. Most likely he would read it after dinner. If he didn't, she would have to show it to him. It wasn't something they could ignore; he had to get the error in the blood alcohol corrected.

Watching her, he said, "You look sad. Is it the money?"

"Not really."

"The house," he said. "All the work you've done."

She shook her head.

"You and the realtor must have finished up early. You left

before the mail came. I have to pick up a piece of certified mail." She didn't respond. "Certified mail," he repeated. "It must be something legal."

"Maybe your dad sent you something."

What did she think his dad would have sent him? "He would have called."

"Maybe it's something from your lawyer. Isn't he supposed to call you?"

If Weems had the police report, he would have called; he wouldn't have sent it certified mail. It had to be something from the court. In his gut Guy had a feeling it would be a civil summons. Now that the liability claim had been denied, the Buon Tos were bound to file suit. Still, he would feel better when Weems got the report. The lawyer said it hadn't been sent over yet, but Guy could tell by his tone that he'd forgotten. Guy would have to call on his break tomorrow to remind him.

He watched Eva dish up the pasta. *He* would feel better when Weems had the report; he didn't know what she would feel. She didn't seem the least concerned about his certified mail, though she'd think about it soon enough when she found out it had to do with money. He wondered how much the Buon Tos would ask. "Maybe you could pick it up for me—the certified mail," he clarified. "I was planning to go back to Dayco. Could you could run by the Post Office tomorrow morning on your way to Gardell?"

"If they'll let me sign for it." She carried the plates to the table. "Remind me though, okay?"

She had never said where she was.

Chapter 15

Eva slept even more poorly than she had these past weeks. She kept flipping to find a position that would soothe her into a restful state, but the covers bound her feet, her pillow was hard, she was hot, then cold, and Guy kept on breathing—she thought the deep, even rhythm would drive her mad, and at the bottom of each breath she tensed in anticipation of the next, the little bubble near the crest that rebounded down her nerves. At last she took a pillow and blanket to the den, but the silence only sharpened her discomfort; the sofa was too narrow, its cushions gave in the wrong places, her shoulders were scrunched. She was worried about H'nghai. At least she thought she was worried about H'nghai. What kept wheeling through her mind was a lunch with Claudia, and whenever Eva's attention to her own wakefulness began to lapse she found herself transported to the table across from Claudia, the unfamiliar, model-thin Claudia whose polished nails played at her hair in a whole new code of tics, though she was asking if Eva had hired her friend Iris and it had been at least three years since Eva had hired anyone. It was a dream, but not exactly a dream because Eva was awake, though she had no more volition than she would sleeping.

This much was true: a few years before Eva had been looking for someone to clean house, and Claudia recommended Iris. All the other female faculty had help; they hired college girls to scrub their bathtubs and run the vacuum. Eva had been thinking about putting an ad up on campus when Claudia encouraged her to call Iris. Iris was from Nigeria as Eva recalled, though she had no recollection of how Claudia had come to know her. Eva had called, but the interview was disappointing. She did not clean bathrooms, Iris told Eva with a brusqueness that belied the beautiful rolling lilt of her voice, she charged ten dollars a room, and it was necessary that the rooms be in order when she got there. But it was the disorder of her house that had led Eva to seek her out! Oh, she understood that she couldn't expect anyone to pick the place up, but what was the point of having someone else clean her house if she still had to scrub the bathrooms? She had a full-time job; she needed someone who would scour sinks and mop floors. In the end she'd employed a college girl who broke her vacuum cleaner and ruined the finish on the bathtub, who left early and came late and couldn't seem to get the hang of a dustrag. After that Eva had been so discouraged she hadn't hired anyone else. For the last two years she couldn't afford to.

Perhaps Claudia had hired Iris to clean her house and passed the recommendation on to Eva. That must have been it, three years ago at least; yet somehow as Claudia sat running her polished nails through her new longer coif she kept asking why Eva hadn't hired Iris. A frown darkened Claudia's eyes. She hadn't hired Iris, Eva explained, because Iris didn't do bathrooms. Over and over she explained—she talked too much, she sounded defensive, though why should she? She had been looking for someone to clean her house—of course she hadn't hired Iris! Claudia pressed a lacquered nail against her chin and gave Eva a long, cool look as she said, "What makes you think the Third World is supposed to clean your bathrooms, Eva?"

It had never happened. It was a dream, a twilight dream, but it made Eva so mad—she felt so frustrated, so misunderstood—that her mind would not stop churning. Who was Claudia to act so holy? She'd had Iris clean her own house, which she'd been after Bill to sell because she wanted to buy a bigger one, an elegant Victorian across the park from Kay and John. Eva clenched her jaw so hard her gums ached; her teeth felt as if they would shatter.

She shouldn't have taken H'nghai home.

She should have been there for Nick. She should have driven him to the orthopedist.

It wasn't her fault Iris didn't clean bathrooms.

She'd been so worried about H'nghai she had forgotten to show Guy the article in the paper, and now the mistake in his blood alcohol was uncorrected. His check was going to bounce. They owed his lawyer. She had to do something about money.

It was nearly light before she fell asleep, and in the morning Guy was out the door before she had time to show him the article in yesterday's paper.

Guy had to locate a phone to call Gordon Weems. He'd been sent to a clean up site. An old textile mill was being dismantled, and his crew was moving the machinery out. Everything was disconnected, there weren't even any lights, and when he asked the receptionist at the offices next door where he might find a pay phone, she offered hers. He had to come around her desk while she scooted backwards in her chair, eyes level with his fly, trying not to stare at his hands, which were black with grease despite the work gloves hanging from his back pocket. She would undoubtedly wipe the phone with a damp cloth the minute he left.

"How's it going?" Weems said.

The receptionist rose to get a cup of coffee.

"Did you get the report?"

"I'm glad you called. Did you see this morning's paper?"

He'd picked it up on his way out and laid it on the breakfast table for Eva.

"No."

"Atwater's on a rampage against drunk drivers. He's thinking about using the felony murder law to try repeat offenders on murder one."

What did that have to do with him? "Did you get the report?" The receptionist had disappeared, but Guy could smell the lingering scent of her hair rinse.

"I don't think it stands a chance of holding up on appeal, but the guy's got a strong record with second degree. Your best bet is to plead to misdemeanor."

He would look at the paper when he got home, but in the meantime—"Look, I can't talk right now, I'm on my break. I just called to see if you got the report."

"Report." Weems's voice was vague.

"The police report. You were going to get the D.A. to send it over."

"Let me pull your file. Can you hold?" Guy waited. There was no clock on the wall, and he didn't have a watch. "Here it is. Hmm. I don't see that list of medications."

Guy felt the cords in his neck tense. "I wasn't on medication. What I...."

"Prescription or OTC. If you took an aspirin, I want to know about it."

"About the report," Guy said.

"The D.A.'s office must not have sent it yet, but you've got no priors, I'm sure I can get him to agree to a plea."

Exasperated, Guy glanced at the receptionist, who had returned and taken a seat in one of the visitors' chairs. She was leafing through a magazine. Her honey-colored hair curled around a face as round and flat as a sand dollar. "Could you check on it? It's been a week. We weren't going to talk about a plea until you reviewed the report."

"Just what was it you wanted to know?"

Twenty thousand dollars, and the man couldn't even get a report sent over. "We were going see what the police report said. My blood alcohol was .02."

"Yes, the BAC. I think I've got that here—just a minute. Like I said, we can challenge it in court, but...here it is, 0.20."

"Point-0-two," Guy corrected.

"No, I've got it right here, 0.20. You don't want to go to court with that. Over 0.1 the conviction rate runs around 90 percent."

A sharp quill of fear shot through Guy's groin. "That's what it says in the report? Zero-point-two-0?"

"It's here in my notes. I had my secretary call the D.A. to check the number. Didn't you see yesterday's paper?"

The receptionist was turning the pages of the magazine too fast. "Look." Guy voice keened. "I'm on my break, I've got to go. Somebody's obviously made a mistake. Just call the D.A. and get the report, would you please?" Just his luck to hire the dyslexic attorney.

"I'll have my secretary ask his office to send it over, but I can tell you right now your best bet is going to be to hope he takes your plea."

"Just get the fucking report!" Guy slammed the receiver, then cast a sheepish glance toward the receptionist. "Sorry," he mumbled, so flustered he forgot to thank her. When he got back to the mill his heart was still knocking so wildly that as he dropped to a squat to fit his arms around a cumbersome piece of machinery he was afraid it would smash itself against his ribs and shatter.

Eva washed two Advil down with her orange juice. She felt ragged after her hour's sleep, but couldn't afford to go back to bed. She'd been away from her office so much lately that she absolutely had to go in to Gardell today and stay. She could call Carole Eisen from her office, but she had no way to call H'nghai. Impatiently she waited for Nick to finish dribbling his cereal over the table and pick up his backpack. Guy had left already for Dayco, and she was anxious to get him off to school because she didn't know what else to do but drive to the apartment. She would have to knock on the door and hope H'nghai would answer, but no matter who came to the door, she would have to find out how H'nghai was, whether Katu had come home or anything else had happened. *Then* she could go to the office.

Nick was dawdling over the comics.

"We need to get going," she prodded.

"Where's Dad?" Her son was wearing yesterday's dirty shirt, but she was too tired to tell him to change it.

"He went to work. I'm going to walk you to the bus stop."

"You don't have to." He didn't object when Guy did it. Guy always brought a football.

"Sure I do."

He sighed. With Guy it was sporttime. With her it was unnecessary supervision. Never mind that his arm was in a cast and he couldn't play ball.

"Change your shirt," she said. "It's filthy."

He sighed louder and went upstairs. She picked up the newspaper. A headline toward the bottom of the City-State section caught her eye.

Try Drunk Drivers for Murder, DA Says

Guilford County District Attorney Adam Atwater has vowed to try habitual drunk drivers on charges of first degree murder in response to Governor Clegg's campaign for safe roads. Following his disclosure of the blood alcohol concentration in last month's fatal accident on Lanyan Road, Atwater said, "The driver who gets in an automobile while intoxicated and uses that vehicle to kill someone is no different from the criminal who picks up a gun. In the hands of a drunk driver, the automobile is a lethal weapon, and we're going to send a message to everyone who drinks and drives: You're not going to get away with murder."

Atwater intends to use the felony murder rule, which stipulates that anyone who kills while committing a felony can be found guilty of first degree murder whether or not there was malice or premeditation. Classifying nonfatal injuries as felonious assaults in an accident that also involved a fatality would permit use of the rule.

Earlier this week Atwater revealed that the blood alcohol concentration of Guy L. Ferrin, who was charged with felony death by motor vehicle in the Lanyan Road accident that killed a 9-year-old Montagnard boy, was 0.20, twice the legal limit.

"Oh, for God's sake," Eva whimpered. Why couldn't they let it rest? She sent a dark look in the direction of the phone. She still had to show Guy yesterday's article. If she'd gone to sleep at a reasonable hour, she would have gotten up in time, but she hadn't gone to sleep because H'nghai's husband dragged her to teach her a lesson and Nick broke his arm. She hadn't shown him last night for the same reason. For a moment her vision turned itself inside out, as if she were looking through the wrong end of a telescope. At the other end she was standing on Kay Courtland's wide front porch with a mint julep in her hand, wearing a straw hat with a challis skirt and linen jacket—all the women were wearing hats, Claudia, Kay, and Sally, hats and voile dresses as they stood chatting in a dapple of late afternoon sunlight that fell through the porch's fretwork, in the background the sound of the post horn on the TV. The image was as sharp as the blade of a knife, but very small and faraway. She hadn't been to the Courtlands' annual Derby Day party in years. Why would that come back to her right now?

She had dreamed about Claudia, though it wasn't until that minute that she remembered Claudia had called yesterday when no one was home and left a message. She wrinkled her forehead. "That's odd," she mused beneath her breath, wondering briefly what Claudia could have wanted.

"Mom!" Nick's voice brought her back. "I'm going to miss the bus."

She checked the clock. "There's plenty of time."

"No, there isn't."

Reluctantly she set the paper aside. "Have you got your homework?"

"I didn't have any."

She should have checked last night. But he'd come in with a broken arm, she'd just taken H'nghai home, and Guy was furious with her, though not half as furious as he would have been if he knew where she had been. She hadn't thought of it.

"Are you sure?"

"I was in the nurse's office all day." He bit the words off.

"Right." She'd forgotten that too. "Well, you'll have to remember to see your teachers and ask if there's any work you need to make up." He didn't answer.

"Well," she said brightly as they left the house, "I bet you're looking forward to school today. You get to show your cast off."

"Big deal." He scuffed his feet on the walk.

"You can get all your friends to autograph it." She and Guy had signed before he went to bed.

"So?"

"Is there anything wrong?" she asked, studying the cowlick at the crown of his brown hair. "Is anything bothering you, honey?"

"No."

"Are you sure?"

He sighed. "Yes, I'm sure."

"It's just you seem a little bit cranky. Does your arm hurt?" Of course his arm hurt. It was broken. She should have asked him first thing, back at the house when she could have given him some Tylenol. She should have been there to drive him to the orthopedist and take him out for ice cream. When he showed up at school in his cast, all his teachers would know that when Nick Ferrin broke his arm his mother couldn't be reached.

What about his father?

But his father was at work and didn't have a phone. She

should have been in her office.

"I'm not cranky!"

His arm didn't hurt then. Whatever it was, he wasn't going to tell her. Probably he'd just gotten up on the wrong side of the bed, or else he was mad because she'd made him change his shirt or because after prodding him to hurry she wanted to read the paper when he said it was time to leave (as it was, they were early; no one else was there yet) or because she'd forgotten he spent yesterday in the nurse's office or because she was walking him to the bus stop instead of his father, or maybe it was more basic than that: he was mad because she wasn't Guy. Or possibly it was because he'd broken his arm and still had to go to school. How was she supposed to know? "I love you," she said.

He uttered the loudest sigh yet, and then they had to stand there in silence forever until the bus came.

As soon as she got home she drove to the apartment complex and parked her car in the driveway behind the courtyard the Buon Tos shared with two other buildings. Nuh and H'nghai had gone in through the back, but again she walked around front. No one answered her knock, and she wondered if she should try the back. The veneer on the door had peeled; it was painted over in the same faded, sickly shade of olive as the asbestos shingles. When she knocked again she heard a rustle.

The woman who opened the door had to be the mother. Her hair hung around her face like smoke; the flesh along her jaw had begun to buckle, and the skin was coarsening to the texture of pulp paper. She was short like H'nghai but heavier, broader through the shoulders, from which a striped shawl was looped in a sling that held a sleeping toddler. Surely she was too old for a baby. The woman stared at her through eyes so dark they seemed to be all pupil.

"Hello. I'm looking for H'nghai." Eva tried to enunciate clearly. "H'nghai Buon To. Is she home, please?"

The woman seemed to gesture that she should come in.

"No, it's okay, I'll wait," Eva said, and after a minute the woman disappeared into the apartment without closing the door, showing Eva a dingy slice of living room, a television and one arm of a slick crushed velvet sofa. From somewhere inside she heard voices speaking Rhadé.

After a few minutes H'nghai appeared, her face crusted. When she opened her mouth to speak her lips seemed to crack through swelling.

"Hello," Eva said.

H'nghai closed the door behind her without looking up.

"Are you okay? How do you feel?" Eva wondered what her parents thought. Even the doctor had known she was lying.

H'nghai's lips moved with caution. "Fine."

"Well, you don't look fine." It was a joke, but H'nghai wouldn't get it; she might even be insulted. "H'nghai, I'm so sorry I couldn't take you home with me. Are you sure you're okay? I worried about you all night."

"Fine."

"Did Katu come home?"

H'nghai cast a skittish glance over her shoulder. "No Katu."

Eva lowered her voice. "He hasn't hurt you any more?"

H'nghai's nods grew rapid. She still hadn't looked at Eva. "Fine, fine. Thank you."

Uncertainly Eva shifted her weight. "Well...."

"Busy," H'nghai said. "Special meal. Many guest today."

"Is it a party?" Eva asked, to prolong the conversation.

"Chicken, porks, rice, vegetable. Many cooking."

"Are you sure you're safe? I'll take you to the shelter right now if you want."

"Help my mother." Her eyes were veiled.

"H'nghai, isn't there anything I can do?"

"Very kind," she said again and turned to go. Beneath the wings of her shouderblades the narrow band of her bra showed through her thin white shirt. She was barefoot.

"Well, I hope you enjoy the dinner," Eva said. Although H'nghai had opened the door, she seemed to hesitate. "Look, if I come by tomorrow, is that okay? Come by to check on you?"

"Okay," H'nghai whispered. She watched Eva descend the stairs and when Eva reached the bottom lifted her arm in a wave. "Bye bye," she called softly.

At Gardell Eva's desk was a mess—she couldn't possibly get everything finished before they left. Especially if she listed the house. Surely she could wait until after the holiday, but having decided she was anxious to get it done. She should call Ravenna Mink. Instead she called Carole Eisen.

"What can I do for you?" the director asked.

"It's about H'nghai," Eva said, "H'nghai Buon To. Remember, you called me last week to give her a ride to Healthcare."

"How did that go?"

"Fine—I mean I got her there, and we filled out the papers. She's pregnant."

"Wonderful. Maybe looking forward to a new baby will help the family cope with their loss."

"Maybe, but she's not very happy with her husband. In fact, she wants a divorce. He abuses her. I had to take her back to Healthcare yesterday after he tied her to his car and dragged her."

There was a quick intake of breath. "Is she...?"

"Well, she's pretty scraped up, but nothing's broken, and the baby's fine."

"You don't know how sick this kind of thing makes me. Everything we try to do—then something like this just reflects back on the whole community." Carole Eisen sighed. "Have you been following the letters to the editor? We did the Montagnard people such an injustice, and they want so little from us."

Eva fingered a stack of loan forms. "Well, I'm really much more concerned right now with her. She wouldn't call the police. She's afraid people will think badly of the Montagnards."

"I wish it didn't work that way."

"The reason I called, I was hoping you could help. She's very unhappy, and she's clearly in danger—her husband seems to be subject to jealous rages. The problem is her parents arranged the marriage—frankly I don't know how they could be unaware of the abuse." H'nghai hadn't looked at her, but she had waved and said bye-bye. Eva hoped it meant she was forgiven. "Her husband's Katu. I believe he paid a bride-price, and she feels that she has to have the money to repay the debt before she can get out of the marriage." The line was silent except for a crackle of static.

"Sorry," Carole Eisen said. "I'm trying to think on my feet here. I'm just not sure there's much we could do, certainly nothing legal unless she wants to press charges. From what you say, she seems to understand the situation—honor is very important to the Montagnards, and they're hyper-aware of the impression they make—they want their friends in the U.S. to help them achieve recognition from the Vietnamese government. It's really not much to ask, but there seem to be a lot of Americans who will grab at any excuse to say we should deny them the little help we've given."

"I understand all that," Eva said. "I want to know what I can do to help *her.*"

"The truth is we try not to intervene in family situations, except to offer assistance in getting family members out of Vietnam. I could try to find an interpreter to make sure she understands her options."

"That might be helpful," Eva said, though she had the feeling that H'nghai did understand, at least enough. She didn't want to press charges for the same reason any American wife who spoke perfect English didn't want to press charges: she was afraid; she didn't want to stir up any more trouble than she already had. "I tried to get her to go to the Women's Shelter, but she wouldn't go."

"That's not surprising. The Montagnards are a proud people. I can refer her to a counselor, but like I say we haven't had much success. You and I are programmed to seek help, but Montagnard culture is community-based, even clannish. In the Highlands everyone had to work together, and then of course there was a wartime situation where people stuck together or else. And here—well, you can imagine. Without that bond they'd feel even more lost. It's really what's enabled them to survive."

Eva wanted to talk about H'nghai, not the culture. "Her husband isn't from the same tribe. He's Katu. They don't even speak the same language."

"Fighting for a common cause really brought the tribes together. That seems to outweigh any differences. We see much more hostility between the Vietnamese and Montagnards than we do between tribes."

"Her husband beats her."

"He may be acting out. I don't think we have any other Katu. It's a remote region. The majority are Rhadé or Jarai. My guess is that he would feel even more lost than most."

"I don't care how he feels," Eva said.

"I'm not trying to minimize your concern. From what you say, it sounds like a very bad situation. It's just that our agency isn't equipped to intervene in a family matter. I'd be glad to put you in touch with some of the other agencies that coordinate volunteers. Understand, it's my job to be an advocate for all the Montagnards." Carole Eisen paused. "Perhaps you could provide her with a place to stay until things cool down. She may be willing to try for a reconciliation."

"I don't think so."

"Either way. It can't hurt for you to put her up. She seems to trust you."

Eva hoped H'nghai would trust her again. "Maybe. The only thing is I can't."

"They're used to close quarters—you wouldn't even need an extra room, just a bed on the living room sofa, even a quilt on the floor."

"I can't."

"Well," Carole Eisen said dubiously, "possibly one of the volunteers could locate temporary housing, though I have to tell you it's scarce."

Eva took a breath. "Look, I'm going to be frank with you." If she had told the truth from the beginning she could have kept her promise to Guy. She would never have met H'nghai. But if she hadn't met H'nghai, who would help her? "H'nghai already knows. The reason I was interested in the family, the reason I can't take her in—my husband was driving the car that killed her brother. We feel terrible about it, but it wasn't his fault. The reports in the paper are completely distorted, all the stuff about his being drunk; he wasn't even drinking. It was raining and Bhan ran in front of the car."

The silence stretched on so long Eva was afraid Carole Eisen would make no response. At last she said, "I don't know what to say."

"The stuff in the paper has been horrible—we've got people calling the house, people seem to think we're in some sort of conspiracy to commit genocide, or else they're calling to congratulate him and say he should have killed them all. Everyone seems to think we did it on purpose."

Again there was a long pause. "I'm sorry, but I really don't know what to say. I don't know the facts."

She couldn't expect sympathy from Carole Eisen. It wasn't even that she, or Nuh's principal, or even Claudia blamed them. Like Carole Eisen said, they didn't know the facts. And when she listened to herself try to explain, she heard what they must hear, facts that could never sound like facts from her mouth; from her mouth they could only sound like excuses and self-pity. "About H'nghai."

"It's our job to advocate for Montagnards. Do you understand? I probably shouldn't be talking to you. We've referred the Buon To family to Legal Aid."

For a moment Eva didn't understand. Then it hit her. Guy had said they would be sued. She wondered if H'nghai knew.

"Maybe you could give me the list of counselors you mentioned, or the list of interpreters, the volunteers." H'nghai would never go to a counselor. "I'll see if anyone else can help with the housing. If she'll go."

"Actually—" Carole Eisen's voice had returned to normal—"maybe the problem should be referred to the Women's Center. They deal with this sort of thing all the time, without the language problem of course, but that's where we could come in, it's probably where we should come in. They can call us if they need an interpreter, but without the girl's cooperation...."

Eva should have thought of the Women's Center in the first place.

Guy had forgotten to remind Eva to pick up his certified mail, but he finished at the textile mill early enough to go by the post office himself. It was the civil summons he expected. He had been named defendant in a wrongful death suit. He folded it back into the envelope, without response. The morning's phone call with Gordon Weems had drained him. He had thought he would carry the burden of the boy's death for the rest of his life, but that organ had died, his sense of responsibility or remorse. His anger, his umbrage at being victimized himself, had killed it, and the only emotions he had left were righteousness and the dull sore that was his rage. They were screwing him—the D.A., his lawyer, the newspaper, the insurance company—and there was nothing he could do about it. That last made him angriest of all. He could feel his soul as a physical presence, a wad of dead tissue inside his chest, with only one shriveled live nerve left, the nerve that might someday transmit guilt again, but a different kind of guilt, a guilt for the death of the grief and guilt he had once genuinely felt over the death of the boy.

At home he propped the summons on the breakfast table for Eva to see, then thought better. He didn't intend to keep it from her, but to leave it where she would find it while he napped, while he was unavailable to discuss it, was mean; she'd done nothing to deserve that, even though he was irked with her. She was losing interest in his predicament, he could tell. In the end it wasn't her problem. No matter how much the family suffered, it was ultimately his problem. Her own worries had begun to crowd his out. The last few days she'd seemed particularly distracted. Instead of realizing that her friends had at last revealed themselves for what they were, she was still brooding. Women relied on their friends; they confided more than men did. His friends were the men he played basketball and softball with, the guys he might call up to go to a sporting event or grab a beer. Really personal conversations among the men he knew were rare.

The light on the answering machine was blinking. Last night, while Eva was in the shower, he'd taken an anonymous call. It had startled him, more than anything else; he had picked up the phone, and an unfamiliar voice had said, "A 'yard saved my life. Don't think you're going to get away with murder." "Who is this?" he had asked, but the caller hung up. Something had been in the paper, Weems said. He glanced at the breakfast table, but the papers were gone. When he got up from his nap, he'd go through the recycling bin. He pushed the button on the machine.

Two messages for Eva from a woman named Ravenna

Mink—she must be the realtor; it had something to do with the house—and one for him from Gordon Weems, who asked him to call in a voice that sounded unaffected by the fact that Guy had lost his temper this morning. Or had the call come before they talked? He remembered what Jerry Beck had said about the innocent: a pain in the ass, never satisfied, slow to pay their bills, because, being innocent, they thought he should defend them gratis. Too bad. For what he charged, Weems could put up with a pain in his ass. He dialed the number half through, changed his mind, and decided to take his nap and call Weems tomorrow. On the other hand, his crew would be back at the textile mill tomorrow, and he didn't want to ask the receptionist next door to use her phone again.

"Thanks for calling," Weems said. "I thought I'd let you know that my secretary's called the D.A.'s office and asked them to send over the accident report. I'm having lunch with Atwater on Friday, and barring any surprises in the report, I'd like to propose a plea. Misdemeanor due caution, a thousand dollar fine—that's stiff for a misdemeanor, but we've got to offer something to sweeten the deal. You'll get two years probation, but you won't do jail time, and there'll be no felony on your record. That's if we can get this matter of the BAC straightened out. How does that sound?"

It was the same deal he'd pushed last week. Guy's fingers tingled with a rise in blood pressure; he had to coax a patient voice up through his throat. "The blood alcohol figures are wrong—they've been transposed. I don't want to talk about a deal until I've seen the printout from the Breathalyzer. If the D.A. doesn't want to send it over, maybe you can get a copy from the police."

"The police don't keep a copy. They send theirs to the D.A. You should have the other."

"I don't have one. Where would I get it?"

"They give you a copy at the time of testing."

Had they? He'd been so shook up he didn't remember. What would he have done with it? Put it on the dining room table, most likely, the same place he left all his stuff: wallet, keys. The phone cord wasn't long enough for him walk to the dining room doorway, but what was the point? It wouldn't be there now. Eva had cleaned house for her mother's visit, they'd eaten dinner at the dining room table every night her mother was there, she'd cleaned it again for the realtor. Ravenna Mink. A woman named Ravenna Mink was selling his house. The name made him think of the animal, but because he didn't know what a mink looked like, he pictured a ferret. "I don't know what I did with it." Maybe it was in his wallet.

"You might want to look for it. Unless you've got proof that this figure—just a minute." Weems shuffled papers. "Zero-point-two-0—that's up there, that's not one or two beers. Unless you've got proof that 0.20 is wrong, the D.A. isn't going to bite. I'll do what I can to keep you out of prison, but at the very least you're going to lose your license for life."

Lose his driver's license for the rest of his life? A man couldn't function without a license. In New York City maybe, but not in Random, North Carolina.

"I'll look for it," he said, impatient to get off the phone and find his wallet. If he could locate the slip of paper, his problems would be over.

"Let me know if you find it. What did you claim the number was?"

"Point-0-two."

"That's a pretty big difference. If it's .02—*if*—we'd have to wonder why you were charged. I'll try to reach the arresting officer, see if I can't interview him and find out his reasoning. What did you say his name is?"

"McThune. Aaron McThune."

"Young, old? What can you tell me about him?"

"He's a black guy. Late thirties, maybe forty. He shaves his head."

Weems seemed to mull this over. "Let me check his record. Maybe that's an angle."

"What do you mean?"

"Well. The victim was a minority; the accident happened on a side of town that's predominantly black. You say you had nothing to drink, you weren't speeding or driving in the wrong lane, you've got a witness who says the kid ran out in front of the car and under the conditions no one could have stopped, but a black officer charges you with drunk driving death and the next thing you know the D.A. has a piece of paper that says you weren't just drunk, you were stinking."

"Are you talking about some kind of conspiracy?"

"Why don't we talk again after you find your slip of paper?"

"Wait a minute," Guy said. "This doesn't feel right. First of all, I said I had a drink before dinner and a glass of wine with—that was more than four hours before the accident, and I definitely was not impaired, but I didn't say I had nothing to drink; I said I wasn't drunk. I've got people calling my house and sending me anonymous letters because the kid I killed happened to be a minority—what do they think, I checked the color of his skin before I hit him? I couldn't *see* the fucking kid. That's why I hit him."

"That's what I wonder," Weems said. "Your BAC is .02, but you get charged with drunk driving death. It makes no sense, unless the officer has some other reason to believe that you were drunk, one, or two, he's got some axe to grind. It can't hurt to check his record. Maybe you sensed hostility. Maybe he did. I notice that when I asked you to tell me about him, the first thing you mentioned was race."

Weems had asked him to describe the cop, for Christ's sake. He'd also mentioned the shaved head, though the officer looked more like Telly Savales than Michael Jordan. Guy pictured the scar on his lip, where maybe fifteen years before on a basketball court Guy had bashed him with his elbow. If it was McThune. The cop hadn't seemed particularly hostile. He hadn't seemed especially sympathetic or unsympathetic, just infuriatingly, impersonally professional. Like Jerry said, he was covering his ass. But that didn't explain the transposed BAC.

"I'm not a racist, Mr. Weems."

"I didn't say you were."

"This is caca," Guy insisted. "I've been around a lot of black people in my life—I play ball with them, I work with them. I know when I'm dealing with someone who hates whites."

"So you weren't drunk and the fellow who arrested you is both an officer and a gentleman, you don't want to take a plea, you want to go to court, and when I get up there to tell the jury you've been framed, you don't want me to step on any toes."

"I'm not going into court and calling somebody a racist just because he happens to be black. I know that."

Weems sighed. "Just find your piece of paper, and give me a call before I meet with the D.A., all right?"

It wasn't in his wallet. He checked the top of his chest of drawers upstairs, but Eva had cleaned that too. The dining room table and the chest were the only places he would have put it.

In the process of looking, he discovered the paper's City-State section from yesterday and today on Eva's dresser. If she had meant to hide the papers from him, she hadn't done a very good job, but she must have had some reason to separate them from the rest. Weems had referred to something in the paper. He scanned the headlines.

Driver in Fatal Accident Was Drunk
Try Drunk Drivers for Murder, DA Says

He didn't even read the articles. He laid both papers and the civil summons out on the breakfast room table for Eva and closed the door to the bedroom so she would know he was taking a nap.

Chapter 16

Guy expected Eva to be waiting for him to wake up, but when he came into the kitchen after his nap she was sitting at the breakfast room table with a pen and legal pad, staring out the window with her lip wrinkled in thought. The newspapers and civil summons had been moved to the side. When he approached, she drew her forearm across the tablet to shield it from his view.

"I'm going for a run," he said. Without looking up, she nodded, which left him nothing to do but run. His legs felt lifeless, he missed his morning zest, but he'd been unable to make himself get up in time to run before he left for work.

When he returned she was at the counter, chopping an onion. He looked at the tablet she'd left on the table, which appeared to hold a list of names and phone numbers. Whatever she was doing, she wasn't brooding about his summons. He had to bring it up himself.

"I saw it," she said, turning her face to one side and wiping a finger up behind her glasses. The spoor of the onion tickled inside his nostrils. "Well, you can't say we weren't expecting it."

"I suppose not." She hadn't said a thing about the newspapers she had—what?—not exactly hidden, but she hadn't thrown them in the recycling bin with the rest of the papers either, nor had she left them out for him to see. "I read the articles," he admitted. She scraped the onion into a skillet and picked up a green pepper. "In the newspaper—yesterday's, today."

"I was saving them to show you. I just didn't have a chance."

"Just my luck, I draw the dyslexic D.A." The skillet began to hiss, and he waited as she stirred the buttery fragrance. "My lawyer thinks I was drunk."

"Obviously we need to get it straightened out."

"You don't think I'm trying?" His sweat was beginning to dry, and he moved a few steps away. "I talked to him twice today. He doesn't seem to be working any too hard on my behalf. He keeps trying to get me to plead."

"Of course he does. It's less work for him."

"You think that's why?"

"Maybe. I don't know. I don't really know a thing about it."

"You must have had a reason for saying it."

She leaned past him to toss the seeds and pith into the garbage. "Not really."

"But you think that's why?" The back of his neck itched. He needed to shower.

Her sigh was shallow. "I told you, I don't know why."

"I know that you don't know why. But...."

"Guy." She turned a warning look on him.

He waited for a minute, but when she didn't say anything else started for the stairs. Halfway there, he turned around. "Have you seen my copy of the readout?"

"What readout?"

"The result of the Breathlyzer."

"It was .02. I remember."

"I know what it was." He took a step toward her. "I want to know if you've seen it."

"Seen what?"

"The piece of paper. I left it on the dining room table." He might have left it on the dining room table.

"I don't remember it. When did you leave it?"

"When we came in."

She turned around. "Are you talking about the night of the accident?"

Of course he was talking about the night of the accident.

She opened her mouth to speak several seconds before the words came out. "That was over a month ago."

"Have you seen it?" He had to have left it on the dining room table. It wasn't in his wallet or his suit pockets. He'd checked.

"Not that I recall." She stirred the vegetables.

"Well, you must have moved it when you cleaned up."

She had her back to him, and he saw her shoulder blades stiffen through her sweater. "I've cleaned up at least twice. I told you—I don't remember seeing it."

She could at least think about it. "I wish you wouldn't move my things," he said.

"I wish I didn't have to move your things," she said.

They were in it now.

"Any time you want them moved, all you have to do is tell me." She set her spoon on the counter. "Did you throw it out?"

She sighed loudly. "No, I didn't throw it out."

"Are you sure? How do you know you didn't throw it out if you don't remember seeing it?"

A scorched smell rose from the stove, and she yanked the skillet from the burner. When she'd set it on the chopping block, she turned to him. "Because I wouldn't throw out a thing like that."

"That's all I'm asking. Where you put it."

She spoke slowly, enunciating each word. "I don't know that I put it anywhere."

All he wanted was the proof that he was innocent. So what if the innocent were a pain in the ass—did she think she would be any different? One cross-eyed look from Claudia, and she'd come completely unhinged. Everyone in the house had been called to suffer.

"This happens to be a very important piece of paper. Without it I might as well have been rip-roaring drunk."

"I don't care what it is. If it was so fucking important, you shouldn't have left it lying on the dining room table."

"I don't think you understand the problem." He took another step forward, disappointed that there was nowhere else to go. "You're so busy making sure the house is spick and span enough to suit you and this ferret woman you can't see this isn't just my predicament. Because it's not just the newspaper that thinks I was stinking, it's the district attorney, the guy who's going to determine whether I go to jail and you have to raise our son alone, and you know what?" He was surprised she didn't interrupt. "It's even the guy we're paying twenty thousand dollars to defend me, the guy who's supposedly on my side." He hadn't mentioned that he was going to lose his driver's license for life; she'd notice that soon enough, when she had to cart him around for the rest of hers.

"That little piece of paper...."

She cut him off. "I wasn't keeping the articles from you. I was going to show them to you—I just didn't get a chance."

"I wasn't talking about the articles."

The burner on the stove was still a dusky red. She turned it off and said, "By the way, we've been getting anonymous calls."

"I know."

She seemed surprised.

"I took one last night when you were in the shower." Another sometime after she had shown him the anonymous letter, and because he'd told her she shouldn't have shown him, he'd had to keep both calls to himself.

She poked at the charred onions and peppers. "I don't know what to say. I never saw the readout, I don't remember your getting it and couldn't tell you what it looks like, but for twenty thousand dollars your lawyer ought to be able to get the decimal point where it belongs."

"The D.A.'s office is dragging its feet. The police don't have a copy—they send theirs to the D.A. That's why I have to find mine."

"Surely the D.A. can straighten it out. I mean they can't just change the number and throw away their copy."

"It's got to be here somewhere."

She flattened her back against the counter. "Guy, I'm cooking dinner. I'm sorry you can't find it. If I had seen it I would have put it on top of your chest in the bedroom or in your desk drawer."

He hadn't thought to look in his desk drawer. He peered past her into the skillet. "What is it?"

She gave her lips a wry tuck. "Onions and peppers. They could have been a lot of things before I burned them."

After that they fell into a habit of not talking. It wasn't a cold silence or even an uneasy one, just odd. She'd become secretive, inattentive, even after that one quarrel agreeable. It occurred to him that she might have a lover, but he was too distraught over his own problems to travel any avenue of thought that led too far from himself. A few years ago the notion might have driven him to obsession—he was jealous by nature, and he could imagine cruising the city for her car, reading her mail, trying to intercept calls, studying her face for clues—but now he only stumbled upon the idea and passed over it without bothering to pick it up to see if light would pass through. If she had a lover it was undoubtedly because he gave her something she needed. How could Guy begrudge her what she needed when he had nothing to give? Or maybe she didn't have a lover but had moved into a new phase of mourning for her friends. Once or twice he even suggested that she call Claudia, thinking she should have someone to talk to since she obviously didn't want to talk to him.

"I'm not going to call Claudia," she said.

"I know she hurt your feelings, but she'd probably welcome the chance to patch things up."

"Well, she's not going to get it," Eva said with a cold finality that told him whatever Claudia had done, Eva had taken it for the basest betrayal and would forever hold a grudge. She was like that. The force of her feeling impressed him, and he wondered, idly, if it had been him would her response have been half so strong.

Vainly he looked for the readout in his desk drawer. He had no more recollection of having seen it than Eva. For all he knew he could have tossed it without ever registering that he had it. He might have left it lying on the desk at the police station. Dropped it in the cab. Maybe McThune never gave it to him in the first place. He tried to reconstruct the cop's demeanor on the night of the accident, but could find nothing telling. The city paid him to be a bastard; actually for a cop he'd been pretty civil. Still Guy remembered the scene at the bar where he'd called to report the accident, the room full of hostile black faces. No black liked whites too much, for all the camaraderie on the loading dock or basketball court. Before McThune had even reached the scene, the odds weren't in Guy's favor.

He got nowhere with the lawyer. Every time he called, the report hadn't come yet or the lunch with the D.A. had been postponed, and soon the secretary started telling him Weems was out—if he wasn't in court he was on another line, he hadn't come back from lunch yet, he'd run an errand. "Would you like him to return your call?" she asked, but Guy was here and there, in and out with Dayco, squeezing calls in on his break. So he hadn't found the readout—shouldn't his attorney interview Eva? She was a witness; she remembered the same BAC Guy did. Why hadn't Weems called Eva? Or maybe Guy had to cough up the twenty thousand first.

He called his broker, an old basketball buddy who had sold him his mutual funds. He didn't ask why Guy wanted to sell. They chatted about the old game for a few minutes, and he told Guy to watch for the check.

A little over seven thousand dollars.

If he'd had the readout, he would remember. It was too important to forget. What did it mean if McThune had never given it to him in the first place? He wanted to talk to Weems again, now that he'd had time to mull the situation over. It was too big a coincidence that the D.A.'s readout should be so wrong and Guy had no recollection of ever having received his copy.

He asked Eva.

"What do you mean?"

"Just what I said—don't you think it's funny I was arrested?

That I wasn't given the readout?" He rubbed the divot of flesh between his nose and lip. "Do you think the cop could have had some secret motive?"

"Like what?"

"You don't think it's strange that the D.A.'s got a piece of paper that says my blood alcohol was twice the legal limit and I can't find the one that would prove him wrong?"

Her nose wrinkled thoughtfully. "Well...."

"What?"

"You said yourself you probably left it lying around."

"Are you sure he gave it to me?"

"I don't know. I was in another room."

"It just seems awfully suspicious."

She frowned. "Well, it is a bureaucracy." What was that supposed to mean? "You can probably expect that mixups are the norm."

He was so mad he wanted to bellow, but he made an effort to keep his voice down. "So you don't think that the fact I'm arrested for no reason and not given a crucial piece of paper, the one piece of paper that if I had it could save my ass, and the D.A.'s got one that says something entirely different and uses my case to start a crusade because next year there happens to be an election...."

She looked up from the breakfast table. "Sweetie, we aren't going to argue about that piece of paper again, are we?"

"I'm not arguing."

"Because anything could have happened to it. You said yourself you don't know where you put it. Around here...." She flung a hand out, but there was nothing to show, no mess to prove her point, because ever since she'd called the realtor she'd been keeping the place like a museum. No reminders, no nagging; everything seemed to jump back into place by magic.

"In other words, you don't think it's weird that I'm arrested for no reason." His voice was flat.

She looked pained. "Well, honey, the boy *died.*"

He couldn't believe it. He had to sit down. "What do you mean?" he finally managed.

The lines cut into her forehead deepened. "I don't mean it was your fault. You know it wasn't. But the cop said when we were leaving the magistrate's office—I mean I think he said—it was something like when you hit a kid you're always at fault."

His jaw dropped. "What did you say? Are you kidding? Why didn't you tell me?"

"I mean he might have said it, I'm not sure. Of course it's weird that you were arrested, but it just seems when something like that happens—well it would be hard for anyone to accept that no one is to blame."

"Do you know what you're saying?' He leapt to his feet. "You think the cop was looking for a scapegoat!"

She looked as if she'd swallowed something spoiled. "I'm not saying anything. I don't know if that's what he said or I imagined it. Nothing from that night is clear anymore—it's like I went over it so many times in my mind it came apart and I can't put it back together. It doesn't even seem real; it's like the whole thing happened in my head."

"Wouldn't that be nice?"

She was near tears as she stood to hug him. "I'm sorry, honey. I love you. We're in this together."

"Weems thinks there might be something up with McThune."

"How?"

"Well, he asked me if the cop was black." He had asked what Guy could tell him. Guy wondered if he had wanted Guy to be the one to bring up race.

She took a step backwards. "What do you mean?"

"Well, the kid was a minority."

"Who is this lawyer?"

"So you don't think...?"

"You think you got arrested because you're white?" Her look was incredulous.

He was ashamed to have mentioned it. He didn't really believe it; he had asked her just to test it out. "No—I mean I don't know, I wanted to know if you think it's possible."

"No."

"Not even possible."

"No."

She was right; he knew it. All the same, the D.A. had the wrong figure, and Guy didn't have his readout, did he?

She eyed him closely, her expression growing matter-of-fact. "I hope that your lawyer isn't nuts enough to try to use a defense like that. Because I don't care whether McThune is Louis Farrakhan, you're the one who'll come off looking like the bigot."

What she said was true. He reviewed the time he'd spent with McThune again. McThune hadn't liked him, but neither did the cop who gave you a parking ticket or told you not to jaywalk. What did he expect, that McThune should forget there'd been an accident and invite Guy to a game of horse just to prove he didn't hold a grudge over his split lip? *If* Guy had been the one to split it.

"Would you at least tell the lawyer I wasn't drunk?" he asked. "Would you tell him you distinctly remember that my blood alcohol was .02?"

"Of course. Why would you think I wouldn't?"

But Weems hadn't asked to talk with her. Guy tried to call the lawyer again. "He's with a client," the secretary said. "Would you like to leave a message?"

Bill Whitt called to invite him to watch the Georgia-Duke game on TV.

"Have a good time," Eva bade him fervently as he left the house. "You deserve one." Two weeks ago she would have been pumping him for anything Bill might have dropped about his separation; she'd have sent him off with a list of questions, and when he got home he would have barely gotten in the door before she demanded he go over every nuance of the evening. She'd been devastated the night Claudia told her she and Bill had split. She'd taken it so hard she'd X-rayed every detail, then turned the details over and X-rayed them again, but now that he was in a position to get fresh information, she showed no interest. He wondered again if she might have a lover.

As it was he didn't get much information. Bill met him at the door in bare feet, a torn white tee shirt, and wrinkled pants, but the house, Guy saw at a glance, had been polished and buffed; it was as neat as his own. Bill hung his jacket instead of tossing it on a chair, and when he melted butter for the popcorn he wiped the stove. He seemed less at home, more aware of where he set his glass down, less inclined to spill salt on the rug, though the house was otherwise unchanged. Even the family pictures were in their familiar places on the mantel,

Bill and Claudia with the kids in happier times. They struck Guy as creepy. The house might be the same, but it was so tidy it felt empty, and Guy's memory of the many evenings the four of them had spent in these same rooms filled that emptiness with absence. Taking turns staying here with the kids, Bill and Claudia seemed to have begun treating the house like a vacation rental, swishing out toilets and stacking the spotless dishes in the cabinets each time they left, in that elaborate veneer of manners that passes for being civil once love and habit turn to hostility. Despite the pretense of the photos, the house had been purged of personality, which expressed itself only in disorder. Guy tucked the observation away to pass along to Eva should she recover herself and ask.

"How's John Courtland?" Guy inquired.

"Good." Bill turned on the television. "He's got a girlfriend." The anger in Bill's voice had abated, and Guy could tell that Bill understood John's girlfriend boded well for him. He might not yet be thinking that if John could find happiness with a new girlfriend so someday would he—"My priority right now is the kids," he said at some point in the evening. "It wouldn't be fair to date." It might be too soon to move into the next stage of his separation, but clearly John's upturn in fortune had permitted him some glimmer of perspective, some sense that one day he too would move on.

For a while the game absorbed them. Bill had graduated from Duke, and Guy wanted to see Georgia kick some ACC ass. He declined Bill's offer of a beer (he would never drink a drop of alcohol before driving again); for a while after Bill made popcorn, Greg joined them in the den. At the end of the half Georgia was up by two.

"How are the kids doing?" Guy asked when Greg went to bed.

"So-so." Bill muted the TV for the commercial and placed his empty beer can inside the ravaged popcorn bowl, picking up a few stray kernels. "They're coming out of the initial shock, but it's going to be a long time before they can accept it, and with the holidays coming up...." He let the thought drift. "Claudia hardly has time to see them, she's so tied up with lover-boy—you'd think it would be enough that the kids are with me four nights a week, but half the time they're with her she's got a sitter." He seemed so resigned that only the last words betrayed the bitterness he still felt.

"That's rough."

"What about you?" Bill turned his head. The game had come back on, but he didn't restore the sound. "How are you doing?"

So he knew. He would. He was too good a citizen not to read the paper. What would he have thought when he read the latest? Whatever, he had invited Guy over and offered him a beer. Would you offer alcohol to someone you thought had killed a kid because he was drunk?

"I'm in a mess," Guy admitted.

"Is it going to work out?"

"I don't know. My lawyer keeps telling me to plead. I wouldn't have to go to jail."

"What happened?"

Guy told him. "But the thing is, I killed the boy—you can imagine how that feels. Everybody thinks you're garbage if you say it wasn't your fault. Sometimes I think I'm garbage. I killed a kid."

"That's a tough one. Is there anything I can do?"

"Thanks," Guy said, gazing around the room, which even in its neatened state had a shabby comfort he'd always liked, slip-covered furniture and tarnished brass lamps with yellowed shades. His eyes paused at a picture of Bill and the staff of the homeless shelter on a bookshelf near the TV. "You haven't had anything to do with the Montagnards in your volunteer work, have you?" He was curious. He didn't know anyone who knew any of Random's Montagnards. The letters to the editor would suggest everyone was in a flap over their presence, but as far as he could tell no one knew a thing about them. Except Eva. At least she wasn't bringing any more books home from the library.

"No. There's an interdenominational group that coordinated housing and employment."

"It seems funny the way Random could just swallow a whole group."

Bill splayed his fingers on the arm of the chair. "We live in the wrong neighborhoods, pal. This town's got a lot more diversity than you think."

Guy had learned that selling papers.

When Bill turned the sound back on Georgia was down by six, and they watched most of the rest of the game without conversation. "Good luck," Bill said when Guy got up to go minutes after Georgia lost. "If you think of anything—if you need a loan—just call. I'm really sorry."

Guy was so grateful for Bill's faith his voice went husky. "I appreciate that."

At the door the light from the nearby streetlamp cast a hard shadow that made Bill's face look haggard, and for a moment Guy wondered if Bill would trade his troubles for Guy's. It was an interesting question. Would he trade his troubles for Bill's? Apples and oranges. There was no comparison.

Eva was in bed by the time he got home, but even the next morning she didn't ask if Bill had said anything about Claudia, and Guy had to volunteer, "Bill seems pretty resigned. I don't think he even hopes he and Claudia will get back together."

"No, I don't suppose they will." She was going through Nick's closet, pulling outgrown clothes and tagging items for a yard sale, though surely she couldn't have a yard sale until they got back from Florida. They were leaving Sunday. Molly and Brian were flying into Jacksonville Monday afternoon. He didn't know whether he was happier about seeing his daughter or just getting away.

"He offered to loan me money."

"That was nice of him." She looked up, though she didn't say anything else. Weeding their possessions, choosing what to sell, seemed to be all she did while she was home, that and making phone calls, though the house was now so clean he thought she must get up to scrub it in the middle of the night. When she did speak, it was usually to suggest that he or Nick divest themselves of this or that, though he didn't have much to sell—the furniture was all hers, he considered, even the paintings and art deco lamp she'd given him, though he might claim his right of ownership if she tried to put those out for the scavengers. All he really had was books, but he didn't want to part with his books, why he wasn't sure. A few of them he might really want, but it wasn't as if he was ever going to sit down and read *The Four Quartets* again; he could hardly claim to need Eric Auerbach's *Mimesis* or *The Annotated Lolita.*

They weren't worth much, but it wasn't so much a question

of money as room, and he couldn't fault her for suggesting he go through them, knowing as she surely did that when he looked back on his years of grad school it was always with distaste, not so much for the experience itself as for the taint his unfinished dissertation gave them. Nor could he make much claim for sentimental value, for those special books—the tattered copy of *On the Road* that had steered him slipperily through his teens, the sturdy gray Scribner's paperbacks of Hemingway and *The Great Gatsby* that had turned him onto literature in college—had long since fallen apart or disappeared. He liked the smell of his books, cheap paper and glue mixed with the prickle of dust and mold, the used hardbacks' starchy buckram bindings. To sell them would be to cancel a part of his past, the years of his devotion to them, especially those years of grad school when, newly divorced, torn between the banquet a sexual revolution seemed to lay before him and the ache of missing Molly, he read long into the night, smoking cigarette after cigarette in the hoop of yellow light that seemed the only warm, indeed the only bearable, spot in his meager room. Like the family photos on Bill Whitt's mantel, his books were souvenirs, reminders of something that might have come to nothing, but was part of him all the same.

Finally she said, "Well, you should probably do whatever you think best." He supposed she meant about Bill Whitt's offer of a loan.

Eva had never liked the phone. As a gawky high school girl she had never learned the habit of languishing around the house in wait of the call that would confer her golden future. And because nothing in her youth had endowed the equipment with magic, throughout her adulthood she'd regarded the home telephone as functional at best, more often a nuisance, for when she did get a call she wanted, it always seemed to come while she was cooking or had just settled in to watch a movie. Briefly a few weeks ago, when it mattered, she had entertained the thought that Claudia might not have dropped her if she had called more frequently, though Claudia had never been much of a phone person either. Now she found herself making call after call, assembling a list of women who volunteered for this or that, trying to locate a place for H'nghai to stay, feeling out the city's resources for battered women. She wanted to place H'nghai safely out of Katu's reach before they went to Florida.

All kinds of plans occurred to her. She would tell Guy and Nick she wasn't going—and in this fantasy, Guy didn't ask why; it was an amicable agreement, he called her Christmas Day, and they chatted merrily, as if it were the most usual circumstance in the world for them to spend their holiday in separate cities. (But she wouldn't get to see Nick open his presents. If they could believe him, he still believed in Santa, and she needed to take him to the mall for his annual visit to the Claus before they left.) A better fantasy was the one in which she took H'nghai with them. Guy had no objections because the accident had never happened.

In these daydreams it wasn't Nick she watched opening presents Christmas morning, but H'nghai, who was as excited, as bright with wonder, as her brothers Bhan and Nuh. Shrieking, laughing, they tossed bows and box lids in the air, glossy red and green paper rained down on them like confetti. Nuh strummed a spangled electric guitar, Bhan eyed a bicycle parked beneath the tree, and H'nghai, a younger H'nghai, dressed a whole sorority of Barbie dolls in evening gowns and power suits, tennis shorts and scuba gear, stuffing their deformed feet into tiny ski boots and pink mules.

She never should have agreed to make the trip. It might be fine to say that if you were going to be in debt it hardly mattered what you owed, but when it came time to pay the bill you would have to scratch the money up one nickel at a time. Motel bills, airfare, Disney tickets, presents. They would have to get something for Curt and his wife and their kids, for her father-in-law and Barry. She hadn't bought a thing for Nick or Guy, and she supposed that she and Guy ought to have a talk about Nick's presents. Nick would understand their situation, but if he really did believe in Santa, they would be the ones to destroy childhood's best illusion. He *said* that he believed—what kind of sucker were they raising?

The only way she could go would be if H'nghai were safe. She called Betty Paxton, who gave her names of tutors. She called the Women's Center, who referred her to the Women's Shelter. She called the Grove Street Ministry, which ran a soup kitchen. She called the Department of Social Services.

Twice she went by the Buon Tos' apartment and stood on the front steps to talk with H'nghai, who refused to meet her eyes as she insisted she was fine, and Eva couldn't tell if she was still disappointed in Eva or just afraid. Twice more she went by without stopping—she was afraid to get H'nghai in trouble—but was too timid to keep cruising the driveway. Two boys who huddled over some kind of game stared as she drove by. A woman on a back stoop turned her head to follow the car. She felt like a teenager with a crush, spying on the boy who doesn't even know her name, strolling by his house, hoping for a glimpse of him tossing a football in the street or taking out the garbage, prepared to die if her sleuthing should be punished by the sight of him standing on his stoop with another girl. Only a few of the parked cars were as old as hers, and the row of colorful plastic bumpers reminded her of the dyed-to-match satin pumps teenaged girls used to wear to proms, as if with her rotting rocker panel and pitted chrome bumper, she'd come clanking to the waltz in a pair of rusty tap shoes.

The first time she talked to H'nghai, the girl bade her wait while she went inside and fetched the clothing to return to Tammi Courts.

"You take," she insisted, and Eva did, but when she returned the neatly folded bundle a nine- or ten-year-old girl who must have been Tammi's older daughter answered the door and accepted the garments.

"Tell your mother thank you," Eva said as the girl began to close the door. She could see the TV flickering inside the dark living room, and a naked Barbie lying near the door.

She bought Nuh a pair of Reeboks. She didn't know his size, but the store promised to exchange them. She put them on her credit card and hid the shoebox in her closet. An hour later she was assailed by second thoughts. The insurance company hadn't settled, Guy was being sued for half a million dollars, and here she was, trying to buy off the plaintiffs' son with a thirty-five dollar pair of Reeboks.

She wasn't, but it would look that way. Or maybe she was and didn't know it. Like her mother, saying in one breath she wasn't prejudiced and in the next that the young black clerk who waited on them in the drugstore was pretty, she had finer features than most colored.

Eva didn't mean to buy him off. He needed shoes, and he

might as well have the kind he wanted. She wasn't stupid enough to think she could have her conscience cleaned that cheap.

She didn't know what to get H'nghai. Clothes were out unless she bought maternity clothes, and they didn't seem like much of a present. Jewelry? H'nghai's silver earrings looked handmade, and Eva wondered if they were an example of Montagnard craft. If there were only a book to help her with her English, though Eva had come to consider her command of the language staggering. Nuh tutored her, H'nghai confided, drilling her on everything he learned in school now that Katu wouldn't let her go to English class herself.

Almost from habit, Eva started to buy Guy a book of essays about baseball, then put it back. Surely it was understood that they wouldn't exchange presents. She picked up the book again—it would do for her father-in-law—but set it down. She should make cookies or candy for everyone and save money. She could get Nick to help her bake. Maybe that was the way to teach him that Christmas wasn't about greed but sharing. They hadn't baked anything together in a long time. When he grew up, she was afraid all he would remember was how she had bitched about fishhooks in the rug. She wanted to do something fun together like they used to.

The third time she stopped to see H'nghai, there was a rounding in the girl's belly visible below the thin yellow sweater now stretched across her bra. More than two weeks had passed since she'd taken H'nghai to Dr. Eudy. She was over halfway through the pregnancy. By now she would have felt the baby move, that little blip so weak at first you could not be sure it wasn't gas. Surely Katu was aware of her thickening waist and swelling breasts. The thought of his hands on H'nghai's narrow flesh enraged her.

"The baby's beginning to show." Eva pantomimed by patting her own belly. "I wish I could take you out to lunch again," she said, remembering that Katu would not permit H'nghai to see her friends, and sure enough H'nghai gave an apprehensive glance over her shoulder. "It would be nice to have some time to visit."

H'nghai took another look over her shoulder. "Wait," she said and went inside. In a minute she was back with her jelly shoes, and she sat on the step to fit them on to her bare feet. The weather had warmed, as it often did in the weeks before Christmas, and she didn't need her parka.

Eva followed her as she moved quickly across the barren front lawn and turned a corner.

"Katu work night. Sleep day." She turned another corner and cut through a field beside a narrow creek toward the hill above Sibley Mills. "Like Vietnam Highland. Walk by river." H'nghai's mouth curved into a mischievous smile as a plastic soda bottle bobbing at the edge caught Eva's eye. "Not so beautiful, American river." When they reached the trestle supporting the dye pipe, H'nghai climbed the hill. From the top they looked down on the sawtooth rooftop of the factory. H'nghai sat on a cement slab beneath one of the pipe braces.

"I come here some time," she said.

"Are you taking your vitamins?" Eva asked.

H'nghai stretched one hand across her belly and arched her back to push the small mound out, then clapped the other hand to her mouth and giggled.

She did want to have the baby. For a moment it made Eva sad. "After Christmas, when I get back, it'll be time to take you back to Healthcare for your checkup."

Quickly H'nghai raised her head. "You go?"

"Just for Christmas, I'll be back before you know it."

H'nghai looked stricken.

"Just for a week," Eva promised, relieved that at least H'nghai seemed to have forgiven her lie.

At once it came to her. Katu might know that H'nghai was pregnant, but even so it would be harder for her to leave once she had the baby. She needed to leave now, before the baby was born, before he could hurt her again; she needed to leave before this weekend so that Eva could go to Florida. She wouldn't go to the shelter, and Eva had had no luck in finding anything else. The perfect, the obvious, temporary housing was Eva's house. It would be vacant for a week. She couldn't believe she hadn't thought of it before. She could wait to list the house till she got back and tell Guy she'd hired a housesitter.

Except he would want to know how she happened to find a Montagnard housesitter, *why* she had found a Montagnard housesitter. She had soothed her guilt over her betrayal by convincing herself he would never see the girl, never know. Her mind skipped ahead—she could call a volunteer to drive H'nghai to the house after they left; H'nghai could stay the week, and Guy would never have to guess that she had been there. What next, Eva wasn't sure, but she had a few days left to think. She waited a moment for her conscience to assail her, and she did feel a little ping, but she was feeling pings every day now, and at each one she felt less repentant and more reckless. Guy would forgive her. He was a compassionate man.

"Where go?"

"Florida."

H'nghai's eyes shone. "Miami Beach. Disney."

Eva couldn't help smiling. "We're going to Jacksonville to see my husband's brother. My stepdaughter's coming." She didn't want to admit that they were going to Disney. Selling their house to go to Disney World, how was that for values? It would be worth it if she could take H'nghai and Nuh, if she could hear their thrilled shrieks and watch them cruise the safe Disney jungle. Nuh would laugh his high-pitched hee-hee-hee and hide his face in embarrassed delight when Mickey Mouse shook his hand. Nick would have a good time and take it all for granted.

"You could help me while I'm gone." A Montagnard who had once lived in a communal longhouse would either understand the concept of housesitting instinctively or not at all, Eva thought. "We don't want our house to be empty, and I thought maybe you would stay there."

H'nghai was frowning.

"H'nghai, the baby's showing. You can't keep it a secret from Katu any longer, and when you have the baby it's going to be harder for you to leave. If you wait he could hurt the baby. And we really need someone to stay in the house. To protect it."

"Protect house?" H'nghai said, and Eva wondered if to her that meant patrolling with an AK-47.

"You wouldn't have to do anything. It's just to make it look like someone's home."

"For robber."

"Exactly." Eva was delighted.

H'nghai looked down. "I do for friend, but...."

Eva's great idea had made H'nghai feel guilty.

"Katu." Sadly H'nghai looked up. "Katu no want cheat."

Fuck Katu, Eva wanted to scream. She'd gotten the same answer from every department and agency she had called: unless the victim was willing.... "Please, H'nghai. It's not for us, it's for you. I'm afraid for you. He could kill you."

"Viet Congs do killing. Destroy our crop, take our animal. The way they do is just destroy our peoples."

"I know." Beside that, Eva supposed, all other danger paled. "But Katu could destroy you too. Even if he doesn't kill you, he'll make you feel like a whipped dog, you won't be able to leave him." She gazed over the factory roof and back at H'nghai.

"Save money. Get divorce."

"You need to leave him now. You can pay the bride price back later."

H'nghai rubbed her hands across her belly and arched her back again. "Big baby. Teach Katu lesson."

Eva saw Nick's fuzzy pink head with the soft spot in its skull as the nurse placed him in her arms. He had been a big baby—nine pounds—but had seemed so vulnerable and small.

"How can I go away and leave you with him?" H'nghai patted her belly again and didn't answer.

Chapter 17

At the last minute Guy accepted Bill Whitt's offer of a loan and paid Gordon Weems, in order not to have his case postponed. The hearing for probable cause was scheduled the morning of January 3, and though he hadn't thought the Dayco crew would know about his case, one of his co-workers surprised him by saying, "You better pay your lawyer, or he get a continuance on Rule 1." And what was Rule 1? "Rule 1 mean he defend you before he get paid he know he never see your money. These lawyers and these judges, man, they all in the same game." Maybe now that he'd coughed up his twenty thou, Weems would get his ass in gear. In Guy's view everything depended upon getting the police report sent over—it was still his hope that the D.A. had simply misread it, and he wanted to go to Florida knowing that his lawyer would be working.

He had never borrowed money from a friend, and he would rather not have, but pride was a luxury no longer within his budget. Though he thought Eva might object, she said nothing, and her silence made him feel more defensive than if she had accused him.

"It seemed like the only thing to do," he said.

"Whatever." Her voice sounded tired. She'd been working too hard, to get ready for the trip, he guessed, that and preparing the house for sale, something he kept forgetting, despite the possessions that kept departing or regrouping—he might close a closet door on a snarl of boots and mittens only to open it again and find a snug row of galoshes beneath a shelf stacked with pairs of gloves. But if Weems did his job—and Guy had paid him to—they wouldn't need to sell.

Not to be a drag on the vacation. That was Eva's New Year's resolution. Not only was she making it ahead, she would keep it in advance. By the time New Year's Day rolled around, she'd be done with self-improvement for the coming year. Except it wasn't funny. Guy was looking forward to the holiday, and though she couldn't have been more unhappy to be going, she didn't want to ruin his trip.

On Friday afternoon she picked Nick up at school and drove him through a sluggish gray rain to the mall, where they stood in line waiting to see Santa. Nick was ebullient: he didn't have to go back to school until next year. From the look of it, he had spent the day gobbling sweets. His mouth was sticky, his fingers black with a residue of peppermint and powdered sugar. The sugar had gone to his head, and in line he kept twitching and pulling on her like the younger children all around him. He'd jumped in a puddle in the parking lot, and his shoes squished against the terazzo floor. "It's hot in here,"he complained. "How come the line's so long?" She took his yellow slicker. He was more than a head taller than any other child there.

"I want a new bike and a pair of roller blades and a fly rod and a Super Mario game and some surprises," he told her.

"Well, sweetie." She had been so preoccupied with H'nghai she hadn't made time to speak with Guy. "First of all, that's an awful lot, and besides we're going...."

"What a chintzy prize," He turned his eyes to follow a family exiting the mall's North Pole, the children decked in paper antlers, this year's souvenir. Since when had he become so materialistic?

"I want a Cignal mountain bike," he said, "not one of those cheap bikes from Kmart."

"But, sweetie, if Santa brought you a bike in Florida, you wouldn't be able to get it home."

"We'll get a bike rack." He jumped in place. If he didn't calm down, he was going to fall and break his other arm. His unbuttoned flannel sleeve flapped against the cast. "Can I have a pretzel?" The mall smelled of wet clothing, unwashed hair, and caramel corn.

"You've had enough junk." He was twisting her wrist. "Honey, stand up and let go." He was acting like he was three, and she wondered, half angrily, if it was an act. He knew perfectly well there was no Santa. He went to public school; you couldn't tell her that some kid on the playground hadn't spilled the beans. "Besides, with your safety record no way is Santa going to bring you blades."

"Besides what?" he said.

"Huh?"

"You said 'besides.'"

"Did I?" She looked at the floor, tracked with muddy water. Outside it was so bleak the streetlights had come on at noon. When she looked up their former neighbor Kappie Kordemeier was standing in front of her, looking like Paddington in a yellow slicker just like Nick's with matching hat.

"Eva! How are you? I really miss the old block." She and her husband had moved up not out. Kappie glanced at Nick and lowered her voice. "I was so sorry to read about Guy in the paper. I never knew he had a drinking problem."

Eva froze.

"Anyway, I hope things work out," Kappie said, giving the words a deeper inflection. "A lot of people really turn their lives around through AA."

As Kappie turned to go, Eva's paralyzed voice returned with a flush of heat. "My Husband Does Not Have A Drinking Problem."

"Mom." Nick was tugging on her arm.

"What?" She looked down at him, her face still hot.

"Move up," he said, and she looked up to see the gap that had opened in front of them as the line trooped forward. "What's the matter?"

She was scowling. Grimly she swallowed the acid that had risen to her throat. "Nothing." The line shuffled another few steps, and the mall's oceanic babble swam past her ears to the domed skylight's roaring echo. The rain trickling down the panes turned the light inside a sickly chartreuse that made the mall seem cramped and crowded. "I hate to see Christmas so commercialized, that's all." She turned to him angrily. "I thought you learned something making those cookies for your teachers. It's about the spirit...." Was she going to ask him to put Christ back in Christmas after she'd dropped out of church? When she glanced at him again, a funny look had come over his face, a pruny stomachache verdigris pulling at his features. "What?"

"I forgot to give them. They're in my cubby."

"Oh Nickie," she was about to sigh, but he looked so young and remorseful that she hugged him instead.

He eyed her warily. "You're not mad?"

"No, I'm not mad." So he was irresponsible. His honesty was touching.

"Boy, that's a relief." As the line moved up he took a sailing leap forward. "I thought you were going to tell me I couldn't have a new bike for Christmas."

But he couldn't have a new bike. "Sweetie," she said.

It was his turn. Though his feet hung to the floor, Santa didn't flinch when Nick hopped onto his knee. "What happened to your arm?" Santa asked, and Nick held his orange cast out for inspection.

"I fell off a bridge."

Santa was impressed. He was a young Santa with wire-rim glasses and a hint of auburn sideburns beneath his snow-white beard. "Did it hurt?"

"Yes and no."

"And have you been good this year?"

"So-so," Nick said, "but I'm improving."

"Good. What would you like me to bring you?"

Eva strained to hear.

"Well, first of all, I'm going to be in Florida," Nick said. "Do you need the address?"

Santa glanced up at her. Did you get that, Mama? his look seemed to say.

"You better write this down. I want a new bike, and I don't want a cheap one, I want a pair of roller blades and a Super Mario game and a fly rod and some new Hardy Boys books and...."

Santa, it seemed, had the same objections Eva did. If Nick couldn't have it all, what would he want most? This Santa was a pro who was murmuring something about his obligations to all the other boys and girls when Nick cut in. "Hey. If you're broke, all you gotta do is say so."

Eva turned away so Nick wouldn't see the tears that sprang

to her eyes. In a second he was back, sans the complimentary paper antlers, hopping on his heels in what she assumed was some sort of super-hero's footwork. "Check it out." He thrust his cast out like a sword. "I got Santa's autograph. Pretty cool, huh?" And he went dancing for the escalator with her trailing, his size 14 yellow slicker bundled in her arms.

The next morning she drove one last time to the Buon Tos'.

The weather had improved, and Nuh was in the yard, squatting in the mud, playing with a group of younger boys. When he saw her, he flung his hand up in a wave and called, "Missy Ferrin." She wondered if he knew that his parents had filed suit against her husband. If H'nghai knew, she hadn't said so, and Eva hadn't wanted to ask. She and Guy had not told Nick though in the Central Highlands children his age worked the swiddens, they hunted and fought the Vietnamese alongside their parents. From the time they rode their parents' backs in slings they were part of the community.

Nuh separated himself from the group while the other children gaped. Each time she drove into the alley that ran behind the Montagnard apartments, she couldn't get over the sensation that the sealed windows were really eyes. She was so conspicuously foreign.

"Hello, Nuh." She smiled as she reached into her shopping bag and held out the shoebox wrapped in red foil. "I brought you a Christmas present."

"For me?" He thanked her profusely, all the while darting looks at the box.

"You can open it," she said. She had bought one size larger than Nick's. "If they don't fit, we can exchange them." She had a present for H'nghai too, though her real mission was to deliver her card. Inside the card was a key to her house and a hundred dollar bill she'd borrowed against her Visa, along with directions and the phone number of a volunteer who'd agreed to give H'nghai a ride. Not until she'd placed the card in H'nghai's hand would she be able to concentrate on her resolution not to spoil the trip.

She had brought a shopping bag full of presents, along with a turkey and two tins of cookies and candy. She felt confidant that H'nghai would not reveal her secret; she planned to let the family think she was a volunteer with Christian Relocation Services, which if she stretched a bit was true. It was hard to believe that less than three weeks had passed since Carole Eisen had called to ask if she would drive H'nghai to the doctor.

For a minute Nuh eyed the wrappings; then with a whoop of delight that stabbed her heart, he ripped through the paper and tore the lid off the box.

There was a moment of silence while the other children gathered. A wad of tissue floated to the ground as Nuh held up one clean white shoe, his face wreathed with joy. "Reebok," he proclaimed. Handing the box to one of the children, he lifted the other shoe. Then he sat on the still damp sidewalk to try them on, meticulously stringing the laces through their virgin holes. He took a few cautious steps, looking down his legs at first one foot and then the other. He pranced. "Reebok," he said again and threw his arms around Eva. "Thank you, Missy Ferrin, thank you."

"You're welcome. If they don't fit...."

Fear hollowed his face. "Fit," he insisted. The children admired his feet as a spasm of nausea closed her throat. She felt like the ugly American, no better than the owner of a deathtrap factory delivering some trinket to the family of the worker his negligence had killed, accepting their thanks as he collected their signatures on the receipt that declared the debt paid in full.

"Is H'nghai home?"

He ran ahead of her to the back door and shouted up the stairs before she could warn him not to call her Mrs. Ferrin.

Inside a small, wiry man with lank black hair to his shoulders was smoking a cigarette and watching TV. He had a long, bumpy face and thick features, and he watched the screen through heavy-lidded eyes. Katu. He had to be. He was too young to be H'nghai's father. She couldn't raise her eyes above the cigarette stuck between his lips.

Nuh had run upstairs. She stood at the edge of the room waiting, but Katu didn't look up. As soon as Mrs. Buon To came down the stairs she said something sharp to him in Vietnamese or Rhadé—at least it sounded sharp, though to Eva's ear the language always sounded emphatic. Then, as H'nghai too came down, half hiding behind her mother, the woman turned to Eva. Her broad smile filled Eva with relief. Nuh hadn't betrayed her.

"Hello. My name is Eva Summer, I volunteer with Christian Relocation Services, and I wanted to bring your family a few Christmas gifts." Did they celebrate Christmas? Eva wondered. She had never asked H'nghai what religion the Buon Tos practiced.

When the woman inclined her head toward H'nghai, H'nghai spoke to her in Rhadé. Nuh too spoke in Rhadé as he lifted first one foot and then the other to show off his shoes. Only Katu didn't speak, but peered around his mother-in-law at the TV. His small yellow teeth slanted inward, and the drooping eyelids made him look stoned. Underneath the odor of tobacco in the room, Eva could detect ginger and garlic.

The woman motioned for Eva to sit and hurried into the kitchen. In a minute she came back with a porcelain mug that she handed Eva with a gesture for her to drink.

Eva took a tentative sip of what turned out to be grape Kool-Aid. "Thank you. It's very refreshing."

The woman conferred with H'nghai, and when she turned back she smiled.

"My mother say you welcome," H'nghai said. "Very kind."

Eva wasn't sure what to do with the mug. Katu's ashtray rested on the arm of his long velvet sofa; she sat on the other, upholstered with plaid Herculon, and finally, after making sure the bottom was dry, she placed her empty mug beside her on the floor. She stole another look at Katu. He wore jeans and a tee shirt pulled tight across his narrow belly. He was small to seem so menacing, but his arms and chest looked hard with muscle.

She emptied her shopping bag to pull the turkey, wrapped in double plastic, from the bottom. Pink water had pooled in the inside bag, and in her hands the cold bird was clumsy. "Can I put this somewhere?" she asked, but first Mrs. Buon To, H'nghai, and Nuh had to poke at the plastic and exclaim.

"Too much my mother say," H'nghai reported. She had been washing something upstairs; her hands were still wet, her sleeves rolled up her arms. A cotton kerchief bound her hair.

Katu had not moved, except to put his cigarette out. Now he said something to H'nghai that caused her eyes to darken and went upstairs. Nuh was nosing in the pile of gifts beside the shopping bag. Eva gave his mother the tins of candy and cookies she and Nick had made. Next were the packages she'd wrapped for the men, a muffler she'd found in perfect condition at the thrift shop and a tie she'd bought two years ago for Guy, a beautiful silk paisley he'd never worn. She'd been disappointed to think he didn't like it; now he'd never miss it. "For your husbands," she murmured, setting the packages beside her on the sofa, hoping H'nghai would not call Katu back. She didn't see the baby. "You have a little one?" she asked, as she held out a pristine stuffed lamb that Nick had long ago rejected. "Baby?"

H'nghai glanced at her stomach as Eva pantomimed the baby riding in Mrs. Buon To's shawl.

"Friend baby," H'nghai explained. "We take care."

Eva handed another package to Mrs. Buon To. Both she and H'nghai bent over it, conferring excitedly, and then Mrs. Buon To draped the long silk scarf over her arm and held it up. It had been Eva's favorite. She and H'nghai exclaimed, and H'nghai reached her hand up to touch her kerchief, then touched her mother's long smoky gray hair and laughed. Her mother disappeared into the kitchen. When she came back she presented a flowered china saucer to Eva.

"I can't take this," Eva protested. "It's very generous, but it belongs to your dishes."

"Must take," H'nghai said.

There was no way out of it. "Thank you. It's beautiful." She had only a small box and the card left.

When she gave H'nghai the box, the girl looked down. The gift seemed to make her sad, and Eva realized she was embarrassed not to have a gift for Eva. She glanced upstairs, and before she would open it, she too went into the kitchen and came back with a ruby-colored shot glass shaped like a beer stein. "You take," she said. Only when she was satisfied that Eva liked it did she untie the red ribbon.

Inside was a sterling silver hair clip crafted by the jewelry maker at Gardell. It was more expensive than Eva could afford; she'd traded a small lithograph from the guest room for it.

"Oh!" H'nghai cried, turning it this way and that. A slender silver bone fit through an intricate filigree cage.

"It's for your hair," Eva explained, and H'nghai's left hand flew to her kerchief. She pulled it off and deftly knotted her hair in the back, then fastened the silver bone through it. Again she glanced upstairs. She turned her head this way and that. After a minute Eva understood that she wanted to look in the mirror, but didn't want to go up. Eva wondered what Katu had said to her.

"You look beautiful," Eva said.

H'nghai kept touching her hair. "Thank you. I love this thing." Eva wanted to give her the card, but was afraid that H'nghai would open it in front of her mother. Nuh had gone outside. The women sat together, but H'nghai seemed shy in front of her mother, and after a few minutes, the mother's silent smile became unnerving.

"Not too much English word," H'nghai explained.

Eva stood. "I have to go anyway." She fingered the envelope tucked in her pocket. "Maybe you could walk me out?""

H'nghai glanced up the stairs. When they reached the sidewalk, Eva said, "I have a card for you, a Christmas card."

"Away in a Manger, Baby Jesus, Silent Night." H'nghai looked solemn. Eva was startled. "Where did you learn about Jesus?"

"Evangelical church." She looked down. "Katu not want

me go." The Katu believed in human sacrifice, H'nghai had confided.

"You worshipped Jesus in Vietnam?"

"Many spirit in Vietnam. Aê Diê, Aê Du, Yang Hruê, Yang Mlan, Yang Liê. All spirit. Jesus. God."

"And are there many spirits here, are...?" She couldn't pronounce the names.

"Spirit everywhere."

"When I come back, will you tell me more? I want to know about your life in Vietnam."

"Very beautiful, Vietnam," H'nghai said. "Very different, very hard, like that."

Eva reached into her pocket for the card. "This is a secret—you know what that word means, secret?"

H'nghai laid a finger at her lips.

"That's right."

H'nghai slit the envelope. As she opened the card both the key and bill fell out, and Eva scooped them from the sidewalk.

"This is to my house; it opens the door. That—" Eva pointed to the phone number written inside the card—"that's the telephone number of a woman named Maggie Davis. She can drive you to my house if you change your mind, if you...." Eva glanced at the second story windows of the apartment. "It's a safe place where you can stay."

H'nghai was turning the bill Eva had returned to her over in her hand. "Dollar."

"A hundred dollars. You need to hide it where no one else can find it."

H'nghai looked confused. "You give me hundred dollar?"

"I want you to have it. You may need it."

"Too much." Tears had come into H'nghai's eyes. "I give you nothing."

"That's not true," Eva said.

Guy had known as soon as he saw his father that he would not tell him about the accident; he was undecided whether he would confide in Molly, but he wanted some time with her. Though he didn't want to worry her, he wanted to close the distance between them. He wanted to feel she was his daughter again, even though he had to suppress a knee-jerk reaction that told him she looked like a freak. Her beautiful dark hair had been cut short as a man's, nearly a buzz with one long forelock and the whole of it dyed an ugly yellow; she had a nose ring and a tattoo. Brian wore an earring. "Holy cow, what happened to you?" had been the first words from his father's mouth, and Curt's new wife, Sherri, kept staring as if she were afraid they were going to rob her house. "Better mind your p's and q's," the old man confided to Guy. "Your brother's gone and married a teetotalling junior leaguer."

Still, even with the cropped yellow hair there was a nubile roundness to Molly's features, a ripe liquidity, that recalled his little girl. He'd hoped to spend the morning with her, but Sherri wanted to show everyone something called the Riverwalk, and as usual his dad was taking over.

"You girls go see it," the old man said. "Us men are going to shoot pool."

"I think Molly wants to see the beach," Eva suggested, and Guy looked at his daughter. "You want to go to the beach?" he asked.

"I'll shoot pool."

"I want to play pool," Nick said. Curt's new stepson Hunter was ten, but something between him and Nick hadn't jelled. Hunter had hugged the transformer to his radio-operated car as if he were afraid that Nick would steal it and gone out to the driveway to play with it alone. "Just think about Disney World," Guy had whispered to Nick in the kitchen. He felt for Curt. Both Hunter and his sister seemed spoiled.

"Hell yes, we're going to shoot pool," his father said. He turned to his granddaughter. "Sorry, sugar. No ladies allowed."

Molly looked a little teed. In any other circumstance Eva might have bristled too, but she was used to Guy's father, and on these family trips she tended to enjoy the time to herself his father's manly excursions provided. Guy was the one with objections. He'd flown his daughter in from Minnesota because he wanted to be with her.

"In the afternoon, I thought maybe we'd drive down to St. Augustine," Sherri said to Eva. "I'm sure Molly would enjoy St. Augustine. They've got such nice antique shops."

"Now you're talking," the old man said. "You gals go shopping."

"Eva?" Sherri said. "Molly?"

"I wouldn't mind seeing St. Augustine," Molly said, "but...."

"There you are. She wants to go. How about we make a little wager, boys?"

Someone, Guy thought, ought to warn his son-in-law. His father was a hustler, and besides that he cheated. His father's cheating used to make Guy so mad he would spend half the holiday fuming, until Eva said, "For God's sake, Guy, it's only a game." It was no wonder the old man insisted on his male-only rituals; he kept his dirty little secret among his sons, and his daughters-in-law adored him.

"Brian's never seen St. Augustine." Molly's voice was doubtful. "Isn't it supposed to be like really quaint or something?"

The old man turned his hawk's eye on Brian. He was willing to overlook the earring in light of the Twins cap seemingly glued to Brian's head. "This here's a Twins fan. He doesn't want to go shopping."

This was it, Guy thought, Brian's make-or-break. He didn't answer, and Guy's father took silence as consent.

"Maybe later you and I can shoot some pool," Guy offered Molly, knowing that later there'd be dinner, and then his father would want to play poker, and the day after that would be Christmas. Maybe when they went to Disney World. She and Brian weren't flying back till Friday. But the issue for her, he saw, was not that she was being kept from her father; it was that her husband was being kept from her. They were still so young, still so besotted that they felt unmoored whenever the other left the room. He looked at Eva, who was sitting in a rattan chair, staring absently through the window at Hunter's radio car circling in the driveway and tried to remember when he and she had been like that, so dependent on each other that without the other in sight each felt like half a person, and with something like a start he realized never. But of course they'd been older.

New Year's Resolution kept, and it wasn't even the new year yet. Eva was as improved as she was going to get for the next twelve months, maybe ever. Working for a college had spoiled her for the little victories of self-help and voluntary privation that other people strove for, the six-week anniversaries of swearing off caffeine or sweets, the courses in aerobics or Tai Chi. To her the language of resolution tasted of committee meetings, stewed in the same pot with self-studies and institutional statements of missions and goals. As a result, she couldn't remember a single resolution she had made since she decided she wanted to have Nick and together she and Guy quit smoking. But now she had actually made a vow to herself and kept it: she'd been a good sport on the trip. In fact, she'd behaved so well that on the drive home Guy remarked, "You had a good time, and that's good. You deserved it."

It was an observation, not a question, and if she'd told him it was an effort, he would think she meant being with his family, steeling herself not to mind when his dad took over or his daughter grew nostalgic about events that had happened while he and Pauline were married, when Barry reneged on his promises to Nick, or Curt began parroting Rush Limbaugh and got into a shouting match with his Democratic father—although those things never fazed her; it was Guy they bothered.

It was an effort not to get along with his family but to remain silent when they asked how everything was and he said fine, and then to be obliged to echo. It was an effort not to object when he insisted on taking everyone out to dinner not to ask if he'd told his dad about the accident, not to inquire if he'd spoken to Molly, though to be fair she didn't think Guy had had one moment alone with his daughter. But most of all it was an effort not to call home to see if H'nghai had taken refuge.

And now, as Guy paid for their gas beneath the bleak white sky that was edging on to evening and she and Nick resettled in the car for the tiresome last leg of the journey, the stunted highways that took them from the interstate at Florence on into

North Carolina and Random, she was out of energy to try. She would maintain that part of the bargain she had made with herself to keep what she was thinking private, but she could no longer keep from thinking, and if that turned her silent or drew shadows across her face, too bad. Because once he pulled into their driveway all bargains were off, and she could no longer keep from wondering if H'nghai would be there and if she was what in the world Eva would say to explain herself to Guy.

The odds were against it. There had been the flashing eyes and emphatic determination to divorce—in the many conversations they had had, H'nghai had never expressed the least affection for her husband; she was not like the abused wife whose real desire isn't to escape the man who hits her but to stay and have him stop, the woman who loves the man but hates his act; she didn't love the man and never had. But she loved her parents and her people, and she was determined not to displease or dishonor either one. Could such a tricky compact be brought about with a hundred dollars? Eva had no idea what price a bride would fetch, but she doubted that Katu would be placated by a refund.

He was jealous—H'nghai had said so. Eva had no way to know if he cared only for his ego or if, in his way, perhaps he loved her. Either way, he was not likely to take the money and let her go, and if she couldn't buy her freedom for a hundred dollars, she couldn't buy it at any price. On the day before their trip, when his mother-in-law had seemed to speak sharply to him in Eva's presence, she'd been pleased to think the mother might not like him. But if his in-laws knew he abused their daughter and did not intervene, then they were unlikely to let her leave either. She couldn't tell what H'nghai had meant when she asked if the parents knew. All she knew was that the father wanted to preserve his culture. It was an admirable idea, but Eva didn't know enough about the culture to know what that entailed. She thought of the African tribes that practiced female genital mutilation, the Chinese women hobbled by their bound feet, the neck rings stacked on the Padaung women featured in the St. Augustine Ripley's. Those were cultural practices too.

Nick had bought a magazine at the gas stop and despite the creeping dusk was reading in the back seat. The sight of his bent head in the visor mirror nipped at her heart. Guy always left the Christmas shopping to her. She had given a hundred dollars to H'nghai and a fishing lure, a couple of Hardy Boys novels, and a book about the Seminoles to her son. The trip, she had explained, was his big present, Santa's present to them all, but it was one thing for Nick to tell the Santa at the mall all he had to do was say that he was broke and quite another for Santa to claim poverty to Nick Ferrin while he lavished a trampoline, CD players, and computer games on Nick's step-cousins. Only a week ago yesterday, after visiting the Buon To apartment, had she broken down and bought the lure. By the time she'd brought the subject up with Guy, who said, "You can't deny an eight-year-old boy his Christmas," it was too late to do more than pick up the book about the Seminoles at the bookshop in the Castillo de San Marcos. She was proud of him. He hadn't uttered a word of complaint when Hunter and his sister Stephanie flaunted their new wealth without inviting him to share. Curt was going to have his hands full with those kids. Even Guy had confided, "I think Curt may be in over his head," and she'd agreed, so determined to be pleasant that she didn't even think *we're in over our heads.* All that talk about real estate with Curt's realtor wife, and only neutrally, as if it were an errand she had to run, did she remember that she and Guy were selling their house. But now that they were nearly home it all came back: she had to finish getting it ready and call Ravenna Mink. Spring semester began next week. At least her paycheck would be deposited on Tuesday. Friday was Guy's court date. He had paid his lawyer, but they might need a short-term loan to tide them over—she would have taken care of it before Christmas if she hadn't been so distracted.

Guy turned the headlights on, and she checked the visor mirror. Nick had put his magazine down and was staring out the window at the dejected winter landscape slipping by them. He might still hope there would be a bicycle waiting to surprise him in their garage, and for a moment she wished there were. What was three hundred dollars compared to the nearly three thousand that they would owe as soon as the VISA statement came? But what if they had given him a bike and then went bankrupt? Probably Guy had been right to insist upon the trip. A vacation couldn't be repossessed.

"Is he asleep?" Guy glanced at her, then back at the road.

In a reverie, maybe. "Huh uh," she said.

"Well, it was a good trip," he said again. "It was nice to have everybody together."

"Umhm." With everyone together, it had been hard to squeeze in a Christmas call to her mother, alone for the holiday in Baltimore. And then when Eva reached her, Ruby didn't want to let her go.

"Molly and Brian seem to get along."

Molly and Brian had strolled the main street of Disney with each other's hands in their back pockets; even Nick had asked why they were always kissing; when either was out of the room the other cast lost glances at the doorway, so exhibitionistically in love they seemed joined at the hip. The Courtlands had been like that. Guy should realize it meant nothing.

But the kids had enjoyed the trip. "Thanks, Daddy," Molly had said at the airport. "We had a great time." Brian had been more formal, and Eva realized that some of his reticence with them came of not knowing how to address Guy. When she joined the family she'd had it easy—everyone called her father-in-law Pop; the name had stuck from his coaching days, and by extension everyone in Ardsley Park had called Guy's mother Mom. Guy called her mother Ruby; she liked to joke that Guy was her favorite son-in-law, though it was the same joke she used to make to Brooks. She wondered if her parents had thought she and Brooks got along. Probably her father-in-law never thought about how Guy and Eva got along; he didn't have to, just as she hadn't had to a mere few months before. That was what she had tried to explain to her mother at Thanksgiving, that she had been so happy to believe she and Guy had reached that place where they trusted not only each other but in the thing itself. There had been such comfort in not having to think about her marriage; it brought a kind of peace that bestowed a freedom that allowed her to feel whole. Or maybe that was just a fancy way of saying they had taken their relationship for granted. For now here they were, back to where every marriage started, wondering if he meant this or she thought that, hoarding secrets, fretting moods and second guessing—oh, but she wanted to say, we're too old for this, we're *tired,* we don't have the novelty of a new union or its relentless daily passion.

"Molly and Brian can't seem to keep their hands off each

other, if that's what you mean," she said.

"I know. They shouldn't do that in public—it's embarrassing."

"They're kids."

"You and I ought to act like kids when we get back," he said.

She rewarded him with a half-laugh. "Is that your idea of a seduction?"

"Well, it's been a while." His voice quickened in defense, but then it softened. "We should make more time for each other."

Startled—she had slipped back into her thoughts of H'nghai—she looked up. "I agree."

As they left the highway and entered Random, she tensed with a familiar apprehension, the traveler's dread that she will round the last corner to see nothing but blackened studs where her house had stood. At first she couldn't see; Guy turned the corner, and ahead in the place where their house should be was a dark gap amid the twinkle of white Christmas lights wound through the neighbor's dogwoods. Then they were braking in the driveway and the solid walls loomed up before them. H'nghai wasn't there.

Chapter 18

It was too late to see H'nghai on the night that they got back, and in the morning, when Eva drove to the Buon Tos' apartment, no one was home. There were only a few cars in the lot, and the courtyards were empty. Like all the faithless, Eva was startled to recall that on Sunday mornings other people went to church. But H'nghai wouldn't be at church; Katu didn't let her go.

For a while Eva drove aimlessly, hoping the Buon Tos would return. Even if she saw H'nghai entering the back door, she would feel better. Just some sign of normalcy, evidence that nothing terrible had happened. She would be willing to wait all day, but Guy was playing basketball this afternoon, and she had to get home for Nick.

Though the air wasn't really cold, a low cloud cover turned the daylight dingy, making her feel trapped inside a long and dreary winter. She saw no one on the streets, and the houses that she passed, small shingled bungalows like the one Tammi Courts lived in, looked deserted for the season, the yards bleached and empty, no sign of life behind the curtains. They reminded her of the houses that the neighbors on East Lombard Street in Baltimore moved up to when they fled the inner city, though the houses of her memory were so new their lawns had barely sprouted, those treeless suburban streets stretching on as far as she could see, whereas the long brick ranches and pastel tri-levels of the upper middle class had seemed confined to the few looped terraces and courts that her mother still asked Guy to drive them through each time they visited, always saying, as if she'd just thought of it, "Want to see how the other half lives?" It embarrassed Eva the more because for years now she had occupied a world in which the reverse seemed true, the domain of the rich and comfortable flung so far and wide that everyone within her horizon seemed to have money. Her experience of Random was every bit as skewed by class as her sense of Baltimore.

She went back to the apartments. As she sat idling in the empty lot, a dented station wagon pulled up. The driver got out and scanned the complex.

"Hello," she cried in a hoarse, briny voice when Eva approached. "Are you here to pick up the stuff for the auction?"

"Auction?" Eva studied the woman's freckled face. Her eyelashes were so pale her eyes looked naked beneath her fizz of long strawberry blonde hair. Eva guessed her to be somewhere near her own age.

"For the festival. It's a fundraiser for the Longhouse Project. They're trying to raise money to build a community center."

What a good idea, Eva thought, gazing around the apartments, which looked even more rundown beneath the soiled sky. "I wondered where everybody was."

"You should come." The woman extended a rawboned hand. "My name's Shirley. My husband was with the 'yards at An Lac."

Eva introduced herself as Shirley surveyed the apartments again. "Do you know which door is Thih's?"

"I don't."

"Well, I'll find it. It's nice to meet you." Shirley started up the walk. "It starts at noon. There's directions in yesterday's paper."

When Eva got home she asked Nick if he'd like to go to a festival. Though she found the directions in one of the papers May Pleasants had saved, she had to stop twice to ask as she drove the uncharted maze of country roads. She'd begun to think that they would just have to give up and go home when she spotted a sign and turned into a lane lined along both sides with cars.

"This sure is a funny place for a festival," Nick observed. He craned his neck for a ferris wheel. Tatters of last summer's kudzu fluttered in the trees overhead. "Will they have rides?"

"I'm not sure," Eva said. "It's a fundraiser for the Montagnards—the people who came over from Vietnam. There'll be native foods and entertainment."

"What kind of entertainment?"

"We'll have to find out. They're trying to raise money to build a longhouse."

"A longhouse?" His eyes brightened. He knew about longhouses from *The Indian in the Cupboard.* "Cool. Are they going to build it here?"

"I don't know. But this is a wildlife club. Maybe there's a lake."

The sound of children at play floated toward them as they crested the hill and saw the cement block pavilion in a small clearing, where a swirl of children ran through the pungent smoke billowing from a pig cooker parked in back. At the edge of the clearing a group of Montagnard men sat on stacks of cement blocks, smoking cigarettes. Eva looked for Katu.

"I don't see any lake."

"Well, you don't have a rod anyway." Satisfied Katu wasn't there, Eva opened the door to the shelter.

"You found us." Shirley looked up from the table where she was collecting money. Eva's eyes went to the flags hung against the opposite wall, an American flag flanked by a red, white, and green striped banner with an elephant in the center and the same black and white POW/MIA flag she'd once seen at a tent near the Vietnam Memorial in Washington. She was eager to see the community in action and taste the native foods, though as she moved into the crowd she felt even shyer that she did at the apartments.

"Look at that dude," Nick said, and Eva looked around to spot a tall, thin, middle-aged man in long gray braids and a leather headband, an American after all, talking to a Montagnard teenager gotten up like a prom queen. Her eyes traveled to the makeshift stage, where a pop-rock band of Montagnards was accompanying a Montagnard woman in a tight red cocktail dress who was singing a Western-style torch song, though the lyrics sounded Asian. Behind the band a hand-lettered white sheet welcomed friends, neighbors, and Dega associates, beside it yet another banner, black with a red shield ornamented with a skull clad in a green beret. The American was wearing what looked to be an army vest covered with buttons, and as Eva began to spot a few other Americans it occurred to her that they must all be veterans of the Special Forces. "If there aren't any rides, what are we supposed to do?"

Looking down, Eva discovered that she had instinctively placed a hand on Nick's shoulder. "I'm not sure. There's a band." Nick gave a disgusted snort, and there was a burst of applause from the crowd of men gathered near the stage as the singer finished and a Montagnard emcee thanked her in English, having mastered not only the language but also the dulcet supper club intonations. Across the room two older Montagnard men with their arms around each other's shoulders were performing some sort of skipping dance step. Blankets were spread on the floor around the room's perimeter, where groups of women sat eating off paper plates. It looked like a big family picnic moved inside for inclement weather. She searched for H'nghai.

Nick tugged at her arm. "Mom! Look at the machete."

The emcee appeared to be announcing the auction. Beside him a large American in an army shirt and green beret held his arms aloft, in one hand the sheath and in the other the long blade.

"Is he selling it?" Nick's eyes were huge, and for a minute Eva thought he meant to ask if they could buy it. At one time he'd been obsessed with weapons, probably because she and Guy had forbidden toy guns, though when they reversed themselves on the saturation theory, his fascination only grew—for years Eva found pistols and rubber knives beneath the sofa cushions and dismembered action figures in the oven; but just when she'd resigned herself to the idea of a military career, his interest suddenly abated. The fixation on guns had waned as the obsession with fishing grew. She and Guy had both been relieved when he failed to develop a companion interest in hunting.

"I'm not sure what he's doing," Eva said as the hippie vet approached them.

"Hi there. Isn't this great? I found out about it on the Net and rode down from New Jersey." Eva stared at his vest, amazed to hear the festival had a web site. The buttons and patches were all about POWs and MIAs. "I'm with Project Homecoming." He produced a pamphlet from a leather pouch at his waist. "We know the POWs are alive. All we have to do is get one out, and the government's going to have to quit lying to the American people."

Eva turned the pamphlet over. "Were you with the Special Forces?"

"Yes ma'am. I trained strikers at Dak Pek. The 'yards are great people. How do you know them?"

"I have a friend." Eva was still searching the crowd for H'nghai. Together they looked toward the stage. The auctioneer had dispensed with the machete and seemed to be demonstrating some kind of martial arts maneuver. "You say they have a website?"

The vet chuckled. "They've come a long way. The first one of these festivals the doorprize was an AK-47."

Eva fingered the ticket stubs in her pocket.

"I'm hungry," Nick said. "You said there'd be food."

"It's outside," Eva said, but he made no move to leave her. Again she scanned the room
for H'nghai.

"Aren't you coming with me?"

She led Nick outside.

"It looks like American food to me," he said as he surveyed the table.

It was American food: hunks of pork and barbecued chicken, baked beans in a big foil pan, bags of buns and bottles of mustard and ketchup, the only sign that it was not the menu for a Fourth of July picnic a crock pot full of rice and a bowl with tiny peppers floating in clear liquid.

At one end of the table there was a warmer full of hot

dogs, and at the other she found a hot box full of sweet potatoes. Behind them the dessert table was piled with brand names, boxes of Dunkin' Donuts and sacks of Oreos, Skittles, and Starlight Mints. Nick ignored everything except the hot dogs and desserts.

Eva had just picked up a plate when H'nghai appeared, carrying a large plastic bowl full of marinated vegetables.

"H'nghai, I'm so glad to see you!" Eva cried.

H'nghai's mouth stretched into a wide smile. Her glossy black hair was knotted into the silver ornament, and she wore a pastel sweater over a slim knit skirt that showed her pregnancy. "My friend!" Her face had healed, leaving shiny pink patches of skin, like a streaky sunburn, but she was all right, she looked fine.

"How you know festival?"

Nick pulled at Eva's sleeve. He was holding his full plate. "I'm hungry." Below the dirty orange cast his hand was filthy.

"Well, then eat," Eva said impatiently and then to H'nghai, "It was in the newspaper. I...." Nick was yanking her arm now.

"Aren't you going to eat with me?"

"In a minute," Eva said. "H'nghai, this is my son Nick."

"Neek." She laughed. "Big boy." Her eyes dropped to Eva's empty plate, and she waved her hand at the table. "Come. Eat."

"What about you?" Eva asked, but H'nghai waved her on.

"Eat," she repeated. "Good," she observed at each selection, "very good" when Eva ladled a generous portion of the chili sauce over her pork and rice. When she was satisfied, she escorted them to a third table at the back of the shelter, crowded with jugs of lemonade and Coke. Eva was surprised to see a keg. She glanced at the men stationed on top of the cement blocks, smoking cigarettes and drinking out of plastic cups. She didn't see Katu.

Eva poured some lemonade. "I went to your apartment this morning, but I guess everybody was here already."

"Like in Highland, women prepare meal, do like group, finish quick."

Inside she took them to a blanket spread on the floor, where Eva had somehow missed Mrs. Buon To. She seemed to be with an extended family of women, who murmured among themselves, not speaking to Eva though they looked up and smiled so frequently that Eva couldn't eat for smiling back. They didn't speak English, she realized. Women, staying home, wouldn't learn the language. H'nghai was an exception, no thanks to her husband.

Gradually the women's attention drifted away. Eva was glad because the chili sauce proved delicious but the pork too tough to chew, and she wanted to dispose of her plate before anyone noticed.

"Is good?"

"Very good." Eva indicated the rice and chilis. She wanted to ask if that was what they ate in Vietnam, but thought of Nuh, telling her how he dug roots and tested drinking water.

"Can I get some candy?" Nick asked. She was surprised he asked, but he was acting clingy. Even with H'nghai's guidance she felt intimidated herself. The language barrier so completely isolated her that whereas she felt conspicuous at the apartments, here she felt invisible.

"You had a lot of donuts."

"I had one."

At least four. "Sure. Have some candy."

"You finish?" H'nghai asked.

Eva looked at the pork still on her plate. "It's delicious. I'm just so full I can't eat anymore." She stood. When she looked back, H'nghai was watching the auction with the other women. They seemed rapt, despite the fact that it was being conducted in English, while Eva, who should have understood, heard only snatches. Looking back toward the stage, she spotted Nuh, sitting where the band had been, playing with the drums, at the same time Nick reached her with a fistful of Now and Laters.

"My friend's here!" he cried ecstatically and ran off. In a minute he was back with Nuh. "Missy Ferrin!" Nuh flashed his grin and pointed to his shoes. A born con man, Eva thought. He could have charmed anyone out of anything. "You have merry Christmas, happy New Year?"

"I did," Eva said, though it wasn't the New Year yet.

"We're going to look for the lake, okay?" Nick asked.

She drained her cup and tossed it in the trash. "Sweetie, I only said...."

"We're just going to look."

It was probably okay, but she didn't want him traipsing through the woods and getting lost. "Honey, you don't have a rod, and besides you're not supposed to get your cast wet."

"I just want to see it."

"But there may not be a lake."

"You said there was."

"I said there might be."

"I find." Nuh cajoled her with a smile.

Eva cast another glance back at H'nghai. "Let me come with you then." She walked them through the door.

"Okay, you came with us," Nick said. "You can go back now."

She frowned and turned her gaze on the men again, catching

her breath when she saw Katu. He was smoking a cigarette and looking at something another man was holding in his hand, although she was certain he hadn't been there before. Probably off pissing in the woods.

"I just don't want you to get lost."

"We're not going to get lost."

She glanced at the children playing at the edge of the clearing. Would she be so nervous if the men sitting on the blocks were a group of white middle class Americans? The moment the question occurred to her she was doomed to let Nick go.

"Okay. But be careful. I don't want you gone too long."

As she watched them set off into the woods, two of the younger children ran up to her. The girl, who was wearing a sweatshirt with one of the narrow handwoven skirts Eva had noticed on a number of the women, held out her hand. "Bullets!" she said and uncurled her fingers to reveal three shell casings. Eva craned after Nick, feeling ridiculous. A wildlife club wouldn't rent its facilities for a picnic if there were hunters in the woods.

"Take our picture." The boy struck a pose.

"But I don't have a camera."

The girl put one arm around the boy, the other hand cupping her treasure, and smiled.

"I don't have a camera," Eva repeated. They stared expectantly until at last she stooped to their level, raised an invisible lens to her eye, and pushed the button. Giggling, they ran off.

"Welcome," a male voice said behind her, and she turned. A short, handsome middle-aged man with a broad smile and thick shock of wavy black hair springing from his baseball cap held out his hand, and Eva rose to shake it. When he introduced himself, she recognized his name, Bo Cao Ya. He was the community leader she had read about in the paper when she was looking up information on the Montagnards.

"I know who you are," she said. "You won a state heritage grant for singing."

His smile turned modest. "What I can, I do it. Dega people love music. We sing, we play the gong, it's very happy." He had walked her back inside, and now he pointed to the flag with the elephant in the middle. "The Montagnard Association flag. Green for our beautiful Highland, the mountain and the forest. White for peace and honesty, red for our blood and Dega struggle."

"What does the elephant stand for?" Eva looked for H'nghai, who was still watching the auction.

"Elephant is symbol of Montagnard people, powerful but gentle. We love elephant. When we have them, we ride them like a car. When we sell them we have money, and then we are happy." Bo Cao Ya smiled again, baring his square white teeth. "You are interested in knowing Montagnard people?"

"Yes."

When he raised his hand to indicate the flag again, Eva noticed the broad scar running from his ear down his neck. "Gold circle around elephant for justice and friendship. We are international association with simple plan, gain a voice, find representation through our American friends. We have Human Rights Platform to present United Nations, United States, and Communist Vietnam." He paused. "See, the way they are doing, the Communist Vietnamese, is just to destroy our way of life and our people."

"I know."

"When the Americans first come to our country, I'm so excited. Now when I come here, I am nervous to learn English but very happy I see my friends."

She nodded.

"You take pictures?"

Eva wondered if, as he approached her from the back while she pretended to photograph the children, he thought she held a camera. "No. The children just...."

"Movie, tape recorder? Maybe you write a book."

She wasn't invisible at all. The other Americans were all either former Green Berets or their wives. As an outsider, she was being given the Montagnard tour. "No, I just read about the festival in the paper."

"You live in Random? Where?"

"Ah." He nodded when she told him. "I try to buy house in that neighborhood, but everything is too expensive. I buy nice house in Carolina Acres cheaper. For my family when they come. I dream to see my wife and children again."

"How long has it been since you've seen them?"

"Ten years. Five children. The youngest I do not see."

"I'm so sorry."

Bo Cao Ya shrugged. "I send more money. Someday they come. You have children?"

"My son's outside. Do you know if there's a lake? He likes to fish."

"You like fish?" Bo Cao Ya's face lit. "All Asian people like fish."

The Homecoming vet approached them and shook Bo's

hand. "So long, Bo. I've got to hit the road, but I'll send you an email.

Bo grinned, his face breaking into a network of cheerful lines. Eva studied his scar as he watched the vet depart. He turned back to her. "You like movie?"

"Sure."

"In Vietnam we watch movie with American soldiers, John Wayne movie. You like John Wayne?"

"I grew up on John Wayne movies."

"John Wayne honorary Dega. Some American people call Dega people Indian, but Montagnard soldiers watch John Wayne. Cowboys, not Indian.."

Eva was so delighted that she laughed.

"Is true," Bo Cao Ya said and threw his head back to laugh with her.

"Remember Dega struggle," he told her when he was done laughing. "You want to make movie, write book, we help you."

"I'll remember," she promised, wondering where Nick was. The afternoon's effort at communication had exhausted her. She needed to talk to H'nghai again and go.

As if she sensed as much, H'nghai fell in step beside her. "You have good time?"

"I did," Eva said, looking at the girl's sweet, earnest, pink-scarred face, wondering if H'nghai had withdrawn to let her mingle because she too found communication draining. They couldn't sit down together and talk about a painting or a book or a friend they had in common, couldn't share a joke or gossip. It was a friendship based entirely in good will. She loved the girl.

"You like Bo? Bo Cao Ya a leader for Dega peoples, very smart with English."

"He's a nice man," Eva said. "H'nghai, are you okay?"

"You have nice son."

"Thank you." Eva tried again. "Are you all right? How are things at home?"

"Okay." H'nghai took Eva's wrist and slipped a beaded bracelet from her arm. "Like John Wayne." As she fastened the bracelet around Eva's wrist, she smiled, and Eva's throat filled. "For you I make. Honorary Dega."

Eva hugged her. "Thank you. Oh, H'nghai, thank you so much!"

On her way out to look for Nick a slender American woman in native skirt stopped her.

She too wore a beaded friendship bracelet. "I'm Pam Martinson. Shirley Prescott told me you might be interested in working on the Longhouse Project."

"I would." She had gone too far to think about Guy. "I don't really know much about it though. What would I do?"

"What can you do?"

Eva was surprised at the strength of her voice. "I run an art gallery. I can design brochures, I can write and edit copy, I can write grant proposals and have experience in fundraising."

Pam Martinson's eyes widened. "*Please* work on the Longhouse Project."

Eva tore a sheet of paper from the memo book in her pocket and wrote her name and number. "I have to go look for my son right now, but will you call and give me more information?"

"I certainly will."

When Eva opened the door, Nick and Nuh were just coming into view. "We found it," Nick announced. Both of them were covered with mud and briers.

"It must have been a way."

Nuh looked down at his muddy Reeboks and tried to wipe them in the grass. He hung his head.

"It was a *long* way," Nick said.

She turned toward the stacks of cement blocks. The light was beginning to fade, and only a few of the younger men were left. Katu was one, and they stared at each other. He raised his chin. He knows that I'm his enemy, Eva thought.

It had been only a week, Christmas week at that, though it felt as if he'd been gone for months, so completely had Guy managed to get away. Yet, when he learned that Weems still didn't have the police report—apparently nothing had been done on his case—all the good the trip had done him was undone, and he felt as if he'd never left Random. He reminded himself of the slow-down a holiday meant in the legal schedule, but it made no difference in his mood. Then on Thursday, the second day of a new year, Weems called to tell him that his probable cause hearing had been postponed.

"Postponed till when?" he asked.

"Postponed."

"It's just that I'd like to have some idea when I can get on with my life."

There was a pause just long enough for an inaudible sigh. "If you want to get on with your life, I recommend we talk to the D.A. about a plea." They were back to that again.

In the meantime he had gone back to Dayco. Wednesday he was off for New Year's, but Monday and Tuesday he cleaned carpets, riding from job to job in a van driven by a pothead with tales of rich, middle-aged nymphomaniacs who snuck up behind you while you worked and opened their peignoirs to show off their sagging breasts and straggly pubes, though the only women Guy saw were a frazzled cleaning woman and a young mother in sweatpants who blathered on the phone the whole time he was there.

Friday he was sent to sweep out a warehouse on the city's southeast side. Driving streets that seemed vaguely familiar from his first stint with Day Labor, which had given him a tour of Random's industrial zones without managing to map those streets and alleys in his brain, he made a wrong turn and passed the East Side Pawn Shop, bleak in the sluggish light of early morning, at the curb an empty bottle with a brown paper sack folded down around it. Only after he'd driven by did he recognize the bar. He circled.

East Side Pawn was dark, except for the faint green disk of a clockface glowing from the depths. He cruised by slowly. The bar had no name that he could see, only the unlit letters of a beer sign in a window bricked in to transom height—not Budweiser or Miller or Amstel Light, just Beer in colorless neon tubes. Varnish was peeling from the solid wood door that opened catty-corner to the dusty street. Three times he drove through the intersection. He was on Lanyan Road, and he followed it until it ended, past warehouses and chain link fences and cracked parking lots, but it looked different in the light, and as hard as he tried he could not determine where the accident had happened.

Chapter 19

As much as Guy hated yard sales—vultures fattening on the dross of people's lives with such mercenary glee he presumed they would enjoy picking dead men's pockets—he also hated clutter. Though otherwise generous, Eva could never bring herself to give anything to Goodwill. Spending money, she had a kid's candy-store excitement that alternately charmed and repelled him. She was forever replacing things with things that she liked better, yet she maintained a complicated fiscal attachment to everything she owned, as if she were unable to justify acquisition unless she could recoup a part of her investment in a sale. Over the years she had crammed the attic with their discards, the refuse of Nick's babyhood—not just crib and high chair but pull toys and puzzles, stained undershirts and sleepers, Tonkas, Tinker Toys, and tiny rubber tools— there were the dishes she was tired of, quilts that no longer matched their walls, faded curtains, dysfunctional electronics, all the prodigal excess she seemed to feel middle class life entailed. She had stuffed the basement, garage, and farthest reaches of their closets, all in preparation for a yard sale she'd never found the time to hold. As a result he could hardly object when, the Saturday after they returned from Florida, she gave her sale.

He even helped her haul stuff down the folding attic stairs, trying not to grumble, but as Friday evening wore on and he descended the ladder over and over without noticeably reducing the attic's freight he felt surly. Though she picked up the relay at the bottom and hauled the junk on out to the garage, the sheer weight of what they'd owned dismayed him, not to mention that he'd loaded trucks all day, his back hurt, he was tired. Eva kept getting distracted as Nick reclaimed his outgrown toys and tried to sneak them to his room. "I wondered where that was," he cried, "I *need* this," until Eva promised he could pocket the proceeds from his own things, which sent him scurrying to his room to fetch more.

"But sweetie," she protested, "you just got that book. Your grandma bought you that. Nick, you can't sell Totter—Totter is your friend!"

Again Guy made her promise that the sale wouldn't start until 8 a.m. Again she said, "I put it in the paper. 'No early sales.'"

At 4 a.m. he woke to someone flailing at the door. "Goddamnit," he muttered as he disentangled his feet from the bedding.

"I'll go," she offered meekly. Already she was cinching her bathrobe.

"You will not." He could never seem to make her sufficiently alert to the world's danger. Both foolishness and feminism start with f, he thought whenever she insisted on her right to walk alone at night or go off hiking by herself or any of a dozen things he agreed she had every right to do though common sense ought to tell her not to. Gruffly he brushed by her, and she trailed him down the stairs.

A bedraggled couple stood beneath the porch light. "Are you having a yard sale?"

"Damnit," Guy said.

The man stepped in front of the woman and gave his

unkempt yellow-gray beard a scrappy tilt. "Don't you curse my wife."

"The sale starts at eight," Guy said. "Eight."

"We'd be glad to have you come back," Eva called from behind him as he slammed the door. He turned on his heel. "I'm sorry." Her voice was tiny.

The woman's wheezy alto crept up the stairs behind them. "Try to distract them. I'll go around the back."

Guy put his hand out to stop her as she turned on the top step. By six the yard was squawking. He took his breakfast at Burger King and didn't come home until 5 p.m.

Eva had never asked Nick not to mention the Montagnard fundraiser to Guy, although on the way home she had considered it. But she couldn't teach her son to lie; she couldn't endow him with the guilt his complicity would bring, though her own experience told her she could not prevent it either. Her mother had never warned Eva not to tell about her trysts; Eva simply sensed that she should not, and so she drank guilt's elixir anyway, not just in the knowledge that she'd been party to a sin, but with the uneasy feeling that somehow the sin had been her fault. All week she waited for Guy to confront her, waited with a fatalistic expectation that was part dread, part need, both relieved when he didn't and then sad, because she had never meant to burden her son. It didn't occur to her that already he didn't tell either of them much or that he might simply have forgot.

She would almost rather that he did tell. Because as long as Guy did not confront her the specter of deceit hovered menacingly between her and the future. It made her edgy, though Guy seemed not to notice. The days dragged on, and nothing happened. Not when she called Ravenna Mink and the for-sale sign went up on their front lawn, not when she had a yard sale and people started banging on the door in the middle of the night. He was grumpy but not really angry, and though she was sure he would have done the same thing in her position, she was not at all sure that he would see that.

The day after the sale Guy played basketball, walking to the court behind the nearby church where he and his friends had begun shooting after the city removed the hoops from the neighborhood parks, though in the last year or so the personnel had changed—his friends had drifted away, aged out or busy, and a younger, more aggressive crowd had moved in. Not one of the old group was there, although so many players had shown up they had to take turns, which gave the game an air of jolting impatience.

He was a Skin, and though it was a mild day, overcast again and slightly gloomy, when he sat beside the court to rest out the next game, he felt a chill poke its damp finger through the sweat-soaked hair on his chest. He was too old for this, he thought, picking up his shirt to mop his brow as a tangle of shoes and tube socks swept by him. His legs felt dead; he'd gone two full-court games, and he was winded; his breath had a brittle edge that stung his throat.

The guy they called Bones went in for a layup. As the ball crashed against the backboard, he came down and took the kid with the knee brace with him. Bones leapt to his feet. "You charged!"

"You undercut me."

"I had position."

"The fuck you did. Your feet were moving."

Tentatively the kid stood, turning on his good leg, blood strung like rubies down his shin. He jabbed a forefinger at Bones, and the argument degenerated into shoves and threats and dirty looks and then a bated pause before the game resumed. Without thinking Guy stood up and started walking. Only when he was halfway home, when he remembered his ball and decided he was too spent to feel like going back to get it, did he form the words "I quit."

Eva thought he was childish. That was the thing about women: if you played they called you immature, and then when you quit they called you childish; what you understood as valediction they called a temper tantrum. Except Eva didn't say anything. She was busy boxing everything that hadn't sold to take to Goodwill, and her face was half hidden behind a cardboard flap. It was in her inattention that he heard the echo of his first wife.

"I just realized I wasn't enjoying it anymore," he insisted.

"Well, it's not like it's something you have to decide." Briefly she looked up. "You should play when you feel like playing, and when you don't, don't."

But it was something he had to decide. He had to know whether he played or not. He didn't.

He might have missed the exercise and camaraderie more if it weren't for the physical routine of Dayco, to which he'd adjusted so quickly after their return that he was surprised to come home from work on Tuesday and hear Gordon Weems's voice on the answering machine.

"Give me a call," Weems said, but when Guy called the lawyer had left for the day, which presented him with something of a dilemma: if he went to work tomorrow, he might be unable to return the call until lunch, at which time Weems himself might be at lunch. And it was almost certain that by the time Guy got home Weems would have again left for the day. On the other hand, if he stayed home just to make the call and all Weems wanted was to propose a plea again, he would have a hard time containing his anger without the distraction of his physical labor.

He went to work and called on his lunch hour. Weems was out.

"Can I have him call you?" the secretary asked.

"I'm not at a phone. Maybe you'd know what he wanted?"

"I'll be glad to have him call you."

"If he could just leave a message that was a little more explicit?"

"I'll have him call you."

It was Thursday before they connected, because on Thursday Guy stayed home. "Did you get the report?" he asked as soon as Weems came on the line.

"The D.A. hasn't sent that over, but I spoke with the arresting officer, and I may have some good news. His name's McThune, Aaron McThune, he's been working Traffic seven years, good record, no suspensions."

Impatiently Guy switched ears with the phone.

"He doesn't recall the exact BAC, but essentially he corroborates your story. He says the BAC was consistent with your account of what you drank."

"It was .02."

"He doesn't recall the figure but says it wouldn't have been over per se."

"Then how come he arrested me?"

"I'm getting to that."

"At least that's something."

"Under other circumstances you might not have been charged, but you did have an accident, which involved a fatality, and you did admit to drinking that evening."

"I was not drinking that evening." Guy's voice sharpened. It was the insistence on the participle that vexed him. "I had a drink. There's a difference." Did he mean to stand up in court and say that the difference all came down to grammar? "I wouldn't have been charged if the kid had been an adult. You told me I was charged because I'm white."

"Whoa," Weems said. "I don't know what gives you that idea. Unless you've got some tangible evidence those are some pretty wild accusations."

Weems had given him that idea! The mealy-mouthed son-of-a-bitch was the one who brought up race. Guy was just trying to make a point—the case made no sense.

"For all I know I was charged because I once fouled the cop in a basketball game."

"In his judgment you were what they call 'slightly impaired.'"

"Ask him. Ask him to tell you where he got that scar on his lip. He was crowding me underneath the basket."

"Mr. Ferrin...."

Guy hated Weems' voice, always reasonable but a little bit tired, as if he had to call attention to the effort patience took. "I wasn't impaired."

"In his judgment...."

"I murdered him in basketball." *Maybe* they had played. "Did he tell you he told my wife it's always your fault when you hit a kid? You told me I wouldn't have been arrested unless the cop had some kind of agenda."

"What did you say?" Weems's tone perked up. "Your wife can verify that he said 'always'?"

"She's not sure," Guy admitted. "She *thinks* he might have said it."

The voice grew weary again. "Why don't you just take your good news? The arresting officer basically corroborates your story."

"Does that mean he drops the charges?"

"Well, I'm afraid that's not up to him. I'll have to talk to the D.A."

"But you think the D.A. will drop the charges."

"I don't know about that."

"The arresting officer is going to testify I wasn't drunk."

"The arresting officer's going to testify you were slightly impaired."

"Oh, for Christ's sake." Guy unclenched the fingers he'd curled around the phone. "No one could have avoided that accident. Haven't you ever had an animal run beneath your wheel?"

"That's not a comparison I'd encourage you to make in court."

Guy sighed. "Look, I'm glad you talked to the cop. It's just that I feel frustrated. I mean, shouldn't the D.A. have to apologize? He's telling reporters I'm a murderer."

"You're charged with felony death."

"I thought I was supposed to be innocent till proven guilty. He's lied about the evidence. He told the *Gazette and Herald* my blood alcohol was twice the legal limit." Weems started to speak, but Guy rushed on. "Isn't that libel?"

"Not my area, but I doubt it. He made a mistake."

"Just get him to drop the charges, and he can make all the mistakes he wants." When they hung up Guy pumped a tentative fist into the air. "All right," he said softly, to see how it would sound. "All right," he repeated. "All right, all right, all right."

The clock ticked loudly. He opened the refrigerator and poured a glass of juice. Ten a.m. His crew would be squatting on the loading dock for their morning cigarette break. He could call Eva at Gardell, but he wanted to break his news in person. He was still standing in the kitchen trying to figure out how to fill the day when he heard someone fumbling at the front door. He arrived in the front hall just in time for Ravenna Mink to push it open.

"Mr. Ferrin." Her face was peevish with surprise. "I left a message." Behind her blowzy body a couple who didn't look old enough to vote were cringing as if he were a burglar.

"I was just leaving," he promised. He retrieved his jacket and his keys, and as he closed the door behind him he heard the fat tart say, "The bathrooms need some work, but you just can't find this kind of charm in your newer houses."

Having nowhere else to go, he drove to the public library, where he joined the derelicts reading newspapers.

Eva and Nick didn't arrive home until six. He waited until their son had plunked himself in front of a cartoon in the den and came up behind her as she opened the refrigerator, which released a vaguely overripe breath. They had never established which of them was supposed to clean it out. "Guess what."

"What?" Her voice was flat, and he frowned at the back of

her head as she bent to examine the contents of the shelves, wondering again if she'd taken a lover. Maybe when he told her his good news she would tell him she was leaving; maybe she'd been waiting for a moment when things were looking up, in order not to be cruel. She wasn't a mean person; she would look for a way to soften the blow. In the space of a moment he convinced himself so thoroughly that he forgot she was waiting for him to speak until she closed the door and turned around, her face creased with impatience. And still it took him a minute to stop waiting for her to deliver the bad news.

"Weems talked to the cop," he said finally.

"And?"

"The cop says I wasn't drunk."

For a moment nothing seemed to register. Then her smile blossomed. "That's wonderful, honey! Are they going to drop the charges?"

"I don't know. He's going to talk to the D.A."

"Oh I'm so glad!"

"You mean it?"

Her smile withered. "Of course I mean it. What kind of question is that?"

He looked to one side of her. "It's just you haven't seemed all that concerned."

"Of course I'm concerned. I just happen to have a lot on my mind right now: I've got two shows to think about, I'm supposed to be getting my tenure file together, classes start Monday and I haven't written my syllabi, I just had a yard sale, there's the house...."

His eyes traveled to the dark window as if he might find in the backyard another version of the realty sign that still startled him at the curb each time he drove up. He wondered if the couple Ravenna Mink had surprised him with that morning would be the new owners of his house—it offended him to think they could afford it. But probably not since the tart had called late that afternoon to say she would be showing it again tomorrow morning.

"If the D.A. drops the charges, we won't need to sell."

"It's already on the market."

"So take it off."

"We can't do that."

Their house was under contract with the ferret; it was if she owned it instead of them.

"Well, maybe nobody will buy it. I don't know what you were in such a rush for anyway."

"We're broke. We owe Bill Whitt twelve thousand dollars."

Or maybe she was in such a hurry because she was anxious to dismantle their life together. They would sell the house, and all that would be left was for her to tell him she'd found someone else. He wanted to ask, but he was afraid she might say yes, that was it, and when she pulled a bag of carrots from the refrigerator to start dinner he lost his nerve. He didn't know what to think when she turned around after setting her pots to simmer and said, "I'm sorry I snapped at you. I'm just tired. I really am glad about the cop, honey."

Eva was startled to hear Claudia at the other end of the phone. She hadn't thought about Claudia much since Christmas, and the bright, energetic sound of her voice as she said, "Eva," caused Eva to glance around her office as if to make certain it wasn't coming from the walls. "It's Claudia! I haven't seen you. I called before Christmas, and you never called me back."

"I forgot." It seemed impossible, but she had.

"I thought maybe you'd want to have lunch. It's time that we caught up."

Eva was annoyed to discover that her heartbeat had quickened. "When did you have in mind?"

"Today?"

Of course. It was already after eleven. For a moment she'd been ready to forget that Claudia had snubbed her. She glanced at her desk again. "Actually, I'm pretty busy."

"Oh." Claudia's voice dulled. "Maybe we could do it another time then."

"Maybe so." Eva was about to add "Thanks for calling" when Claudia cried, "It's just I miss you. I feel like I've been abandoned by my friends."

So she was feeling sorry for herself. Eva shifted with impatience as a muffled sniffle came through the line.

"This has been the worst week."

"I'm sorry." Eva was unable to keep her voice from sounding cold.

"Is something wrong? You sound so distant. Are you mad?"

Eva didn't want to go into it. "Maybe we can have lunch some other time."

"But why? What have I done?"

"I'm not mad." She wasn't mad. *Mad* wasn't the right word.

"I called you before Christmas. You didn't call me back."

"I was busy."

"Why won't you tell me what I've done?"

Because you should know, Eva thought, suddenly very

tired. "Claudia, I'm at work."

"Is it because I haven't called more often? I just offered to see you."

And what about all the times I offered to see you, Eva thought. What about the day I told you we killed a child and all you could say was *Sorry, good to see you, got to run.*

Another sob leaked from Claudia's throat.

Eva sighed. "We can have lunch tomorrow, okay?"

"Tomorrow?" Claudia said, her tone so doubtful that Eva halfway expected her to add, "No, tomorrow's not good for me, couldn't we make it today?" The truth was that Eva would just as soon get it over with, but she didn't want to give Claudia the satisfaction of meeting on her terms.

"I have a free hour tomorrow," she said firmly. "I can meet you then."

"I know today's late notice but...."

"Yes, it is."

Again Weems left a message for Guy to call him but was gone for the day by the time Guy got home and checked the machine. This time there was no deliberation. He called Dayco to say he wouldn't be available tomorrow. Eva had left a note reminding him she had a dinner this evening, one of those affairs where she had to chat up rich collectors, and to pick up Nick at the Y. Since he'd gone back to Dayco he'd fallen into the habit of going to bed early, and even though he wasn't working in the morning he went upstairs before she got home. As a result they nearly collided on the stairs at 7 a.m.

"I'm not going in today," he explained, adding when he got back from walking Nick to the bus stop, "I have to call my lawyer."

She was reading the paper, which rattled as she lowered the front page. "Do you think he's talked to the D.A.?"

"I hope so."

She took a deep breath. "This is it then? We'll know today what's going to happen?"

"If I'm lucky." He picked up his cold coffee cup. "Weems hasn't exactly beat down any doors." But he couldn't imagine that Weems would have called to offer the same old plea.

"Will you let me know? Call me at the office."

"Sure."

"As soon as you've talked to him." She reached across the table to touch his hand. "Good luck, honey. I'll keep my fingers crossed."

"Thanks."

"I mean it. I'm sorry I've been so distracted. It's just...." She looked away. She had dressed for work before she came downstairs, in a putty-colored knit dress, and he could see the faint outline of her nipples through the jersey. She looked pretty, though he wished she would wear her hair loose the way she used to. "He'll have to drop the charges, won't he? What time do you think you'll call?"

"He ought to be in by nine. By the way, that ferret woman called. She's showing the house again this morning."

"Did you talk to her? Damn." She took a hasty inventory of the kitchen's condition. "What time?"

"She didn't say. I ran into her the last time. The couple she had with her looked like they were all of sixteen." His voice was bouncy. He was feeling so optimistic he couldn't even think of an objection to the ferret.

"Then let's hope they have rich parents." She rose. "You'll call me? I'll be in my office till noon." She raised an eyebrow. "I'm having lunch with Claudia."

He was so astonished his mouth fell open. Eva shrugged. "Well, that's good," he said, recovering. "I mean I assume you're glad."

"She called me yesterday. Actually she wanted me to go to lunch right then, and when I said I couldn't she started crying about how mean I was and asking what she'd done." Eva drew her lips out in displeasure.

"So what are you going to tell her?"

"The truth, I guess."

"You could just let bygones be bygones. After all you were friends for a long time."

She had paused to tidy some things on the kitchen counter, and she turned back to him, narrowing her eyes. "I thought you didn't like her."

"I never said that."

"You were the one who was always warning me not to trust her."

And look what happened. "All I said was...look, if it makes you happy, go ahead and let her have it."

"I'm not going to let anybody have it." She was riled. "She asked me to tell her what she's done."

He shook his head, glad he didn't have to be Claudia today. "You're a hard woman, you know that?"

"Honestly." Annoyance flickered in her eyes, but she looked more exasperated than angry. She lifted her coat from the rack. "Promise you'll call me just as soon as you've talked to the lawyer."

"You'll be the first to know. By the way—" in his excitement after Weems's message he'd forgotten—"you had another house call. Somebody named Martinson wants you to call her about the Long house."

She turned. An emotion he didn't recognize roused her face. "Did she leave a number?"

"I put it on the desk in the living room. Are you looking to buy a smaller house?" He was curious, but she wasn't listening. She'd grabbed the number off the desk and was gone.

Eva tried Pam Martinson as soon as she reached Gardell but didn't reach her and decided to wait to call again until she'd heard from Guy in order to keep the line free. It had to be good news. And if it was good news it might not even matter that she was volunteering for the Montagnards. He would be so relieved it wouldn't matter that she'd betrayed him. He would relax; they both could. They could stop quarreling all the time and go back to the way they used to be. She would help her son remember to pick up his things and do his homework instead of flying off the handle.

She jumped each time the phone rang, but the only calls were for the gallery, and when she tried to call him she got the machine. At 11:45 she still hadn't heard. She was reluctantly reaching for her keys when the phone shrilled again, and she snatched it, thinking this is it, this is it through a hammering of her heart so loud she had to ask Ravenna Mink to repeat what she had said. The realtor had an offer.

The Carolina Cafe was in an old house near Gardell, and Eva toured the second floor to make sure Claudia wasn't there before returning to the first and taking a table near the front window. She was only a few minutes late, having promised to call Ravenna Mink back after she'd had a chance to consult Guy, though there wasn't much to consult about. The realtor had two offers, one at the asking price, so the only thing to decide was whether they would leave the washer and drier. She checked her watch and wondered if she should try to call Guy again. Most likely he just hadn't reached the lawyer yet, though she was afraid he had, afraid he hadn't called because the D.A. declined to drop the charges.

She was about to ask if the cafe had a pay phone when Claudia's clogs rapped up the wooden front steps. She disappeared into the foyer, then reappeared in the archway that led to the front room. The same scuffed leather jacket she'd worn the night of the Hines opening hung loosely from her shoulders, and Eva was struck again by how dry and gray her skin looked.

"Hi, sorry I'm late," she said, looking around, at the pressed tin ceiling and burlwood columns framing the mirrored bar. "Did you order?"

"I was waiting for you."

Claudia picked up the menu. "What's good?"

"They do nice soups. I like the Portobello sandwich."

Claudia ordered a bowl of soup and water. "How's Nick?" she asked, spreading her polished nails out on the table. Without waiting for an answer she began to fill Eva in: Caroline had a dance recital; Gregory was building a volcano for his science project. "Don't you just hate the science fair? They might as well assign the project to the parents," Claudia said. "It's so depressing when you see all these projects on display boards with computer labels that were probably printed by their father's secretaries, and over on the table in the corner there are all these hand-lettered projects on torn shirt cardboards from the project kids, and if that's not bad enough they go and give the rich kids ribbons."

Eva had observed as much herself. She hadn't thought to ask Nick what he was planning, which undoubtedly meant he wasn't planning anything. She had no idea when it was due. She was tempted to ask Claudia. If there was still time, she could help him—they could have fun with it, something they could do together.

Claudia had gone on, but Eva was only half-listening.

"By the way," Claudia said, "Kay and Sally both say hi."

Eva was startled back to the present. Liar, she thought. Had she ever been friends with Sally and Kay? They seemed like distant acquaintances; even Claudia seemed like a ghost from her past, though once they'd been so close they didn't even knock at each other's doors. H'nghai was her friend now, whom she hadn't seen since the day of the festival because she couldn't keep thinking of excuses to drop by, and she was afraid to get H'nghai in trouble. She touched her Dega bracelet. "How are they?" she said listlessly.

"Great. Just great. We had dinner this weekend." Claudia's voice bounced without a trace of yesterday's anguish. "Did you know Sally's teaching at Siler? The art teacher went on maternity leave."

Eva wondered if Sally was teaching Nick. The idea made her almost angry.

"It's a lot of work. Teaching is hard."

"I know."

Claudia didn't seem to catch the irony. "Kay's been having to substitute. We'll none of us ever get decent jobs in Random, but we're stuck here on account of the kids. You don't know how lucky you are to have a career."

Kay and Sally were *from* Random.

"How's Nick?" Claudia asked again.

"Fine."

"I bet he's grown a foot. I'm afraid Gregory's going to be short like Bill." Claudia paused. "Greg really misses Nick, they were such good friends." They were friends who didn't live in the same neighborhood and went to different schools. "I wish I weren't going out of town this weekend—Greg would love to have him spend the night. I just hate that they don't get to see each other any more." Claudia lowered her voice. "Derek and I had a little tiff, but he's been so sweet since we made up. We're going to the mountains this weekend."

Yesterday, Eva realized, surprised to feel stung, you made up after you called yesterday. Otherwise you wouldn't have called. She hadn't thought Claudia still had the power to wound her.

"I wish there was some way the boys could spend the night." Eva stared. "Did you and Guy have plans for Friday?" Claudia flashed a smile that showed her perfect white teeth and took a sip of soup.

"I don't think so," Eva said.

"That's great! Greg will be so happy when I tell him."

"I mean I don't think it would be a good idea for Greg to spend the night."

Claudia's eyes dimmed. "Oh, are you going out of town too?"

"We've been out of town. We went to Florida for Christmas."

"How was that?"

"Okay."

"Great." A small sigh slipped through Claudia's lips,

punctuating the awkward silence.

"We're selling our house. We have to get up and get going Saturday mornings so the realtor can show it." But the house had already sold, or at least it would have as soon as she talked to Guy and called Ravenna Mink. Why did she think she owed Claudia an explanation?

"Selling your house? You mean you're moving?"

"Looks like it."

Claudia's sleeve caught her soup bowl, and she pushed it aside. "I'm just surprised, I guess. You didn't tell me."

Eva didn't answer.

"I know I haven't seen you. It's just—with the kids, and Bill—he can't—it's hard." Claudia paused. "Did you buy another house? Surely you're not leaving Random."

Would you care? Eva wondered, wishing for a moment that she could say yes, we're leaving Random. We're leaving and we didn't tell you. But that was petty, and she didn't want to be petty, even if Claudia had called her yesterday just to wangle an invitation for Greg to spend the night. She forced herself to speak. "No, we're not leaving Random. We need the money. Guy had an accident, remember?" She wondered if Claudia knew that Bill had loaned Guy money.

"I wondered what happened," Claudia said. "I just didn't want to ask."

"I'm surprised you haven't read about it. There's been quite a bit in the paper."

"I don't get the paper." Claudia's shoulders made an apologetic little shrug. "I guess I just hoped it all worked out."

"It hasn't been a very good time."

"For either of us, I guess. The kids are so cold to me, and

Bill...." Claudia tapped a finger against the table. "I just wish he'd quit acting so angry."

"I could have used a friend."

"I'm having to do all those things I should have learned how to do twenty years ago—pay bills, get health insurance. Sometimes I just feel overwhelmed. But I'm sorry about your house. I know how much you loved it."

"Thanks." Eva looked at her watch. "I'm going to have to go pretty soon. Guy was going to call me today after he talked to his lawyer."

"Actually I've got to find a new place myself—it's time I got settled somewhere big enough to have the kids stay over." Claudia sighed loudly. "Part of what's made it so hard is having to go back to the house and look at all those pictures. It makes me feel like I wrecked everything."

Well, didn't you? Eva thought as she watched Claudia slip a packet of crackers into her pocket. "You asked me to tell you what you'd done." Claudia frowned. "Yesterday, when you called."

"Oh, that's okay." Claudia waved her hand. "Yesterday was a bad day. I thought you were mad at me."

"I am." Claudia's eyes turned flinty as Eva folded her arms on the table. "I know you've had a hard time, and I'm sorry, but it was your choice to leave, and you have a boyfriend—you'll get over it. I don't think you can begin to imagine what we've been through. What I resent is that you haven't even tried."

"It's not my fault my feelings changed. I can't make myself feel something I don't even if Bill blames me."

"That's probably true," Eva admitted. "But you can't expect him to get over it just like that because you want him to."

"It's not just Bill, it's my kids—at least your son doesn't hate you."

"I don't know whether he does or not. This has changed us so much I don't know how he feels. Sometimes he seems like such a brat I can't stand to be around him. I love him more than anything, but I act like I hate him. Wait." Eva lifted a hand as Claudia opened her mouth. "I wish I could say this has made us better people—and there are times I think it has." What did she mean? It hadn't made either one of them a better person. "Bad things don't necessarily bring out the best in people.

"Wait," she said again as Claudia opened her mouth. "I'm not finished. You can't ask someone to tell you what you've done, and then not let them speak. I've had a terrible time these past two months, almost as bad as Guy. I needed my friends too. You were my best friend, and that night at the Hines opening, you snubbed me."

"So what if I haven't called you? I haven't called anybody.

"You called Kay and Sally." Eva couldn't stop, though she kept her voice low. "You put me off and manipulated my sympathy and refused to give me any in return. You forgot that Guy and I killed a nine-year-old boy and that he's been charged—and if you could be bothered to get outside your own skin long enough to read the paper you'd know the D.A. is talking about trying him for murder." A clumsy fear coiled itself around Eva's heart. Surely Guy had talked to Weems by now.

"I never snubbed you. I called you before Christmas, and you didn't call me back."

"The only times you called me were when you wanted me to babysit."

Claudia rose. "I can't see I've done anything wrong, but

I'm sorry you have those feelings."

"So am I," Eva said.

Chapter 20

"Why didn't you call me?" Eva descended the basement steps, ducking her head to peer into the corner where Guy was pulling laundry from the drier. "Did you talk to the lawyer?"

"I didn't reach him until fifteen minutes ago. He was in court all morning."

"What happened? What did he say?"

"The D.A.'s agreed to check the file. He'll get back to Weems."

Disappointment wobbled her legs. "But it's been over eight weeks!" she wanted to cry.

She might have thought it would seem like yesterday, but instead the accident seemed like years ago, years and years, too many to be no closer to a resolution. The overhead bulb hollowed pockets beneath his eyes. He looked like a man so worn down and cornered he would badger his wife over a piece of paper and leap on the idea that he was a scapegoat. How long did the District Attorney and Weems think he could go on without a meltdown? Or maybe that was the idea; they would slowly change him into someone so reproachable he might as well be guilty. "Well, I suppose it's better than nothing."

He bent to retrieve a fallen sock. "How was your lunch with Claudia?"

She rolled her eyes.

"There's a message from the realtor."

"I talked to her at work." She turned to let him follow her upstairs, waiting until he had cleared the placemats from the breakfast table and begun to fold the freshly laundered briefs and tee shirts. "She sold the house." A look of sharp surprise snapped his face up. She shrugged. "I told her I'd talk to you. She got two offers, one for one forty-nine nine and they want us to leave the washer and drier. The other's one forty-eight five." She reached for a tee shirt. "Actually we're pretty lucky. A lot of houses sit for months." She couldn't help wondering if it hadn't sold so quickly because Ravenna Mink had underpriced it. She should have found another realtor. *He* should have found another lawyer.

"I don't know what to say." He turned back to the pile of unmatched socks.

"It's your house too."

"You bought it. I never wanted it in the first place." It was true, though he hadn't objected. He wouldn't have wanted any house because he never wanted anything. It used to make her mad.

"How soon do you suppose the D.A. will get back to Weems?"

"I don't know."

She pressed her face into the tee shirt, inhaling its clean, warm fragrance. "What do you want me to tell Ravenna Mink?"

"It's your decision." Which made it her responsibility. "Have you thought about where we're going to live?"

She hadn't. She'd expected the house to sit on the market; she had thought there would be months. "There are always apartments."

"I think you better start looking," he said.

Still, there was plenty of time, she assured herself throughout the following week; they wouldn't close until the middle of

March, and there were bound to be apartments. She didn't want to make a decision until Guy's fate had been decided, but one day followed the next and Weems failed to call Guy back.

She kept busy. The longhouse committee, three Americans and five Montagnards, met in Pam Martinson's living room the evening after she agreed to sell the house. Bo Cao Ya welcomed her so warmly she felt welcome. By the end of that first meeting she felt useful, no longer the tourist at the festival or self-conscious foreigner cruising the apartment driveway. Of course, they didn't know who she was, but when she reminded herself of this she felt only a twinge of guilt.

When she went to see H'nghai the next day, there was a fresh bruise along one cheek.

"Do your parents know he beats you?" Eva demanded again, thinking of the Montagnards she'd met the night before, all smiles and jokes. She hoped the answer was no, though the thought of Katu filled her with fury. It was as if he'd hit her too. He knew that she was watching.

"No at home," H'nghai said shrilly, "no at home," and averted her eyes.

She could mean they didn't know. They might be like any family who didn't want to know. Without realizing that they did so, they might let her lie and turn their backs on all the signs. It was hard to believe that she could do the same if it was Nick who was in danger, though nothing was so fallible or foolish as innocence, that smug, untested virtue.

"You belong in the shelter, H'nghai."

"Slow. Katu tell me bring, too slow." H'nghai touched her cheek. "Not so bad."

"And what about next time?"

H'nghai stroked her pregnant belly.

"The baby won't protect you," Eva said, wishing H'nghai wasn't so adept at lying to herself, though H'nghai's sense of honor seemed so genuine that she thought what H'nghai had to rationalize away was not cowardice but courage.

H'nghai averted her eyes again. "Save money. Get divorce."

"Sooner or later I'm going to convince you." Eva stroked her bracelet. It was later that she worried about.

Guy took his coffee from the microwave and brought it to the table, wondering how many hours he and Eva had spent in these same chairs, reading the paper, eating breakfast, eating dinner, exchanging that quotidian of dialogue whose very banality is the mark of intimacy: *We're out of birdseed. The upstairs toilet is leaking. Our mice are back.*" They had occupied the house for over a decade, but in the last week its air had changed more definitively than if Eva had hired a contractor to knock out walls. In less than two months the new owners would take possession, though Eva had informed him they wouldn't actually move in until a master bath addition and renovations to the old baths and kitchen were completed. The knowledge disturbed him in a way he had not anticipated, for rather than feeling loss or anger he'd been overtaken with unease. He and Eva had yet to talk about the future, such tacit agreements not to talk seeming more and more required of them these days. But that was not the only source of his discomfort. He felt violated, as if his privacy had been invaded, as if by mere virtue of their contract the new owners—not teenagers after all but a pair of young lawyers, according to Eva—had already been installed, spying on his habits and his marriage from behind the curtains or inside the walls. Standing at the toilet or cursing a stubbed toe, he felt his very breath made loathsome by their verdicts.

"Have you found an apartment yet?" he asked her.

"There's plenty of time." She was wearing her abstracted look, and it occurred to him that she might be annoyed to have him linger at the table.

He pushed his coffee cup aside. "Actually I was thinking," he said, which was a lie—he hadn't been thinking at all; it seemed to him as if it had been months and months, maybe even years, since he had experienced anything as coherent as a thought. "What if we left Random?"

Her forehead creased.

"It's the perfect time—we've sold the house; there's nothing keeping us." He warmed to the idea, which seemed in the suddenness with which it had announced itself, in its simplicity and wholeness, a gift. If they left they truly could start over. Providing, of course, he did not go to jail, but he refused to consider the possibility of prison. "We could go out West—you always said you liked that landscape."

"I don't want to leave Random."

"Because of the gallery?" He should have thought about her job; even though she claimed to have soured on it, he shouldn't have dismissed it so quickly. With some justification she would feel belittled. He studied her face for a sign of irritation, but as usual her eyes seemed focused somewhere else.

"Not really."

"I know how hard you've worked—I know you don't want to feel it came to nothing, but it hasn't come to nothing. If it weren't for you, Gardell wouldn't even have a gallery." He paused. "We could take an apartment here in town until you finished the school year. That would probably be the best thing anyway for Nick." Her face was expressionless now, which caused him to rush on. "I was thinking you might like somewhere like Santa Fe, you know, some place that attracts a lot of artists. It doesn't have to be out West. We could go to New York. Or Washington—there must be a hundred art museums there." She would never go to Washington; it was too close to her mother. "You can find a gallery where you don't have to kowtow to a bunch of picayune administrators."

"No such thing." She allowed a wry smile to nibble at her lip. "Anyway, we can't afford to live in New York or Washington or Santa Fe."

He understood her to be pointing out the fatal flaw in his idea, which had revealed itself to him the instant he ceased to speak. He hadn't mentioned what he was going to do, and she might easily be thinking that he meant to move them someplace where she could find a job she liked so well she wouldn't notice that her husband hadn't bothered to seek employment. No wonder she was unreceptive. But he couldn't tell her what he planned to do because he didn't know, though now that this idea had come he knew he'd figure something out. He had to leave; it amazed him not to have realized that sooner.

"Plenty of poor people live in cities."

The shape her mouth took was less amused and more pointedly sardonic. "Indeed they do."

Okay, so they didn't want to crowd into some tenement, though if they'd been younger, if they didn't have Nick—for a moment he let a bittersweet nostalgia for lost youth and the opportunities he'd let pass wash through him. So it didn't have to be a major city—even Raleigh had a good art museum, though

Raleigh seemed too close, too claustrophobic. He needed to get out of North Carolina, maybe even the South, where, except for those few years in Pittsburgh and the occasional vacation, he had managed to spend his entire life, a fact that suddenly seemed stifling, though he'd always been the one who loved the South, who was secretly delighted that her career had brought him back, while she had never been more than lukewarm.

"Anyplace you want to go. I'll find some kind of work—I always do. There's not a gallery in the country that wouldn't be glad to get you."

"Not true, but it's sweet of you to think so." She turned an uncharacteristically frank and steady gaze on him. "Actually I've been thinking about getting out of the art biz."

She would never leave it. She'd quit painting, but the business kept her hand in. "You never said anything."

"I've said it a million times."

"You've said you were sick of your job. That's not the same thing."

She shrugged. "Even if I wanted to stick with it, I'm obsolete. The climate's changed—art's not about art anymore; it's all politics and social statement."

"It stinks."

"Actually a lot of it is very powerful, but it's just not the way I see. Actually...." Her eyes shifted. There had been other things, they implied, more urgent things, that affected how she felt. "I guess you're right. I haven't said anything. But I've begun thinking about going back to school."

He would do nearly anything except go back to school.

"Don't laugh, but I've been thinking about social work."

It would never have occurred to him to laugh. He was too

astonished.

"I can't picture it," he said finally.

"Neither could I a couple months ago." Another smile licked at her mouth. "My mother's always saying that's what you should do."

"Social work?" He felt his face fold into a frown. "I'd hate it."

"I know you would."

"But if that's what you want...." His voice picked up. "Let's do it. It's perfect timing. We can find an apartment while you and Nick finish out the school year and you apply to programs."

"I said I'm thinking about it. I don't know. Anyway, UNCR has a program."

"You don't have to go to UNCR." His only connection to the state campus in the middle of Random was a bunch of haughty professors who used to come out for softball—you would have thought they'd invented the homerun the way they acted, as if they'd theorized the double play and every other triumph inside the ugly brick architecture of their fifth-rate ivory towers. To him the university was just a traffic jam. "You always said you only came South for the job."

"I know what I said." She smoothed her placemat. "But I'm used to it. We live here."

"You don't want to leave your friends, is that it?"

She gave him a starched look. "I'm not friends with my friends anymore, remember?"

"You had lunch with Claudia. I thought maybe...."

"That was over a week ago," she said as if it had been a year.

"What then?" Frustration squeezed his vocal chords. "What

in the name of God is here for us? It's not friends, and it's not the house, and if it's not your job it sure as hell isn't mine, sweeping warehouses with a bunch of derelicts and dropouts. I need to think about something permanent."

"What?" she asked.

"I don't know. I just know I can't find it here."

"Are you thinking about looking for another paper?"

"Maybe. I never minded sales." But with all the newspapers that were folding jobs in sales were drying up. Those that survived were revamping themselves to resemble *USA Today.* It made him sad to think that he lived in a world where the newspaper might become extinct. He turned his head toward the window as a squirrel leapt to the empty birdfeeder. "Bastard!" he yelled, hearing an echo from Cheever as he rapped his knuckles against the window. *Rapscallions! Varmints! Avaunt and quit my sight!* That's what grad school had done for him. His unwritten dissertation had been on Richard Yates, and when he fought with his wife he sometimes cringed to hear how pathetically he resembled that hapless wimp, Frank Wheeler. Whatever he did, he would not go back to school. "If I wasn't so old I've actually thought about giving sportswriting another try."

"That's a great idea."

"Well...." He paused. "The hours are lousy, and the pay is worse."

"So what?"

"And there can't be many papers looking to hire a rusty forty-seven-year-old reporter."

"You could find out."

But she'd just said she didn't want to leave Random. Did she expect him to apply to the *Gazette and Herald?* For all he knew she might think that was how the paper could make amends. Guardedly he watched her for a clue. "Are you saying you want to stay and have me go?"

A ribbon of pain rippled through her eyes—he should have known not to ask her so directly. As she turned away, he felt a wider band of pain wrap itself around his stomach.

"I'm saying I can't leave, that's all. Not now."

First she didn't want to; now she couldn't. His heart wedged into his throat with a sound like a low growl.

Her face gave, and she looked at him. "Of course I don't want you to go."

"What then?"

"Just I can understand the way you feel. Anybody would."

The pain loosed a chill inside his torso that hit him in the bowel. He had thought ever since they got back from Florida that she might have a lover. He hadn't dwelled on it—he had even thought he could accept it, though that was a deception of not having pursued the idea; perhaps he had thought if he didn't think about it it would go away. Nausea scalded his throat; he felt sick all over.

And then he was angry. She could say something like that and then just sit there coolly, waiting to see how he reacted. She might as well have sent Sally DeMik to tell him at the grocery.

"Have you been talking to your friends?" His voice came out a roar. "Your pals, your cronies, the divorcées? Bill Whitt warned me—I should have known they'd go to work on you. And here I felt sorry for you the night you were wailing all over the house because Claudia hurt your feelings, when I should have known what that meant was you cared more about those bitches than you did about me."

She was squinting at him with a frown that seemed less irritated than baffled. "What are you talking about?"

He was on his feet. "I guess you're happy now—you can join their little club."

Her voice crisped with impatience. "I told you, I'm not friends with my friends anymore."

"You had lunch with her!" He hit the table. "Don't lie to me!"

Eva's frown had grown more exasperated. "Are you talking about Claudia?"

"Hell yes, I'm talking about Claudia. Did she put you up to this?"

"I haven't even seen her except that one lunch. And you know what happened? You want to know what she said?"

"Is that why you found a boyfriend?"

"I don't have a boyfriend," she said in a flat voice. "I'll tell you what happened. She wanted me to invite Gregory to spend the night so she and her boyfriend could go away for the weekend, and I told her no—I told her, what a bad time it was and how lonely and abandoned I felt, and you know what she said? She said she was sorry I had those feelings." Eva's face worked. "Jesus."

"I'm not interested in Claudia."

"In that case, why don't you quit yelling about her?"

He took a step back and examined her face. "You don't have a boyfriend?"

Impatiently she flipped her hand. "Whatever gave you that idea?"

He moved back in, leaning across the table to look down at her. "You don't—you aren't involved with someone else?"

Her eyes faltered, and she looked away.

So he was right after all. Only now that he knew, he no longer tasted anger. He felt weak and more like weeping. Tears thickened in his throat, and he had to swallow them to speak. "What about our son?"

"It isn't what you think."

"What then?"

"It's not a man." Quickly, she turned back to him. "I mean—it's not anybody I'm in love with, it's not like that. Anyway, you were right about Claudia, and I was wrong."

He didn't care about Claudia.

"I told her off, but you know what? It didn't make me feel better. I guess I realized that even though I listened to her problems—which is more than she was willing to do for me—I didn't really sympathize, maybe because they meant she was too preoccupied to be sympathetic to mine." She paused. "What I mean is when she left Bill I felt like she'd done something to me."

If he let her, she would talk about Claudia all day.

"What is it then, if it isn't a man?" Nobody she was in love with. *Not like that.* What did that mean? "Why can't you leave?"

The phone rang. Neither of them moved to answer, and her own voice looped back to them from the answering machine on the counter. They waited out the beep. Then Gordon Weems asked Guy to give him a call.

After a minute Eva looked up. "It's your lawyer. You'd better call him."

"Why won't you leave Random?" She bit her lip. "Why?" His teeth ached, and his voice ground against his skull.

"I love you. I wouldn't take another lover."

"Why?" He grabbed her wrist, and still she let him wait.

"I'm sorry," she whispered when he let go. "This was just something I had to do."

"What?"

She turned to him but didn't meet his eyes. "I've been working with the Montagnards. They want to build a longhouse—it's sort of a community center."

His tongue was thick. "You're working with the Montagnards?"

For a second she looked up. "I know you told me not to get involved, but...." Guiltily she looked down. "It's really the Montagnards who got me started thinking about social work."

"That's why you don't want to leave? The Montagnards?" He felt stupid.

She wrapped the fringe of her placemat around her fingers.

All this time while his case went on pending—he had nothing *against* the Montagnards, but he didn't want anything to do with them, he didn't want to be reminded. He'd told her what the insurance adjustor said. And she'd done it anyway, done it knowing how he felt, knowing it could harm him.

"One thing, the *only* thing I asked...." She opened her mouth, but he cut her off. "The District Attorney has been talking about trying me for murder!"

Mechanically she said, "You should call your lawyer."

"I told you...." He could barely speak.

"It's not their fault—any more than the accident was yours. It's not their fault that you got blamed."

She was asking him to be reasonable. After everything that had happened, she was asking him to be reasonable. "You would leave me before you'd leave the Montagnards." He had to sit. It wasn't reasonable to ask him to be reasonable.

"If it was just the group...." Her face wrenched. "I can't leave her."

"Who?"

"His sister."

"Whose sister?"

She looked down. "Bhan's, Nuh's. The boy we killed."

The depth of her betrayal hit him in the chest. He felt as if all his wind had been kicked out.

"I'm sorry." She was crying. "You don't know how sorry I am."

He strode to the kitchen doorway. "I'm sick of that word."

Eva wiped her glasses. "Her name is H'nghai. She's sixteen or seventeen years old, and she's going to have a baby. Her husband beats her, but she can't seem to leave him because her parents arranged the marriage, and he paid a bride-price to her family, or maybe it was a dowry they paid him, it's confusing. She won't go to the women's shelter or report him to the police because she's afraid it will reflect badly on the community. I think she would have come here, but...." She looked up. "Guy, she knows who I am. She forgives us."

"Forgives us?" He took a step back into the room. "Would you please tell me what the hell for?"

"We killed her brother."

"It was an accident," he said.

"You would have done the same thing if you'd been me." She looked away. "I can't abandon her."

"Instead you'd abandon me. You think if you had asked me to do one thing for you, just one thing, I would have betrayed you like that?"

"All I meant was you would have tried to help her."

"Not at your expense." He crossed to the table, where he stood over her. "What about our son?"

"I didn't set out for this to happen."

He hadn't set out to kill Y Bhan Buon To either, but he had to suffer the consequences, didn't he? It wasn't his fault his guilt had turned to anger. He *felt* that failure. One more consequence he had to suffer. "Look, okay, forget the Montagnards. I need to leave— you can understand that, can't you? I need to get the fuck out of Random, okay?"

"I do understand that."

"All right then."

But it wasn't all right. She was going to explain herself whether he wanted her to or not.

"Right after the accident, when Nuh kept coming to the house? He kept saying he wanted American insurance to help his sister. I wanted to know more about him and about his brother, about the Montagnards, I had to know, it was the only way I could deal with what happened, so I went to the Christian Relocation Services. I told them I couldn't volunteer, but, well, it's a long story. They needed me to give one of the women a ride to the doctor. I didn't know it would be Bhan's sister."

"Do you have any idea," he said slowly, "any idea at all what I'm going through? Do you know how many times I've had to ask myself what if I didn't have that glass of wine at dinner? I mean if you're so damn determined to be a do-gooder, can't you find someone else? There's a big, cruel world out there, they're not the only hurting people."

He waited. "What about our son?" She rested her head on the table. "Have you thought about our son?"

"No," she whispered. "I haven't."

He paced. When he paused in front of her again he said, "You would tear this family apart because you can't leave this girl, and you haven't even thought about what will happen to your own son?" His head felt hollow.

She lifted her face. "I don't want for this to happen."

"Neither do I," he snapped. "What do you think you're going to do for her anyway? You said yourself she won't leave or call the cops. You get between them, he's likely to come after you."

"I've thought of that. But somehow I don't think so. Like you say, there's almost nothing I can do."

"All right then." He picked up his cold coffee.

"Be there."

"Be there," he repeated in disgust as he took the mug to the sink and poured the coffee down the drain. He rinsed it out and drew a cup of water, which he set on the counter. "This is it then."

After a minute he picked up the cup, sipped, and wiped his chin. "And Nick?" he prodded.

She looked at him. "I couldn't make you leave him. I would never do that to you." Her eyes filmed again. "I think I've known ever since that night that I would lose him. He was the only thing...."

"What is that supposed to mean? What kind of self-pitying, melodramatic, fatalistic kind of crap is that? You want to feel sorry for yourself, don't you dare—don't you *dare* use our son to do it!"

She tried to catch his eyes. "All I mean...."

"I know what you mean! And it's bullshit, do you hear me?"

She hung her head.

He had balled his hands into fists. Carefully he unclenched them, feeling for a moment the sting of the white crescents his nails had dug into his palms before he placed them on the counter. He didn't know whether he'd meant to strike her or not. "It's stupid."

He stared at his hands as if they belonged to someone else, the squared off nails, a white fleck in the right thumbnail, the puckers of skin at the knuckles, and swirl of hair above his wrists. He had always lived under the assumption that hitting a woman was something he would never do.

There wasn't any more to say. He went upstairs to call Gordon Weems.

Eva was still sitting at the breakfast table when Guy returned. She felt shrunken. Though he'd been gone only a few minutes, she was afraid to look up, afraid he might already have a suitcase in his hand. Her life of the past weeks had been shown to her for what it was, not so base as his anger had taken it to be, not the evil of commission that he thought, but a betrayal far worse. Though she could not take back her involvement with H'nghai—that she would do again; she could see no way around it—she had managed to deny the consequences of her actions so completely that he had surprised her with her sin. All these weeks she had feared that he would be so angry he would leave her, and still she had not thought about their son.

Something in the way he continued to stand in front of the table without speaking forced her to raise her eyes. His face wore such a dull mask of shock a prickle of fright crept down her neck. "What?"

"I just talked to Weems," he said numbly. "The D.A.'s reduced the charge. I'm going back to District Court."

Chapter 21

Driver Convicted; Fined $100 for Fatal Wreck

U.S. District Court Judge Richard Chambers fined Guy L. Ferrin of Jefferson Road $100 after Ferrin was convicted yesterday of failing to exercise due caution in the November accident that killed a 9-year-old Montagnard boy.

Y Bhan Buon To died of injuries sustained when the car Ferrin was driving struck him while he was walking on an unlit section of Lanyan Road Nov. 16. Ferrin, who maintained that the boy ran in front of the car, admitted to police he had been drinking that evening. He was charged with felony death by motor vehicle.

According to District Attorney Adam Atwater, Ferrin's blood alcohol was .20, twice the state's legal limit. Atwater considered trying Ferrin on a murder charge until the results of the Breathalyzer disappeared from Ferrin's file. Atwater called the disappearance mysterious, saying, "Without that crucial piece of evidence, we just couldn't take it to Superior Court."

Rather than dismiss the charge, Atwater reduced it to failure to exercise due caution, a misdemeanor, so that Ferrin could be tried in District Court.

The judge imposed the $100 fine but did not sentence Ferrin to prison or rescind his driver's license. Nor did he require Ferrin to undergo alcohol education.

"It's a shame, but under the circumstance the

court did what the law allows," Atwater said. "Too often there is nothing a judge can do to prevent a drunk driver from getting behind the wheel of a car and killing again."

A civil suit against Ferrin filed by the boy's parents is still pending.

Eva set the newspaper aside. "So much for 'innocent until proven guilty,'" she murmured. So this was how it ended, she thought, not yesterday in the courtroom when the judge pronounced the sentence and the lawyer turned to shake Guy's hand, not even afterwards when they rode the elevator to the ground floor and the courthouse door released them into a glorious afternoon and their own letdown relief, but now, finalized, given shape, made real by a few column inches in the paper. Guy, who had skimmed the piece without comment before turning to the sports page, didn't look up. His countenance was that of a man whose confrontation with the misdemeanors at his core had etched his face with a permanently subdued sense of sorrow. "I suppose you could sue for libel." Her tone was halfhearted. Even if he had a chance of winning such a case he would never bring it; the last thing he would want was to drag an epilogue out.

And in her heart she believed what Weems had posited in the hallway as he walked them to the elevator. It was a mistake; everything that had happened was in all probability no more than a mistake. Someone in the district attorney's office, a secretary, an assistant, even the D.A. himself, had likely misplaced the Breathalyzer readout; in recollection the D.A. had transposed the figure. It was an error that held more logic than the truth; after all, Guy had been charged with felony death.

The governor was campaigning for safe roads, and the D.A. was coming up for re-election. They could hardly expect the him to admit his office had screwed up, for by the time Weems talked to McThune—though Eva maintained that was the first thing both the lawyer and the district attorney should have done—Atwater had already shot his mouth off about trying drunk drivers for murder. He had never said that he meant Guy; he had only allowed the public to infer it. McThune had looked at neither of them as he testified briefly to the facts, the estimated speed of the vehicle, the adverse weather conditions, but had freely acknowledged to Weems that the BAC he recalled was consistent with Guy's account. She had known it was a mistake even before the case was heard, as they sat together in the crowded District Courtroom while the D.A.'s office called the docket and the various petty criminals in the room mumbled pleas while babies wailed and relatives went in and out, making so much noise the assistant D.A. complained he couldn't hear them with a smirk that said he didn't expect to. She read the graffiti carved into the hard wooden benches, and it struck her that while they waited for the disposition of their cases these penny-ante vandals sat here committing more crimes. It was a system built to facilitate mistake.

A dimpled sunlight lay across the table. Yesterday, when they emerged from the courthouse, they had paused a moment on the steps while she retrieved her sunglasses from her purse, a little dazed by the brilliance of the early afternoon sun. The soft fingers of a breeze stirred her collar and lifted her hair. It was the last day of January, but the air suggested spring. They did not speak. Only after he had paid the attendant and pulled from the courthouse lot into the street, did she turn to him and say, "I'm glad it's over," though what she had felt at that moment wasn't gladness or closure, but the same dull sense of remission she felt now. She had wanted to reach across the console to touch him but didn't feel as if she were allowed.

"You need to call the insurance company," she said. Now that he had been found criminally liable, the company would have to review the claim, and if they wanted to accept the settlement the Buon Tos would have to drop their suit. Legally, she thought, it could not have worked out better.

"I know."

But they had killed a child. It wasn't possible to feel glad or exonerated.

"Everybody knows you didn't do anything wrong," she cried. "Even the D.A. and the judge know as much. Why do you think it got to court so fast once the charge was reduced? In the end everybody just wanted it over with."

She couldn't find the words that would bridge the quarrel that lay between them, though what had happened was not really a quarrel but something else, something that seemed beyond reconciliation. The news that the case was being sent back to District Court had postponed its resolution, forcing a suspension in the way a death might, any event so significant it required a temporary truce, that polite, uneasy lull that interrupted war. They had been together too long for either of them to think she would not see him through his trial. In a way, she supposed the vague torpor she had felt since leaving the courthouse yesterday was only the same exhausted apathy that followed any fight. Things had moved more quickly than she had thought legal matters could once the charge had been reduced, but in that ensuing week before the trial the two of them had moved as sluggishly as if underwater, as if their limbs were freighted with thick air. She had hoped somehow that the lull would have changed things, but the longer he did not speak, the more palpable the distance she'd put between them grew.

She could not part with her son. But she had said she would, and he would not forgive her. She tried to recall other things she had said in heat over the years. Their arguments had not been frequent, at least not before the past few months, but they had been explosive, less disagreements than eruptions, impossible to forestall or to reconstruct. Rarely had she and Guy made up; after a day or so they simply resumed without referring to their fight. For her it was if the quarrels had never happened, and she was distressed to discover that he remembered every one, in lacerating detail. More than remembered: he bore her accusations like wounds no longer visible but never fully healed. Words did not mean the same things to them. They had different temperaments.

Probably she had said "I hate you"; no doubt she had at some time called him a bastard. In one argument she recalled she had stood facing him in their bedroom and cried, "I was so happy in my little apartment, and you moved in and trashed it!" She couldn't remember what had detonated the quarrel, only the aftermath, the days or weeks during which he had been so assiduously tidy, until somehow they had fallen back into old habits. She had left a sweater on a chair or perhaps it was a pair of shoes beside the sofa; she was responsible; she had given him permission. She was responsible for the words she chose. Nor could she claim she did not mean them, for as she spoke she believed them. But it was not in anger that she had said she would give up Nick; it was in sorrow. She had been doomed from the night of the accident not to lose him, but to say so. That unredeemed sentence was the climax the long first paragraph of her grief had required. It was the crime at her core, the unredressed flaw of her character, that fatalism, the need to find a shape in every labyrinth of feeling.

"I know you're still angry with me," she said. "But I wish you would forgive me."

His sigh was a weary exhalation. "Eva."

"I love you," she said, as if that were all.

He rose. He crossed the kitchen and stood at the sink. For a long time neither of them spoke.

"I want it back," she said, her voice as childish as the longing, that absurd and inexpressible desire to travel back through accidents and failures, disappointments and quarrels, through knowledge, guilt, and resignation, to reclaim a single day of youth, with its innocence, its tender light, fragrant smells and gentle air and all its ignorance and promise.

"Don't we all?"

"What will you do?" she asked.

"I don't know."

"Will you leave?"

He turned to look at her. "Will you?"

"I can't leave you or Nick."

"What about your Montagnard friend?"

She looked away. "I can't leave her either."

"Choose," he said.

"I wish you would forgive me." She could not say it.

"All I can tell you is what I feel now," he said and turned away.

She crossed the room and took his hand. "I know."

“Choose,” he said again.

Everything depended on a word she could not find. There was no word for anything as complex as marriage. He would not forgive her. They would not quickly heal. But she loved him. She had his hand, and she held on.

Cover photo by Lee Zacharias
Author photo by Janice Wald Friedman
Book Design by Les Butchart

About the Author

Lee Zacharias is the author of *Helping Muriel Make It Through the Night* (short stories) and the novel *Lessons*, winner of the Sir Walter Raleigh Award. Her work has appeared in *The Southern Review*, *The Gettysburg Review*, *Shenandoah*, *Southern Humanities Review*, numerous other journals, and *The Best American Essays*. Recipient of fellowship awards from the National Endowment for the Arts and the North Carolina Greensboro, she is Professor Emerita at the University of North Carolina Greensboro and a past editor of *The Greensboro Review*. She lives in Greensboro with her husband Michael Gaspeny.

Made in the USA
Charleston, SC
21 February 2013